"The Golden Nugget is a permanent fixture here in Thunder Canyon. I'm not."

At Mia's words, Marshall's spoon paused in midair as he frowned. "You're not leaving soon, are you?"

His finger slid beneath her chin and lifted her face up to his. The serious look she saw on his handsomely carved features sent her heart into a heavy rapid thud.

"We're just getting to know each other, Mia. I'd really like you to stay longer."

His voice tugged at her every feminine particle. "I—uh—I'll think about it."

Suddenly his head was bending toward hers, and the whisper that passed his lips skittered down her spine.

"Maybe you should think about this."

Longing held her motionless as his lips descended onto hers....

Dear Reader,

I was thrilled when asked to do a MONTANA
MAVERICKS book, and when I learned the
theme—striking it rich—I knew it was a subject
that would touch everyone. After all, haven't we all
wondered what it would be like to hit the lottery or
fall into sudden fortune? Ahh, the things we could
do with all that money. Shopping till we dropped.
Traveling around the world. Indulging ourselves
with anything and everything we've ever wanted.
Sounds good, huh? Sounds like all our problems
would be solved. Or so my heroine thinks.

After scratching her way through years of poverty,
Mia believes money is all she needs to fix the
troubles in her life. But when a fortune suddenly
befalls her, she slowly and painfully begins to see
that being rich in money is not nearly as great as
being rich in love.

I hope you enjoy reading how Mia finds the real
treasures in her life!

God bless you with life's true riches,

Stella Bagwell

STELLA BAGWELL

sold her first novel to Silhouette Books in November 1985. She still loves her job and says she isn't completely content unless she's writing. She and her husband live in Seadrift, Texas, a sleepy little fishing town located on the coastal bend, where the water, the tropical climate and the seabirds make it a lovely place to let her imagination soar and to put the stories in her head down on paper.

She and her husband have one son, Jason, who lives and teaches high school math in nearby Port Lavaca.

To my family—the real golden nuggets in my life.

Chapter One

Was this his lucky day or what?

Using the back of his arm, Marshall Cates wiped the sweat streaming into his eyes and peered a second time at the woman sitting on a boulder some twenty feet below. From his precarious position on the rock ledge, the only view he had was of a portion of her back, the long fall of her raven-black hair and her nipped-in waist; but those tempting glimpses were enough to tell him it was *the heiress*.

For the past three weeks every male employee at Thunder Canyon Resort had been talking and fantasizing about the mystery guest. So far Marshall had only gazed at her from afar and wondered what a beautiful young woman with money to burn was doing here alone in

Thunder Canyon. True, the small western Montana town was growing in leaps and bounds and Thunder Canyon Resort, where he worked as staff doctor, was garnering a reputation for fine hospitality surrounded by scenic splendor. The clientele was becoming ritzy, flying in from all corners of the nation. Still, Marshall couldn't help but figure a woman with her apparent class would rather be vacationing on the French Riviera than in the middle of a cowman's paradise. The fact that she appeared to be here without an escort intrigued him even more.

This morning, Marshall had risen early, wondering what to do with his off-duty time. With his brothers and his buddies all tied up with other interests, he'd eventually decided to do something he loved, climbing, and had headed up one of the mountains near the resort. When he'd set out on this trek, he'd never dreamed that the chance to meet Ms. Heiress would present itself on the edge of a rocky bluff. Since he'd only ever spotted her lounging around the lodge, he hadn't figured her for a nature girl.

Quickly, he rappelled the last few feet of the layered rock until his boots hit solid ground. Once there, he gathered up his climbing equipment and left his ropes, rings and anchors in a neat pile with his backpack.

As Marshall walked over to the woman he noticed she was sitting near an opening in the trees, looking out toward the endless valley that swept away from the mountain range. The view was majestic, especially to someone who'd never seen the landscape before. But this woman didn't appear to be enjoying the scenery;

she was deep in thought. So much so that she was completely unaware of his presence.

Fearing his approach might scare her so badly she'd fall from the boulder, he stopped ten feet from her and called out.

"Hello there."

The moment she heard his voice, her head whipped around and her palms flattened against the rock in preparation to push herself to her feet. Surprise was etched upon her parted lips and wide eyes, telling him she'd definitely believed herself to be totally alone on this particular piece of mountain. She was dressed in khaki shorts that struck her mid-thigh, a pale pink T-shirt that hugged her breasts and sturdy brown hiking boots. Her hair hung like shiny satin against her shoulders.

An enchanting princess sitting on her throne, he thought, as he felt every male particle in him begin to buzz with excitement.

"Sorry if I scared you," Marshall went on before she could gather herself enough to speak. "I saw you sitting here and thought I'd say hello."

Slowly, warily, she eased her bottom back on the boulder and her dark eyes carefully monitored his movements as he came to stand a few feet beside her. Marshall wondered if he really looked that sinister. It was an odd thought for a doctor who'd taken an oath to save lives, not harm them. But Ms. Heiress didn't know him and he supposed she was wise not to trust a strange man out in the wilderness.

Finally, she returned his greeting with a faint nod of her regal head. "Hello."

Spoken quietly, that one word was clear and without a hint of accent, giving little clue as to where she might live. However, it did tell Marshall that she'd not traveled up to Thunder Canyon from a Southern state.

Giving her the sort of smile he reserved for skittish female patients, he asked, "Enjoying the warm weather?"

Actually, it had been downright hot. Not an unusual occurrence for August, but it would take a native like himself to know the nuances of Thunder Canyon climate and right at this moment he wasn't ready to let this beautiful sophisticate know he was a born-and-bred local. She might just snub her straight little nose at him and walk off, and he was too curious about the woman to take that chance.

"Very much," she quietly replied.

Marshall took two steps forward, all the while feeling her dark eyes gliding over him, weighing him as though she were trying to decide if he was worthy of conversation. The idea irked Marshall just a bit. Especially since he was accustomed to women smiling warmly at him, not studying him like a bug on a leaf.

"The view is beautiful from here," she suddenly went on. "The sky seems to go on forever and I was thinking about hanging around to see the sunset this evening, but I suppose being caught out here in the dark wouldn't be wise."

At least the woman had a little common sense to go with all that beauty, he thought, as his gaze covertly slid down a pair of long shapely legs. Her skin was slightly kissed by the sun and the warm gleam told him it would be butter smooth beneath his hand.

Trying not to dwell on that pleasant thought, he shook his head. "No. I wouldn't recommend being here on the mountains after dark. Black bears and mountain lions are spotted in this area from time to time. You wouldn't want to meet up with any of those."

Glancing at the forest surrounding them, she said, "I've noticed the warnings signs on the hiking trails and read the information posted in the lodge." She lifted one hand and shook a bracelet adorned with sleigh bells. "Just to be safe I wore a bear bracelet. I was told the sound would scare the creatures away."

"So they say." He didn't go on to tell her that as a teenager he'd had his own run-in with a black bear and that the sow had refused to back down until his brother had shot a round from his hunting rifle over the angry animal's head. Scaring the woman would hardly be the way to entice her into further conversation.

To Marshall's surprise, she suddenly climbed down from the rock and stood within an arm's length from him. The short distance was enough to give him a clear view of her face. High rounded cheekbones, a dainty dimpled chin and full lips were perfectly sculpted out of creamy skin. Her eyes, which appeared dark from a distance, were actually a blend of earthy green and brown, outlined by a thick fringe of jet-black lashes. Above them, delicate brows of the same color arched into a smooth, wide forehead.

At the moment, the corners of her pink lips were curved faintly upward and Marshall could hardly tear his gaze away.

"You've been mountain climbing?" she asked, her gaze sweeping past him to the mound of equipment he'd left beneath the rocky bluff.

"Since this morning," he answered. "I didn't make it all the way to the top, but far enough for a good workout."

Her gaze pulled back to him and he could feel it sliding over his sweaty face and down to the damp patch in the middle of his black T-shirt. Normally when a woman looked at him, Marshall didn't give it a second thought. But Ms. Heiress was studying him in a way that left him close to blushing. Something he hadn't done since his sophomore year in high school.

"I hiked up this far, but when I ran into the rock bluff I realized this would be as far as I could go," she said a bit wistfully. "Is this something you do often?"

His smile crinkled the corners of his eyes and exposed a mouthful of snow-white teeth. "You mean, find a beautiful woman up in the mountains?"

The faint flare of her nostrils said she didn't appreciate his flirty question and Marshall inwardly sighed. He should have known the woman would be cool. Rich, pampered women usually were. The words friendly and down-to-earth probably weren't in her vocabulary.

"No. I mean rock climbing," she said a bit curtly.

"Oh. Well, actually I do quite a bit of climbing and hiking. Along with biking and kayaking. Once the snow leaves the slopes, that is."

She looked faintly interested and Marshall felt momentarily encouraged. Maybe the woman was approachable after all.

"You obviously like outdoor sports," she said.

"Yeah. Skiing is my first love. I could do that every day of the year. But of course, my wallet would get pretty empty if I didn't work once in a while," he added with a grin.

Like the flip of a light switch, her back went ramrod straight and her lips compressed to a tight line. Her gaze shifted from him to a magpie squawking from a branch on a nearby spruce tree. Apparently she preferred the bird's talk to his.

After a moment, she asked in a cool tone, "Or find a willing woman to pay for your sporting games."

Stunned by this abrupt change in her, Marshall stared at her profile. She might look like an exotic princess, but that didn't mean he was going to let himself be insulted. Hadn't she ever heard of a joke?

"I beg your pardon?" he asked.

Her head swiveled back around and she stared down her straight little nose at him. "Oh, come on, I'm sure you do this all the time. Strike up innocent conversations with single women, turn on the charm and eventually get your hand in their pocketbook. Isn't that the way your game is played?"

So she thought he was after her money. Marshall was so incensed he would have very much liked to turn her over his knee and whack that pretty little bottom of hers until she apologized. But he wasn't about to use caveman tactics on a woman. She'd probably miss the point of a spanking anyway.

"Sorry, Ms.—uh—Smith, isn't it? Mia Smith?"

A mixture of surprise and suspicion suddenly crossed her face. "How do you know my name?"

"I'm Marshall Cates—the staff doctor for Thunder Canyon Resort. I've heard your name mentioned by some of the other staffers. And in case you didn't know, there are people, like me, who can make it just fine in life without a pile of riches. My salary easily takes care of my wants. I certainly don't need a woman to take care of me financially," he added coolly.

Completely stunned now, Mia stared at the man standing a few steps away. She'd assumed he was also a guest at the resort. She'd jumped to conclusions and figured he'd heard she was a single woman with money and thought she would probably be an easy prey to his good looks. To learn that he was a doctor at the resort— no doubt a well-to-do one—both rattled and embarrassed her.

Hot color washed across her face as her fingertips flew up to press against her lips. Too bad she hadn't kept them shut earlier, she thought. No telling what the man was thinking of her.

"Oh, I—I'm sorry, Dr. Cates. I don't know what else to say." Glancing away from him she let out a loud, inward groan. Why couldn't she do anything right anymore? Is that what inheriting money had done to her? Turned her into a mistrustful snob?

Drawing in a deep, bracing breath, she turned her

gaze back to him and once again felt the jolt of the man's presence. He wasn't just a good-looking guy in a pair of sweaty shorts and T-shirt. He was so masculine that she could almost feel the sexuality seeping from him. Waves of coffee-brown hair naturally streaked by the sun were tousled around his head. Eyes the color of a chocolate bar peered at her from beneath thick, hooded brows. A straight nose flared slightly over a pair of lips that at the moment were compressed into a tight, angry line. A faint shadow of evening stubble covered a strong jaw and a chin that jutted proudly forward, telling her more about his personality than his words.

At the moment he appeared to be waiting for her to explain the meaning of her insulting comments and she supposed he deserved that much from her. Yet how could she really explain without telling the man things about her that she didn't want anyone to know?

"I thought— I took it for granted that you were a guest, Dr. Cates, and I was afraid— Well, you see I've had to deal with the problem of men…approaching me for financial reasons." Her features crumpled with remorse. "I'm sorry I was so quick to misjudge you. Please accept my apology."

He continued to study her with a guarded eye and Mia realized he was weighing her words and her sincerity. She couldn't blame him for that. Even so, she didn't know why his opinion of her should matter so much. She wasn't at Thunder Canyon Resort to find herself a man, even a respectable man like Dr. Cates. In fact, she'd run almost blindly to this area of Montana, hoping that no one from her past would be able to follow. She'd come here seeking peace and privacy, nothing more.

"I'm curious, Ms. Smith. Just exactly what is it about me that made you think I was a gigolo?"

More hot color washed up her neck and over her face and her gaze dropped guiltily to the toes of her hiking boots. "There wasn't— You don't look like a gigolo, Dr. Cates. I guess it was that flirty line about finding a beautiful woman in the mountains that set my alarm bell off."

She glanced up to see the doctor folding his arms across his chest while studying her with curious amusement.

"I'm sure a woman like you runs into flirty men on a daily basis. I hope you don't insult them all the way you just did me."

So he wasn't going to make this easy for her, Mia thought. Well, it didn't matter. She had apologized to him. He could accept her offer or not. Either way, she'd probably never see the man again.

Stifling a sigh, she reached up and shoved back a strand of hair being tossed about by a lazy wind. "Look, Dr. Cates, I've apologized. There's not much more I can say."

He grinned at her in much the same way that he had earlier and, in spite of the rigid resistance she'd been trying to hold onto, she felt herself drawn to the man.

He said, "Except that you'll walk down the mountain with me."

His offhand invitation took her by surprise. Even though that flirty smile of his was aimed straight at her, she wasn't expecting him to take this meeting between them a step further. And though her first instinct was to withdraw and tell him she preferred her privacy, the feminine side of her was intrigued and flattered by his overture.

"That is," he added, "if you are ready to leave the mountain. I wouldn't want to rush you away from this spot. Not after the laboring hike it took to get up here."

The idea that he appreciated her physical effort to climb to this particular shelf of the mountain warmed her even more and she found herself smiling back at him.

"It was quite a trek for me to make it this far," she admitted. Twisting around, she bent down and picked up a small backpack lying at the base of the boulder. As she shouldered it on, she said, "But I am ready to go. The sun is beginning to dip."

"Great," he said with a smile. "Just let me get my things and we'll head down the trail together."

Mia followed him over to the rock ledge and waited while he shoved his climbing equipment into a vary large backpack. After he'd secured the straps over his shoulders, he gestured toward the direction of the trail.

"Shall we go?"

Nodding, Mia fell in step with him and was immediately staggered by his nearness. Since less than a foot separated their shoulders, she was close enough to pick up the faint spicy scent of cologne mingled with sweat, an odor that was extremely masculine, even erotic. And for the first time in ages, Mia found her senses distracted by a man.

"I guess getting outdoors is a nice break from working in an office," she commented as they picked their way down the rocky trail.

"I'd go crazy if I couldn't get out and do something physical," he told her. "But I do enjoy being a doctor."

She glanced at him from the corner of her eye. Looking at his lean body, Mia could plainly see he got plenty of strenuous exercise. His arms and legs were roped with hard muscles.

"Are you a general practitioner?"

A hint of amusement grooved his cheeks and Mia couldn't help but wonder about his odd reaction to her question. Did he think being a general practitioner was a joke? She hated to think he was one of those specialists that went around with their nose up in the air.

"No. There's not much need for one of those at the resort. I specialize in sports medicine. Twisted ankles, broken bones, strained muscles and pulled tendons. We have lots of skiers and hikers here."

For some reason, she could easily imagine him examining a blond ski bunny's strained leg. She'd bet a pile of money that the majority of his patients were female. But she wasn't about to suggest such a thing to Dr. Cates. She'd already stuck one foot in her mouth this afternoon. Mia wasn't about to try for a second.

"What about sniffles and fever? Can you treat those, too?"

He tossed her a wide grin. "Sure I can. Why? You're not feeling ill, are you?"

Her nostrils flared at his suggestive question. "I feel

very well, thank you. I was just wondering about those guests that might get colds or tummy aches."

He chuckled and Mia realized she liked the warm husky sound that rolled easily past his lips. It said he was happy with himself and his life. She was envious. Desperately envious.

"Well, wonder no more, Ms. Smith. I can do what any general practitioner can do, plus a little more."

The teeny thread of arrogance in his voice was just enough to give him an air of confidence rather than conceit. And she realized she liked that about him, liked the self-assurance he possessed. If only she could be that sure of her own abilities and decisions, she thought wistfully. Maybe then she could step out and begin to live again, instead of hiding herself here in Thunder Canyon.

"If that's the case, the resort must be getting a lot for their money."

He chuckled again. "I like to think so."

The trail suddenly turned a bit steep and treacherous, forcing them to focus on their steps rather than their conversation. But despite her best effort, Mia's boots slipped on the loose gravel.

Her arms were flailing about, snatching for any sort of bush to help her regain her balance, when she felt the doctor's arm wrap around her waist and his strong hand grip the side of her waist.

"Careful now," he said in a steadying voice. "I've got you."

Breathing deeply from the physical scramble to stay

upright, she tucked her long hair behind her ears and darted a grateful glance at his face.

"Thanks," she murmured between quick breaths. "I...almost went over head first."

Their gazes collided and Mia felt as though everything around them were slowing to a crawl. Except for her heart, which suddenly seemed to be going at breakneck speed, pumping hot blood straight to her face.

"It would be a steep tumble from here," he said, his voice husky. "I'm glad that didn't happen."

His brown eyes left hers and began to glide over her face as though they were fingers reverently touching a beautiful flower. The idea so unsettled Mia that she nervously swallowed and looked away from him.

Tall, pungent spruce along with white-barked aspen grew right to the edge of the hiking trail. The branches blocked out the sun, making it appear later in the evening than it really was and leaving Mia feeling as though the two of them were cocooned in their own little world. She wasn't ready for that much togetherness with a man who took her breath away each time she looked at him.

"Uh, we should be going," she quickly suggested. "The shadows are getting longer."

"Let me go first so I can help you down this rough patch," he told her.

To her relief he released his hold on her waist and carefully eased down the path a few feet in front of her. Once he found solid footing, he reached a hand up to her.

"Take my hand. I don't want you to fall."

She could have sat on her rump and scooted down the washed out part of the trail, but that would have been a little humiliating to do in front of a man who climbed mountains. Besides, he was only watching out for her safety, not merely trying to find an excuse to touch her, she told herself.

Leaning forward, she latched her fingers around his and with a firm grip he steadied her as she maneuvered over the last few treacherous steps.

"Thanks," she told him. "I've got to admit I was dreading going over this area again. I had to practically crawl on my way up."

He nodded. "I think this washout needs to be reported. The resort has maintenance people for repairing just this sort of thing. It might save a guest from a bad injury."

Mia suddenly realized he was still holding her hand and she was letting him.

Feeling like a naive teenager, she disengaged her fingers from his and carefully stepped around him. To her relief, he didn't try to delay her. Instead, he followed a few steps behind her.

She was trying hard to focus on the trail and the birds flittering among the limbs of the aspens, rather than the man behind her, when his voice suddenly sounded again.

"Are you a Montana native?"

His question put her on instant alert. If his questions grew too personal she didn't know how she could evade them without coming off as snobbish.

"No. Actually, I'm from Colorado."

"Oh. Then you're used to the mountains," he casually commented.

Truthfully, she'd grown up in a southern area of the state where most of the land was flat and used for farming and ranching. But that was more information than she wanted to give this man. He might inadvertently say something to other employees at the resort and if Janelle, her mother, just happened to be searching for her, the information might put the woman on her trail. And seeing Janelle right now was the very last thing Mia wanted in her life.

"Well, you could say I'm used to gazing at them from afar. I...uh, live in Denver."

He chuckled. "There're hundreds of beautiful vacation spots all over your state and you chose to come to Thunder Canyon. I'm amazed."

Put like that it did sound strange, even ridiculous. But she wasn't about to explain her motives for coming to Montana. Dr. Cates was obviously a man with wealth and prestige, maybe even a family. He would be outraged if he knew the real Mia. Mia Hanover. Not Mia Smith. That name was just as phony as the person she was trying to be.

Stifling a sigh, she said, "I'd never been up here. I wanted to see more of the state than just pictures."

Her simple excuse sounded reasonable enough. Lord only knew it was a mistake for a man to try to understand the workings of a woman's mind. Still, something about Mia Smith being here didn't feel right to him. Even so, he wasn't going to press her with any more questions. Something about the clipped edge to her words told him not to pry, at least, for right now.

"I'm glad you did. I hope you're having a nice stay," he told her. "Do you have plans to stay much longer?"

Long moments passed without any sort of reply from her and Marshall had decided she was going to ignore his question completely when she suddenly paused on the trail and looked over her shoulder at him.

"I'm…not sure. I'm taking things a day at a time."

A day at a time? Most normal folks went on vacation with a planned date of arrival and departure. They allotted themselves a certain amount of time for fun and mentally marked a day to go home. Work, school and other responsibilities demanded a timetable. But then Mia Smith wasn't like "normal folks." She was obviously rich. She didn't have responsibilities, he reminded himself. More than likely she was a lady of leisure. She didn't have to worry about getting back to a job.

She's out of your league, Marshall. You'd do well to remember that.

The tiny voice running through his head made sense. But it also irked him. He wasn't a man who always wanted to play it safe. He liked excitement and pleasure and getting to know Mia Smith would definitely give him both.

The next five minutes passed in silence as the two of them carefully made their way to the bottom shelf of the mountain. Here the ground flattened somewhat and the trail they'd been traveling split, with one path looping by the river before it headed back to the resort. The other trail was a more direct path to the ski lodge.

Shifting his backpack to a more comfortable position, Marshall paused at the intersection of trails to look at her.

"Would you like to walk down by the river?"

Her gaze skittered over his face before it finally settled on the horizon. Even before she spoke a word, Marshall could feel her putting distance between them.

"Sorry, but I have a few things I need to do back at my cabin. In fact, if you'll excuse me, I think I'll get on down the trail." She reached to briefly shake his hand. "Thank you for helping me with the trip down. Goodbye."

Before Marshall could make any sort of reply, she quickly turned and headed down the beaten path that would lead her back to the lodge.

Amused by her abrupt departure, Marshall stared after Mia Smith, while wondering where he'd gone wrong. He wasn't accustomed to women walking away from him. In fact, most of the time he had to think up some polite excuse to get rid of unwanted advances.

Mia Smith had just given him a dose of his own medicine and though the idea should have had him throwing his head back and laughing at the irony of it all, he could do nothing but stare down the trail after her and wonder if he would ever have the chance to talk with her again.

Chapter Two

Thunder Canyon Resort's infirmary was a set of rooms located on the bottom floor at the back of the massive lodge. When Caleb Douglas, wealthy businessman and cattle baron of Thunder Canyon, decided to build the resort, he'd spared no expense. The multistories of wood and glass spread across the slope of mountain like a modern-day castle. By itself, Marshall's office was large enough to hold a Saturday night dance. In fact, he'd often thought how perfect the gleaming hardwood floors would be for boot scootin' and twirling a pretty girl under his arm. Not very professional thoughts for a doctor, Marshall supposed, but then he hardly had the job of a normal doctor.

One whole wall of his office was constructed of

glass; it was an enormous window to the outside world. His desk, a huge piece of gleaming cherrywood, had been placed at the perfect angle for Marshall to view the nearby mountains and a portion of the ski slope. At this time in the summer, it wasn't rare for him to look up from his paperwork to see elk or mule deer grazing along the slopes.

Yes, it was a cushy job. One that Marshall had never dreamed of having. At least not while he'd been trudging through medical school, burning the midnight oil over anatomy books while his friends were out partying.

When Marshall had finally received his doctorate, he'd come home and taken a job at Thunder Canyon General Hospital. At the time some of his friends had wondered about his choice. They had all continually reminded him that his specialty in sports medicine could possibly open up big doors for him. Wouldn't he like to work for a major league team in baseball or the NFL where he could make piles of money?

Marshall would be the first to admit that he liked money and he'd gone into the medical profession believing it was a way to make a fortune without breaking his back. But he hadn't necessarily had his eye on a job that would take him away from his hometown.

By the time he'd finished medical school and his internship, he'd been too homesick to even consider going off to some major city on the East or West Coast to look for a job. Instead, he'd returned to Thunder Canyon, never dreaming that his hometown was about to undergo a sudden and drastic change.

A little over two years ago the discovery of gold at the Queen of Hearts mine had quickly changed the whole area. Businesses, mostly catering to tourists, were sprouting up in Thunder Canyon like daffodils in spring-time. The resort, which had started out as a single lodge with a ski slope, had expanded to an upscale, year-round tourist attraction with all sorts of indoor and outdoor enticements for the young and old. And the resort was continuing to build and expand. Under the management of Marshall's longtime buddy Grant Clifton, the recreational hot spot had become a gold mine itself. And Marshall was definitely reaping part of the rewards.

This morning, as soon as he'd entered his office, his assistant Ruthann had placed a steaming cup of coffee along with a plate of buttered croissants on his desk. The woman had been a registered nurse for nearly thirty years and three years ago had just settled into retirement when her husband suddenly died of a heart attack. The tragedy had put her in financial straits and when Marshall had heard she'd needed a job, he'd decided she'd be perfect as his assistant.

Now after a year of working with her, he realized he'd been more than right about the woman. She was an ex-cellent nurse with plenty of experience, plus he didn't have to worry about her ogling him as something to take home to meet mother. In fact, in her early fifties, Ruthann was more like a mother to him than an assistant.

"Surprise, surprise. You actually have three patients this morning," she said with dry amusement as she watched him chomp into one of the croissants. "Any clue as to when you'd like to see them?"

"Are any of them critical?" he asked, even though he knew if any patient had arrived with serious injuries, Ruthann wouldn't be standing around gabbing.

"A sprained ankle, a cut knee and a jammed finger. I think the finger case is just a ruse to see you. She's young and blond and drenched with designer perfume."

"What a suspicious mind you have, Ruthie," he scolded playfully.

Her laugh was mocking. "I see the sort of games that go on in this infirmary. Frankly, it amazes me how brazen women can be nowadays when it comes to you men."

The memory of Mia Smith's aloof, even shy behavior toward him yesterday had been something entirely different from the sort of women Ruthann was describing. Maybe that's why he couldn't get the heiress out of his mind.

"Okay, Ruthie, I'll forget my breakfast and go see if Ms. Blonde really has a finger problem."

The petite woman with short red hair and a face full of freckles snorted with playful sarcasm. "That's no way for a doctor to eat."

Grinning, he retorted, "Then why did you put it here for me?"

"Because I knew you'd sleep instead of get out of bed and make yourself breakfast."

Marshall shook a finger at her. "I'll have you know I was up early this morning. I just didn't make breakfast because I was chasing Leroy halfway down the mountain. He dug a hole last night beneath the backyard fence. Guess he was mad at me for not taking him hiking yesterday."

Marshall's Australian blue heeler was often so adept at understanding his master that it was downright eerie. No matter how he tried, Marshall couldn't fool the dog.

"You went hiking? I thought you were going to help your dad paint that workshed of his."

Shaking his head, Marshall wiped bread crumbs from his fingers and picked up the three files Ruthann had placed in front of them. Since they all belonged to current guests of the lodge, each of the manila folders held only a single sheet inside them. Being a doctor at a place where people resided for only a few days or weeks didn't allow the opportunity to make longtime patients. Temperature and blood-pressure readings didn't tell him much about a person. But that was okay with Marshall. He'd never set out to be one of those kind family doctors who knew all the townsfolk by name, made sure they kept all their routine checkups and often served as their counselor and therapist. That sort of doctoring took commitment and he was too busy enjoying himself in other ways to chain himself to an office.

"He and Mom had to do something with some friends—something about an anniversary celebration. We've planned the painting day for another time."

He rose to his feet, a signal to Ruthann that it was

time for them to get to work. As they walked to the door, he said casually, "I met the heiress yesterday."

Pausing, Ruthann twisted her head around to give him a bemused look. "The heiress," she repeated blankly. "What are you talking about?"

He rolled his eyes. Normally Ruthann was the one who kept him up on resort guests. He couldn't believe she was unaware of Mia Smith.

"*The heiress.* You know, that black-haired beauty that everyone has been talking about. The one that's always alone."

Ruthann's brows suddenly lifted with dawning. "Oh, that one. I didn't realize she was an heiress. Where'd you get that information?"

"Well, I don't know for a fact that she's an heiress. Grant was the one who insinuated that she must be from a rich family. She's been here more than two weeks now. Only a person with money to spare could afford that much time at a luxury resort. He said she rented a safety deposit box for her jewels, too."

"Grant! Isn't he supposed to be engaged to Stephanie? What's he doing gossiping about a female guest?"

Marshall sighed. Yep, Ruthann was just like a mother, he decided, maybe worse. "Don't go jumping to the wrong conclusions. I was the one asking Grant about Mia Smith."

Ruthann shot him a frown of disgust. "I should have guessed." She clucked her tongue in a disapproving way. "A grown man, a doctor at that, prying for information about a woman you don't know from Adam. Shame on you, Marshall Cates. Now what was she like?"

Marshall laughed at the nurse's abrupt turnaround on the sins of gossiping. "Cool. Very cool," he told her. "But as pretty as the rising sun. I got the sense, though, that she's like that beautiful actress, uh—" he paused as his mind searched for the name "—Greta Garbo. She wants to be alone."

Nodding shrewdly the nurse said, "In other words she didn't fall for any of your nonsense."

Reaching for the doorknob, Marshall yanked it open and taking Ruthann by the shoulder ushered her over the threshold.

"Don't count me out yet, Ruthie. Besides, for all you know the woman has been pacing her room, wondering how she can get a second chance with me."

Ruthann chuckled. "I'm sure she's tearing her hair out for an opportunity to get her hands on you."

That was the last thing Mia Smith was probably doing, Marshall thought wryly. But then he wasn't going to let her snub get to him. He'd never had to beg or cajole any woman into having a date with him and he'd be a fool to start now.

With a good-natured chuckle, he nudged Ruthann on toward the first examining room. "Let her pine. Why would I need a beautiful heiress when I have you?"

Behind the lodge, several hundred feet farther up the mountain, Mia paced through the suite of rooms she'd been living in since she'd arrived at Thunder Canyon Resort. A day ago she had considered the luxurious log cabin as a refuge. But now, after the encounter on the mountain with Dr. Marshall Cates, her peace of mind had been shattered.

She'd gone there hoping the quietness and the beauty would allow her to meditate, maybe even help her decide what to do next with her life. But then *he* showed up and her senses had been blown away by his charming smile and strong, masculine presence.

Now she was afraid to step out of her cabin and especially leery of walking down to the lodge, where the infirmary was located. The lodge meant maybe running into Dr. Cates and Mia didn't want to risk seeing him again. He was trouble. She'd felt it when she'd first looked into his eyes and felt her heart race like a wild mustang galloping across a grassy plain.

So what are you going to do, Mia? Stay in your cabin for the next month?

Groaning with self-disgust, Mia sank onto a wide window seat that looked down upon the lodge and the cluster of numerous other resort buildings, imagining what it would look like in the dead of winter. Everything would be capped with white snow and skiers would be riding the lifts and playing on the slopes.

Suddenly, her cell phone rang, the shrill sound jangling her nerves. She stared warily at the small instrument lying on an end table.

There were only a handful of people that had her number and she'd left all of them behind in Colorado. She'd told what few friends she had that she was taking an extended vacation and didn't know when she might return. As for her mother, Mia hadn't told Janelle Josephson anything. She'd simply left the woman a note telling her that she was going away for a while and to please give her the space she needed.

That had been nearly three weeks ago, and Janelle had rang Mia's cell phone every day since. And every day Mia had refused to take her call.

Mercifully, the ringing finally stopped and Mia left the window seat to look at the caller ID. Just as she expected. Janelle wouldn't give up. She wanted to be a part of her daughter's life. And as much as Mia hated to reject her, right now she couldn't even think of Janelle as her mother. As far as she was concerned her mother was dead and nothing, not even a pile of money, would ever bring her back.

There are people, like me, who make it just fine in life without a pile of riches.

Dr. Marshall Cates' words had pierced her heart like a flaming arrow and even a day later they continued to haunt her, to remind her of the awful, selfish choices she'd made in her life.

Money. She desperately wished that she'd never needed or wanted it. She wanted to take what she had of it and throw it into the nearest river. At least then maybe she would feel clean. At least then maybe she could start over. But something told her that even that drastic measure wouldn't heal the wounds she was carrying.

Angry with herself, she put down the phone, walked over to the dining table and grabbed the handbag she'd tossed there earlier. Seeking privacy didn't mean she had to totally hide from life. And if she did cross paths with Dr. Marshall Cates, she could handle it. After all, he was just a man.

A man who would look at you with disgust if he knew you'd once been Mia Hanover, a woman who'd killed her own mother.

For a brief moment, Mia shut her eyes tightly and swallowed hard as the memory of Nina Hanover's death filled her mind like a dark cloud. Her adoptive mother had been a woman who'd worked hard as a farmer's wife, who'd always tried to give Mia the best in life. She'd been a sweet, loving woman until the alcohol had taken her into its awful grip.

With a groan of anguish, Mia shook her head and hurried out of the cabin, wallowing in guilt and self-pity wasn't going to fix anything. She had to get out and get her mind on other things.

A half hour later, in downtown Thunder Canyon, she parked her rental car in front of the Clip 'N' Curl. Even though Mia had made use of the fancy beauty salon and spa located on the resort, she felt much more comfortable here in this traditional, down-home beauty parlor. Here the women dressed casually and everyone talked as though they were all family.

Since the majority of the women at the resort appeared to use the Aspenglow for their beauty treatments, Mia figured the patrons of the Clip 'N' Curl were local residents. In fact, a few days ago when she'd visited the place, she'd heard a couple of the women complaining about the traffic problems that the influx of tourists had brought to Thunder Canyon.

Since Mia was one of those tourists, she'd simply sat quietly and listened to the other customers discussing the Queen of Hearts mine and how the recent discovery of gold there had turned the town topsy-turvy. Several of the women felt that the new money was a wonderful thing for the little town, but others had spoken about how much they hated the traffic, the crowds and the loss of Thunder Canyon's quaintness.

Money. Gold. Riches. The subject seemed to follow Mia no matter where she went. If she could manage a walk-in appointment today, she hoped the shoptalk would be about something different. The last thing she wanted to think about was the money Janelle, her birth mother, had showered upon her and how drastically it had changed Mia's once simple life.

Leaving her small rental car, Mia walked into the Clip 'N' Curl and waited at the front desk. The small salon was presently undergoing major renovations. Only three stations were up and working amid the chaos of working carpenters. And today all three styling chairs were full while only three empty chairs remained in the small waiting area.

Figuring she'd never get an appointment, Mia turned to leave the shop when one of the hairdressers called out to her.

"Don't leave, honey. We'll make a place for you. Just have a seat. There's free coffee and muffins if you'd like a snack while you wait."

"Thank you. I'll be glad to wait," Mia told her, then took a seat in one of the empty plastic chairs.

As Mia reached forward and picked up one of the style magazines lying on a coffee table, the woman sitting next to her said, "Your hair looks beautiful. I hope you're not planning to cut it."

Easing back in the chair, Mia glanced over to see it was a college-aged woman who'd given her the compliment. Short, feathery spikes of chestnut hair framed a round face while a friendly smile spread a pair of wide lips.

Mia smiled back at her. "No. Just a shampoo and blow-dry. I've tried short hair before and believe me I didn't look nearly as cute as you."

The young woman let out a quiet, bubbly laugh. "Thanks for the compliment, but compared to you I'm just a plain Jane." She thrust her hand over toward Mia. "Hi, I'm Marti Newmar."

Mia shook Marti's hand and as she did she realized it had been months, maybe longer since she'd felt a real need to communicate with another woman just for the sake of talking and sharing ideas. Dear God, maybe this quaint little western town was beginning to help her heal, she thought.

"Mia Smith. Nice to meet you."

Marti's nose wrinkled at the tip as she thoughtfully studied Mia. "I think I've seen you somewhere. You live around here?"

Trying to push away the cloak of wariness she constantly wore, Mia said, "No. I'm a guest at Thunder Canyon Resort."

Marti's lips parted in an *O*, then her fingers snapped with sudden recognition. "That's it. That's where I've seen you. In the resort lounge."

Mia relaxed. She should have known this young woman had to be a local and not someone from Denver or Alamosa, Colorado, where she'd lived for most of her adult life.

"Yes, that's probably where it was," Mia agreed.

"I just started working at the coffee shop in the lounge a few days ago." She laughed. "I'm still learning how to make a latte. I grew up on a nearby ranch and the only kind of coffee my parents ever drank was the cowboy kind. You know, throw the grounds and water into a granite pot and let it boil. This fancy stuff is all new to me."

Warmed by the woman's openness, Mia smiled at her. "I'm sure you'll learn fast."

"I hope so. Grant Clifton, the guy that manages the resort, was kind enough to give me a job doing something. You see, I'm trying to get through college and the cost is just awful. I got a partial scholarship on my grades and this job should help with the rest of the expense."

Marti's situation was so familiar to Mia that she almost felt as though she were looking in a mirror. Five years ago she'd entered college with hopes of getting a degree in nursing. But at that time her father had already passed away and, using what little money she and her mother could earn at menial jobs, she'd had to settle for taking one or two classes at a time. Those years had been very rough and discouraging. It had been during those terribly lean times in her life that her priorities had gone haywire. She'd begun to think that money could fix everything that was messed up in her life. She'd been so very, very wrong.

"Whatever you do, don't give up," Mia encouraged her. "It may take you a while to find your dream, but you will."

Nodding, Marti said, "Yeah, that's what my mother keeps telling me." Tilting her head to one side, she continued to study Mia. "Have you met many people at the resort?"

The young woman's question instantly brought the image of Marshall Cates to Mia's mind.

"A few. I'm not…much of a social person."

"Hmm. Well, there're all sorts of good-looking men hanging around there." She gave Mia an impish grin. "But I only think of them as eye candy. I'm not about to let some smooth-tongued devil change my plans to become a teacher."

"I'm sure some day you'll want to marry. When the time is right for you," Mia told Marti, while wondering if that time would ever come for herself. At one time, Mia had dreamed and hoped for a family of her own. Now she would just settle for some sort of peace to come to her heart. Otherwise she'd never be able to give her love to anyone.

Marti shrugged in a ho-hum way. "I don't know. I've seen my older sister get her heartbroken over and over again." She looked at Mia. "You know Dr. Cates? The hunk that works at the resort?"

Every nerve in Mia's body suddenly went on alert. What was she going to learn about the man now?

"Vaguely," she said, not about to elaborate on the surprise encounter she'd had with the man.

Marti sighed, telling Mia that the young woman definitely considered Marshall Cates eye candy. "Gorgeous, isn't he?"

"He's, uh—a nice-looking man."

"Mmm. Well, my sister, Felicia, thought so, too. They dated for a while and she was getting wedding bells on the brain."

Mia was afraid to ask, but she did anyway. "What happened?"

Wrinkling her nose, Marti said, "She found out the good doctor wasn't about to settle for just one woman. Not when he had a flock of them waiting in line."

So the man was a playboy. That shouldn't surprise her. No matter where he was or who he was with, the man was bound to turn female heads. The best thing she could do was forget she'd ever met him. Still, she couldn't help but ask the question, "Is your sister still dating Dr. Cates?"

Marti chuckled. "No, thank goodness. She finally opened her eyes wide where Marshall Cates was concerned. She recently moved to Bozeman and got engaged to another guy."

Across the room, one of the hairdressers called out. "Marti, I'm ready for you, honey."

Smiling at Mia, the young woman hurriedly snatched up her handbag and jumped to her feet. "Nice meeting you, Mia. Maybe I'll see you at the coffee shop. Come by and say hello, okay?"

Nodding, Mia returned Marti's smile. "Sure. I'll look forward to it."

Later that afternoon, at the resort lodge, Marshall finished up the small amount of paperwork he had to do, then left Ruthann in charge of the quiet infirmary and headed down to the lounge bar for a short break.

Three couples were sitting at tables, busy talking and sipping tall, cool drinks. One older man with graying hair and a hefty paunch was sitting at the end of the bar. He appeared to be sleeping off his cocktail.

Lizbeth Stanton was tending bar this afternoon, and the pretty young woman with long auburn hair smiled when Marshall slid onto one of the stools.

"Hey, there. I was about to decide you weren't going to show up today." She glanced at the watch on her wrist. "This is late for you."

Marshall chuckled. "I'm so relieved that at least one woman around this place is interested enough to keep up with my comings and goings."

She shot him a sexy smile. "Awww. Poor Marshall," she cooed. "Had a bad day?"

With an easy grin, he raked a hand through his dark, wavy hair.

"I've never seen so many patients in one day. Several were suffering from altitude sickness and one had taken a nasty fall on a hiking trail. But they'll all be okay."

Not bothering to ask if he wanted a drink, Lizbeth

went over to a back bar and began to mix him a cherry cola. At one end of the work counter, a small stereo was emitting the twangy sounds of a popular country music tune.

"Well," Lizbeth said to him, "that *is* what you're paid for. To doctor people who have more money than sense."

Yeah, he thought, that's right. But sometimes in the darkest part of the night, when everything looks different, he wondered if he was just as shallow as some of the guests he treated. He'd not gone to school for eight years intending to doctor women who'd ripped off nail beds trying to rock climb with false fingernails. But on the other hand, Marshall was making an enormous salary and most days he hardly had to lift a hand to earn it. He'd be crazy to want anything else. Wouldn't he?

Lizbeth carried the tall glass over to the bar and placed it on a cork coaster before she pushed the frosty drink in front of him.

"Here, since you can't drink anything alcoholic on the job, maybe this will perk you up."

"Thanks, beautiful. Remind me to do something for you sometime." Giving her a wink, he took a sip of the drink, then lifted the stemmed cherry she'd placed on top and popped it into his mouth.

As he chewed the sweet treat, Lizbeth's brown eyes studied him in a calculating way. "Well, if you really mean that you could take me out to dinner tonight. I'm getting tired of taking home a sack of fast food and eating it in front of the television."

Marshall chuckled a second time. He doubted Lizbeth ever had to spend a night alone, unless she wanted it that way. Even if she was known as a big flirt, she was pretty, bubbly and enjoyable to be around, the perfect type of woman for Marshall, who didn't want any sort of clingy hands grabbing hold of him.

"If you'd really like to go out to dinner tonight, then I'm all for it."

A faint look of surprise crossed her face. "You really mean that?"

Marshall shrugged. He and Lizbeth both knew that neither of them would ever be serious about each other, but that didn't mean they couldn't enjoy an evening together. Besides, eating dinner with a warm, appreciative female was better than being snubbed by a cool, beautiful heiress.

"Sure," he answered. "Let's splurge and eat at the Gallatin Room. The grilled salmon is delicious."

Lizbeth's brown eyes were suddenly sparkling and Marshall wondered what it would take to see Mia Smith react to him in such a way.

Damn it, man, forget the woman, Marshall scolded himself. You've got plenty of female distraction around here. You don't need to get hung up on a woman who's apparently forgotten how to smile.

"Oh, this is great, Marshall! I can wear my new high heels. Just for you," she added with coy sweetness. "What time shall we meet?"

"When do you get off work?" Marshall asked.

"Six this evening. But I can ready by seven."

"Okay, I'll meet you in the lounge at seven-thirty," he told her. And by then he was going to make damn sure that the winsome Mia Smith was going to be pushed completely out of his thoughts.

Chapter Three

Mia wasn't at all sure why she'd bothered going out to eat this evening, especially at the Gallatin Room. Before she'd found Janelle, Mia had never been inside a restaurant where the tables were covered with fine linen and the food was served on fragile china. After her father, Will Hanover, had died of a lung disease, she and her mother had been lucky to splurge on burgers and fries at the local fast-food joint. The sort of life she was experiencing here at Thunder Canyon Resort was the sort she could only dream about back then.

Today at the Clip 'N' Curl, her brief visit with Marti Newmar had reminded her even more of how simple and precious those years on the farm had been with her adoptive parents. Maybe she'd not had much in the way of material things, but she'd been wrapped in the security of her family's loving arms. Mia had learned at an early age that she was adopted; yet that hadn't mattered. She'd been a happy girl until her father had died. And then things had gotten tough and she'd made all sorts of wrong choices. She'd begun to believe that money was all it would take to fix everything wrong in her life. Well, now she had it, but she was far from happy.

With a wistful sigh, she realized the Gallatin Room was the sort of restaurant that a woman should visit with her husband or lover. The small table where Mia sat near a wall of plate glass gave a magnificent view of the riding stables and several corrals of beautiful horses. Far beyond, near the valley floor, a river glistened like a ribbon of silver in the moonlight. Yet the pleasant sights couldn't hold Mia's attention. Instead she was imagining what it would be like if the handsome Dr. Cates was sitting opposite her, reaching across the fine white linen and clasping her fingers with his.

"Ms. Smith, your steak will be ready in a few minutes. Would you like more wine?"

Mia looked around to see a young waiter hovering at her elbow, willing to jump through hoops, if necessary, to please her. After the first few days at Thunder Canyon Resort, Mia had become aware that some of the male staff seemed to bend over backward in an effort to make her happy. She'd not been fooled into thinking they were at her beck and call because they liked their job. No doubt they'd heard gossip or simply assumed that she was rich. The fact that she *was* rich, only made her resent their behavior even more.

"Yes, I will take more wine, thank you," she told him.

The young man filled Mia's goblet with the dark, fruity wine she'd selected, then eased back from the table. As he moved from her sight, Mia got a glimpse of movement from the corner of her eye. Turning her head slightly to the right, she was shocked to see the handsome doctor and a sexy redhead taking their seats several tables over from hers.

Mia stared for a moment, then purposely looked away before either of them could spot her. She'd seen the redhead before, but where?

Recognition hit her almost immediately. She was the bartender here at the lounge. Mia had visited the bar on a few occasions, just to enjoy a cocktail and a change of scenery from the rooms of her cabin. The redhead had always been working behind the bar, but Mia had never seen Dr. Cates there. Were the two of them an item? It certainly appeared that way to Mia. But from what Marti Newmar had told her at the Clip 'N' Curl earlier today, the man liked women in the plural form. The bartender was probably just one in a long line waiting for a date with Dr. Smooth.

Across the room, at Marshall's table, he and Lizbeth had ordered and the waiter was pouring chilled Chablis into Lizbeth's stemmed glass when he looked slightly to the left and spotted *the* woman. She was sitting alone and, even over the heads of the other diners, Marshall couldn't mistake the black-haired beauty. It was Mia

Smith, wearing a slim pink sheath and black high heels with a strap that fastened around her ankles. Her black hair was swept tightly back from the perfect oval of her face and knotted into an intricate chignon at the back of her head. She was a picture of quiet elegance and Marshall found it hard not to stare.

"Dining here in this posh part of the resort is quite a treat for me, Marshall. You must be feeling generous," Lizbeth teased.

Jerking his head back to his date, Marshall plastered a smile on his face. Lizbeth was the sort of woman who'd be happy to let a rich man take care of her for the rest of her life. Since it wasn't going to be him, he could afford to feel generous.

"Maybe I just felt as though I had earned my paycheck today," he told her.

She laughed. "Oh, Marshall, you're so funny at times. I hope you never go serious like that brother of yours. He should have been a judge."

Marshall had three brothers. At thirty, Mitchell was four years younger than him. And then there were the twins, Matthew and Marlon, who were just twenty-one and trying to finish up their last year of college.

At one time in their young lives both Marshall and Mitchell had walked somewhat on the wild side. And while the two boys had lived on the edge, they'd both loved a passel of ladies and broken more than a few hearts. But age had slowed both of them down, Mitchell especially. He'd founded a farm and ranching equipment business and spent nearly all his time making the place turn big dollars.

"That's why Mitcheil has made a big success of Cates International," Marshall said to her. "He takes his business seriously. When I'm out on the slopes skiing, he's usually at work. That's the difference between him and me."

Lizbeth playfully wrinkled her nose at him. "What's the use of money if you can't have a little fun with it?"

Marshall sipped at the beer he'd ordered, then licked the foam from his lips. He would surely like to ask Mia Smith that question, he thought. But then maybe she was having fun. Maybe being alone was how she liked things.

He looked back to the table where Mia was dining and before he could catch himself he was gazing at her again. At the moment she was eating one slow bite at a time. There was something very sensual in her movements, as though she was a woman who savored each and every taste. Marshall could only imagine what it would feel like to have those lush lips touching him.

"In case you don't know, her name is Mia Smith."

Lizbeth's comment doused him with hot embarrassment and he quickly jerked his attention back to his dining companion.

"You caught me. What can I say, Lizbeth, except that I'm sorry?"

Laughing lightly, she reached over and touched the top of his hand. "Don't bother. I know when a man considers me just a friend. It might be nice if you looked at me the way you're looking at her. But you don't."

Relief washed through him. Jealous women were

hard to handle, especially in a place that required good manners. "Thanks for understanding, Lizbeth," he said wryly. "I guess I'm pretty transparent, huh?"

"Well, if I knew the Gettysburg address I would have had time enough to recite the whole thing while you were staring at Ms. Smith."

Shaking his head with a bit of self-disgust, he said, "I'm sorry. It's just that—well, I met her yesterday. On the mountain while I was hiking."

Intrigued by this morsel of news, Lizbeth leaned forward. "Really? Did you exchange words with the woman?"

The two of them had exchanged words, glances, even touches, but apparently none of it had affected Mia Smith the way it had Marshall. She'd walked away from him as though he were no more than a servant.

"A few."

"That's all? Just a few?"

"The lady is cool, Lizbeth. She—uh—wasn't interested in getting to know me."

Picking up her wineglass, Lizbeth laughed, which only caused the frown on Marshall's face to deepen. "That's hard to believe. I've talked with her at the bar and she seemed friendly to me."

Now it was Marshall's turn to stare with open curiosity at Lizbeth. "You know the woman?"

Shrugging, Lizbeth said, "She comes in the bar fairly often. Drinks a piña colada with only a dash of alcohol."

"Does she ever have anyone with her?"

"No. She's always alone," Lizbeth answered. "Can't

figure it, can you? The lady is beautiful. Men would swoon at her feet, but apparently she won't let them. Maybe you ought to ask her for a date. If anyone can change her tune about the opposite sex, it would be you, dear Marshall."

He chuckled with disbelief. "Me? Not hardly. I offered to buy her a drink. She pretty much gave me the cold shoulder."

"Maybe you should try again. That is—if you're really interested in the woman."

Unable to stop himself, Marshall glanced over at Mia's table. At the moment she was staring pensively out the window as though she were seeking something in the starlit sky.

"Frankly, I wish I wasn't interested. I have a feeling the lady is trouble. She doesn't come across as the other rich guests around here. She's different."

Lizbeth smiled coyly. "And maybe that's why you can't get her off your mind. Because she *is* different."

He thoughtfully studied his date. "Hmm. Maybe you're right. And maybe once I got to know her, I'd find out she's not my type at all. Then I could safely cross her off my list."

Lizbeth let out a knowing little laugh. "You'll never know until you try."

The next morning on his way to work, Marshall entered the lodge by way of the lounge and headed to the coffee shop. After the busy day in the infirmary yesterday, he wanted to pick up one of those fancy lattes and present it to Ruthann when she walked through the door. No doubt the surprise treat would make his hard-working nurse want to whip out her thermometer and take his temperature, he thought wryly.

At this early hour, the coffee shop was full of customers sitting around the group of tiny tables, reading the *Thunder Canyon Nugget* and the daily newspaper from nearby Bozeman while drinking ridiculously expensive cups of flavored java. Marshall found himself waiting at the back of a long line and wondering if he had time to deal with getting the latte for Ruthann after all, when a vaguely familiar voice spoke behind him.

"Looks like we have a long line this morning."

Turning, he was more than surprised to see Mia Smith. She was dressed casually in jeans and a white shirt with the sleeves rolled back against her tanned arms. Her black hair was loose upon her shoulders and the strands glistened attractively in the artificial lights.

The sight of her put an instant smile on his face. "Yes. Everyone must have had the same idea for coffee this morning."

Mia could feel his gaze sliding over her face and down her throat to where her shirt made a V between her breasts. The sensual gaze made her wonder if he'd looked this same way at his date last night. Then just as quickly she scolded herself for speculating about the playboy doctor. The man's private behavior was none of her business.

Even so, she couldn't stop the next words out of her mouth. "How did you like your dinner last night at the Gallatin Room?"

His brows lifted ever so slightly. "I didn't realize you saw me there."

This morning he was obviously dressed for work in a pair of dark slacks and a baby-blue button-down shirt. A red tie with a blue geometric print was knotted neatly at his throat. She could see that he'd attempted to tame the wild waves of his thick hair, but several of the locks had already fallen onto his forehead. Just one look at him was probably enough to cure most of his female patients.

"I...uh—spotted you and your date when you were arriving."

"Oh. Well, Lizbeth wasn't actually a date. I mean— she was—but we're basically just friends. Actually, she was the one who asked me out."

Mia shot him a droll look. Was this the sort of line he handed out to all unsuspecting females?

"Good for her."

The line of customers began to move forward and she tried to peer around his shoulder to gauge how much longer the wait would be, but the man held her gaze.

"I stopped here at the coffee shop this morning to pick up a latte for my nurse," he explained. "She's always treating me so I thought I'd do something for her."

Figuring his nurse was a twenty-something blonde with long eyelashes and a come-hither smile, Mia said, "Why settle for just a coffee? Perhaps you should take her to the Gallatin Room, too."

To her amazement a look of dawning swept over his face and he nodded in agreement. "You know, that's a wonderful idea. Ruthann has been a nurse for more than thirty years and she's always taking care of other people, even when she isn't on the job. Her husband died of a heart attack about three years ago and she's having a hard time making ends meet with just his social security to help her along. Dinner at the Gallatin Room would be something really special for her. Thank you, Mia, for suggesting it."

Feeling suddenly like a heel, she hoped he never guessed that her suggestion had been given in sarcasm. Damn it, why did she continually want to believe this man was only out for himself? Because Marti had described him as a ladies' man? Or because a user could always spot another user, she thought dismally.

But you're not a user, Mia. Everything you have has been given to you freely. You haven't taken anything from anybody—except your adoptive mother's life.

Trying to shut away the guilty voice inside of her, Mia gave him a hesitant smile. "I—uh—think that would be a very nice gesture for your nurse."

"Well, I'm not always as thoughtful as I should be. Blame it on my male genes."

The grin on his handsome face was as wicked as the images going through Mia's head. She'd never been around a man who continually made her feel like she needed to take deep breaths of pure oxygen. Dr. Cates was making her think things that definitely belonged behind closed doors.

Smiling in spite of herself, she said, "I'm sure your nurse will think you're very thoughtful."

At that moment a customer carrying a portable

cardboard holder filled with several cups of coffee was attempting to work his way through the crowd. As he jostled close to Mia, the doctor's hands closed around her shoulders and quickly set her out of the customer's path.

The abrupt movement brought her even closer to Marshall and he realized her thigh was pressed against his and the thrust of her breasts was almost touching his chest. His breathing slowed, while the faint scent of gardenia filled his head like a gentle breeze on a hot night.

"I—uh—thought that man's drink was going to topple right on you." Reluctantly, he eased his grip on her shoulders. "Sorry if I startled you."

He watched a pretty pink flush fill her cheeks. "I— it's okay. Better to be a little startled than scalded."

The line ahead of them moved again and Marshall quickly glanced over his shoulder to see he was next to place an order. If he was ever going to make his move on this woman he needed to do it now and fast.

"You— I noticed you were dining alone last night and I was wondering if you might like some company tonight? I'm free if you are."

Faint surprise crossed her face, an expression that puzzled Marshall. Surely a woman who looked like her was used to men asking her out to dinner.

"Actually, I don't think I could take the Gallatin Room two nights in a row. It's a little stuffy for my taste."

Hope sprang up in him like an exploding geyser and he wondered what the hell was coming over him. The world was full of pretty women and willing ones at that.

Why had getting a date with this one suddenly become so important?

"Mine, too. I only took Lizbeth there because she— Well, she enjoys that sort of thing, but she can't really afford such a splurge on her own." Another quick glance over his shoulder told him the customer was about to step away from the counter. He turned a beseeching look on Mia. "We could go downtown and maybe grab a burger or pizza. How does that sound?"

She opened her mouth as though to speak, then just as quickly her pink lips pressed thoughtfully together. Behind him, the coffee shop attendant said, "Dr. Cates, it's your turn to order now."

With his eyes riveted on Mia's face, he tossed over his shoulder, "A large latte with plenty of foam."

His dark brown eyes were pulling her in, making her forget there was a crowd of people around them. In the back of her mind, she understood he was a man who would be dangerous to any woman's heart. Yet there was something about his smile that made him impossible to resist.

"Sure," she heard herself saying. "A burger would be nice."

"Great. Where shall I pick you up? Are you staying here in the lodge?"

Not yet ready to give him that much information, she said, "I'll meet you here at the lounge."

A wide smile suddenly dimpled both cheeks and Mia felt her insides go as gooey as warm taffy.

"Great. I'll be here. Six-thirty okay?"

Why not, she thought. It wasn't like she had anything

important to do and maybe it was time she did something about this aimless path she'd been on for the past few months. "Six-thirty is fine. I'll see you then."

After he'd picked up his latte and given her a quick farewell, Mia found herself standing at the counter staring straight into Marti Newmar's smiling face.

"Hi, Mia! I didn't expect to see you here so soon. What can I get you this morning?"

"Hi yourself," Mia greeted the bubbly young woman. "I'd like a cappuccino with sugar and a pecan Danish."

Marti repeated the order to another worker who was busily preparing the drinks and rang in Mia's purchases.

While they waited on the cappuccino, Marti leaned slightly over the counter and said in a hushed voice, "Looks like Dr. Cates has his eye on you. Be careful, Mia. I wouldn't want you to end up like my sister."

Shaking her head, Mia smiled at the young woman's earnest face. "Don't worry, Marti. I'm not about to let the doctor turn my head."

"Yeah, well that's what Felicia said, too."

Thankfully, a worker set her order on the counter and Mia quickly scooped it up. Now that she'd agreed to a date with Dr. Cates, the last thing she wanted to hear were warnings about the man's character. She'd rather find out such things for herself than listen to gossip.

"I'll keep that in mind. See you later, Marti."

At the back of the lodge, in Marshall's airy office, Ruthann sipped leisurely at her latte while Marshall playfully tap-danced around her chair.

"Have you lost your mind, doc?" she asked with a

laugh. "First you surprise me with a cup of coffee that cost more than my wristwatch and now you're trying to imitate Fred Astaire. What else do you have planned for today?"

Laughing, he grabbed her swivel chair and spun her in a wild circle that had her yelling for him to stop.

"How about a date with the heiress? That's what I have planned."

She planted her feet on the hardwood floor and stared at his smug face. "Oh. So that's what this display of joy is all about. You've proved me wrong and talked the mystery beauty into a date. I should have guessed. How did you do it?"

Still smiling, he sauntered over to his desk and took a seat in his plush leather chair. "Frankly, Ruthie, I don't have a clue. I ran into her at the coffee shop and—" He stopped and held up a hand. "Wait a minute, I'd better tell you about last night first. I saw her, the mystery beauty, dining at the Gallatin Room last night."

Ruthann lowered her coffee and frowned at him. "It's a good thing we don't have any patients waiting this morning, cause I'd like to hear what you were doing having dinner in the Gallatin Room. You have so much money that you've decided to start throwing it away?"

His expression suddenly sheepish, Marshall shrugged. "I took Lizbeth out to dinner."

Ruthann groaned out loud. "Oh, Lord, Marshall, what were you thinking? She's nothing but a big flirt."

He batted a dismissive hand at her. "Never mind Lizbeth. I'm not serious about her."

Ruthann's expression turned incredulous. "And you are serious about the mystery woman?"

Marshall chuckled at his nurse's question. "Ruthie, you know me, I don't have plans to get serious about any woman. Why should I? I'm having too much fun."

She smirked. "Why indeed? Have you ever thought of children? Of someone to spend your golden days with?"

Marshall's barked laugh said he was worried about Ruthann's sanity. "Just how old do you think I am, Ruthie? I've got years ahead of me before I think about anything like a family. Right now I've got mountains to climb."

She leveled a thoughtful look at him. "And what are you going to find when you reach the top?"

Tilting the plush chair to a reclining position, he linked his hands at the back of his neck and let out a smug sigh. "The satisfaction of getting there. That's what I'll find."

"Satisfaction, huh? Well, you go on climbing, doc. I'd rather have two loving arms around me."

Chapter Four

Later that evening, before it was time to meet Marshall, Mia sat on the bed in her cabin and slowly sifted through the stack of photos in her hand. She wasn't at all sure why she'd packed the snapshots when she'd left Colorado.

Maybe she'd brought them along as a reminder of all she'd left behind. The photos were the only images she had of herself with her birth mother. They'd been taken during Mia's twenty-sixth birthday party, which had been held at Janelle's lavish home.

A frown tugged at the corners of her mouth. She still couldn't think of the mansion in Denver as her home. But for nearly two years Mia had lived there with her birth mother. During that time she'd tried to fit into Janelle's rich social life and accustom herself to the role of an heiress. All of which had been a drastic change for the young woman who until then had been struggling to work her way through school.

With a sigh, Mia stared at the snapshot in front of her. No one could mistake the identity of the tall woman with her arm draped affectionately around Mia's shoulders. She was almost the mirror image of Mia, only older. One minute Mia had been a young woman in nursing school who longed for the safe and secure home she'd had when her father had still been alive and working their potato farm, a young woman on a long and seemingly fruitless search for her birth mother. The next minute she'd not only found Janelle Josephson but she also discovered the woman was unbelievably rich. After that, Mia and her adopted mother's life had taken a drastic turn.

For years Mia had hunted her birth mother and for just as many years Nina had tried to dissuade her from the search, insisting that Mia's birth mother didn't want to be found. But Mia had felt driven to find the woman who'd signed her baby girl over to a stranger.

In the end, both Janelle and Mia had been shocked at the occurrences that had separated mother and daughter. Controlling parents had led a teenage Janelle to believe her baby was stillborn. She'd had no idea that her daughter was alive and searching for her. As for Mia, it was difficult for her to absorb the fact that she had a wealthy mother, one who seemingly loved her and was only too happy to lavish her with all the treasures and resources that money could buy.

What happens when a person goes from poverty to riches? Mia was a good example of that age-old question. Suddenly she could have any material thing she wanted, but none of it had made her happy.

For a moment the turmoil in Mia's heart brought a stinging mist to her eyes. But then she determinedly pressed her lips together and shoved the photos in the nightstand drawer.

Right now she needed to put her troubled reflections away and put on the cheeriest face she could muster. It was almost time for her to walk down to the lodge and meet Dr. Cates. And she wanted to give the jovial, flirty doctor the impression that she was just as carefree and happy as he.

Minutes later, Mia walked into the lounge and spotted her date sitting on the end of a plush leather couch. He was focusing intently on the BlackBerry in his hand and for a brief moment Mia paused to study his sexy image.

Even after she'd become an heiress, she'd never dreamed a man of his stature would show interest in her. But she realized that if the doctor knew the real truth of her past, he wouldn't be sitting here waiting to have an evening with her.

Tonight, however, she wasn't going to dwell on that, she wanted to have fun and see if she could remember how to enjoy herself on a simple date.

Mia was walking across the lounge and had almost reached the couch where he was sitting, when he happened to look up and spot her approach.

The quick leap of her heart surprised her. For so long now she'd felt numb. Incapable of feeling anything.

Smiling broadly, he rose to his feet and shoved the BlackBerry into the pocket of his blue jeans. As she walked toward him, he quickly closed the last few steps separating them.

"Hello, Ms. Smith," he said warmly.

His voice was just rough enough to be sexy and she wondered what it would sound like if he were to whisper in her ear.

Smiling in return, she thrust her hand toward his. "Please make it Mia. Calling each other Ms. and Dr. over a burger would be a little ridiculous, don't you think?"

"And shaking hands with a beautiful woman is more than ridiculous for me," he said. And before she could guess his intentions, he leaned forward and placed a gentle kiss on her cheek. "There. That's a much better greeting, don't you think?"

His dancing brown eyes held hers, and Mia realized she was far too charmed to scold him for being forward. The skin along her cheekbone tingled where his lips had touched her and she was getting that breathless feeling all over again.

Deliberately avoiding his pointed question, she said, "I hope you haven't been waiting long."

"Not more than five minutes," he answered. "Are you ready to go? Or would you like to have a drink at the bar before we leave the lodge?"

"Actually, I'm hungry. Let's save the drink for another time." If there was another time, she reminded herself. If Marti's opinion of this man was correct, he'd probably have a different woman on his arm tomorrow night.

"Great," he said. "Let's go. My Jeep is waiting outside the lodge."

Figuring his "jeep" would be one of those plush SUV's that could comfortably haul seven, she was surprised to find his vehicle was one of those compact two-seaters built high off the ground and generally used to traverse rough terrain.

After helping her negotiate the lofty step up, Marshall skirted the hood and quickly slid beneath the wheel. While he buckled his seat belt and started the engine, Mia glanced around the small interior. Behind them, a small bench seat was loaded down with a canvas backpack and a pair of boots caked with mud. An assortment of empty bottles that had one time held water and sports drinks lay on the floorboard below. In front, a small crate of CD's was wedged between the console and the dash. Hanging from the rearview mirror was a small dream catcher made of black and white feathers.

"I promise I cleaned the dog hair from your seat before I drove over here to the lodge. The rest of the mess I hope you'll forgive. I get busy doing things I enjoy and put off all the tasks I hate."

Actually she was relieved that he hadn't shown up in some sleek, spotless luxury car. This vehicle made him seem far more human and closer to the lifestyle Mia had been accustomed to before Janelle had taken her in and presented her with a treasure trove of riches.

"It's fine," she assured him as she adjusted the seat belt across her lap. "You say you have a dog?"

He shoved the floor shift into Reverse and backed out of the parking slot. "A blue heeler named Leroy. He's spoiled worse than I am."

Mia smiled faintly as she glanced over at him. "I take it you spoiled him, but who spoiled you?"

He grinned that sexy grin of his and Mia was suddenly reminded of their close quarters. If she were so minded, she could easily reach over and curl her hand over his forearm.

"My mother insists she ruined all of her boys. Much to Dad's dismay," he added with a chuckle.

Interest peaked her brows. "You have brothers?"

"Three. Mitchell. He's thirty. And the twins, Matthew and Marlon, are twenty-one."

Three brothers and a complete set of parents, Mia couldn't imagine having a more wonderful family. "Where do you fit in among the bunch?"

"I'm thirty-four, the oldest of the Cates brood. My parents live north of town, not too far out. Maybe you'd like to meet them before you leave?"

Meet his parents? No. She didn't think so. Making too many memories here might make it that much harder to leave. And she would have to leave soon, she reminded herself. She couldn't continue to hide from Janelle much longer.

"Maybe," she answered.

By now they were leaving the resort area and the Jeep was heading south on Thunder Canyon Road. Ahead of them on the far horizon, the sun was sinking, spreading a golden-pink glow over the mountain basin.

"I guess all the hoopla over the Queen of Hearts mine is what drew you to this area? Or did you choose to stay at Thunder Canyon Resort for other reasons?"

The only reason she'd ended up in Thunder Canyon was because she'd gotten lost on her way out of Bozeman. Originally she'd been intending to travel all the way into Canada. But Marshall Cates didn't need to know the story of her life.

"I thought it would be beautiful and peaceful. And when I saw your little town with its Old West storefronts and flavor, I was enchanted. I didn't know anything about gold being found in Thunder Canyon until I'd been here a few days. From what I hear, the discovery has turned the place upside down."

With a wry twist to his lips, he nodded. "I never realized money could make people go so crazy. People who've been friends around here for years are now fighting over choice lots in town. Everyone wants to get their hands on a piece of the fortune that's coming in from the crush of tourists."

I never realized money could make people go so crazy, thought Mia.

Marshall didn't know it, but he could have spoken those very words about her. For a while money had slanted her every thought and controlled every choice she'd made. Now having the stuff was more like a dirty little secret that she couldn't hide or discard.

Stifling a sigh, she said, "Well, I've overheard several

women in the Clip 'N' Curl beauty salon talking about all the changes that have come to this area. Some of them like the opportunities the gold find has brought about. Others seem pretty resentful of all the traffic as well as all the strangers clomping up and down the sidewalks of their little town. How do you feel?"

Shrugging, he glanced at her and grinned. "Personally, I don't understand these people that want to hang on to the past. Hell, before the gold rush, lots of folks around here were hurting for jobs and an income of any kind. Now most of them are doing better than anyone ever thought possible, including me. And frankly, I don't see anything wrong with a man wanting to do better for himself."

No, Mia thought, doing better for oneself was hardly a crime. Unless somewhere along the way the rush for riches harmed innocent people. The way Mia's desperate need for financial security had ultimately harmed her dear adopted mother.

"I guess it's all in the way a person sees things," she murmured thoughtfully.

He tossed her another grin. "That was put very diplomatically, Mia. Maybe you should referee some of Thunder Canyon's town hall meetings," he added teasingly. "There's been so much feuding going on that the police have to hang close just in case a fight breaks out."

"No, thank you. I'm not into politics, local or otherwise."

She'd hardly gotten the words out of her mouth when the outskirts of town appeared in the distance. In a few short minutes they were passing the town's outdoor ice rink, now a quiet arena in the summer heat; then just around the corner was the Wander-On Inn, a stately old hotel that had originally been built and operated by Lily Divine, Thunder Canyon's own lady of ill repute.

As Mia studied the landmark, Marshall said, "Lily Divine first built that old hotel. If you've read anything about Thunder Canyon's history, you probably haven't forgotten her name. She's been called everything from a wicked madam to a noble suffragette. Her great-great-granddaughter Lisa Douglas owns the Queen of Hearts mine." He shook his head as if that fact was still hard to believe. "Now there's a rags-to-riches story. A couple of years ago, the woman was as poor as dirt and then she finds out she's the owner of a lucrative gold mine. I can't imagine how that sudden catapult must have felt."

Mia could have told Marshall exactly how finding sudden fortune felt. One day she'd been wondering if she could make two meals out of a package of wieners and the next she was eating steak from a gold-rimmed plate. The drastic change in her life had sent her emotions spinning in all directions.

Careful to keep her expression smooth, she asked, "This Lisa…is she happy now?"

Something in her voice pulled Marshall's glance over to her. She looked wistful, even hopeful, and Marshall could only wonder why she would be so interested in the outcome of a person who was a total stranger to her.

"I suppose so. She married one of the Douglases, a

family that probably owns half the valley. In fact, his old man built the resort where you're staying. She'll never want for anything again."

Her lips pursed and then her gaze dropped to her lap and a curtain of black hair swung forward to hide her pained expression. "You can't be sure of that," she said quietly. "People die—things change."

"Yeah. But she'll always have the money."

Her head jerked up and she glared at him as though he'd just uttered a blasphemy. "What does that mean? You think money can take the place of a loved one? Well, it can't!"

Her voice was quivering with outrage and Marshall was befuddled as to why she'd reacted so strongly to his comment. With his right hand he reached over and gently touched her forearm. "Whoa, Mia. Don't get so bent out of shape. I just meant that she'd always have financial security. I like money just as much as the next guy, but my loved ones mean more to me than any-thing—even a gold mine, if I had one."

His gaze left the road long enough to see her release a long breath and her pretty features twist with regret.

"I—I'm sorry, Marshall. Having money has made me too touchy, I guess. But people say insensitive things, especially when they don't understand that we have problems, too."

He wanted to ask her what sort of problems she was talking about, but he could see she was hardly in the mood. Besides, he sensed the woman needed joy and laughter in her life and that was the very thing he wanted to give her.

"You're right, Mia. People are too quick to judge. But let's not have a philosophical discussion about human nature right now. I want to have fun with you tonight. Okay?"

She nodded jerkily and he was relieved to see a faint smile cross her face.

"Sure," she said. "I didn't mean to suddenly get so serious on you. Let's start over, shall we?"

Marshall gave her a broad smile. "Okay, we'll start over. Good evening, Mia. What would you like to eat tonight?"

"Burgers and fries. I'm sure you advise your patients not to eat such things, but maybe you can forget about the fat and calories for one night."

Glad to see she was going to follow his suggestion and lighten up, he chuckled. "Believe me, Mia, doctors don't always practice what they preach. Burgers and fries sound great to me."

At the next intersection, he made a right onto South Main. As they passed the town square with its shade trees and park benches, he said, "There's a little place right down here where I used to eat in all the time when I worked at Thunder Canyon General. They serve plain home-cooked meals and the burgers are great. You can even have a buffalo burger if you'd like."

Her nose wrinkled playfully. "I'm afraid I'm not quite that adventurous. I think I'll stick to plain ole beef."

Moments later Marshall parked the Jeep near a small bar and grill. As they walked down the rough board sidewalk, Mia noticed the front of this particular building was made to look like an Old West saloon, complete with swinging doors.

As they entered the dim interior, she could feel Marshall's hand flatten against the small of her back. And though she'd expected his touch to feel warm and strong, she'd not expected the wild zings of awareness spreading through her body.

Bending his head down to hers, he spoke close to her ear in order to be heard above the country music blaring from the jukebox in the far corner.

"We seat ourselves here at the Rusty Spur," he said. "How about a table over by the wall?"

"Fine with me," she answered.

Tonight the bar and grill appeared to be the popular place to be. Most of the round wooden tables and chairs were filled with diners and beer drinkers. Everyone was dressed casually and seemed to be laughing and talking and generally having a good time. Quite a contrast from the elegant Gallatin Room, she thought wryly.

As soon as Marshall helped her into a chair and took his own seat, a fresh-faced young waitress with a blond ponytail stopped at the side of their table to take their orders.

When Mia requested a soda to go with her food, Marshall said, "They serve beer here that's made at a nearby brewery. It's really good. Wouldn't you like to try one?"

Mia tried not to outwardly stiffen at his suggestion. She wasn't a prude, but after seeing Nina become dependant on alcohol she preferred to limit herself.

With a shake of her head, she said, "No. Soda is fine. But you please go ahead."

While Marshall gave the waitress their order, Mia looked around the L-shaped room. The ceiling was low and crisscrossed with dark wooden beams; the walls were made of tongue and groove painted a pale green. Not far from the swinging door entrance, a long bar, also fashioned from dark wood, ran for several feet. Swiveling stools with low backs of carved wooden spokes served as chairs; at the moment they were all filled with customers.

As the waitress finished scribbling onto her pad and hurried away, Mia turned her attention back to him.

"This seems to be a popular place. You say you used to eat here when you worked at Thunder Canyon General. You worked at the hospital before you took the job at the resort?"

He nodded. "I went to work there right after I finished my internship."

Mia thoughtfully studied his handsome face and realized there were more layers to the man than she'd expected to find.

"What sort of medicine did you practice there? The same thing you do at the resort?"

As Mia watched the corners of his mouth curve upward, she could feel her heart flutter like a happy little bird. Which was totally ridiculous. She'd had men smile at her before, even good-looking men. But they'd not made her blood hum with excitement the way that Marshall did.

"Mostly E.R. work."

"Did you like doing that?"

For a moment he was thoughtful, as though he'd never stopped to ask himself that question. "I suppose. There was always something different going on."

Easing back in her chair, she said knowingly, "But you like your job at the resort better."

His laugh was a mixture of amusement and disbelief. "Of course. Why wouldn't I? It's a cushy job. On most days I only see a handful of patients. I'm provided with a great nurse and the resort pays the astronomical cost of medical liability for me."

The waitress arrived with their drinks. After Mia had taken a long sip of her soda she said, "Is that what you went to medical school for? To get a job like you have at the resort? Or did you become a doctor so you could help people?"

Laughing lowly, he shook a playful finger at her. "Now, now, Ms. Smith. We weren't going to have philosophical discussions, tonight. Remember?"

Blushing faintly, she smiled. "Okay. I won't dig at that anymore. So tell me about your siblings. Do you get along with them?"

"Sure. We're all good buddies. 'Course, with Mitchell and I being closer in age, that made us a little tighter, I suppose. We love our twin brothers, too, but growing up they were just a little too young to do much with us."

"Any of them like sports as much as you?"

"Kind of, the twins are into baseball and football, sports of that sort. But Mitchell is more of a brain than an athlete. I couldn't pay him to climb a mountain with me."

"I don't blame him," Mia said. "It's dangerous stuff."

"Not if you know what you're doing." He leaned toward her, his dark brown eyes twinkling in a way that warmed her blood even more. "I could teach you."

Mia laughed and as she did she realized this was the first time since her mother had died that she'd felt this good. Before she realized what she was doing, she reached over and squeezed his hand with her fingers.

"You must be an optimist, Marshall, if you think you can teach me to climb a mountain. I'm too awkward and certainly not strong enough."

His thumb reached out and curved over hers. The touch was ridiculously intimate, but although Mia told herself to pull away, her body wouldn't obey her brain's instructions. His touch made her feel secure, even wanted. Something she hadn't felt in a long time.

"You hiked all the way up to the bluff on Hawk's Home. That's a pretty stiff climb."

His compliment put a warm blush on her cheeks. "Thank you for the confidence. But that's hiking. That's not what you do with the pulleys and ropes and such."

"I can teach you all that. In baby steps, of course."

The grin on his face deepened, showcasing his dimples. It was hard for Mia to concentrate on their conversation; her senses were spinning, her mind conjuring up all sorts of sexual images.

"I—don't know. Maybe before I leave you can take me on a baby climb."

Surprise and then pleasure swept across his face. "I'd like that, Mia. You'd be the first woman to go climbing with me."

She shot him a skeptical look. "You don't really expect me to believe that, do you?"

"Why not? Most of the women I've dated don't like to do that much outdoor strenuous stuff. A bicycle ride maybe. But not mountain climbing."

For some reason, Mia didn't want to be compared to his other dates. Nor did she want to think of him as a playboy or herself as just one of many women who'd sat across a table from him and held his hand.

Easing her fingers away from his, she said, "Shows you how much sense I have."

The grin on his lips eased to a pleased curve. "No, it means you're unique. Just like I imagined you'd be."

She was unique, all right, Mia thought wryly. If he looked for a hundred years, he wouldn't find another woman who'd turned her back on the loving mother who raised her. He wouldn't find another woman stupid enough to think that financial security would fix all the ills in her life.

Yes, Mia was unique, all right, but in all the wrong ways. Hopefully, Marshall Cates wouldn't discover any of those terrible things about her until long after she'd left Thunder Canyon.

Chapter Five

Before Mia and Marshall left the Rusty Spur, he insisted that the two of them needed dessert and asked the waitress to get them a container of Golden Nugget to go.

Later, after Marshall had paid for the meal and the two of them had left the building, she looked suspiciously at the brown paper sack in his hand.

"What is that—did you call it Golden Nugget?"

His grin mischievous, he helped her into the Jeep. "I did. They conjured up this stuff shortly after the gold strike. You'll find out what it is when we get to where we're going to eat it."

"A man of mystery," she said teasingly. "Well, I suppose I'll just have to wait for this surprise dessert."

Once he'd pulled away from the bar and grill, he

turned the vehicle toward North Main. While he nego-
tiated the busy narrow streets, Mia realized she hadn't
felt this warm and mellow in a long time. Like their
meal, their conversation had been simple and comfortable. She was enjoying being with the man far more than
she had expected.

To Mia's surprise, Marshall drove them straight to
Thunder Canyon Road and stopped the Jeep in the large
graveled parking lot of the ice rink.

"What are we doing at an outdoor ice rink in August?"

Marshall's chuckle was suggestive enough to lift
her brows. "We're going to eat our dessert, what
else?" he asked.

Picking up the brown paper bag, he left the vehicle
and came around to help her down to the ground. As Mia
placed her hand in his she felt a rush of naughty excitement. After nearly three years of avoiding men alto-
gether, being out with a man as sexy and sensual as
Marshall was like having a plateful of cherry pie after
a long stretch of dieting. Sinful, but delicious.

Once she was standing on the ground, he slipped his
free arm around the back of her waist and guided her
toward the rink, which was surrounded by a chain-link
fence and dimly lit by one lone lamp standing near a
small building that was used as a warming room. The
gate was unlocked and once they were inside the
compound they walked over to one of the wooden
benches looking out over the rink.

A huge cottonwood tree shaded the seat while
overhead the fluttering leaves were making soft music

in the evening breeze. In the far distance, the mountains surrounding Thunder Canyon Resort loomed like majestic sentinels robed in deep greens and purples. Mia sighed with pleasure as she sank onto the bench.

"It's pretty here. I'll bet it's really nice when the rink is frozen over and skaters are whirling about. Do you skate?" she asked.

"Sure do. Our parents taught all of us boys how to skate long before we ever went to kindergarten." He smiled fondly out at the now empty rink. "I've had some really fun times here. Even when I cracked my wrist."

He began to open the paper bag and pull out a quart-sized paper carton. When he pulled off the lid she could see it held something that looked like ice cream.

"Oh. A cracked wrist doesn't sound like fun to me."

He handed her one of the two plastic spoons.

"Several of us skaters had made a dandy whip and I was getting a heck of a ride out on the tail end. It was a blast until the g-force finally got me and I flew completely off the ice and crashed into a bench like the one we're sitting on. My wrist was in a cast for six weeks."

Mia gave him a knowing smile. "Sounds like you were a little daredevil. I'll bet you gave your mother plenty of gray hairs."

"Probably more than a few," he admitted with a wry smile. "But my parents always encouraged us to be independent and adventurous. I think it stuck on me the most."

He thrust the container toward her. "Dig in. I can't eat all this by myself."

Mia followed his example and spooned up a bite. As the ice cream melted on her tongue, she closed her eyes and savored the taste. "Mmm. You were right. This is scrumptious."

"See, the streaks of caramel are supposed to represent veins of ore and the chunks of almonds are the gold nuggets. This is definitely one good thing that came out of the Queen of Hearts striking it rich. Next to you, that is," he added with a wink.

Mia understood his words were just playful flirting, but she also considered how nice it would be—and more than flattering—for a man like him to look at her in a serious way. When her father had still been alive and her life had been fairly secure, she'd been smart enough to know that she'd never belong to the elite of the world. She didn't dream of marrying a prince or even a doctor or a lawyer. She'd always pictured herself with a farmer or, at the very most, a man who made his living working outdoors, like Lance, who'd worked as a Colorado forest ranger.

But after a tumultuous year of dating, Lance had walked away from her, she thought grimly. He'd tired of her obsessive search for her birth mother, then later he'd hated the woman she'd changed into after finding Janelle and her inheritance.

Trying to shake away that dismal thought, she lifted her gaze to Marshall and gave him a lopsided smile. "You need to remember that Golden Nugget is a permanent fixture here in Thunder Canyon. I'm not."

His spoon paused in midair as the corners of his

mouth turned downward in an exaggerated frown. "You're not leaving soon, are you?"

This past week Mia had been telling herself that it was time to go, time to get back to reality and finally make a few painful decisions concerning her relationship with Janelle. But then she'd met Marshall on the mountain and now she was foolishly looking for any reason to stay at the resort a few days longer.

Dropping her gaze to the ice-cream container wedged between their thighs, she murmured, "I don't suppose it's necessary for me to leave in the next few days. But I—really should."

The last word had hardly died on her lips when his forefinger slid beneath her chin and lifted her face up to his. The serious look she saw on his handsomely carved features jolted her; her heart pounded heavily.

"We're just now getting to know each other, Mia. I really would like you to stay longer."

His gravelly voice was a soft purr and the sound tugged at every feminine particle inside of her. "I— uh—I'll think about it."

Suddenly his head was bending toward hers and the whispered words that passed his lips skittered a warning down her spine.

"Maybe you should think about this."

Mia wasn't totally naive. She knew what was coming and knew she should jump from the bench and put a respectable distance between herself and the handsome doctor. But longing and even a bit of curiosity held her motionless as his lips descended onto hers.

Cool and sweet from the ice cream, his hard lips moved gently, coaxingly over hers. Mia's senses quickly began to tilt. In search of an anchor, her hands reached for his shoulders and she gripped the muscles as the lazy foray of his kiss went on and on.

By the time he finally lifted his head, Mia was breathless and her face was burning.

"A man isn't supposed to kiss a woman like that on their first date," she said as primly as she could, while inside she was quaking, shocked that she could feel such connection from a single kiss.

A crooked grin spread across his face and even in the semidarkness she could see that his brown eyes were shining as though he'd just conquered a dragon and laid it at her feet.

"Well, I was pretending that this was our second date. Forgive me if I was too forward."

She swallowed as emotions tangled into a ball in her throat. "You were. But that's my fault. I should have stopped you in the first place."

Before he could make any reply, she jumped from the bench and began walking around the edge of the rink. The deep reaction she'd felt to Marshall's kiss had left her almost frantic and she told herself she should have never agreed to this date in the first place. It was clear that nothing meaningful could ever happen between them. Being with him was asking for trouble.

Her mind was spinning with all sorts of agonizing thoughts when his hand came down on her shoulder and stopped her forward motion.

"Mia, wait. Don't be angry."

Quickly, she turned to face him and when she spoke Marshall was surprised to hear her voice was almost contrite. As though she were apologizing for kissing him. The idea stunned him.

"I'm not angry at you, Marshall. I—"

Before she could react, he wrapped his arms around her and pulled her close against him. "You're a beautiful woman, Mia. I've wanted to kiss you ever since I met you. There's nothing wrong in what just happened between us."

Even though it had been more like an earthquake than a kiss, Marshall thought. His head was still reeling, but he was wise enough to know that he had to play down the whole thing. She was already trying to run from him and he couldn't let that happen. One way or the other he was going to make her his woman—at least for a while.

Her fingers fluttered against his chest while farther down her thighs were brushing against his. Desire surged through him like a prairie wildfire.

"Marshall, I'm just a tourist. The most we can ever be is friends. And friends don't touch each other like this."

She started to push him away, but he held her for a moment longer. "You and I are going to be more than friends, little darlin'. You might as well take my word on that."

Frowning, she stepped out of the circle of his arms and marched back in the direction of where they'd been sitting. Marshall tempered his long strides to match hers.

"Are you this—this arrogant and cocky and overly confident with your other dates?" she demanded.

He laughed. "I don't know. My other dates have never stirred me up like this."

She shot him a glare. "Then you'd better give yourself a pill to get unstirred, doc. Because I have no intention of becoming one of your many lovers!"

By now they were back at the gate that would lead them to the parked Jeep. As her hand reached to open the latch, Marshall caught it with his.

"Whoa now, Ms. Smith. Somewhere along the way things have gotten way out of hand. I'd like to know where this 'many' came from?" he asked crossly. "How would you know how many women I've bedded?"

Her lips pressed tightly together, then she deliberately turned her head away from him. "I shouldn't have said that. I'm sorry. It's none of my business anyway."

More frustrated than he could ever remember being, Marshall raked a hand through his hair and blew out a weary breath. "Okay. I'm sorry, too. I shouldn't have thrown that taunt at you. I just—well—I like you, Mia. I really like you." His voice was a low, gentle murmur as he dared to step closer. "And I do want us to be more than friends. There's nothing wrong in being honest with you, is there?"

Her head turned back to his and he was disappointed to see that her expression was carefully guarded, as though she didn't trust him enough to allow him to see what she was actually feeling and thinking. It wasn't the first time he'd noticed the curtain she pulled across her features and he suddenly vowed to himself that he was going to learn what was behind those beautiful eyes, no matter how long it took or how painstaking the effort.

"No. I do appreciate your being up-front with me," she said finally. "I'm just trying to tell you that I'm not in the market for a brief affair."

His fingertips made gentle circles on the back of her hand. "Why? Do you have a boyfriend or fiancé waiting for you back in Denver?"

Her lips parted and she hesitated for a split second before she replied, "No. There's no significant man in my life."

Marshall didn't realize how much her answer meant to him until she said it. Relief poured through him like a warm spring rain.

"Look, Mia, I'm not asking you to have an affair with me. I'm just asking you to spend time with me and see where it takes us. That's all." Taking her hand between his, he gave her a pleading grin. "I think we can have fun together, Mia. And I have a feeling you could use a little of that."

A few stilted moments passed before she let out a soft sigh and the stiffness in her body melted away.

With a halfhearted smile, she said, "I'm sorry, Marshall. I shouldn't have overreacted the way I did."

"Forget it. I'm just as guilty." His fingertips tenderly touched her cheek. "What do you say we go finish the ice cream?"

Her quiet laugh warmed his heart.

"It's probably melted by now."

Draping his arm around her shoulders, Marshall turned her back toward the ice rink. "Then we'll drink it."

Two days later, Marshall's Thursday turned out to be a busy day at the infirmary. He'd tended everything from strained knees to poison ivy to bee stings. However, the last patient he examined didn't have the usual external problems he normally encountered. The middle-aged woman he was treating complained of stomach complications. She was dressed in casual but expensive clothes and her jewelry shouted that her bank account was overflowing. Yet Marshall didn't miss the fact that her ring finger was conspicuously empty.

"I really think it's just a virus, doctor. If you could just give me something for the pain—my stomach feels like it's clenching into a tight ball."

Stepping back from his patient, Marshall studied her face. She'd obviously had a face-lift at some point. The job wasn't a bad one, but as a doctor he could easily pick up on the telltale tightened skin. Her light blond hair had been manufactured at a beauty salon, probably to cover the gray that was beginning to frost her temples. Yet on the whole she was an attractive woman, or would be, he decided, if her eyes weren't filled with such sadness.

Is that why you went to medical school? To get a cushy job? Or did you become a doctor so you could help people?

Mia's pointed questions suddenly hit him like a brick. Normally, he wouldn't have taken the extra time to dig into this patient's problem. In the past Marshall would have simply written her a prescription to relieve her symptoms and sent her on her way. She obviously needed more help than he could give her. But now, with Mia gnawing at his conscience he felt compelled to do more for this woman.

"Ms. Phillips, I have my doubts that your stomach problem is a virus. Something like that usually lasts no longer than a couple of days and you tell me this problem has been going on for two or three weeks."

She nodded. "That's right. It started while I was still home, but I ignored it. I thought once I got here at the resort I'd feel better. You know, getting out and away from…things always makes a person forget their aches and pains."

Thoughtfully, he placed the clipboard he was holding on the edge of a cabinet counter. "Do you have a family, Ms. Phillips?"

A nervous smile played upon her carefully lined lips. "Call me, Doris, doctor. And yes, I have…a daughter. She's grown now and just married this past spring."

"That's nice. And what about your husband?"

She suddenly looked away from him and her fingers fiddled nervously with the crease of her slacks. "I'm not married anymore. We're divorced. He—uh—found someone else."

"Oh. I'm sorry. Guess that's been hard on you."

Her short laugh was brittle. "Twenty years of marriage down the drain. Yes, it's been a little worse than hard. Now my daughter is gone from the house and—and the place is really empty. I decided to come here to the resort to be around people and hopefully make new friends."

Marshall gave her shoulder an encouraging pat. "It's good that you're trying to change your life, Doris, and things will get better. In the meantime, I'm going to give you a prescription that will help ease your stomach. I have an idea that all the stress you've been through is causing the problem and I want to give you this anti-anxiety medication." He pulled a small pad from his lab coat pocket and began to scribble instructions for the pharmacist. "But I want you to come see me again before you leave. If this doesn't help, we'll take a closer look, okay?"

A bright look of relief and gratitude suddenly lit the woman's face. "Yes, doctor. Thank you so much."

Marshall left the examining room with a warm feeling of accomplishment and was still smiling when he met Ruthann at the end of the hallway.

"What's the grin all about?" the nurse asked. "Happy that you've finished the last patient for the day?"

Frowning, he thrust Doris Phillips's chart at her. "Put this away, will you? And no, I'm smiling because I think I just made someone actually feel better."

Rising on her tiptoes, Ruthann placed her palm on his forehead. "Yeah, you're a little flush. One of the patients must have passed a bug to you."

The frown on his face deepened. "Quit it, will you? I am a doctor, you know. My job is to make people feel better."

He pushed her hand away and stalked toward his

office. Ruthann hurried after him. "I was only teasing, doc," she said as he took a seat at his desk. "What's with you, anyway?"

Picking up a pen, he tapped the end against the blotter on his desk as he regarded his concerned nurse. "Nothing is wrong, Ruthie. Aren't I supposed to enjoy my job?"

"Well, yes. But I never remember you—well, you mostly get to the point and send the patients on their way. You were in there so long with Ms. Phillips I was beginning to think she'd attacked you or something."

Was that how Ruthann saw him? Effective but without compassion? Marshall realized he didn't care for that image. But then he had no one but himself to blame.

"The woman has stomach problems and I was trying to get to the root of the matter. She thought she'd picked up a virus but the real germ she's dealing with is an ex-husband."

"Oh. You got that out of her?"

It had been easy, Marshall realized, to get his patient to open up. So why wasn't it easy with Mia Smith? After their date last night, he'd realized that she truly was a mystery woman. She didn't talk about her family or her past and the shadows that he sometimes noticed clouding her eyes meant that whatever troubles life had thrown her way were still haunting her. But what were they and why did he feel this need to help her?

Seeing that this new, more compassionate side of him was putting a look of real concern on Ruthann's face, he laughed and gave her one of his usual winks.

"Ruthie, I haven't lost my touch with women yet."

Seeing him back to his normal self, Ruthie rolled her eyes with amusement. "And I'm pretty certain you never will." She walked over to a door that would take her into another room where hundreds of charts, most of them from one-time patients, were stored. "Ready to call it an evening? Dr. Baxter should be here any minute."

Dr. Baxter was the doctor who worked evenings and remained on call all night long. The man had much less to do than Marshall, but Grant insisted that medical personnel be available to the guests twenty-four hours a day—just one of the added conveniences that set Thunder Canyon Resort apart from the competition.

"Go ahead, Ruthie, I think I'll stop by the lounge and have a drink before I head home."

Her expression suddenly turned thoughtful as she walked over to his desk. "I hope you're not stopping by to see Lizbeth Stanton. That girl doesn't need any encouragement. She has her eye on you and any man that could give her a home on easy street."

Marshall dismissed Ruthann's remark by batting a hand through the air. "You're being a little too harsh on the woman, Ruthie. She's really not all that bad. She just needs to grow up a little and get her head on straight."

"Well, just as long as you're not the one doing the straightening," Ruthann said.

Laughing, Marshall turned off the banker's lamp on his desk, then rose to his feet and pulled off his lab coat. "Ruthie, I can't go around fixing all my girlfriends. Now," he said, curling an affectionate arm around her shoulders, "how would you like to go to dinner with me at the Gallatin Room some night soon?"

Ruthann practically gaped at him. "Me? With you? At the Gallatin Room?" Before Marshall could answer, she let out a loud laugh, then patted his arm in a motherly way. "I couldn't step foot in that place. Not with the clothes in my closet. But thank you for the gesture, Marshall. It's sweet of you." Leaving his side, she opened the door to the chart room. After she stepped inside, she stuck her head around the door and added, "Listen, doc, that mystery heiress you were so enchanted with the other day is the kind you need to be taking to the Gallatin Room. Why don't you ask her?"

Because something told him that Mia needed more than glitz and glamour and a meal at a ritzy restaurant.

Thankfully, Ruthann didn't expect any sort of answer from him and Marshall didn't give her one. Instead, he quickly hung his lab coat on a nearby hall tree and told his nurse goodbye for the day.

A few minutes later, Marshall entered the lounge. For an early weekday evening, the place was unusually full of guests. But he didn't pay much attention to the people relaxing on the tucked leather couches and armchairs covered in spotted cowhide. Instead, he made his way straight to the bar where Lizbeth was busily doling out mixed drinks to a group of barely legal young men.

Marshall slung his leg over a stool at the end of the bar and waited for her to finish placing a tray of drinks in front of the lively group.

"Hey, what does it take for a guy to get any service around here?" he called when she finally turned in his direction.

Smiling with apparent pleasure at seeing him, Lizbeth waved and hurried to his end of the polished bar. "Doctor, all you have to do to get a woman's attention is just throw her a grin."

Not where Mia Smith was concerned, he thought. She seemed immune to those things that normally charmed women. Looking at Lizbeth, he inclined his head toward the boisterous group of men at the other end of the bar. "You've got me confused with those young guys."

Resting her forearms on the bar, Lizbeth leaned slightly toward him and lowered her voice so that only he could hear her words. "They just think they know how to flirt with a woman, but they're still wet behind the ears. Unlike you, Dr. Cates."

Any other time Marshall would have laughed at Lizbeth's flirtatious remark, but this evening it only made him feel old and even a bit shallow. It was a hell of a thing when a man was more noted for being a playboy with the women than a doctor to the sick.

"Give me a beer, Lizbeth. Something strong and cold."

"Sure." All business now, she started to push away from the bar, but at the last moment paused and gave him a thoughtful look. "Just in case you're interested, I saw that *heiress* of yours a few moments ago walk out to the sundeck. She was carrying a book of some sort. You might still find her out there reading. Or maybe she's just pretending to read and really looking at the scenery." To make her point, Lizbeth glanced at the young men she'd just served.

Marshall's head whipped around and his gaze studied the far wall of glass that separated the lounge from the large wooden sundeck. From this vantage point, he could see several people lounging on the bent-willow lawn furniture, but Mia wasn't one of them.

Quickly, he slipped off the stool. "Forget the beer, Lizbeth. I'll catch one later."

As he strode away, he heard the bartender call after him. "Good luck."

Luck? It was going to take more than that for him to get inside Mia Smith's head and delve into her secrets, he thought as he stepped onto the sundeck. Or was it really her heart that he wanted to unlock and hold in the palm of his hands?

Chapter Six

Marshall was asking himself how a question of that sort had ever gotten into his mind when he spotted her. She was stretched out in a lounger, her long legs crossed at the knees, her shiny black hair lying in one thick, single braid against her shoulder. A book was open on her lap, but her gaze was not on the pages. Instead she was staring straight at him and the tiny smile that suddenly curved her lips hit Marshall smack in the middle of his chest.

If he'd been a smart man he would have turned and run in the opposite direction just as hard and fast as he could. But when it came to the opposite sex, Marshall was as weak as a kid in a candy shop. And Mia Smith was definitely one delectable piece of candy.

Feeling like a man possessed, he walked to her chair

and squatted on his heels near the arm so that his face would be level with hers.

"Hello, Mia."

"Hi yourself."

Her voice was soft, sweet and husky. The sound shivered over him and for one fleeting moment he felt like a humble knight kneeling to the princess fair.

"Lizbeth told me I might find you out here. Been reading?" He glanced briefly at the hardback book in her lap, then back to her face. There was a faint hint of color on her cheekbones and lips, but for the most part it was bare of makeup, giving him a hint at the natural beauty he would see if he were to wake and find her head pillowed on his shoulder.

"Trying. But the story is rather slow. And there's a bit too much distraction around the lodge," she added with a pointed smile.

"That's me. A distraction," he jokingly replied while everything inside of him wanted to reach for her hand and bring the back of it to his lips. He wanted to taste the soft skin and watch the reaction on her face.

Folding the book together, she swung her legs over the side of the lounger where he was still crouched. She was so close that the flowery scent of her perfume drifted to his nostrils and the palm of his hand itched to slide up her bare thigh.

"Are you finished with work for the day?" she asked.

He nodded, then with a nervousness that was totally foreign to him, he asked, "Do you have plans for the evening?"

Marshall's question made Mia realize just how unplanned her life was at this moment. Staying here at Thunder Canyon Resort was easy and pleasant. But she was living in limbo and sooner or later she was going to have to step over the dividing line.

A sardonic smile touched her lips. "I don't really have anyone around here to make plans with."

"You have me."

His simple words unsettled her far more than he could ever know and, to cover her discomfiture, she rose to her feet and walked over to a low balustrade that lined the edge of the sundeck.

Slanted rays of the sinking sun painted the distant bluffs and forests a golden green. Below them, guests ambled around the manicured grounds of the resort. As her senses whirled with his blatant comment, Mia carefully kept her gaze on the sights in front of her.

"That is—if you want me."

She hadn't realized he'd walked up behind her until his murmured words were spoken next to her ear. She tried not to shiver as his warm breath danced across the side of her cheek.

"I—uh—enjoyed last night," she admitted. In fact, Mia had lain awake most of the night, reliving the connection she'd felt when Marshall had kissed her. It had been more than a fiery meeting of lips. The kiss had been full of emotions so ripe with longing and sensuality that she'd felt it all the way to her heart. And that scared her.

His body eased next to hers and she felt his warm arm encircling the back of her waist.

"So did I," he said lowly.

Part of her started to melt as his fingertips slid back and forth against her forearm.

She was trying to think of any sensible thing to say when he spoke again.

"And I was wondering before I ever left my office if you'd like to have dinner with me again."

All sorts of skeptical thoughts raced through her head. What could a successful man like him find attractive about her, she asked herself. She was not a raving beauty or a sexy party girl. She wasn't even much of a conversationalist. As far as she was concerned she was totally boring. She was also a fake. How long would it take him to figure her out, she wondered dismally.

"Dinner tonight?"

He nodded and she couldn't mistake the sensual glint in his green-brown eyes. As his gaze traveled slowly over her face, the suggestive sparkle warmed her cheeks.

"Sure. Have you eaten yet?"

If Mia had had any sense at all, she would have lied and told him she'd just stuffed herself at the Grubstake, a fast-food grill located in the lounge. At least that way she'd have an excuse to politely turn him down. But the awful truth was that she didn't want to turn the man down. Being with him was too exciting, too tempting for her lonely heart to pass up.

"No. Before you walked out here I was thinking about grabbing a salad at the Grubstake."

His nose wrinkled with disapproval. "You need more than rabbit food. How about letting me grill you a steak at my place? I'm pretty handy as a chef." A corner of his lips curved up in a modest grin. "An outdoor chef, that is."

She hesitantly studied his face. "At your place?"

The grin on his face deepened, saying she had nothing to fear, and when his fingertips reached out to trace a lazy circle on her cheek, she knew she was lost.

"Yes, my place. I live here on the resort, not far from the lodge. I'd like for you to see it. And while you're there you can meet Leroy. He loves company."

Seeing his home, meeting his dog—did she really want to let herself get closer to this man? Especially when she knew she could never have a meaningful relationship with him.

"I…Marshall…"

As she began to hesitate, he wrapped his arm around hers and led her away from the balustrade toward a set of steps that would take them off the sundeck. "I'm not about to let you say no," he said. "So don't even try."

"Okay, okay," she said, laughing. "But I need to go home and change first."

He glanced pointedly at her denim shorts and pale yellow T-shirt. "Why? You look great to me and I'm the only one who's going to see you. Besides, this is going to be a casual affair."

Knowing she'd already lost, Mia groaned with surrender and allowed him to lead her around to the back of the massive ski lodge to the private parking area where his Jeep was parked.

The drive to his home took less than five minutes on a winding road that spiraled up the mountainside.

Spruce and aspen trees grew right to the edge of the road and shaded patches of delicate blue and gold wildflowers nodding in the evening breeze.

Suddenly the road widened and the Jeep leveled onto a wide driveway. Mia leaned forward at the sight of a large log structure with a steep red-metal roof nestled among several pines and cedars.

A graveled walkway lined with large white stones led up to a long, slightly elevated porch made of wooden planks. Ferns and blooming petunias grew in baskets hanging along a roof that was supported by more thick logs. Double doors made of wood and frosted glass served as an entrance to the charming structure.

"Wow, is this the sort of housing all the employees at the resort get?"

His chuckle was almost a little guilty. "No. I'm an exception. When the resort was first being constructed, this house was actually built to rent as a honeymoon suite. But for some reason that was nixed and I ended up getting it for my digs."

She glanced at him curiously as he parked the Jeep in front of the house. "Why? Because you're the resort's doctor?"

His expression a bit sheepish, he answered, "No. Grant Clifton, the manager of the resort, is a good friend of mine. We grew up together and attended the same school. It helps to have friends in high places."

Had it helped her to have a mother in high places? Mia asked herself. She'd be lying to say it hadn't. She was no longer scraping pennies to buy gas for a clunker car to carry her from a ratty apartment to the college campus, or wondering how she was going to find enough in the cabinets to cook a meal for her adoptive mother and herself. But in most ways Janelle's massive wealth had only caused Mia grief and more trouble than she could have possibly imagined. From the moment she'd found Janelle, the woman had smothered her with love and money. By themselves those two things would have been good, but along with the love and money, Janelle had also wanted to hold on to Mia and control her every step. Having spent years believing her baby girl had been stillborn, she now clung to the grown daughter that had miraculously been resurrected before her eyes.

"Well, it's a beautiful place," she finally said to him. "I'm sure you must love it here."

"It's nice" was his casual reply before he opened the door and climbed out to the ground.

After he helped her out of the vehicle and they began the short walk to the porch, Mia glanced expectantly around her. "I was expecting your dog to run out to meet us. Where is he?"

With his hand at her back, he ushered her up the three short steps to the porch.

"The backyard is fenced. That's where Leroy has to stay. Otherwise, he'd follow me down to the lodge and harass the guests."

"Oh," she said warily. "He bites?"

Marshall laughed. "No. But he'll knock you down trying to get your attention. I suppose I should send him to obedience school, but I'd miss him too much. And besides, none of us behave perfectly. Why should I expect Leroy to?

None of us behave perfectly. He couldn't have gotten that more right, Mia thought. But if he could see into her past behavior she doubted the doctor would have that same lenient compassion toward her.

Don't think about that now, Mia. Just enjoy the moment and bank this pleasant time in your memory. Once you leave Thunder Canyon and face your real life again, you're going to need it.

"We all have our bad habits," she murmured. "I'm sure Leroy is a nice boy."

Chuckling, he opened the door and ushered her over the threshold. "You've got it all wrong, Mia. I'm the nice boy around here and Leroy is the animal."

They passed through a small foyer furnished with a long pine bench and a hall tree adorned with several hats and jackets that she supposed would be needed once autumn came and the cold north winds began to blow across the mountains and plains.

"Oh, this is nice and cozy," she commented as they walked into a long living room with a wide picture window running along one wall.

Rustic pieces of furniture fashioned of varnished pine and soft butter-colored leather were grouped together so that the spectacular mountains could be viewed from any seat. Brightly colored braided rugs covered the oak flooring while the chinked log walls were covered with paintings and photos. Potted plants sat here and there around the room and from their lush appearance Mia figured he must have a green thumb along with his eye for the ladies.

"Well, I'm sure it doesn't compare to your home," he said, "but it suits me."

Pretending to study the view beyond the window, Mia looked away from him and hoped the mixed feelings swirling through her didn't show on her face.

It was true that Janelle's home was a mansion and large enough to hold several houses this size. But the last ratty apartment that she'd shared with Nina had been more of a home to her than any of those opulent rooms in Janelle's house. Funny that she could see that so clearly now when only a couple of years ago she'd believed Janelle was welcoming her into a castle in paradise. Dear God, she'd been so naive, so gullible, she thought.

"I think it's beautiful," she said, then turned to him and smiled in spite of the tears in her heart. "Where's the kitchen? I'll help you get things started."

"Whoa, slow down, pretty lady. We're going to relax and have a drink first. That is, after I change out of these work clothes. Why don't you have a seat and I'll be right back."

She was far too nervous to simply sit while she waited for him to return. Clasping her hands behind her back, she said, "I think I'll just wander around the room and see how good you are about keeping things dusted."

"Lord, I'd better hurry," he said with a laugh and quickly darted through an open doorway.

Once he was gone from the room, Mia ambled slowly along the walls, curiously inspecting the many paintings that depicted the area and the cherished photos that were carefully framed and lovingly displayed. Eventually she discovered one of four smiling boys and an adult man, all of them dark-haired and all possessing similar features. The group had to be the Cates brothers and their father.

As she quietly studied their smiling features, she felt a pang of total emptiness in her heart. If Mia had been lucky enough to have siblings, her life would have no doubt taken a different track. Certainly she wouldn't have felt such a driving need to search for her birth mother. And with a sibling to lean on, Mia mightn't have been so profoundly influenced by Janelle. But ifs didn't count. And she'd not been as blessed as Marshall Cates.

Moments later, Marshall stepped through the door and spotted Mia at the far end of the room. Just seeing her there filled him with strange emotions. He'd never invited one of his girlfriends here before and he wasn't exactly sure why he'd felt compelled to blurt the sudden invitation to Mia. Something about her seemed to make him lose all control and throw out all the dos and don'ts he carefully followed with other dates. The fear that he might be headed for a big fall niggled at the back of his mind, yet the sight of her slim, elegant body standing in his living room was somehow worth the risk.

Obviously lost in his family photos, she didn't hear him approach until he was standing directly behind her. Resting his hands lightly on her waist, he said in a teasing voice, "I see you found the Cates brood. What do you think? That we could pass for the wild bunch?"

She didn't answer immediately. Instead, she turned and gave him a smile that was wobblier than anything. The glaze of moisture in her eyes completely dismayed him.

"You have a nice-looking family, Marshall," she said huskily. "You must love them very much."

Before he could say anything, she eased out of his grasp and stepped around him. As Marshall turned to follow, he could she was wiping a finger beneath her eyes. The image hit him hard and he was stunned to discover his throat was knotted with emotion. Why would seeing a photo of his family affect her like this? he wondered. And why was her tearful reaction tearing a hole right in his chest?

Clearing his throat, he caught her by the shoulder and gently pulled her to a standstill. "Mia? Are you okay?"

She lifted her face up to his and the smile he found plastered upon her delicate features was really just a cover-up and they both knew it.

"Of course I'm okay. I...I just get silly and sentimental at times. Don't pay any attention to me. Women get emotional. You ought to know that, doc."

Of course he understood women were emotional creatures, but as far as he could remember none of his dates in the past had ever shed a tear in front of him. The women he squired were more likely to have fits of giggles, a sign he must be dating good-time girls, he thought, then immediately wondered why that fact should fill him with self-disgust.

He glanced back at the photo of his family. Then, looking questioningly to her, he asked, "Do you have siblings?"

Shaking her head, she said, "No. I'm an only child."

She tried to smile again and this time her soft lips quivered with the effort. Marshall was stunned at how much he wanted to pull her into his arms and soothe her. Not kiss or seduce her, but simply quiet her troubled heart. Something strange was definitely happening to him.

"I'm—sorry, Mia," he murmured. Then, quickly deciding he needed to put an end to the soppy moment between them, he urged her forward. "Come on," he said a bit gruffly. "Let's go have a drink and start dinner. I don't know about you, but I'm famished."

She seemed relieved that he'd suddenly changed the subject and by the time they reached the kitchen, she appeared to have pulled herself together. Marshall did his best to do the same as he went to the cabinet where the glasses were stored.

"Would you like a beer or a soda? I have a bit of everything stashed around here," he told her.

After a long pause, she answered. "I—uh, I really don't care much for alcohol."

Marshall looked over his shoulder to see she was resting her hip against the kitchen table, her long bare legs were crossed and she was studying him through lowered lashes. The provocative sight forced him to draw in a long, greedy breath of air.

"Oh. Since you visited the lounge, I didn't figure you had anything against drinking."

"I—" suddenly she straightened away from the table and glanced at a spot over his shoulder "—I have a weak cocktail on occasion. And I don't mind other people enjoying themselves. But it bothers me when it's abused."

Had she had trouble with overdrinking herself, Marshall wondered, then quickly squashed that question. She didn't seem the sort of woman to lose control over anything—even though that kiss they'd shared at the ice rink had been hot enough to sear his brain cells.

"Well, unfortunately we humans abuse a lot of things. Even food," he said.

"And people," she added in a small voice.

"Yeah, and people," he grimly agreed, then quickly shrugged a shoulder and grinned. "But we're not going to ruin our evening together by fretting over the ills of the world. Why don't I fix you a soda and I'll have a beer?"

Her smile was grateful. "Sounds good. Let me help."

Happy to change the solemn mood, Marshall gave her a glass to fill with ice then showed her where a selection of sodas was stored in the pantry. Once they had their drinks in hand, he ushered her out the back door and onto a wide deck made of redwood planks.

Almost instantly, she heard loud happy barks and turned around to see a stocky dog with a bobbed tail bounding onto the deck and straight at them.

"Leroy! Don't even think about doing your jumping act," Marshall warned the animal. "You sit and I'll introduce you to our guest."

The blue-speckled dog seemed to understand what his master was saying and Mia was instantly charmed as Leroy sat back on his haunches and whined happily up at her.

"Oh, you're gorgeous," she said to the dog, then glanced questioningly at Marshall. "Is it okay if I pet him?"

Marshall laughed. "That's what he's waiting for. But beware. He'll smother you if you let him."

Placing her soda on a small table, Mia leaned down and with both hands lovingly rubbed Leroy's head. "You're just a teddy bear," she cooed to the dog. "I'll bet you wouldn't hurt a fly."

"Maybe not a fly," Marshall said with amusement, "but he'd love to get his teeth around a rabbit or a squirrel."

Mia stroked the dog's head for a few more moments then picked up her soda. Marshall waited until she'd settled herself on one of the cushioned lawn chairs grouped on the deck before he took a seat next to her.

Leroy crawled forward to Mia's feet, then rested his muzzle on his front paws. Smiling affectionately at the dog, she said to Marshall, "I'll bet he's a lot of company for you. Have you had him long?"

"Close to two years. I got him not long before I came to work here at the resort."

Mia glanced over at him and felt her heart lurch into a rapid beat. She'd been around handsome men before, but there was some indefinable thing about Marshall that sparked every womanly cell inside of her. It was more than the nicely carved features and the ton of sex appeal; there was a happiness about him that filled her with warm sunshine, a twinkle in his dark eyes that soothed the gaping wounds inside of her. Being with him filled her with a sense of worth, something she'd not felt since her father had died years ago.

Like Marshall, Will had been a happy man with a love for life. He'd always made a point of telling Mia that she was special, that she could do or be anything she wanted. He'd made her smile and laugh and look at the world as a place to be enjoyed. When she'd lost him, she'd also lost her self-confidence and security. But she wasn't going to think about that tonight.

"When was the resort built? There's so much to it that I figured the place had been here for several years."

Marshall shook his head. "Mr. Douglas didn't start building Thunder Canyon Resort until after gold was discovered in the Queen of Hearts mine, and that was about two years ago."

"Wow. He must have lit a fire under the contractors to have gotten the place up and running in such a short time."

"Yeah, well money talks and having plenty of it makes it easier to get things done quickly. Did you know there's a golf course in the makings, too? Construction is supposed to start on it next summer. Maybe when you come back to Thunder Canyon for another vacation we can play a game together. Have you ever played?"

Golf? Mia almost wanted to laugh. As far as she was concerned that was a rich man's sport. Even when Will, her father, had still been alive, the Hanovers hadn't been well off. The potato crops he'd harvested every year had been enough to keep them comfortable but not enough for luxury. Then after Will had died, she and Nina couldn't have afforded a set of used clubs from a pawnshop, much less the fees to belong to a country club. That was the sort of life Janelle enjoyed. It was the sort of life she wanted Mia to experience. But try as she might, Mia couldn't make herself comfortable with Janelle's money or lifestyle. How could she, when everywhere she looked she saw Nina Hanover's troubled face?

"No. I— Golf was never an interest at my home." At least that was the truth, she told herself.

The crooked smile on his face melted her. "Well, that will give me a good reason to get you out on the course and teach you."

If she ever returned to Thunder Canyon, Mia thought grimly. What would he think if he knew she was only here at the resort because of a missed turn on the wrong road? That she was running from herself and hiding from her mother? God, she couldn't bear to imagine how he would look at her if he knew the truth. That her actions had caused her mother to drink and then climb behind the wheel of a car.

Trying to shake the disturbing thoughts away, she sipped her soda and glanced around the small yard fenced with chain link. On the west side three poplars shaded them from the red orb of the sinking sun. To her left, in one corner of the grassy space, a blue spruce towered high above the roof of the house. Even from a distance, the pungent scent of its needles drifted to her on the warm breeze.

Near one end of the deck was a doghouse made with traditional clapboard and shingles. Nearby, a small wading pool meant for children was full of water—for Leroy's amusement, she supposed. A few feet farther, in the middle of the yard, a black gas grill was positioned near the end of a redwood picnic table.

The only thing missing in the family-friendly setting was a colorful gym set and a couple of laughing kids playing tag and wrestling with Leroy. The dreamy picture floated through her mind and filled her heart with wistful longing. Would there ever be a place like this for her? she wondered. Would there ever be a man who could love her and want a family with her in spite of her faults?

"Mia. Are you okay?"

His voice finally penetrated her thoughts and with a mental shake of her head, she glanced at him. Apparently she'd been so lost in her daydreams that she'd not heard his earlier remarks.

"Oh. Sorry. I was just thinking…how quiet and pleasant it is here on the mountainside." Her expression turned wry. "But to be honest, this is not the bachelor pad I expected to find."

His eyes wandered over her face as he grunted with amusement. "What were you expecting? A round bed and mirrors on the ceiling?" His eyes crinkled at the corners. "Maybe I should remind you that you haven't seen my bedroom yet."

He was teasing and yet just the mention of his bedroom was enough to make Mia jump nervously to her feet and rub her sweaty palms down her hips. "Uh—maybe we should start dinner. I'm actually getting hungry."

Marshall set aside his empty beer glass, then slowly rose from the lawn chair. It was all Mia could do to stay put as he closed the short distance between them.

"Mia, Mia," he said softly as his hands slipped over the tops of her shoulders. "You really do think I eat women for breakfast, lunch and dinner, don't you?"

Embarrassed now, her gaze dropped to her feet. "Not exactly. But I'm sure you've had plenty of—female friends up here and—"

Before she could finish, his forefinger was beneath her chin, drawing her face up to his. "You're wrong, Mia. Very wrong. Yes, I've had plenty of female friends over the years. But not one of them has been here at my home. Until you, that is."

Something deep inside her began to quiver and she didn't know whether the reaction was from the touch of his hand upon her face or the surprising revelation of his words.

"Marshall, you don't have to tell me something like that. I mean— I'm not expecting special treatment from you."

Frowning now, his hand fisted and his knuckles brushed the curve of her cheekbone. Everything inside Mia wanted to close her eyes and lean into him. She wanted to taste the recklessness of his lips again, feel the strength of his arms holding her tight, crushing her body against his.

"You think I'm lying, don't you?"

Her head twisted back and forth until his fingers speared into her hair and flattened against the back of her skull. With his hands poising her face a few inches from his, everything in her went completely still. Except for her heart and that was beating as wildly as the wing of a startled bird.

"Marshall—it doesn't matter what I think."

"Doesn't it?"

She swallowed as emotions threatened to clog her throat. "Soon I'll be gone and you and I will probably never see each other again."

Even saying the words brought a wretched loneliness to the deepest part of her heart and she suddenly realized she was in deep trouble with this man. It was painfully clear that he was becoming a part of her life, a part she didn't want to end.

"Mia," he said in a gravelly whisper, "when are you going to stop thinking about *leaving* and start thinking about *staying?*"

She couldn't stop the anguished groan in her throat. "Because I— Oh, Marshall, there's nothing to keep me here."

Mia had hardly gotten the words out when she saw a wicked grin flash across his face and then his lips were hovering over hers.

"What about this?"

His murmured question wasn't meant to be answered. At least not with words.

Mia closed her eyes and waited for his kiss.

Chapter Seven

Leaves rustled as a soft breeze blew down from the mountain, carrying with it the faint scent of spruce. Birds twittered overhead and across the deck Leroy lifted his head and watched in fascination at the couple with their arms entwined, their lips locked.

As for Mia, she was hardly aware of her surroundings. Marshall's kiss was spinning her off to a place she'd never been before, a place where everything was warm and soft and safe. The wide breadth of his chest shielded her, his strong arms girded her, cradled her as though she were something very precious to him.

Back and forth his lips rocked over hers, while inside tiny explosions of pleasure fizzed her brain, transmitting streaks of hot longing throughout her body.

Her hands were clinging tightly to his shoulders and she was wondering where she was ever going to come up with enough resistance to end the kiss, when he suddenly lifted his head. As she gulped for breath, his eyes tracked a smoldering trail across her face, down her neck, then still lower to the perky jut of her breasts.

"See, you do have something to keep you here," he murmured, his voice raspy with desire. "Me. This."

Mia was smart enough to know that Marshall wasn't an old-fashioned man. He considered a kiss as nothing more than a sexual pleasure between a man and a woman, a sweet prelude for something more intimate to come. It wasn't a pledge of love or even a promise of fidelity. For him it was a carnal act, plain and simple.

With every ounce of strength she could muster, Mia gathered enough of her senses to push away from his embrace and walk across the deck. Bending her head, she stared unseeingly at the grains in the wooden planks while asking herself what she was doing here at Marshall's home. Pretending that she could have that fairy-tale life she'd once fervently dreamed of? No. She'd learned the hard way that fairy tales weren't the heavenly fantasies she'd thought them to be. The reason she was here was far more basic. Marshall made her momentarily forget, made her feel as if she'd soon discover sunshine over the very next mountain.

She was blinking at the haze of moisture collecting in her eyes when Leroy's head appeared in her line of vision. The dog must have sensed her troubled mood.

He looked up at her and whined, then promptly began to lick her ankles.

The warm, ticklish lap of the dog's tongue against her skin had Mia suddenly laughing and she squatted on her heels to stroke his head.

"You're a funny fellow," she crooned to Leroy.

Walking up behind her, Marshall put a hand beneath her elbow and eased her up to her full height. Slowly, she turned and met his somber gaze.

"I wish I could make you laugh like that," he said quietly. "It sounds nice. Really nice."

Feeling slightly embarrassed now, but not fully understanding why, she directed her gaze to the middle of his chest.

"I guess I'm not the most jovial person to be around, Marshall. I—" Pausing, she lifted her gaze back to his face. There was a smiling warmth in the brown depth of those eyes, a tenderness that she'd not expected to see and her heart winced with longing. "I really don't understand why you'd want to be around a person like me."

With a wry slant to his lips, his hand reached up and stroked gently over the shiny crown of her head then down the long length of her thick braid.

"A person like you? What does that mean? You're a beautiful, desirable woman. Any man would be crazy not to want your company."

Her nostrils gently flared as his fingers reached the end of her braid and lingered against her breast.

"Like I told you before, I'm not a party girl."

His palm flattened against her breast and Mia's pulse

quickened as heat pooled beneath it and spread to the center of her chest.

"What makes you think that's the type of girl I want?" he murmured huskily. "Maybe I'm tired of party girls."

Why did she so desperately want to believe him? Mia wondered. Why did the foolish, wishful part of her want to believe that he might actually come to care for her, when every sensible cell inside her brain understood that once her past was revealed he'd run faster than Leroy after a rabbit?

She sighed as a faint smile curved her lips. "That kiss you just gave me didn't feel like a man who was looking for a woman to share an evening of political theories. But I— I'll hang around Thunder Canyon for a while longer. Just don't expect me to fall in bed with you. That isn't going to happen."

To her surprise, a wicked grin flashed back at her. "What about jump into bed with me? Or leap? Yeah. Leap sounds better. That would get us there faster."

He was teasing and Mia was glad. It gave her a chance to step away from him and end the awkward intimacy that constantly seemed to sizzle between them.

"You're crazy," she teasingly tossed over her shoulder. "And right now I'm wondering if you actually know how to cook or if you're going to let me starve."

Chuckling, he draped his arm around the back of her waist and guided her down the steps and onto the grassy lawn.

"C'mon," he urged. "You can watch me start the grill

and then I'm going to cook you the best rib-eye steak you've ever eaten."

Once Marshall got the charcoal burning, the two of them went inside the kitchen to prepare steaks, potatoes and corn on the cob for grilling. As Mia worked alongside him at the counter, she tried to push the heated memory of their kiss aside. She tried to convince herself that being in Marshall's arms hadn't really been that nice. But she couldn't lie to herself. Not when his very nearness begged her reach out and touch him.

They ate the simple meal on the picnic table while Leroy sat near Marshall's feet and begged for scraps. By the time they pushed back their empty plates, the sun was casting long shadows across the lawn.

"There's a little sunlight left," Marshall said as the two of them sipped the last of their iced tea. "Do you have enough energy for a walk? There's a beautiful little spot I'd like to show you. It's just a short distance up the mountain."

With a hand against her midsection, she groaned. "It had better be a short distance because I'm stuffed."

He extricated his long legs from the picnic bench and rose to his feet. "I promise the exercise will be good for your digestion," he said impishly, then held his hand down to her.

She curled her fingers around his and he helped her to her feet. "What about Leroy? Can he walk with us?" she asked as he led her over to a gate where they could exit the backyard.

Since the heeler was already bounding eagerly

around their feet, Marshall didn't have the heart to order the dog back to the porch. Besides, Mia seemed to enjoy Leroy and whatever made her happy was what he wanted to give her.

Hell, if he ever admitted his sappy feelings to his brother and longtime buddies, the group of men would fall over with laughter, Marshall thought. Either that or warn him that he was in danger of losing his bachelorhood.

"If I didn't let him go, he'd probably dig out from beneath the fence," Marshall told her, then to Leroy he said, "okay, boy, you can go. But no running off and hiding in the woods or I'll leave you out for the bears to eat."

Leroy barked as though he was big enough to take on any black bear that happened to cross his path. The moment Marshall opened the gate, the dog shot through the opening like a rocket on four feet. Mia laughed as the animal raced far ahead of them.

"Boy, you've certainly got him trained."

"Yeah, he follows my directions about as well as my patients," he joked.

Marshall ushered her through the gate and onto a small trail leading out to the dirt road that ran past the house and on up the mountain.

"You mean we can walk on the road?" she asked with surprise. "We don't have to go into the woods?"

"For about a quarter of a mile we'll stick to the road," Marshall told her. "Then we'll turn into the woods. It won't be far then."

"And what will I see there?" she asked curiously.

He wagged a finger at her. "If I told you now, it wouldn't be a surprise when we got there. Don't you like surprises?"

When the surprises were nice, Mia thought. Like the ones her mother and father used to give her on her birthday: a kitten with a bow around its neck, a sweater with a fur collar and shiny pearl buttons, a small cedar chest to hold all her cherished trinkets. Yes, those had been precious surprises and gifts worth more than all the gold in the Queen of Hearts mine. She'd just been too naive to realize it at the time.

"Sometimes," she said.

They were walking close together and every few moments the swinging gait of their arms caused them to brush together. Mia made herself widen the distance between them, but Marshall countered her move by reaching for her hand and dragging her even closer to his side.

As he threaded his fingers through hers, he said with a provocative little grin, "We're not on a military hike, Mia dear, we're on an after-dinner stroll."

The feel of her palm flattened against his and their fingers locked together was all it took to send Mia's blood singing through her veins. It was crazy, she thought. They were only holding hands, yet the connection she felt was almost as if they were kissing all over again. She wanted to pull away even while she wanted to draw closer to his side.

"It's a good thing," she said in a breathy voice. "Because I need to take this uphill grade slowly."

He was teasing her about being out of breath when they suddenly heard voices, then muffled whimpers. The sounds appeared to be coming farther up the mountain from them and Mia and Marshall paused long enough to exchange watchful glances.

"That sounds like someone in distress," Marshall said. "Is that what you heard?"

Concerned now, Mia nodded. "Is it unusual for anyone else to be on this road?"

"Not really. It's on resort property and some hikers like to go up the mountain the easy way rather than the narrow trail that winds through the woods. C'mon. Let's go see if we can find them."

He tugged on her hand and the two of them hurried up the steep road. Around a sharp curve, they spotted a boy no more than eight years old with taffy-brown hair and a smattering of freckles across his nose, sitting in the ditch. Tears were streaming down his face as a young woman with a light brown ponytail was trying to untie his hiking boot.

Mia shot Marshall a glance of concern, then rushed forward. The woman looked up in surprise as Mia practically stumbled to a stop in front of them.

"Oh, thank God," the young woman said with a desperate note of urgency. "Can you help us?"

"What's happened?" Mia asked quickly as she knelt down next to the woman.

"I'm not sure how it happened. Joey and I were walking through the woods and the next thing I knew he was on the ground screaming in pain."

"I was trying to jump a stream," the boy said in tearful explanation. "The next thing I knew I landed on a rock and it rolled beneath my boot. I fell and now my leg hurts something awful."

A grubby little hand rubbed down his shin and stopped somewhere near his ankle. Mia's heart ached for the little fellow. Apparently he'd taken quite a tumble. There were deep scratches on his knees and legs. Mud and dirt was smeared on his chin and alongside his nose.

The woman said fretfully, "Wouldn't you know it, this is the one time I didn't bring my cell phone with me. And Joey is too heavy for me to carry off the mountain."

Giving the boy a soothing smile, Mia reached into a pocket on her shorts and pulled out a clean tissue. Gently, she dabbed at the tears rolling down his cheeks, then went to work wiping away a trickle of blood from his knee. "You're a brave boy. Don't cry," Mia told him, turning toward Marshall who stood behind her. "This man is a doctor," she told Joey. "He'll take good care of you."

"A doctor!" Jumping to her feet, the woman stared at Marshall in disbelief. "Really?"

Marshall thrust his hand toward her. "I'm Dr. Marshall Cates. I'm the staff doctor at Thunder Canyon Resort."

A look of relief crossed her plain features. "Oh. I'm Deanna. Deanna Griffin." She gestured down to the boy who was grimacing with pain. "And this is my son, Joey. We're not resort guests. We're staying in town at the Wander-On Inn. We just decided to drive out to the mountains and then Joey wanted to climb. I guess someone will probably charge us with trespassing."

"Don't worry about any of that," Marshall tried to assure her. "You're not going to get into trouble for being on resort property." Quickly, he broke off the conversation and kneeled down beside Mia and the boy. "Okay, Joey, can you show me where it hurts?"

The boy glanced to Mia for reassurance, then with a short nod pointed to his right ankle. "Somewhere down there. But it kinda just hurts all over. Is it broke?"

"I don't know, son. We'll have to take X-rays of your leg before we know that," Marshall told him.

Carefully, he cradled the bottom of the child's boot in both hands while anchoring his thumbs on the top. "Mia, can you loosen the laces while I keep his foot steady?" he asked.

Without hesitation she nodded, then gave the boy a conspiring wink. "Sure. We're gonna get through this together, aren't we, Joey?"

Gritting his teeth, Joey reluctantly nodded and Mia quickly went to work easing the bootlaces. Eventually she loosened them enough for Marshall to slip the shoe from the boy's foot. A thick white sock followed.

When Joey's foot was finally exposed, Marshall ran his fingers over the already bloated joint. "Mmm. The ankle is beginning to swell and turn blue. I don't feel anything broken." He glanced up at Joey's mother. "But there could be a fissure that can't be felt. We need to get him down to my office for X-rays."

Close to tears now, Deanna Griffin groaned with misgivings. Mia looked away from Joey and up to his mother. Although the woman was dressed in a decent-looking pair of Capris and a tank top, the look on her face spoke volumes to Mia. She'd seen that frantic what-am-I-going-to-do expression many times before on her own face. The fear in Deanna Griffin's eyes said she saw a mound of cost suddenly thrown at her, a cost she couldn't meet.

"Look, Dr. Cates, I think—maybe—I'd better have you take Joey to the county hospital. I'm not insured and, well, I hate to sound ungrateful but I don't think I can afford your services. At the hospital…"

The deep grimace on Marshall's face was enough to cause the woman to pause. "Ms. Griffin, this isn't about money," he said with rough impatience. "This is about your son's leg!"

Stunned by Marshall's attitude toward the woman, Mia touched him on the shoulder to get his attention. "Marshall, could I speak with you a moment? Alone?" she asked pointedly.

He hesitated for only a moment, then, leaving Joey, he followed Mia several feet away from the mother and son.

"What is it?" he asked before she could say anything.

Her lips pursed at his impatience. She was seeing a different side of this man and she wasn't at all sure she liked it.

Tossing back her tousled hair, she lifted her chin to a challenging slant. "For your information, Marshall, not all people are blessed with plenty of money like you. She's probably barely able to make ends meet and I doubt there's a man around to help her in any way. Now you bark at her as though she's an unfeeling mother!"

A look of impatience came over his face. "Unfeeling! Mia, I was trying to tell the woman not to worry—that money isn't the issue here."

Stepping closer, she tapped a finger against the middle of his chest. "You still don't get it. Money *is* an issue with her. She doesn't have it. And medical care—the kind you provide—ain't cheap! Now do you get the picture?"

Frustration marked his features as he glanced over his shoulder at Joey then lowered his head to Mia's. "This woman is a stranger to you. How could you possibly know anything about her situation?"

Because she'd been there, Mia thought grimly. In that same dark, terrifying place with nowhere to turn and no one to help. Mia understood how humiliating and humble it felt to have to throw herself on the mercy of a total stranger. But she couldn't tell Marshall Cates about that part of her life. He wouldn't understand. No more than he could empathize with Ms. Griffin.

"It's…easy. I—I'm a woman and I can…just tell these things. And if she needs financial help, I'll be glad to pay for Joey's care."

Shaking his head with dismay, he raked a hand through his hair. "Mia, look. It's very generous of you to make the offer. But even if the kid has to spend time in the hospital, I have connections—I can make sure the bills are taken care of. Does that make you feel better?"

"Much better." Rising on tiptoe, she kissed his cheek, then hurriedly stepped past him and over to Joey's mother.

The woman turned a harried look on Mia. "Dr. Cates

is right. Joey's leg is the first concern here. It's just that I have to be…uh, practical. And—"

"You don't have to explain, Ms. Griffin," Mia swiftly interrupted. "And there's nothing to worry about. Marshall meant to say that Joey will be treated and you're not to worry about the cost."

Her eyes blurred with grateful tears, Ms. Griffin reached out and gave Mia a tight hug. "I don't know what to say," she murmured. "Except thank you."

Mia was about to tell the woman that no thanks were necessary when Marshall approached the two women. "I think the best way to handle this is for me to jog back down the mountain and get the Jeep," he told Mia. "Can you wait here with Ms. Griffin and her son?"

"I'd be glad to."

His nod was grateful and as he turned to go, Mia thought she spotted a flicker of surprise in his eyes. As though he'd expected her to come up with some sort of excuse to quickly extricate herself from these people's problems. But Mia had learned that when a person cried out for help, someone needed to be there for them. This was one tiny way of making up for her mistakes.

"Good. I'll be back in a few minutes. In the meantime, make sure Joey doesn't try to move or stand. If he does he could hurt himself even more."

"We'll make sure he stays put," Mia assured him.

Two hours later Mia and Marshall were sitting on the deck behind his house, drinking coffee and watching the stars come out.

Only minutes earlier on the lodge steps, they had

waved goodbye to Joey and his mother. Thankfully, the boy's ankle had only been badly sprained. Marshall had ordered ice packs for the swelling and had made a point of giving Ms. Griffin samples of pain medicine rather than writing her a prescription.

"I'm sorry that we didn't make it to the special place I wanted to show you," he said to Mia. "We'll have to try again another day."

The two of them were sitting on a cushioned glider and every now and then Marshall would use the toe of his shoe to keep the seat rocking. The lazy movement, along with Marshall's nearness had lulled her to a dreamy state of mind and for the first time since Lance had left her, she felt herself drawing closer and closer to a man.

"I'm just glad we happened to run in to Joey and Deanna. The boy would have probably panicked if she'd left him there to go after their vehicle."

"Hmm. Well, I'm just glad the boy didn't have a broken bone. He was lucky." Marshall leaned forward and placed his coffee cup on the floor, then squared around to face Mia. "Now that things have quieted down, I want to compliment you on the way you handled Joey. A real nurse couldn't have done it any better. Where did that come from? Have you cared for children before?"

Mia very nearly laughed. The number of children she'd babysat to make extra money was too high to count. But heiresses didn't do those menial types of jobs, so she simply said, "I like children. I guess it's just a natural thing."

"I wouldn't say that," he argued. "When we walked up on them, his mother was getting nowhere at quieting him down."

She looked away from him and up at the blanket of stars twinkling across the endless Montana sky. There was so much she wished she could say to Marshall; so much she'd like to share with him, if only he would understand.

"That's nothing unusual. Most kids respond better to someone other than a relative. And I... Actually, at one time I was studying to become a nurse."

She glanced over to see he was staring at her in total surprise. What now?

"A nurse! Really?"

She swiftly sipped at her coffee to cover her nervousness. She didn't know why she'd blurted that bit of information about herself. "Yes. I'm very serious."

"You said you were studying. What happened? Why did you stop?"

What could she say, other than finding a rich mother had suddenly put a stop to all the goals and dreams she'd set for herself. Somehow she'd allowed Janelle to slowly take over her life, to push her into believing that being rich was all that was required for happiness.

Bitterness rose in her throat, but Mia did her best to swallow it down before she answered. "I guess in the long run you could say I stopped because I was weak. Too weak to fight my mother. You see, she, uh—she didn't want me doing something as blue-collar as being a nurse. To her a nurse does nothing more than hand out pills and empty bedpans."

Even though it was dark, there was enough light coming from the kitchen window for her to see that his brown eyes were searching her face as though she were a different woman than the one who'd first sat down beside him. As she sat there waiting for him to speak, she felt totally exposed and fearful that he was seeing the real Mia. Mia Hanover.

"I'm sorry she feels that way. I have a feeling you'd make a great nurse."

A nervous laugh escaped her lips and she quickly turned her head away from him. When she spoke her voice was wistful. "I wouldn't know about that, but I do think I would enjoy caring for people who…need me."

A few silent moments passed and then she felt him shifting on the seat and his arm settling around her shoulders.

"What about your father, Mia? Doesn't he have any say about this?"

This is the sort of thing that happened, she thought, when she let one little thing about herself slip. It always led to more questions. Questions that she didn't know how to answer without exposing her dirty secrets; questions that were too painful to contemplate.

Her next words were pushed through a tight throat. "My father died a long time ago."

"Oh, that's too bad, Mia. I can't imagine not having my father around. He's like an old tree trunk. I know I can lean on him if things ever get bad." His hand gently kneaded her shoulder. "Guess you have to do all your leaning on your mother."

Janelle wasn't the type, Mia thought. She wanted to lead her daughter rather than support her. Besides, she wasn't a mother to Mia. Not as Nina had been a mother. Nina was the one who'd bathed, diapered and fed Mia as a baby. She was the one who'd taken on multiple jobs; scraped and sacrificed to make sure Mia had a roof over her head and food to eat.

"I try not to do much leaning," she said. Then, with a smile she was hardly feeling, she quickly turned to him. "Let's not talk about such serious things, Marshall. You haven't offered me dessert yet. Do you have anything sweet hidden in your kitchen?"

"Sorry. The only thing I have is a package of cookies that has to be at least two months old."

Mia wrinkled her nose. "We could drive into the Rusty Spur and share a carton of Golden Nugget," she suggested.

The last thing Marshall wanted to do was leave this quiet porch where Mia was practically sitting in his lap. From the moment they'd sat down together on the glider, the warmth of her body had been tempting him; the scent of her soft skin and silky hair cocooned him in a sensual fog. For the past half hour his mind and certain parts of his body had been zeroed in on making love to her. The idea of having her in his bed, her naked curves just waiting to be explored, was enough to leave his stomach clenched with need. It was all he'd been able to think about. Until she'd shocked him with that bit about nursing school.

Marshall had gotten the sense that she'd not intended to give him that information about herself, but now that she had, he only wanted more. He was beginning to see that there were layers to this woman he'd not even begun to see and he wanted to peel them away almost as much as he wanted to peel away her clothing.

But tonight was too soon to push her. She'd agreed to stay on at the resort for a while longer. For now Marshall had to be content with that.

Stifling a wistful sigh, he rose from the glider and offered a hand down to her. "Whatever my lady wants, I'm here to give."

84

she'd thought she was fine. It took Daniel's words and Brooke's question to make her realize she was far from a full recovery.

She'd made a start with her sister's help and she intended to go forward now. Sarah felt as if she'd been living in a darkened room and some-one had suddenly opened a door, letting in the fresh air and sunshine. She could feel its warmth slowly seeping into the coldest part of her. The feeling was liberating. She realized it was only a small step and she had a long way to go, but she was ready to face life again with Serena and her family behind her.

All too soon, they were saying goodbye and Sarah experienced a moment of sadness for all the years she and Serena had missed. But they ad each other now and that's what She held

PRINTED IN THE U.S.A.   © 2006 HARLEQUIN ENTERPRISES LTD.
® and ™ are trademarks owned and used by the trademark owner and/or its licensee.
Publisher acknowledges the copyright holder of the excerpt from this individual work as follows
THE RIGHT WOMAN Copyright © 2004 by Linda Warren. All rights reserved.

The Silhouette Reader Service™ — Here's How it Works:

Accepting your 2 free Silhouette Special Edition® larger print books and 2 free gifts places you under no obligation to buy anything. You may keep the books and gifts and return the shipping statement marked "cancel". If you do not cancel, about a month later we'll send you 6 additional Silhouette Special Edition® larger print books and bill you just $4.74 each in the U.S. or $5.49 each in Canada, plus 25¢ shipping & handling per book and applicable taxes if any.* That's the complete price and – compared to cover prices of $5.50 each in the U.S. and $6.50 each in Canada – it's quite a bargain! You may cancel at any time, but if you choose to continue, every month we'll send you 6 more books, which you may either purchase at the discount price or return to us and cancel your subscription.

*Terms and prices subject to change without notice. Sales tax applicable in N.Y. Canadian residents will be charged applicable provincial taxes and GST. Offer limited to one per household. All orders subject to approval. Books received may vary. Credit or debit balances in a customer's account(s) may be offset by any other outstanding balance owed by or to the customer. Please allow 4 to 6 weeks for delivery.

If offer card is missing write to:
Silhouette Reader Service, 3010 Walden Ave., P.O. Box 1867, Buffalo, NY 14240-1867

SILHOUETTE READER SERVICE
3010 WALDEN AVE
PO BOX 1867
BUFFALO NY 14240-9952

BUSINESS REPLY MAIL
FIRST-CLASS MAIL   PERMIT NO. 717-003   BUFFALO, NY

POSTAGE WILL BE PAID BY ADDRESSEE

NO POSTAGE
NECESSARY
IF MAILED
IN THE
UNITED STATES

Chapter Eight

The next evening, after Marshall had gotten off duty, he was walking through the lounge searching for any sight of Mia when his cell phone rang.

Flipping the instrument open, he was surprised to see it was his brother Mitchell calling. Quickly, he pushed the talk button as he continued to amble through the several couches and armchairs grouped in front of the massive fireplace.

"Hey, Mitch, what's going on?"

"What the hell do you mean, what's going on? We're all over here at the Hitching Post. Have you forgotten that it's our night to meet?"

Pausing at one of the empty cowhide-covered chairs, Marshall sank onto the padded arm. His brother's question had literally stunned him. How could he have forgotten boy's night out? For years now, Marshall, Mitchell, Grant and Russ and Dax had all gotten together once a month at the Hitching Post to drink beer, play pool and sit down to a game of poker. It was their time together, to relax and forget about any problems they might have. Just the idea that he'd been concentrating on Mia instead of his normal routine was enough to worry him.

"I suppose I had forgotten. Are you guys already gathered up?"

"Hell, yes. We were waiting on you to start the poker game, but the rest of the guys gave up and decided to play pool. What's the matter, did you have some sort of emergency this evening?"

"I'm still here at the lodge, I just stayed late to do a bit of paperwork." And to wait around and see if Mia made an appearance at the lounge, he thought wryly. Last night after they'd eaten ice cream, he'd dropped her off at her cabin and given her a chaste good-night kiss. He'd not wanted to press his luck and ask her for another date tonight, but he'd damned well wanted to. Dear Lord, if he'd missed boy's night out because of a date, the guys would never let him live it down. "Just hold my place, Mitch. I'll be there in a few minutes."

Friday night at the Hitching Post was always a rowdy affair with drinking, loud laughter and even louder music. The popular nightspot located on the southwestern edge of town was Thunder Canyon's version of an

Old West saloon, complete with live country bands on Friday and Saturday nights and hardwood floors with plenty of space for boot stompin' and two-steppin'. A restaurant serving everything from steaks to burgers was situated on one side of the building, while on the opposite side was the original bar that had once graced Lily Divine's sporting house. And over the back bar, above the numerous bottles of spirits and rows of shot glasses, hung a painting of Thunder Canyon's most infamous lady.

Marshall, along with every guy who'd ever visited the Hitching Post, had often gazed at the nearly naked Lily and wondered if she'd really been as bawdy and decadent as the good folks of the town had depicted her to be back in the 1880s. There were always two sides to every story and he figured the truth of Lily's past would never be understood. The beautiful madam was a mystery. Just like Mia Smith, he thought, as he skirted the edge of the crowded dance floor and shouldered his way toward the bar. She was another beautiful mystery that he seriously wanted to unravel.

After wedging his way past the crowd packed around the busy bar, Marshall spotted his brother standing near one of the several pool tables located just off the dance floor.

He worked his way toward his brother while the band's rendition of a popular country tune rattled the rafters and forced people to communicate with hand signals rather than conversation. For one brief second, as he waited for a big burly cowboy to step aside,

Marshall longed for the quiet sanctuary of his back porch, the glider and his arm around Mia.

Hell, what was coming over him, Marshall wondered as he finally reached the pool table where his brother and friends were racking balls for a new game. He'd always loved the nightlife, the louder and wilder, the better. The Hitching Post had given him some damn good memories and getting together with his brother and buddies was a tradition since their high school days. This was his idea of the good life and he didn't want to change a damn thing about it.

"Hey, buddy, you finally made it," Grant Clifton called to him from the opposite end of the table. "Want to play this game?"

Russ Chilton, the rancher of the group, took the pool stick he'd been leaning on and offered it to Marshall. "Go ahead. I've already lost one game to the stud down there." He motioned his head toward Grant. "Why don't you see if you can wipe that smug smile off his face?"

"Aw, Russ, the smile on Grant's face doesn't have anything to do with beating you at pool." Dax Traub, spoke up over another blast of loud music. "The man is in love. Real, true love."

Marshall looked across the table at Dax, who owned a motorcycle shop in the old part of town. The remarks he'd made about Grant's love life had held more than a hint of cynicism, but that was to be expected from Dax. He was six foot of brooding sarcasm since his marriage to Allaire had hit the skids.

"How do you know so much about Grant's love life?"

Marshall asked at the same time as he signaled to a nearby waitress.

Dax jerked his thumb toward Grant. "The big manager of Thunder Canyon Resort has been telling us all about his upcoming wedding to his cowgirl. I've advised him to take her spurs off first, though. Otherwise she might trip on her way down the aisle."

By now the waitress had reached Marshall. He quickly ordered a beer, then turned and walked to where Grant was resting a hip against the edge of the pool table.

"Sounds like Dax is giving you a hard time about becoming a husband," Marshall said with faint amusement.

Grinning, Grant tossed his pool stick to Dax. The other man quickly positioned himself over the table and busted the triangle of balls.

With the game going again, Grant moved a few steps away from the table and Marshall followed.

"I wouldn't expect anything else from Dax. He's jaded."

Marshall blew out a lungful of air. Even though he'd known that Grant was engaged, the idea that his old buddy would soon be married shook him in a way he'd never expected. Grant's bachelor days were coming to an end.

Marshall glanced shrewdly at his longtime friend. "Maybe Dax is concerned that you'll end up getting hurt—like him. But I'll have to say you don't look like a worried man."

Grant chuckled. "Worried. Why should I be? I'm

marrying the woman I want to spend the rest of my life with. I couldn't be happier."

Marshall slapped a hand on Grant's shoulder. "If you're happy, then I'm happy for you."

"Thanks. Maybe you can deliver our children when they come," Grant added jokingly.

With a wry shake of his head, Marshall said, "I'm a sports doctor, Grant. Remember? I don't do babies."

Grant's calculating laugh was loud enough to be heard above the music. "Maybe not in the delivery room. But you might just make a few—if you meet the right woman."

Marshall didn't think he'd ever seen his longtime friend so buoyant and happy. Nor had he ever heard him talk so openly about love and kids, subjects that normally would have made both men squirm. Now Marshall could merely look at him and wonder.

Glancing toward the other members of their group, Marshall said, "You know me, Grant, I'm never really looking for the *right* woman. But I—I'm half afraid that I may have found her anyway."

The waitress arrived with his beer and he tossed a few bills onto the serving tray before she hurried off to deliver more drinks.

As he gratefully sipped the dark draft beer, Grant edged closer. "What do you mean? I didn't realize you'd been seeing one certain woman."

Feeling more than a little foolish, Marshall shrugged. "I hadn't been. But then I ran into Mia and we—uh— we've gone out a few times." He glanced at Grant and appreciated the fact that his friend wasn't grinning like a possum. "This is probably going to sound crazy, Grant, but I think I'm falling for this girl."

Grant's dark brows lifted with surprise. "Mia? Do I know this woman?"

"You should. Her name is Mia Smith. She's one of the high-toned guests at the resort. I remember you said she rented a safety deposit box for her jewelry."

Grant's lips formed a silent *O*. "Yeah, I remember now. The mystery heiress that all the staff was chattering about when she first arrived. You've been seeing her?"

Marshall nodded. "Believe me, Grant, I never thought she'd give me the time of day. Now that she has I—well, all I want is to be with her. And if I'm not with her I'm thinking about her. Does that sound like love to you?"

Frowning, Grant said, "Marshall, from what I've heard about Mia Smith, she keeps to herself. No one around the resort knows where she came from or anything else about her. Do you?"

What little Marshall knew about Mia was hardly enough to fit in his eye, yet he'd learned enough to tell him she was a good, decent person and that being with her made him happy. Wasn't that really all that mattered, he asked himself. To Grant he admitted, "I've learned a little about her, but not as much as I'd like to."

Slapping a comforting hand on Marshall's shoulder, Grant said, "Well, I wouldn't worry about it, ole buddy. You're probably just infatuated with her because she's a mystery. Once you give yourself time to really get to know the woman, your feelings might change completely."

After a long gulp of beer, Marshall glanced out at the crowded dance floor. For the life of him he couldn't imagine Mia laughing and kicking up her heels like the women here at the Hitching Post were doing tonight. She'd said she wasn't a party girl, but Marshall instinctively felt there was more to her reserved mind-set than what she was telling him.

"You may be right, Grant. The only thing I'm sure about now is that I'm going to keep seeing her—until she leaves the resort."

Several loud shouts suddenly sounded from the pool table and both men returned to the group of friends just in time to see Dax send the last ball on the table rolling into a corner pocket.

Looking for anything to get his mind off Mia, Marshall said, "Give me that cue, Russ. Somebody needs to knock Dax off his throne."

More than an hour later and after several games at the pool table, the five guys found seats and ordered pitchers of beer.

As for Marshall, he tried to keep up with the bits and pieces of conversation flowing back and forth across the table, but all the while he was wondering what sort of believable excuse he could come up with to leave the party early.

He could always pull out his cell phone and pretend he had an emergency message from the resort. But with Grant being the manager, he'd eventually find out the truth and then his departure would need even more explanation. Damn it, why couldn't he just sit back and enjoy himself like he usually did at these gatherings?

The next thing Marshall knew, Dax was waving a hand in front of his face. "Hey, buddy, are you with us?"

Realizing he'd been caught daydreaming, Marshall placed his beer mug on the table and glanced around the table. "I'm here," he answered a bit sharply. "I was just thinking about a patient," he lied. "Did you ask me something?"

"Yeah, we want to know about your date with Lizbeth Stanton. What was that all about?"

Grimacing, Marshall asked, "How did you know about that?"

Russ laughed. "Since when did anything stay a secret around Thunder Canyon? You ought to know Dax hears a stream of gossip in his motorcycle shop."

Marshall shrugged. "Well, there wasn't anything to it. She asked me out to dinner and I accepted. No big deal. She's really more of a friend than anything."

"Sexy as hell, though, don't you think?" Dax tossed a wink at him. "And she's just your style—a big flirt."

Marshall was about to tell him to go jump off a cliff when he spotted Mitchell staring at him like a hound dog with perked ears.

"You say Lizbeth asked you out?" his brother asked. "Not the other way around?"

"That's right," Marshall answered. "But like I said, the two of us are just friends. In fact, while we were having dinner she encouraged me to go after Mia Smith."

"I see."

Marshall thoughtfully watched his brother tip the pitcher of beer over his near-empty glass. If he didn't know better, his brother seemed unduly interested in Lizbeth Stanton, but that idea was ludicrous, he thought. Mitchell was the serious one. Flirty, flighty Lizbeth would be the last woman to fit his needs.

"Oh, so you've already moved on to this Mia now?" Dax asked. "Maybe we should be asking about her instead of Lizbeth."

Rising to his feet, Marshall pulled several bills from his trouser pocket and tossed them onto the table to pay for his portion of the beer.

"Sorry guys. I've had a long day and there's a patient I want to check on before it gets too late."

"A patient! Are you kidding?" Grant exclaimed. "Since when did you ever worry about a patient after working hours?"

Since he'd met Mia, Marshall silently answered. Aloud, he said, "There's a first time for everything, guys."

He walked away, leaving every man at the table staring after him.

The next morning Mia had just stepped out of the shower and was toweling dry when she heard a knock on the door of her cabin.

Puzzled that anyone would be trying to contact her, she quickly pulled on a blue satin robe and knotted the sash at her waist as she hurried to the living area.

Even though the resort was basically safe and away from the dangers that lurked in city living, she still opted to use the peephole before simply pulling the door open to a stranger. But to her surprise the visitor wasn't a stranger. It was Marshall, dressed in a green short-sleeved shirt and faded blue jeans. The tan cowboy boots on his feet reminded her that even though the man was a doctor, he still had a bit of Montana in him. And it was that rough edge that made him just too darn sexy for a woman's peace of mind.

Her pulse fluttering wildly, she thrust strands of wet hair off her face and pulled open the door to find him smiling back at her.

"Good morning, beautiful," he said softly.

The sweet, sensual greeting knocked her senses for a loop. Embarrassed that he'd caught her in such a disheveled state, she clutched the folds of her robe chastely together at the base of her throat.

"Hello yourself," she replied while her mind spun with questions. What was he doing here at her cabin so early in the morning? And why did the sight of him make her heart sing? She was clearly losing control with him—and herself.

"Uh—I know it's early. I tried to call, but there was no answer." His dark gaze left her face to travel downward to where her puckered nipples were outlined by the satin, then farther down to where the edges of the fabric parted against one naked thigh. "I guess you were in the shower—or something."

Just before Mia had stepped into the shower she'd heard her cell phone ringing, but even though she'd given her number to Marshall the other night after they'd dealt with Joey's sprained ankle, she'd figured the only person who would be calling so early was Janelle. And Mia was still far from ready to talk to the woman.

"Yes, I was in the shower," she repeated as though she didn't have an ounce of brain cells. Then, realizing she couldn't keep him standing on the small porch, she pushed the door a bit wider. "Would you like to come in?"

The grooves in his cheeks deepened as he stepped across the threshold and past her. "I thought you'd never ask," he said as he glanced thoughtfully around the small but luxuriously fitted cabin.

Her hands shaking, she shut the door behind them and then adjusted the front of her robe to a more modest position.

"This is quite a surprise," she said. "I wouldn't have expected you to be up so early on a Saturday morning. Would you like coffee?"

She moved around him and into the kitchen. Thankfully she'd turned on the coffeemaker before she'd stepped into the shower and now the brew was ready to drink.

"I'd love a coffee," he said as he followed her behind an L-shaped bar and into the small kitchen area. "And this might surprise you, but I'm not one to lay in bed on my days off. There's too much to enjoy and life's too short to sleep it away."

Grateful that the task of finding cups and pouring the coffee gave her a moment to collect herself, she said in a teasing voice, "Oh. Well, I figured with your nightlife you'd need the rest."

He chuckled. "Nightlife? Now who's been talking

about me? I don't have that much of a nightlife. Even though I was out last night—at the Hitching Post with my brother and friends."

Turning, she handed him one of the mugs. Their fingers met and at the same time their gazes clashed. For a brief moment Mia's breath stopped, as arcs of sizzling awareness seemed to zip back and forth between them.

"Friends?"

She realized the question was personal, that it was the same as saying *I'm interested in you,* but she couldn't stop herself. If he'd been out with another woman last night, then his showing up here this morning wouldn't be anything for her heart to sing about. Maybe it wasn't anything to sing about anyway. But she couldn't seem to get her heart to go quiet. Instead it was thumping and jumping joyously around in her chest.

"My old high school buddies." A corner of his mouth slanted upward. "Guys—just in case you're wondering."

Feeling a blush coming on, she lifted the cup to her lips and sipped while she waited for the heat in her cheeks to subside.

"I guess it's time to confess that I have heard gossip about you."

One of his dark brows arched with amused speculation. "Really? Where?"

She lowered the cup and tried to keep her voice casual. "The Clip 'N' Curl."

Marshall laughed. "The beauty salon in town? Mia, you're *supposed* to hear gossip at a beauty salon. Something would be wrong if you didn't."

She did her best to chuckle along with him. Yet these past few days she'd not been able to completely dismiss what Marti had revealed about her sister and Marshall.

"This particular person I met there seemed to know you quite well. Or, at least, her sister did."

His amusement turned to outright interest. "You don't say, Well, who was this person?"

"Marti Newmar. She works at the coffee bar in the lounge."

Sudden dawning crossed his face and then he glanced down at the cup in his hand, but not before Mia glimpsed something like regret in his eyes.

"Hmm. Marti. Yes, I'm acquainted with her. And yes, I dated her older sister, Felicia. It was nothing serious, though, and she's gone on to other things. In fact, I don't even think she lives here anymore."

He sounded so casual, almost too casual. And a prick of warning sent a cool shiver down her spine. If he was that flippant about his past girlfriends, then who was to say he'd be any different with her?

But you don't want him to be serious about you, Mia. You're a fake, a phony. Even if he did grow to love you, the truth would end everything. No, a mild flirtation is as far as this thing with Marshall could ever go.

Sighing, she leaned against the bar and stared across the expanse of living room. "Marti seems to think that her sister was in love with you."

She could hear his boots shifting slightly, but she didn't turn to look at him. If she saw another dismissive look on his face she didn't think she could bear it.

"I couldn't help that, Mia. Felicia was—she wasn't my type. I'm at fault for dating her in the first place."

"Why wasn't she your type?" Mia asked stiffly. "Because she was poor?"

"Poor? You think that's why I ended things with her?"

There was such indignation in his voice that she glanced over her shoulder at him. He was glowering at her and she knew she'd hit a nerve, but at this moment she didn't care. Maybe it was time Dr. Playboy was questioned about his dating ethics.

"I don't know," she said. "From the way Marti describes her home and family, it doesn't match up to yours."

"Well, the Newmars' financial situation had nothing to do with anything," he countered. "Felicia was— naive. That was the whole problem."

Mia's lips twisted. She'd been naive before, too. She'd been foolish to believe that Lance had loved her enough to stick with her through the good and the bad. But even worse, it had been silly, perhaps even child-like, to believe that Janelle and her stacks of money could buy happiness.

"Why?" she asked, her voice brittle. "For believing a guy like you could care about a girl like her?"

He groaned. "Why are you trying to make me look like a cad?"

With a shake of her head, she said, "I'm not trying to do anything. Maybe you've already done it to yourself."

There was a pregnant pause and then she heard a rough sigh escape him.

"Look, Mia, you're probably right in thinking that I

hurt Felicia. I'm sure I did. But I didn't do it intentionally. I never led her on or tried to make her believe she
was *the* special woman in my life. She was simply a
pretty girl, a fun date. But she obviously wanted more
than I was prepared to give. When I finally saw where
her feelings were headed, I quickly ended things. If that
makes me an unfeeling bastard, then I guess I'm guilty."

Feeling a bit raw without even knowing why, she
said, "Forget it, Marshall. I shouldn't have brought the
matter up anyway. You and I are just friends. And your
past dating habits are no concern of mine. No more
than mine are yours."

Chapter Nine

Before Marshall could say any more on the subject of Felicia Newmar or any other women he'd dated, Mia turned toward him and gestured to one of the tall bar stools pushed up against the varnished pine counter.

"Have a seat," she invited.

He pulled out one of the bar stools and slung a long leg over the padded seat. Mia placed her coffee mug on the bar, then carefully climbed onto the stool next to him. As he sipped at his coffee, she pulled a wide-tooth comb from the pocket of her robe and began to smooth the wet tangles away from her face.

As Marshall watched her deal with the mass of black hair tousled around her head, he couldn't help but wonder why she'd confronted him about an old girlfriend and why he'd felt so compelled to defend himself. Before Mia, he'd not really cared what anyone thought of his dating habits. If a heart got broken here and there, he'd justified his part in the malady by telling himself the woman had learned a lesson about men, albeit the hard way. But now, to even think of breaking Mia's heart troubled him deeply. Dear God, what was she doing? Taking a freewheeling bachelor and turning him into a conscientious but boring gentleman?

"I thought you might like to know that I stopped by the Wander-On Inn last night and checked on Joey," he commented. "His ankle is coming along nicely."

She looked at him with surprise. "You mean you interrupted your night on the town to check on a patient?"

A wry smile twisted his lips. "You see, I'm not all bad, as you seem to think."

"I never thought you were *all* bad."

Their gazes clashed and her eyes darted nervously away from him. He watched her put down the comb and pick up her coffee.

"I would offer to make you breakfast," she said after a moment, "but I don't have any food in the house. I'm afraid I've been doing too much eating out, letting others do the cooking."

"Don't worry about it. I actually stopped by to invite you out, anyway. I thought we could grab some breakfast at the Grubstake and then do a bit of climbing."

Her gaze swung back to him. "Climbing? As in mountain climbing?"

He grinned at her wariness. "Sure. You're up to it, aren't you?"

Even though he had mentioned the two of them going climbing together before, Mia had never believed he'd actually get around to asking her. Taking an inexperienced person on such a strenuous trek would be like taking a toddler on a shopping excursion.

"I don't know." She licked her lips as she weighed his invitation. Mia Smith, the heiress who wanted to stay hidden from the world, knew it would be wise to politely decline and send him on his way. But she was getting so weary of being that woman, so tired of pretending. And more importantly, it didn't matter to her what this man's motives to spend time with her were; being with Marshall simply made her feel good. And right now she needed that very much.

She said, "You've surprised me."

"Good. A man shouldn't be predictable." His eyes sparkled with all sorts of innuendos. "At least, not to a beautiful woman."

Her nostrils flared as her pulse fluttered. It would be so much easier if she could forget the taste of his lips, forget the feel of his strong arms wrapped around her, but she couldn't and now as she looked at him her senses buzzed with erotic memories. This was probably how Marti's sister had felt, she thought, charmed, helpless, ready to give the man anything he wanted.

"I'll go climbing with you. Just as long as you don't try to take me up something like Pike's Peak."

Marshall chuckled. "The highest mountain in

Montana is Granite Peak and it's many miles east of here. We'll go up a baby mountain here on the resort. Promise." He used his forefinger to make a cross against his chest, then leaning toward her, he wound a strand of wet hair around the same finger. "You ought to know I wouldn't hurt a hair on your head."

Even though Mia desperately needed to draw in a deep breath, the air lodged in her throat. "I'm—um. It's not my hair that I'm concerned about. It's my bones."

A deep chuckle rumbled up from his chest and his finger left her hair to slide down the stretch of thigh exposed by the part in her robe. "I'm a sports doctor, remember? I can fix broken bones."

Yeah, but what about broken hearts? Don't think about it, Mia. Just go. Have fun. Forget.

Carefully, she caught his wayward hand and placed it safely on his knee. "All right, doc," she conceded. "You've talked me into it. What time did you want to go?"

His smile was a picture of pure triumph. "Great! I'm ready right now."

Mia glanced pointedly down at her robe. "Well, I'm not. You're going to have to give me time to get dressed. What should I wear?"

"You might want to settle on loose-fitting shorts. It's going to be a warm, sunny day."

Mia quickly slipped off the bar stool. "Give me five minutes," she told him.

Just as she was walking across the living room, her cell phone began to ring. Mia glanced at the small table where the device was lying and felt her spirits sink. Janelle had been ringing and ringing, no doubt determined to make Mia pick up and talk to her. So far, she'd not found the courage or determination to confront her mother.

"Go ahead," Marshall spoke up from his seat at the bar. "I'm not in that big of a hurry. Answer your phone."

Knowing it would look odd if she didn't acknowledge the ringing, Mia picked up the phone and flipped it open. The caller ID flashed the name Janelle Josephson and her heart sunk all the way to her toes.

Snapping the phone shut, she said, "I— It's nothing important. I'll return the call later."

The ringing stopped and Marshall watched her place the phone back on the table. Her features, which only a moment ago had been smiling, had rapidly gone pensive, then guarded. Who could the caller be, he wondered. A family member? A lover? All along he'd sensed that something was going on with Mia Smith, something that she wanted to keep hidden.

He figured the answer could be found if he sifted through the call history information on her telephone. A name. A number. Someone from her past was obviously still reaching out to her. He desperately wanted to know, but he couldn't push her. He had to be patient and wait to see if she would ever feel close enough to confide in him.

"Are you sure? We have all day for climbing," he tried to assure her.

Suddenly she snatched the instrument up from the table again and this time slipped it into the pocket on her robe. "It's nothing important, Marshall," she said in a firm voice, then whirled and started out of the room. "Just let me change and we'll be on our way."

Marshall was still thinking about her odd behavior when she emerged from the bedroom a few minutes later wearing a pair of black khaki shorts and a white tank top. A white scarf secured her wet hair into a ponytail at the nape of her neck.

Even with a bare minimum of makeup her face was lovely, but at the moment it wasn't her features that had snared his attention. With a will all their own, his eyes slid an appreciative gaze down her long, shapely legs and ended as her trim ankles disappeared into a pair of heavy brown hiking boots. The sight of all that honey-tanned skin was enough to distract him from the earlier phone call and he put it entirely out of his mind as he slid from the bar stool and walked over to her.

"Ready to go?" he asked.

Nodding, she patted the back pockets of her jeans. "I think I've taken everything I needed from my handbag." She glanced eagerly up at him. "Is Leroy going to come with us?"

Laughing, he placed a hand at the small of her back and guided her toward the door. "Not this time. I want to devote all my attention to you, dear Mia."

After a quick breakfast of hotcakes, they left the Grubstake and climbed into Marshall's Jeep for a short drive to the north edge of the resort. Before they reached the base of the mountain, a meadow carpeted with pink and yellow wildflowers came into view and Mia gasped with delight.

"Oh, how beautiful! Can't we stop here for a few minutes, Marshall?"

An indulgent smile curved his lips. "We'll make a visit here on the way back," he promised. "I'm afraid if I let you wander out in all those flowers now, I'll never get you up the mountain."

She sighed as she gave the splendorous sight one last glance before she turned her gaze on his profile. "You're probably right, doc. Most women tend to prefer picking flowers to climbing rocks. But I'm game and I'll try to keep up."

Reaching across the small console, he picked up her hand and gently squeezed. "You're a good sport, Mia. I like that about you. Believe it or not, you're the only woman who's been brave enough to go climbing with me."

His admission warmed her heart, even though she told herself it shouldn't mean anything.

"Maybe you mean the only woman *crazy* enough to go climbing with you," she said with a wry smile.

His fingers tightened around hers. "You're not crazy, Mia. You're an adventuress. I knew that when I first saw you sitting on that boulder on the side of the mountain. A weaker woman wouldn't have even attempted that much of a climb. You not only made it, but you made it alone. I was impressed."

Mia's lashes fluttered downward to partially hide her mixed emotions. He'd called her an adventuress and that much was true. Even before she'd graduated high school, she'd set off on a quest to find her real mother. In spite of having limited funds, even more limited

means of searching and her adopted mother's disapproval, she'd been determined, almost relentless in
reaching her goal. She'd been brave enough to make
calls to total strangers and badger those persons holding
the key to private records. Yet once she'd actually found
Janelle, her bravery and independent nature had melted.
She'd allowed the woman and her money to very nearly
swallow her up. It had taken Mia months and months to
realize that her weakness had not only caused her to lose
Nina and Lance, it had also caused her to lose herself.

Lifting her head, she did her best to push the dark
thoughts from her mind. "You didn't give me any impression that you felt that way," she replied.

"I didn't know you well enough. And you weren't
exactly inviting me to strike up a personal conversation."

No, she thought miserably, when she'd first arrived
at Thunder Canyon Resort, she'd gone out of her way
to keep every encounter with staff and guests to a totally
impersonal level. It was easier to maintain her guise as
Mia Smith that way. But now Marshall was digging at
the doors she was hiding herself behind and every
moment she was with him she had to fight to keep from
flinging them open and letting Mia Hanover pour out.
The only thing stopping her was knowing the deluge of
truth would end their relationship.

"So," she said carefully, "do you think you know me
now?"

To her surprise, he lifted her fingers to his lips. "Not
as much as I'd like to, but enough to make me want you
beside me."

No one had to tell her that Marshall Cates was a dangerous flirt, a smooth charmer. Yet none of that seemed to matter whenever he touched her or flashed her one of his sultry grins. Mia realized she was losing herself to him and there didn't seem to be any will inside her to stop the fall.

Moments later, he steered the Jeep onto a dim, washed-out road that led up the base of the mountain. When the going finally became too rough for the vehicle to handle, he steered it off the path and parked beneath a huge pine.

She helped Marshall unload the climbing equipment from the back of the Jeep, then stood to one side and watched as he strapped on a heavy backpack.

"What about me?" she asked. "Do I need to carry something?"

"You can be in charge of our water. Since I only brought two bottles, they shouldn't be too heavy."

"Two bottles? The day feels like it's going to be hot. Won't we be needing more water than that?"

He glanced at her as he adjusted the pack to a more comfortable position on his shoulders. "You're right, but trying to carry too much of it will only weigh us down. I've brought a filtration device along, too. And once we climb higher, there are several falls and pools where we can get water."

She looked at him with fascination. "There are pools of water up on the mountain?"

"Several," he answered as he took her by the arm and urged her away from the Jeep. "And one of them will make your flowered meadow look humdrum."

"I'll believe that when I see it," she said with a laugh.

The day was bright and sunny, the breeze warm and gentle. The first two hundred feet of their climb were strenuous but fairly easy to maneuver with plenty of hand- and footholds. Thankfully Mia was accustomed to jogging in the high altitude of Denver, so her breathing was no more labored than Marshall's as they levered and worked their way upward. During the slow climb he'd made sure to stop at frequent intervals to give her some lessons on the basic techniques. Apparently his instructions had been a big help to her, because each time he'd glanced over his shoulder to make sure she was keeping up and each time she'd surprised him by being right on his heels.

Eventually he paused long enough for her to join him on a small rock ledge. "I think it's time I made our trail a little more difficult," he said. "This is no challenge for you."

Groaning, she shrugged off the small pack she was carrying and dug inside for one of the water bottles. "C'mon, Marshall, give me a break. I'm already covered with sweat."

While she took a long drink from the bottle, a cunning grin flashed across his tanned face. "You haven't done any real climbing yet. We're going to get out the anchors and ropes and make our way up that bluff."

Mia's gaze followed the direction of his index finger. When she spotted the bluff he was talking about, her jaw dropped. The red layers of rock appeared to be shaved off evenly without even the smallest of ledges to give a climber a toehold.

"You're crazy!" she squeaked. "I can't make it up there! Just look at my boots, they don't have spikes!"

"Neither do mine. In fact, I wore these old cowboy boots today and they're slick on the bottom and hell to climb in."

Mia rolled her eyes. "Then why did you wear them?"

"For a challenge. And to put me on an even keel with you."

She let out another groan. "And here I was patting myself on the back for keeping up with you. I didn't have a clue that you'd handicapped yourself."

Chuckling, he reached out and cupped the side of her face with his palm. "You're doing great, honey. I'm proud of you."

Shaken by the sweet sensation of his touch, she handed the water to him, then turned away to gaze out at the quaint town of Thunder Canyon spread beneath the endless stretch of blue Montana sky. Months ago, after Lance had walked away and her mother had died, she'd believed that no spot on earth would feel like home again. But this place was beginning to tug at her heart.

Or was it the man standing beside her?

"Maybe you'd better wait until we tackle the bluff before you say that," she told him.

He moved closer and Mia's eyelids drifted down as the back of his hand moved against her bare arm.

"You're going to make it," he murmured. "We'll make it together."

Together. It was difficult for Mia to remember back to a time when she'd thought of herself as a part of a team. She had a few female friends back in Denver, but they were Janelle's sort, spoiled and out of touch with the real world. They'd readily accepted her into their circle and all of them were basically nice to her, but she'd never felt a connection with any of them and she'd quickly come to the conclusion that she didn't want an idle life without goals or dreams. As for the young men who'd tried to court her, she'd felt frozen by their flippant attitude toward life and money and family.

"Mia? You've grown awfully quiet. Are you all right?"

She glanced over her shoulder and up at him. The look of concern on his face warmed her and made her wonder what it would be like if he really did care about her, even love her.

"I was just thinking," she said, then before she could stop herself, she twined her arm through his. "Tell me about your friends, Marshall. The guys you went out with last night. Are they—special to you?"

A look of real fondness swept over his features. "Very special. We all grew up together—went to high school together and even now we make sure we all get together at least once a month. 'Course, I call Mitch my brother and my friend. He's four years younger than me and a hell of a lot smarter. He owns and runs Cates International in Thunder Canyon."

"That's some sort of business?"

"Farming equipment." His expression turned wry. "Not everyone around here has a gold mine where they can harvest nuggets."

"Is your brother married?"

Marshall's laugh was robust to say the least. "No. He's as serious as a judge. I'm not sure any woman could deal with him."

"What about your friends? Do they have families?"

He thought for a moment. "Not exactly. Dax used to be married to Allaire, but their marriage didn't last. Now he runs a motorcycle shop down in the old part of town. Then there's Grant, I think I told you about him. He manages the resort. He's a workaholic, but he's finally managed to get himself engaged to the woman who runs his ranch, Clifton's Pride. Russ has a ranch outside of town. He's from the old school—hates everything the gold rush has brought to Thunder Canyon. He used to be married a long time ago and has a kid—a son—but he never sees him."

Mia frowned. "How sad."

"Yeah. I think his ex didn't want the connection— I'm not sure. Russ doesn't talk about that part of his life. Anyway, he's definitely single and I don't see him changing."

"So that's all of them? Your friends, I mean."

"No. There's also Dax's brother, DJ, but he took off to Atlanta and has been living down there for a while. He owns a bunch of barbecue places and we've been trying to talk him into coming back to Thunder Canyon. What with the gold boom, a barbecue joint around here ought to do handsprings."

Mia smiled wistfully. "You're lucky to have friends and especially lucky that you've stayed together for so long."

"I'm sure you must have good friends, too." He

grinned impishly. "I'll bet you were the prom queen or the cheerleading captain—someone that all the girls envied."

Mia had to stop herself from snorting out a laugh. She'd been tall, skinny and gawky. Her clothes and shoes had mostly come from thrift stores and her hair had been worn with thick bangs and chopped off straight at the bottom because that was the only way her mother could cut it. A visit to the beauty salon had been out of the question. Necessities came first and there was rarely a dollar left over for luxuries. No, none of the girls she'd gone to school with had envied Mia Hanover.

Now Mia probably had more money than all of those young women put together. But it meant nothing. She'd give every penny of it away to go back to being that poor Mia whose mother was still alive and cutting hair with not much skill, but a whole lot of love.

Blinking at the mist of tears that had gathered in her eyes, Mia quickly looked away from him and adjusted the pack on her back. "We'd better be going, don't you think?"

The abrupt change in her took Marshall by complete surprise. Moments ago she'd seemed eager to hear about his friends and then when he'd barely mentioned hers, she'd dropped a curtain and went off to someplace he wasn't invited.

For a moment he considered taking her by the shoulders and asking her point blank about her life, her past. But so far the day had gone so well that he didn't want to push his luck. There would come a time for him to gently pry at her closed doors and when that time arrived he would know it. Right now he was going to be content with her company.

For the next hour, as the two of them slowly made their way up the rough crags of the mountainside, Marshall tried to forget about the empty look he'd seen on Mia's face when he'd suggested she'd been a star attraction in high school. He didn't like to think that her past had been less than happy, but he wasn't blind. In a sense she was like Doris Phillips, who'd come to his office for help. She was putting on a brave pretense at happiness, but underneath her smiles there was a wealth of pain.

But what had caused it? Marshall wondered, as he hammered an anchor in between two slabs of rock. A man? With Mia's striking looks he'd be a fool to think a man hadn't been a serious part of her life at some point. Hell, for all he knew she could already have been married and divorced. That notion left such a bitter taste in Marshall's mouth that he felt almost sick.

With the last anchor in place, Marshall attached a strong rappelling rope and slipped it through a ring on his belt. In less than a minute, he'd swung himself down to the narrow ledge of rock where Mia was patiently waiting.

"I really think I've lost my mind. Are you sure I can do this, Marshall?"

Her question came as he girded a belt around her hips, then tested the buckle with a hard tug to make sure it was secure.

Straightening to his full height, he forced himself to rest his hands on his own hips rather than the sweet tempting curve of her behind. "We'll take the easiest route. Just remember everything I've taught you. And once you begin climbing, don't start staring down at the floor of the canyon. You might get vertigo and then we'd be in a hell of a mess."

"I don't get vertigo," she said with a frown. "See, I'm looking down now and nothing—"

Before she could get the remainder of her words out, she felt as though the top half of her was swaying forward. Frantic that she was about to tumble head over heels down the mountainside, she snatched a death grip on Marshall's arm.

He reacted instantly by snaring her with both arms and wrapping her tightly against his chest.

"Mia! Why did you do that?" he gently scolded as he cradled the top of her head beneath his chin. "If you'd lost your balance I might not have been able to catch you!"

Shivering with delayed fright, Mia clung to him and pressed her cheek against the rock hard safety of his chest. "I—I'm sorry, Marshall. I thought— I didn't think it would bother me. I've never been affected by heights before."

And Marshall had never been so affected by a woman before. It didn't matter that the two of them were precariously perched on a small shelf of mountain or that jagged edges of rocks were stabbing him in the back. All he could think about was covering her mouth with his; letting his hands explore the warm curves pressed against him.

"Oh, honey, don't scare me that way." Anguish jerked

his head back and forth as unbearable images flashed through his head. "If you'd fallen, I would have had to jump after you."

Slowly her head tilted upward until her troubled gaze met his. "Don't say such things, Marshall. I'm—I'm not worth trying to save, much less dying for."

Softly, he pushed away the black strands of hair sticking to her damp cheek. "Why not? I wouldn't be worth much without you."

To Marshall's surprise tears suddenly gathered in her eyes and he could feel her trembling start anew, as though his words scared her even more than her near fall.

"Don't say something that serious, Marshall, unless you really mean it."

It suddenly struck him that he'd never been more serious. Losing Mia for any reason was something he couldn't contemplate.

"I couldn't be more serious, Mia."

Disbelief flashed across her face, but Marshall didn't give her time to respond. Instead he gathered her chin between his thumb and forefinger, then lowered his head to hers.

"Don't argue with me, Mia," he murmured huskily. "Don't say anything. Just let me kiss you."

He could see questions shouting in her eyes, but her lips were silent, waiting to meet his. He groaned as a need he didn't quite understand twisted deep in his gut, then his eyes closed and his lips fastened hungrily over hers.

Chapter Ten

Two hours later, after climbing nearly to the timberline of the mountain, then descending back to their starting point, Mia and Marshall returned to the Jeep and were now traversing the rough track of road that would eventually carry them back to the resort.

Mia was hot, tired and thirsty. Her knees were scraped raw and she'd cut a painful gash in her palm, but those problems were minor discomforts compared to her spinning thoughts.

The kiss Marshall had given her on the rock ledge had frightened her with its intensity and she was still wondering what had been behind it and his suggestive words. He couldn't be getting serious about her. They'd only known each other a few days. On top of that, he wasn't a man who wanted to get serious about any woman. And even if he were, she was carrying a trunk full of baggage. All he had to do was open the lid to see she wasn't the sort of woman he'd want to gather to his heart.

"Are you too tired to stop by the meadow?"

Marshall's voice interrupted her burdened thoughts and she glanced over to see he'd taken his eyes off the road and was directing them at her. Just looking at him pierced her with a longing that continued to stun her. She'd never expected to feel so much desire for any man. Even Lance, whom she'd believed that she'd once loved, had never elicited the hungry need she felt for Marshall. What did it all mean? And where could it possibly lead her, except straight to a crushed heart?

"I'm tired, but I did want to take a closer look at the flowers."

The corners of his lips turned softly upward. "Good," he said. "There's something I want to talk with you about before we get back to the resort."

Her brows lifted with curiosity, but she didn't have time to ask him to explain further. By now the road had leveled and they were quickly approaching the flower-filled meadow.

Moments later Marshall parked the Jeep along the side of the road. As she waited for him to skirt around the vehicle to help her out, she made a feeble attempt to smooth her mussed hair. She was trying to do something about the dirt and blood caked on her palm when he jerked open the door.

"What's the matter?" he asked as she quickly closed her hand away from his sight.

"Uh—nothing. I just gouged my hand a little on a rock. I'll clean it up later, when I get back to my cabin."

With a frown of concern, he gestured for her to give him her hand. "I'm the doctor around here, remember. Let me see."

Mia was reluctant to let him treat her, even for a basic scratch. Something had happened to her when he'd kissed her up there on the mountain ledge. It was like he'd woken her sleeping libido and turned it into a hungry tigress. Letting him touch her, for any reason, was enough to send her up in flames. But she could hardly explain any of that, so there was nothing left for her to do but place her hand upon his palm.

"Mia!" he exclaimed as he gently probed at the deep gash. "Why didn't you tell me you'd hurt yourself? This is going to have to be cleaned. Otherwise the dirt might cause infection. It might even need a stitch or two. And you're going to need a tetanus shot. We need to go to the office where I have the equipment to deal with this."

With a nervous laugh, she swung her legs over the side of the bucket seat and pulled her hand from his grip. His gaze dropped instantly to her raw knees and he shook his head with misgiving.

"You look like you've met up with a grizzly bear and lost the fight. I'm sorry, Mia. When I asked you out this morning it wasn't with the intention of getting you hurt."

"I'm not hurt, doc. Just scraped a little. Now help me

out. You can take care of my wounds later. After I take a look at the flowers."

Seeing he wasn't going to deter her, he took a firm hold on her arm and helped her to the ground.

"Don't even think about trying to get away from me," he told her as he guided her into the deep grass of the meadow. "I don't want any more cuts and bruises on you."

The two of them walked several yards into the quiet meadow before they found a seat on a fallen log bleached white by years of harsh elements.

Mia sighed with pleasure as she looked around at the thousands of tiny pink and yellow blooms carpeting the surface of the meadow. "It's like a fairy-tale world," she said in a hushed voice. "I don't think I've ever seen anything so pretty."

"I have."

"You mean the pool of water you showed me up on the mountain? Well, it was beautiful," she admitted with another sigh. "But not as much as this."

Without warning, his hand came against her face and he turned her head so that she was facing him. Her heart jolted at the tender glow she found in his brown eyes.

"I'm not talking about the pool on the mountain," he murmured. "I'm talking about this."

His fingers brushed against her face, as though her cheek was a rose too delicate to touch. Mia couldn't stop the strong leap of her heart or the blush that crawled up her throat and onto her face.

"You're a terrible flatterer, Dr. Cates. I never know what will come out of your mouth."

The faint grin on his face was both wry and wistful. "I never know myself. Sometimes I get into trouble for saying what I'm thinking. And right now I'm thinking I'd like to lay you down in all these flowers and make love to you."

His admission shattered Mia's composure and for a moment all she could do was stare at him. Then suddenly she realized she had to get away from him, before she fell into his arms like a complete fool.

Quickly, she started to push herself up from the log, but he caught her by the arm and tugged her back beside him.

"We'd better go. Now!" she blurted sharply.

"Calm down, Mia. I'm not going to act on my words. I was simply telling you what I felt. Surely it isn't a surprise to you that I want to make love to you."

Mia slowly breathed in and out as she tried to still the rapid beating of her heart. She could have told him that it wasn't him she was afraid of, but rather herself. Yet to do that would only reveal that she was falling for him, that she wanted the very same thing he wanted—to make love to him in a bed of flowers.

Bending her head, she said in a thick voice, "You're right, Marshall. I'm not some innocent young woman. I'm twenty-six years old and I—I've had a man in my life. We were close for a long while—very close. And I...don't want to give myself to anyone like that again."

She looked up to see his brown eyes searching her face and she felt a little more of her resistance slip, a little more of the hidden Mia screaming to come to the surface.

"What happened? He wouldn't make a commitment?"

No, he'd gotten tired of her obsessive hunt for her mother, Mia thought. Tired of her putting their relationship on hold while she'd pored over names and telephone numbers, searched through stacks of birth records and driven miles to strange places with the mere hope that she'd find a lead. By the time she'd actually found Janelle and fell into her newfound fortune, her relationship with Lance had suffered greatly. Yet she'd thought, hoped, that having financial security would change everything for the better and that she and Lance could finally be happy, marry and start a family. But the money had only caused more of a wall between them. He'd walked away, but not before accusing her of being selfish and unfeeling. Dear God, he'd been right, she thought sickly. And that was the hardest part she'd had to live with.

Bitterness coated her tongue when she answered, "He made a commitment, but then…changed his mind."

Silence settled around them until the raucous screech of a hawk lifted Mia's gaze toward the blue sky. The predator was circling, searching for a weak and easy prey to wrap his talons around. Only the strong survived in this world, she thought sadly. And she wasn't strong. She'd been weak and needy enough to allow Janelle to get her hooks in her, to draw her away from Nina, the only mother she'd ever known.

"I'm sorry you had to go through that, Mia. But I can tell you why it happened."

Her nerves went on sudden alert as she dared to look at him. Did he know? Had he guessed at the terrible mistakes she'd made?

"You can?" she asked in a strained voice.

His smile was gentle, almost loving, and her hammering heart quieted to a hard but steady pound.

"Sure I can. Call it what you want. Fate or the hand of God. That thing you had with the other guy ended because you were supposed to wind up here—with me."

Hopeless tears poured into her heart until she was sure it was going to burst, but she carefully hid the pain behind a wan smile.

"Marshall, you're just so…"

When she couldn't finish, Marshall did it for her. "Sweet? Romantic? Yeah, I know," he said, his eyes twinkling. "I just can't help myself."

Sighing, she slipped off the log and bent down to pick a handful of delicate wildflowers. Marshall watched as she lifted the blossoms to her nose and wondered why the more he learned about her, the more he was growing to love her.

Love. Was that what it was? This endless need to see her face, hear her voice, have her beside him? He'd never felt like this before. Never felt so protective of a woman, so mindful of her feelings. He wanted more than just sex from her. He wanted to cradle her in his arms, wipe away the sadness from her eyes and cherish her for the rest of his life. If that was love then he'd fallen like a rock tossed into a river.

"My parents are having a little farewell dinner for my twin brothers this weekend," he said suddenly. "I'd like you to go with me."

She turned to stare at him and he could see doubts

running rampant over her face. He wanted to reassure her with promises that he'd never hurt her, but he figured anything he might say right now would ring hollow. He was going to have to earn her trust. Show her that he wasn't the same sort of man that had changed his mind and walked away from her.

"Where is this dinner going to be?" she asked finally.

"At my parents' home."

As she chewed thoughtfully on her bottom lip, Marshall rose to his feet and laid a hand on her shoulder.

"Don't worry, Mia, it'll be a casual affair. And my parents are nice, laid-back people. You'll like them." He squeezed her shoulder. "And I know they'll like you."

Her eyes drifted up to his. "I'm not sure it would be a good idea."

"It would mean a lot to me," he said softly. "A whole lot."

She drew in a shaky breath and then a wobbly smile slowly spread across her lips. "All right, Marshall."

Leaning his head back, he gave a loud yip of joy.

That Saturday, as Marshall drove the two of them to the Cates homestead on the west edge of town, Mia continued to ask herself what in heck had possessed her to agree to this outing. Meeting a guy's parents was a serious thing. Or, at least, it was where she came from. She wasn't sure that Marshall meant anything signifi-cant by his invitation. But if by some odd chance he did, then she was digging herself into a deeper grave. She couldn't continue to let Marshall believe she was simply a rich young woman who'd been raised in a nice, wealthy family. Yet to confess would only mean the end of their time together. And her hungry heart just wasn't ready for that yet.

The Cates home was a brick two-story structure set on five acres of a gently sloping property dotted with large shade trees. A wooden rail fence cordoned off a large front yard landscaped with beds of blooming perennials and neatly clipped shrubs. A concrete drive led up to a double garage. Presently the garage was closed and Marshall parked his Jeep next to a white pickup truck with logos on the doors that read Cates Construction—Built to Your Needs.

As Marshall helped her out of the vehicle Mia stared at the professionally done sign. "I thought you said your brother's business was called Cates International. That says Construction."

"That's another Cates," he said with a laugh. "The pa of the herd. Dad's been in the building business since he was a very young guy. Started out with his dad—my grandfather. Before the gold strike most of their business was over in the Bozeman area. The economy in Thunder Canyon was so slow that the city did well to build picnic tables for the town square. But now Dad and his employees can't keep up with all the contracts being thrown at them from a number of townsfolk. He thinks it's great, but Mom isn't so happy. For years now she's been planning for them to take a trip from coast to coast, but that's been postponed until Cates Construction catches up or the town goes bust."

"Marshall, quit dallying around and come in! We've all been waiting for you!"

Mia looked over her shoulder to see a middle-aged woman with chin-length pale blond hair standing on the small square of sheltered concrete that served as the front porch. She was dressed casually in tan slacks and a white sleeveless blouse. The warm smile on her face made Mia feel instantly welcome.

"Coming, Mom!" he yelled, then wrapping an arm around the back of Mia's waist, he urged her toward a wide sidewalk that bordered the front of the large house.

"You're a true doctor, son. Always late," Edie Cates fondly teased as Marshall guided Mia up the steps.

"I like to keep with tradition," he joked back, then quickly thrust Mia forward. "Mom, this is Mia Smith. She's a guest at the resort. And, Mia, this is my mother, Edie, the beautiful female of the bunch."

"The *only* female of the bunch," Edie said with a laugh.

"It's very nice to meet you, Mrs. Cates."

Expecting the woman to shake hands, Mia was surprised when she slung an arm around her shoulders and began leading her toward the door. "It's Edie, my dear. Don't make me feel any older than I already do with that *Mrs.* stuff. And I'll call you Mia, if that's okay with you."

"Of course," Mia told her. "And thank you for having me as a guest tonight."

"It's our pleasure," she said. She opened the door and ushered Mia inside while leaving Marshall to follow. "None of our sons have been brave enough to bring a girl home to meet us until now. Marshall has definitely treated his parents by inviting you."

Mia tossed a look of surprise at Marshall, but he merely winked and grinned.

Edie ushered them through a small foyer, a formal sitting room, then on to a den where the rest of the Cates family was congregated in front of a large television. A major league baseball game was playing on the screen, but the sound was turned low, telling Mia that the four other Cates men had been doing more talking than watching.

Over the next few minutes Mia met Marshall's father, Frank, a tall, well-built man with salt and pepper hair and a jovial attitude that reminded her of Marshall. Mitchell, the second oldest son, was an attractive man with the same dark coloring as his brothers, but very quiet. Especially when she compared him to Matthew and Marlon, the young twins, who were continually telling animated stories and swapping playful swings at each other.

After all the introductions were over, Edie passed around soft drinks and Marshall directed Mia to take a seat at the end of a long couch. If anyone noticed that he tucked her into the crook of his arm, they didn't let on, but Mia was riveted by the warmth of his torso pressed against her side, the weight of his hand lingering on her upper arm.

He was treating her as though she were someone special in his life and he wanted his family to know it. The idea was a thrilling one to Mia. Even though she knew this time with him couldn't last forever, she decided that this evening she was going to relish it. After all, leaving Thunder Canyon would come soon enough.

After a few minutes of light conversation and much bantering between the four brothers, Edie rose from her husband's side and announced she was heading to the kitchen to check on dinner. Wanting to feel useful, Mia instantly rose to her feet and offered to help.

"I can manage, Mia," Edie said. "But I'd love the company."

With a smile for Marshall, Mia quickly eased out of his gentle clasp and followed the woman out of the room and down a short hallway.

"Mmm, something smells delicious," she exclaimed as the two women pushed through a swinging door into the large, brightly lit kitchen.

"Lasagna. I hope you like Italian food. All the boys love it. Frank prefers steak, but since this is the twins' last night at home, he wants them to be treated."

"I love pasta of any sort," Mia told her as she watched the other woman open the oven door on a gas range and peer into the hot cavern.

"I do, too. And it shows in all the wrong places." Chuckling, she patted one shapely hip.

"I think you look beautiful," Mia said sincerely. "And you certainly don't look like you've had four children." Nor did she look as though she'd had the nips and tucks from a plastic surgeon that Janelle and thousands of other women chose to have in order to appear youthful.

Edie removed the large glass casserole dish full of bubbling lasagna and carefully placed it on the top of the stove. "You're very kind, dear. And very pretty. I can see why you caught Marshall's attention."

Feeling more than awkward, Mia let the woman's comment slide. "Is there anything I can do to help? Make a salad? Ice glasses?"

With a knowing chuckle, Edie glanced at her. "Don't want to talk about that, huh? Well, don't worry, I'm not a nosy mother. Now that the boys are grown, I stay out of their private lives unless I'm asked advice." She moved on down the counter and began to pull silverware from a drawer. "It's better that way. Otherwise they resent the interference." She laughed. "'Course there are times I'd like to tell them plenty."

Mia joined her at the cabinet counter. "I wish my mother were so understanding."

Edie glanced up from counting a handful of forks. "Does she live close to you?"

In the same house, but Mia wasn't going to admit that. It made her sound like a child who was now all grown up but too indolent to leave home. When actually the circumstances of living with Janelle were nothing close to that. Mia had fought against moving into the Josephson mansion. She'd wanted to keep her independence and privacy. But Janelle had played on Mia's soft heart by pointing out that she'd gone for twenty-five years believing her baby had died, surely living in the same house with her was not too much to ask. Not wanting to hurt her mother any more than she'd already been hurt, Mia had agreed and moved into the stately house. Ultimately that move had been a mistake, one that she was still paying for.

"Yes. And she can be very controlling. That's one of

the reasons I've been vacationing here in Thunder Canyon," she admitted before she could stop herself. "Sometimes a person needs a little breathing room." She slanted a regretful glance at Marshall's mother. "That sounds pretty awful, doesn't it?"

Her expression empathetic, Edie reached over and touched Mia's arm. "No. It sounds perfectly human to me." She smiled warmly and with an ease that totally charmed Mia, she quickly changed the subject by pointing to a cabinet above her head. "Now if you'd like to ice the glasses, you'll find them there. Looks like there're seven of us tonight. A nice lucky number."

Midway through dinner it struck Mia that the Cates were the sort of family she'd always dreamed of being a part of. Marshall and his siblings were close enough to bicker and tease without fearing that their love for each other could ever be shaken. They had parents that still adored each other after decades of marriage. Obviously Edie and Frank had raised their four boys with love and that love had stood as an anchor for them as they'd grown into men. If either parent was the controlling, smothering sort, it wasn't evident to Mia. Of course, with a guest present, she assumed that everyone was probably on his or her best behavior. Still, as far as she could see, there were no taut undercurrents or furtive glances of impatience between family members. All Mia could see was genuine affection and it filled her heart with golden warmth, like a treasure chest spilling over with incomparable riches.

As the group dined on plates of lasagna accompanied by hunks of garlic bread, Mia drank in the easy ambiance like sips of wine to be savored. With Marshall at her side showering her with attention and affectionate glances, it was easy to let herself dream that she was home and she was loved.

"Did you make any extra lasagna, Mom?" Marlon asked as the meal began to wind down. "You know Matthew and I will need something to eat once we get to the dorm."

The roll of Edie's eyes was tempered with an indulgent smile. "I'm sure there's not a place on campus that sells food," she teased. "That's why I made an extra pan. When you get to your dorm room just make sure you keep it in the refrigerator. You can't leave it sitting out, then rake off the mold expecting it to be good."

Mia looked at Matthew, who was sitting directly across the table from her. Marlon was striving for a career in business agriculture while Matthew was working his way toward a law degree. Both twins appeared eager to head back to school, although she could sense they were going to miss being home. "When will you two be leaving?" she asked.

"In the morning," Marlon spoke up before his twin could answer. "As soon as I can kick Matthew out of bed."

"Hah!" Matthew tossed at his brother. "I'll be the one doing the kicking. You don't even have your bags packed."

Marlon shot him a droll look. "That's because I'm not the dandy you are. I don't need trunks of clothing or hours to pack it. Five minutes to fill a duffle bag will be enough for me."

From the end of the table, Frank chuckled. "Well, I know one thing," he said to the twins. "Both of you are going to miss having your mom do your laundry and cooking."

Edie smiled at her two youngest sons, then settled a privately shared gaze on her husband. "Oh, Frank, you know I've spoiled the twins the same way I have you and Marshall and Mitchell. And just like you three, they take it all for granted. Once they get back to college, they'll forget all about their ole mom and everything I've done for them."

Both twins groaned with loud protest and everyone around the table began to laugh. Except Mia. She wasn't hearing the laughter or seeing the teasing faces. She was suddenly back in Denver and Nina Hanover was begging her to come home, which at that time had been a little apartment in Colorado Springs. Nina, a little drunk and full of a whole lot of pain, had accused Mia of forgetting her mother, the mother that had raised her from a newborn, the mother that had worked and sacrificed to keep a roof over Mia's head and food on their table.

The memories were suddenly too much for Mia to bear and, as tears began to blur her vision, she frantically realized she had to get away from the dinner table before she broke down completely.

"Please excuse me," she mumbled, then before Marshall or the rest of the family could respond in any way, she scraped back her chair and rushed from the room.

Chapter Eleven

Mia's abrupt departure from the dining room halted all laughter and Marshall stared in stunned silence at his parents and brothers.

"What happened?" Mitchell was the first one to ask. "Did somebody say something wrong?"

Edie looked across the table at Marshall who was already tossing down his napkin and rising to his feet. "Son, you'd better go see about her. I got a glance at Mia's face as she turned away from the table and I thought she looked sick. Dear heaven, I hope my cooking hasn't upset her stomach."

Marshall headed out of the dining room. "Don't worry, Mom," he tossed over his shoulder. "I don't think it's anything like that. The rest of you finish dinner and I'll go check on her."

After checking the guest bathroom and finding the door open and the light off, Marshall hurried to the den. When he didn't spot her there, he stepped through a sliding back door and onto a small patio. During dinner, the sun had fallen and now golden-pink rays were slanted across the backyard.

At first glance he didn't notice the still figure standing with her back to him in the shadow of a poplar tree. But as he turned to step back into the house, a flash of her coral-colored blouse caught his eye.

Quickly, he made his way across the yard to where she was staring out at the ridge of nearby mountains. If she was aware of his approach, she didn't show it, even when he came up behind her and gently placed his hands on her shoulders.

Through the thin fabric of her blouse, he could feel her trembling and concern threaded his softly spoken words. "Mia. What are you doing out here? Everyone is worried."

Several moments passed and then she reached up and wiped at her eyes. The realization that she'd been crying hit him hard.

"I'm…sorry, Marshall," she said in a raw, husky voice. "I—didn't mean to upset your family. They've all been so wonderful to me. Too wonderful."

The painful cracks in her voice struck Marshall right in the heart and he slowly turned her to face him. Tears rimmed her beautiful eyes and spilled onto her cheeks. Marshall wiped them away with the palm of his hand.

"If everything is so wonderful then why are you out here crying?"

Bending her head, Mia stared at Marshall's boots. She'd gone and done it now, she realized. There was no way she could easily explain away her behavior. Not without giving away the past she desperately wanted to keep hidden. But he was expecting an explanation and she was so sick of the deception she'd been playing.

"I—uh—guess I just got swamped with memories, Marshall. Your family is so nice and I guess it hit me all over again that mine is gone."

"Gone?" he repeated blankly. "I remember you saying your father died long ago. Are you telling me that your mother has passed away, too?"

She lifted her gaze and the concern she saw in Marshall's eyes gave her the strength to release the words bottled in her throat. "Yes. About a year ago. She—uh—was killed in an auto accident. And I—I've been having a hard time dealing with—the whole thing. I miss her terribly. Her death—" She paused, swallowed, then tried to keep her voice from breaking. "Her death has left a hole in me, Marshall, and I—just don't know how to fill it back up."

With a gentle shake of his head, he said, "I'm so sorry, sweetheart. I know that doesn't mean much, but I really don't know what else to say. If I told you that I understand what you're going through, I'd be lying. I've been blessed. I don't know what it's like to lose a loved one."

She blinked furiously at the fresh tears that threatened to spill onto her cheeks. "My parents were like yours, Marshall. They loved each other very much and they loved me—maybe more than I realized— until they were gone. It troubles me that I didn't appreciate them as much as I should have."

He reached out and smoothed a hand over the crown of her head. The soothing touch caused Mia's eyelashes to flutter down and rest against her cheeks. If only she could always have him by her side, she thought longingly. To soothe her when she hurt, to laugh with her when she was happy, to simply love her for who and what she was.

"We're all guilty of that, Mia. I hate to admit it but there have been plenty of times that I've taken my family for granted and forgotten to show them how much they mean to me. Fortunately they know that I love them anyway. I'm sure your parents knew that you loved them, too."

Over the past months Mia didn't think her heart could hurt anymore than it already had, but the pain ripping through the middle of her chest was so deep it practically stole her breath.

"I hope so," she choked out. "But it's different for me, Marshall. My family...well, I wasn't raised up like you."

"I never expected that you were," he countered. "Dad has always made a nice living for his wife and children, but I'm sure it can't compare to your family's wealth."

She shook her head viciously back and forth and the truth, or at least part of it, demanded to be let out. "No—

you have it all wrong, Marshall. I wasn't born into wealth. Will, my father, raised potatoes and alfalfa hay and Nina, my mother, was a simple housewife. We lived in a modest farmhouse outside of the little town of Alamosa down in southern Colorado. We weren't rich—just rich in love. It's—" she paused long enough to draw in a deep breath and lift a beseeching gaze up to his "—it's taken me a long time to realize that, Marshall. Too long."

Marshall would be lying if he said that her admission hadn't taken him by surprise. Learning she wasn't a born heiress was the last thing he'd expected to hear. But her stunning declaration couldn't compare to the emotions piercing him from all directions. He'd never imagined that he could feel someone else's pain this deeply. It had emanated from her like a tangible thing and wrapped around his heart like an iron vice. And like a flash of lightning, Marshall suddenly realized he was just now learning what it truly meant to be a doctor to the needy and a man to the woman he loved.

"Oh, Mia. I'm glad you told me. And if you think it could make me care about you less, then you've got it all wrong. I don't care that you weren't born into wealth. None of that matters. All I want is for us to be together."

He *cared* about her? Dear God, maybe it didn't matter to him that she'd come from a modest background, Mia thought. But he couldn't begin to imagine the whole story. And he wouldn't be nearly so understanding if he found out she'd caused her mother to turn into a drunk driver. Nina Hanover had turned to a bottle of vodka to drown out her sorrows. First to forget that she'd lost her husband, then more heavily because her daughter had deserted her for a pile of riches. Or at least, that's the way it had seemed to Nina. Actually, Mia hadn't ignored her mother because she'd stopped loving her. She'd simply grown weary of dealing with Nina's drinking and whining and pleading. It had been easy to let Janelle shield her from all of that and give her a quiet haven away from Nina's emotional problems. But Mia couldn't forsake Nina entirely and one day she'd agreed to meet her for lunch. She'd had plans of talking her mother into entering rehab and finding the help she needed. But Nina had ended any and all of Mia's hope when she'd climbed behind the wheel of a car and crashed on her way to meet Mia.

"Marshall, I…" The rest of her confession lodged in her throat like pieces of poisoned bread. She couldn't tell him the rest. Not tonight. Maybe she was wrong, even greedy for not telling him everything. But she wanted this fairy-tale time with Marshall to keep going for as long as possible. "Thank you for understanding," she finally whispered.

For long, expectant moments, his dark gaze gently skimmed her tear-stained face and then suddenly his head was bending down toward hers, blocking out the last bit of twilight.

When his lips settled over hers, she didn't even try to resist. The taste of his tender kiss was the very thing she needed to soothe her aching heart and before Mia realized what she was doing, she rose up on tiptoes and curled her arms around his neck.

Marshall was about to place his hands on her hips and draw her even tighter against him, but thankfully, before their embrace could turn into something more passionate, he caught the sound of footfall quickly approaching from behind.

With supreme effort, he quickly lifted his head and turned to see his mother watching them with a frown of concern.

"Sorry, I didn't mean to intrude," she quickly apologized. "We were all getting a little worried about Mia. Is everything all right?"

Clearing his throat, Marshall arched a questioning brow down at Mia. Of course *everything* wasn't okay with Mia, he realized sadly. It was going to take her a long time to recover from the recent loss of her mother. But at least for the moment her tears had dried and a wan smile was curving the corners of her lips.

Mia stepped toward Marshall's mother. "I'm fine, really, Edie. And I'm so sorry that I ruined the last of your dinner. Please forgive me. I guess—I got a little too emotional thinking about my own family."

Edie closed the short distance between them and wrapped Mia's hand in a warm clasp between the two of hers. "Don't bother yourself one minute over it. You didn't ruin anything. We've loved having you. Would you like to come back in now and have coffee? I'm afraid that the twins have already dug into the brownies, but there're plenty left."

Mia glanced back at Marshall and all he could think about was taking up their kiss exactly where they'd left off.

"I think Mia's had enough of the rowdy Cates brothers for one night," he told his mother. "If you and Dad won't mind, I'm going to take her home."

Edie's understanding smile encompassed both Mia and her son. "Of course we won't mind. As long as you two promise to come again soon."

"You can bet on it," Marshall told her, then bent and placed a kiss on his mother's cheek. "Tell everyone goodbye for us, will you?"

"Sure."

Edie turned and disappeared through the patio doors. Marshall took Mia by the arm and led her around the house to where his Jeep was parked.

Before he opened the door to help her in, he gathered her back into his arms. Then resting his forehead against hers, he whispered, "I hope you don't mind that we're leaving. Do you?"

The suggestive tone in his voice set her heart thumping with anticipation. "No. I'm ready to go if you are."

He placed a quick, but promising kiss on her lips. "I couldn't be more ready."

Once they were in the Jeep driving back to the resort, Mia stared, dazed, out at the darkened landscape. Marshall had said he cared about her. He couldn't *love* her, she mentally argued. Could he? Especially now that he knew she wasn't a born-and-bred heiress.

She didn't realize he'd passed her cabin and had

driven them on up the mountain to his house until the vehicle came to a final halt and she looked around her at the encroaching pine forest.

"This isn't my cabin, it's yours," she stated lamely. "What are we doing here?"

He shoved the gearshift into first and pulled the key from the ignition. "I didn't think you needed to be alone right now. And I wasn't sure you'd invite me in if we stopped at your place."

Her heart melting at the tender look on his face, she reached over and touched his hand with hers. "I was going to invite you in. But this is just as good."

Leaning toward her, he slipped a hand behind her neck and pulled her face toward his. His lips were warm and searching, inviting her to forget everything but him.

Mia was about to wriggle closer when Leroy's loud barks caused her to flinch away from him.

"Oh. Leroy scared me!" she exclaimed.

"Damn dog," Marshall muttered. "He has no timing at all."

"Yes, but he's a sweetheart," Mia crooned as she looked toward the front-yard gate. The dog was reared up on his hind legs, pawing eagerly at the wooden post where the latch was located.

Mia laughed and Marshall shot her a droll look. "Hey, beautiful, you're confused. I'm supposed to be the sweetheart around here. Not Leroy."

She was still laughing as they crossed the yard and entered the house with a happy Leroy trotting behind them. But the moment he shut the door and drew her into his arms, he swallowed up her chuckles with a kiss hot enough to curl her toes.

"I think Leroy is watching," she whispered when he finally lifted his lips a fraction from hers.

"Not for long."

She was trying to guess his intentions when he suddenly bent and scooped her up in his arms.

"Marshall!" she squeaked. "You're going to drop me!"

"Then you'd better hang on," he warned with a chuckle.

Flinging her arms around his neck, she clung to him tightly as he began to walk out of the living room. When his route took them down a narrow hallway it was obvious he was headed to a bedroom and she wasn't so naive that she had to ask why. For the past few days, she'd felt the two of them drawing closer and closer, ultimately leading them onto this path and this very moment.

Seconds later, Marshall entered a room, kicked the door shut behind them, then set her on the floor. Black shadows filled the corners and shrouded most of the furniture, while faint shafts of light sifted through the windows and slashed across part of the bed and the upper half of his face. The illumination was enough to give Mia a glimpse of his heated gaze and it arced into her like a sizzling arrow.

Her heart was suddenly pounding, pushing heated blood to every inch of her body as his hands came up to cradle her face.

"You can tell me you're not ready for this, you know," he whispered gently. "But I hope you are."

He was giving her the opportunity to walk away from

him and the intimacy he was offering. He was giving her a moment to analyze her feelings and consider the consequences of making love with him. But Mia didn't need the extra moment to question the rightness or wrongness of being here. She was sick of analyzing and agonizing over every decision she made, tired of guarding her true feelings. She wanted to be a woman again and for tonight that was enough to justify stepping into his arms.

Slipping her arms around his waist, she rested her chin in the middle of his chest and tilted her face up to his. "I want you, Marshall. Here with you is the only place I want to be."

Groaning with a mixture of relief and need, he skimmed his hands down the sides of her arms. "I want you, too, baby. So much."

Her breath caught as his head slowly lowered down to hers and then she forgot all about breathing as his lips settled over hers and his hands clasped her waist and drew her against the length of his body.

Like a desert wildfire, his kiss raged through her body, turning her insides to molten mush. His tongue pushed its way past her pulsing lips and then she was lost, groaning with abandoned pleasure as he explored the dark cavern of her mouth, the rough edges of her teeth.

In a matter of moments a tight ache started somewhere deep within her and began to spiral outward and upward until she was twisting and clinging, fighting to find the relief his body would give her.

Fueled by her heated response, Marshall continued

to kiss her as his hands quickly went to work releasing the buttons on her blouse and finding his way to the warm flesh beneath. Her skin was smooth beneath his fingers. He couldn't touch her enough as his hands slid upward, along the bumps of her ribs, then around to her spine where they climbed until his thumbs snared in the fastener on her bra.

With deft movements he unhooked a pair of eyelets and the garment fell apart, the loosened tails dangling against her back. He broke the kiss and their gazes locked as he slowly pushed the blouse from her shoulders, then slipped the straps of her bra down her arms.

Beneath the trail of his fingers, he could feel goose bumps breaking out along her skin, telling him just how much he was affecting her. As for him, he felt like an awkward teenager, touching a woman for the first time. His heart was pounding. Blood was rushing to his head, fogging his senses, filling his loins to the aching point. He'd never wanted so much. Needed so much.

He was asking himself what it could mean when the bra fell away from her breasts and the perfectly rounded orbs were exposed to his gaze. The lovely sight of puckered rose-brown nipples momentarily froze him and then slowly, seductively, he raked the pads of his thumbs across the delicate nubs.

Almost instantly Mia's head fell back. A moan vibrated in her throat. Bending his head, Marshall slid parted lips along the arch of her neck, over the angle of her shoulder, then lower until he was tasting the incredibly soft slope of her breasts.

When his mouth finally fastened over one taut nipple, Mia was panting, thrusting her fingers against his scalp, urging him.

When he finally lifted his head, he was shaking from the inside out and wondering if he was in some glorious dream that would end at any moment. But Mia's warm flesh brushing against his was enough to remind him that she was real and waiting to become his woman, his lover. The implication brought a tremble to his hands as he reached to undo the front of her jeans.

"Let me do this," she whispered as his fingers fumbled with the button at her waist. "It will be faster."

Not in any condition to argue with her, Marshall eased away from her and while he struggled to fling aside his own shirt and jeans, he darted hungry glances at Mia until she finally pushed the denim off her hips.

With his own clothes out of the way, he stood watching as she stepped from the pool of fabric. The sight of her plump breasts and tiny waist, the curves of her hips and the long firm muscles of her thighs just waiting for him to touch and taste was enough to leave him just short of speechless.

"Mia. Oh, Mia," he whispered.

Stepping forward he lifted her onto the queen-sized bed, then followed her onto the down comforter. As he enfolded her in his arms, she pressed her cheek against his and the sweetness of her gesture pierced his heart, filling it with something warm, something that had nothing to do with sex and everything to do with love.

The idea scared him, but the feeling was so thrilling that he couldn't stop. Couldn't look back.

"Marshall, I didn't know how much I wanted this—you—until tonight. But when you kissed me out in your parents' yard…I don't know. Everything felt different—right. Does that make sense?"

At this moment nothing made sense to Marshall except the extraordinary need to kiss her, hold her, feel his body sliding into hers.

"Making sense doesn't matter," he said thickly. "You and me together—that's all that matters."

Rolling her onto her back, Marshall used the next few minutes to make a feast of the mounds and hollows of her body and each nibble, each tempting slide of his tongue sent shivers of longing down Mia's spine. In a matter of moments she forgot everything except the desire that was surging higher and higher, begging her body to connect with his.

When she began to moan and writhe beneath him, he eased back enough to slip the scanty piece of lace from her hips. The black triangle of hair springing from the juncture of her thighs beckoned his fingers. For a moment he teased the soft curls and then, lifting his gaze to hers, he stroked lower. Her eyes widened with surprise, then closed completely as he gently, coaxingly touched the intimate folds between her thighs.

"Marshall, Marshall," she said on a thick, guttural groan. "Don't torment me like this. I need—"

The rest of her words stopped on a gasp as one finger slipped into the moist heat of her body. Stock still, she waited, barely breathing as he stroked and explored that secret part of her. But after a few short moments the teasing rhythm of his movements was too much for her to bear.

Crying out with a mixture of intense pleasure and pain, she reached for the boxers riding low on his hips and, hooking her thumbs in the waistband, pulled them down around his thighs.

"Make love to me, Marshall. *Please.*"

The urgency of her whispered plea was like throwing accelerant on an already raging fire. On the verge of losing all control, Marshall forced himself to move away from her and over to a chest of drawers where he fished out a small packet and quickly tore it open.

When he returned to her, Mia hardly had time to notice that he'd been dealing with protection. All at once his knee was parting her thighs and his hands were slipping beneath her buttocks, lifting her up to meet the thrust of his arousal.

A sudden rush of fiery sensations brought a keening moan to the back of Mia's throat and, seeking any sort of anchor she could find, her fingers latched a tight grip around his upper arms. Bending forward, he began to move inside her and when she slowly began to move with him, he brought his lips to hers and growled out her name.

"Mia. Mia. Touch me. Love me."

Happy to comply with his sweet request, she swept her palms over the hard muscles of his chest, down his ribs and abdomen, then back up until her fingertips lingered at his hard nipples.

With each bold foray of her hands, she heard his

breath catch, felt his thrusts quicken. Frantic to keep pace with him, she wrapped her legs around his and clung to his sweat-drenched shoulders.

At some point the room around her spun away, leaving a black velvety place where only she and Marshall existed. With each rapid plunge, he drove her to a higher ledge, where her heart was hammering out of control, her lungs burning with each raspy breath.

They took the climb together, racing frantically toward the peak of the mountain where a crescent moon poured silver dust and lit their pathway to the stars.

She was straining, her body screaming for relief, when Marshall's lips came down over hers to swallow up her cries and nudge them both over the last precipice of their journey. He drove into her like a man possessed, his hands and hips gripping her to him as he spilled his very heart into her.

His throaty groan of release launched Mia even higher and, like a rocket gathering steam, she shot straight through a bright, molten star. She cried his name as lights glittered behind her tightly closed eyelids. And then she was drifting, glowing, falling back to earth on a cloud of emotions.

When Marshall's senses finally returned, he was still breathing raggedly and sweat was rolling into his eyes and down his face. Beneath him Mia's body was damp and lax, her face covered with a tangle of black hair.

With a groan that sounded like it belonged to someone else, Marshall rolled to her side and reached to push the veil of hair away from her cheek. As his fingers brushed against her neck, he could feel her pulse hammering and he bent and pressed a kiss to the throb of her heartbeat.

"I'm not sure I'm alive," he murmured. "Are we in heaven?"

The corners of his lips tilted into dreamy smile. "I think I just went there."

Slipping a hand over her belly, he latched onto her hip bone, then rolled her onto her side and against the length of his body. After cuddling her head in the crook of his shoulder, he pillowed his jaw against the crown of her hair and closed his eyes in exhausted contentment.

For the first time in Marshall's life words seemed inadequate to describe what he'd just experienced. Joy was swimming around inside him, warming him like bright sunshine. Maybe that made him a sappy fool. But he didn't care.

"I knew it would be good with us," he murmured, then silently cursed himself for emitting such a stupid remark. Hell, good was a long way from portraying the connection he'd felt to Mia. Why couldn't he tell her that? Because he was a chicken, he realized. Because even though she'd made love with him, his hold on her was still too fragile. Any remark suggesting a future together would send her running.

"Mmm. How did you know that? Experience?"

Sliding a finger beneath her chin, he tilted her face up to his, but the darkness of the room hid her expression. He touched the pad of his forefinger to the middle of her lips.

"Oh, Mia, I thought I knew what being with a woman was all about. But making love with you—" He shook his head, then chuckled with wry disbelief. "It felt like the first time. No—not the first time. The *only* time."

Her heart wincing with regret, she lifted her fingers to his face and slid them along the length of his jawline. "You'll feel differently about that in the light of day. Especially if you see me when I first wake up," she tried to tease.

His arms moved around her back and hugged her even closer. "I hope that means you're going to stay here with me tonight."

She was wondering how to best answer that question when his arms tightened around her even more.

"Don't bother answering," he said, "because I'm not going to let you out of this bed for any reason. Except breakfast, maybe."

She tried not to let the possessive tone in his voice thrill her, but it did. Everything about the man thrilled her. And tonight she needed to be close to him, needed to let herself believe that she could be loved.

Bringing her lips up to his, she kissed him softly, temptingly. "Will you be doing the cooking?"

His sexy chuckle fanned across her face and curled her toes.

"Just tell me what you want."

Chapter Twelve

When Mia woke the next morning, she was momentarily startled by the strange room, but as she sat up in Marshall's bed, everything about the night before came rushing back to her. And the memories were enough to send a scarlet wave of heat across her face.

Oh, my, oh, my. She glanced at the empty spot where Marshall had lain beside her. Never had she behaved with such abandon. She'd responded to Marshall as though he'd been her lover for years rather than hours. Nothing had inhibited her. Nothing had stopped her from showing him how much she wanted him.

Well, she could be thankful she hadn't made a slip of the tongue and confessed that she loved him, she thought dryly, as she climbed from the bed and snatched up her clothing from the floor. At least she'd still have a shred of pride to hang on to whenever he eventually sent her packing.

Minutes later, after a quick shower in the private bath of his bedroom, she jerked on her jeans and blouse and hurried out to the kitchen. Marshall spotted her just as he was ending a call on his cell phone.

He snapped the instrument shut and hurried over to place a quick kiss on her lips.

"Good morning," she murmured shyly, then glanced at the phone he was dropping into pants pocket. It was six o'clock. She wouldn't expect him to be getting calls at this early hour. "Is anything wrong?"

He grimaced. "Afraid so. One of the guests is having some sort of chest pains. He thinks he pulled a muscle while rowing on the river yesterday. His wife is afraid it's his heart. I'm going to check him out. You can't be too careful with something like this." He glanced regretfully down at her. "There goes our breakfast for now. But I did have a chance to make coffee before the call came through. Why don't you have some and I'll be back as soon as I can. If I don't have a line of patients waiting on me, we could go to the Grubstake later for breakfast."

Mia quickly shook her head. "Don't worry about me. Go. Tend to your patient. That's the most important thing. I'll walk home to my cabin after I have a cup of coffee," she assured him.

Relief washed across his face. "You're too understanding, Mia." He planted another brief kiss on her lips, then turning to go, he tossed over his shoulder. "I'll see you later. This evening. Promise."

She waved him out the kitchen door and seconds later she heard the Jeep drive away.

Later that morning, after Marshall had determined that his early bird patient was suffering from a pulled ligament rather than a heart attack, he wrote the man instructions for care at home, along with a prescription for inflammation. The couple was just leaving his office when Ruthann arrived for work.

The redheaded nurse stared at Marshall as though the sight of him had sent her into shock. "What are you doing here?"

Marshall shot her a droll look. "I'm the doctor around here, Ruthie, remember? Marshall Cates, M.D."

Rolling her eyes at him, she marched over to his desk and dropped a white sack full of sugary doughnuts and cream-filled pastries. "Shouldn't you add BS to that?"

He followed after her and snatched up the sack. As he pulled out a doughnut, he asked, "What does that mean?"

Ruthann banged the heel of her palm against the side of her head. "Do I have to spell it out for you? It's something you shovel out of the barn and you're full of it."

He bit off half the doughnut and swallowed it down after a few short chews. "Hell! That's not what I mean! Why are you insulting me by implying that I work banker's hours? I am a doctor," he reminded her pointedly. "I do have emergency calls."

Her brows shot up. "I thought you regulated those to Dr. Baxter."

"Not anymore."

"Since when?" she countered.

Frowning, he dropped into his desk chair and pulled another pastry from the sack. "Since a few days ago," he answered with a tinge of annoyance. "Since I decided I needed to do more around here to earn my pay."

Ruthann slapped a palm against her forehead and sank into a chair angled toward the front of Marshall's desk. "My God, let me sit down! I think I'm hallucinating—I think I'm actually seeing a doctor with a conscience."

He leveled a gaze at her. "Sometimes it stuns me that you can be such a mean woman."

She started to laugh and then another thought must have struck her because she frowned at him in confusion. "What was the emergency that called you out of your bed this morning?"

"Chest pains. But it was nothing serious. The patient and his wife were very relieved. And grateful. Made me feel good to help them. Even if I did have to miss cooking breakfast."

This time Ruthann did laugh, although the sound was more like a snort.

"Yeah. Sure, Marshall. You slave over the stove every morning, then eat a sack of pastries after you get to work."

Dusting the powdered sugar from his hands, he leaned back in the cushioned leather chair. He was exhausted. But it was the most pleasant sort of exhaustion he'd ever felt in his life. Mia had kissed him, touched him, whispered to him, turned him inside out with her lovemaking. He felt like a new and different man. And suddenly all the things he'd considered unimportant in life were now shouting at him to take a second look.

"Ruthie, do you think I'd make a good father?"

The startled nurse scooted to the edge of her chair. "Did you get drunk last night?"

Only on love, he thought. It was crazy. Foolish. He'd never imagined that the bug would bite him. He'd thought he was immune. But he felt like a grinning idiot and it was downright glorious.

"No. And I asked you a perfectly logical question," he shot at her.

She drew in a long breath and slowly released it. "Don't you think you ought to be a husband first?"

He pondered her question as he reached for another doughnut. "Yeah. That would be the way to do it, wouldn't it? A husband and then a father. Yeah. I could do it. Just follow after my dad."

"Well, I have to admit that Frank Cates is probably the best example of both. But as for you—you're thirty-four years old. You've gone through women like a stack of cotton socks. No," she said with a shake of her head, "if you had a wife you'd only end up breaking her heart and then I'd really hate you."

"I wouldn't do any such thing," he countered.

She snatched up the bakery sack before he could reach for the last pastry. "You're not only crazy this morning, you're eating like a hog. Why in heck are you so hungry?"

A wicked grin spread across his face. "Exercise, Ruthie. You ought to try it some time."

With a roll of her eyes, she left the room, carrying the last sugary treat with her.

Later that day, Mia sat on the porch of her cabin, trying to read, trying to forget the endless times Janelle had rung her cell phone today and, even more, trying to come to terms with the fact that she'd fallen in love with Marshall.

An objective friend would probably tell her that she was simply still glowing after a night of good sex. But Mia didn't have a close friend here on the resort to confide in. And even if she did, she wouldn't go along with that reasoning. Yes, being in Marshall's arms had given her a glimpse of ecstasy, but it hadn't just been sex. Not with her half of the partnership. The only reason she'd allowed him to carry her to his bed was the love that had been growing in her heart, building until she'd been unable to shut it down or hide it away.

Now what was she going to do about it? she wondered miserably.

Fool! There's nothing you can do about it. Marshall believes you're a sweet girl who unfortunately lost her parents. Once he gets the real picture of who you are, he'll turn his back and walk away.

Painful emotions knotted her throat and misted her eyes, making it impossible to read the open book on her lap. She was trying to compose herself and will the attack of hopelessness away when the sound of an approaching vehicle caught her attention and she looked up to see Marshall's Jeep braking to a halt next to her rental car.

Desperate to hide her turmoil from his perceptive gaze, she quickly dashed the back of her hand against her eyes and rose to her feet. By the time he'd jogged up on the porch to join her, she'd managed to plaster a bright smile on her face.

"Hello, doc."

His lips tilted into a sexy grin, he slid his arms around her and locked his hands at the back of her waist.

Mia's heart fluttered with happiness as he brought a soft, sweet kiss to her lips.

"Hello, beautiful," he murmured.

"My, that's a special greeting."

The grin on his lips deepened. "You're a special girl. My girl," he added softly.

Her heart winced at the sincerity in his voice. The idea that he was actually starting to care for her only made matters a thousand times worse. It would be wrong to lead him into a relationship that could go nowhere. Yet she wanted him so. Needed him so. Oh, God, help me, she silently prayed.

Dropping her gaze away from his twinkling eyes, she buried her cheek against the middle of his chest. "How did your emergency go this morning? I hope everything turned out okay."

"It did." He rubbed his chin against the top of her head. "The guy's heart checked out perfectly fine. He had a pulled ligament."

"That's good."

"Yeah. I'm just sorry it interrupted our breakfast together. That's one reason why I'm here. I thought I'd make up for it by taking you to the Grubstake for a quick bite. And then…"

His suggestive pause had her tilting her head back to look up at him. The sultry squint of his eyes told her he'd already planned a repeat of last night and Mia realized if she wanted to avoid an even bigger heartache, she'd turn tail and run. But she couldn't. Not when everything inside her was hungering to be back in his arms.

"Then what?" she softly prompted.

"We're going on a bike ride."

Her eyes widened. "A bike ride! Where?"

He chuckled at the surprise sweeping across her face. "Up the mountain from my house. Where we found Joey and his mother. I never got to show you my special spot up there. Are you up for it?"

At this moment she felt certain she could run for miles. As long as he was by her side.

Smiling, she eased out of his arms and picked up the book she'd left laying in her lawn chair. "Just let me change into some jeans. The last time I went up a mountain with you my knees were ground into hamburger meat."

Laughing, he followed her into the cabin.

Two hours later, after eating hearty sandwiches and fries at the Grubstake, Mia and Marshall rode up the mountain, two miles past the spot where they'd found Joey, then left their bikes at the side of the road to walk into the woods.

When they first ventured into the thick forest of tall aspens and fir trees, Mia expected a long steep hike over treacherous boulders, but it turned out to be more of an easy stroll along a lightly beaten path.

"Do other resort guests know about this place of yours?" she asked as she closely followed him through a stand of aspens.

"I doubt anyone else has ever found it. I've never seen anyone else climbing up this far."

"Hmm. Well, no one else is a mountain goat like you are," she teased.

"Just wait. You'll see that this trip was worth it."

Moments later they rounded another stand of trees and suddenly an open area appeared before them and Mia gasped with shocked pleasure.

There before them were slabs of red rock towering at least fifty feet above their heads. Water was spilling over the top of the ledge, falling and tinkling against the rocks until it reached a natural pool edged with tall reeds and blooming water lilies. The spot was so incredibly beautiful that it seemed more fairy tale than real.

Mia's first instinct was to rush forward to get an even closer look, but before either of them took a step, Marshall grabbed her arm and silently pointed to a mule deer with a fawn at its side slipping quietly from the trees and over to the pool's edge.

As mother and baby drank, Mia looked up at Marshall and smiled gratefully. "Thank you for bringing me here," she silently mouthed up at him, so as not to give away their presence and startle the animals.

Marshall responded by bending his head and pressing his lips to hers. The kiss was full of tenderness and something else that Mia had never felt before. It tugged at her heart and filled her chest with such emotion that she could scarcely breathe.

When he finally lifted his head, they both turned their heads to see that the doe and fawn had disappeared. Marshall slipped his arm against her back and urged her toward the waterfall.

"Come on," he said quietly. "Let me show you where I come when I really want to think."

When they returned to Marshall's log house later that evening it was no surprise to Mia that the two of them ended up in his bed. Nor was it a surprise that their lovemaking was even more earthshaking for her than it had been the night before. Her heart was well and truly entangled with the man and each time she'd given her body to him, her very soul had gone with it.

This morning after cooking her a leisurely breakfast, he'd dropped her off at her cabin on his way to work. He'd kissed her goodbye with the promise of calling her later in the day to talk over plans of getting together tonight.

Since that time, Mia had been prowling around her cabin, unable to relax, unable to concentrate on anything except this impossible situation she'd fallen into.

Situation. No, it was far worse than a situation. It was a complete and utter disaster. This thing between them was snowballing, racing along so quickly that she didn't know how to put on the brakes, much less stop it. But stop it she had to. Now. Tonight. Before Marshall found out she was really Nina Hanover.

The ring of her cell phone interrupted her pacing and for a moment she simply stared in dread at the instrument. If Marshall was calling what was she going to say? Just enough to put him off without alerting him that something was wrong? Yes, she thought, frantically. If she had tonight alone, then maybe she could figure out how she was going to deal with him tomorrow.

For once she wished that the caller actually was Janelle. But the ID number glaring up at her was Marshall's and she was forced to answer. Otherwise, he'd wind up on her porch and she wouldn't be able to find the resistance to stay out of his arms.

Swallowing hard, she pushed the talk button and spoke. "Hi, Marshall."

"Hi, darlin'. I'm five minutes away from leaving the office. Tell me where you'd like to eat dinner. How about driving over to Bozeman? I doubt you've been off the resort since you first arrived."

It was true. Once Mia had decided to temporarily settle at Thunder Canyon Resort, she'd ventured no farther than town. She'd not wanted to show her face on any of the major cities along the interstate, just in case Janelle had private investigators out looking for her. And there was little doubt in Mia's mind that the woman had been searching for her. Since finding Mia's note explaining that she was taking an extended trip to give herself time to think, Janelle had probably whipped into action, doling out money to anyone who'd make a con-centrated effort to find her runaway daughter.

"Uh—no, I haven't been to Bozeman." Her voice sounded strained even to her own ears, but she couldn't help it. Her heart was breaking and all she really wanted to do was throw down the phone and sob until she couldn't shed another tear.

"Is something wrong, Mia? You sound strange."

She swallowed again as her throat clogged with a ball of guilt and regret. "I—well, actually there is some-thing wrong. My head. I—developed a migraine this afternoon. And it's really cracking. I don't think I can make it out of bed."

"Mia, honey! You should have called my office earlier! I can prescribe you something for the pain or if necessary give you an injection. Just hold on. I'll be there in five minutes."

"No!" she blurted, then realizing how frantic that sounded, she added, "I mean, there's no need for you to come over. I took something a few minutes ago and I'm going to try to sleep."

Several moments passed before he finally replied. Mia got the feeling that this sudden change in plans had really taken him aback. Well, it had done more than that to her. The pain that had started in her chest was now radiating through her whole body, leaving her numb and dazed. If there was some sort of painkiller that could wipe out this love she felt for him, then she desperately needed it.

"All right, Mia. But I'd feel much better if you'd let me examine you."

"Don't be silly, Marshall. It's just a headache. I'll be fine tomorrow. I'll call you then."

She could hear him drawing in a rough breath. The sound brought tears to her eyes and she swiftly squeezed them shut.

"I—I was really planning on us being together tonight," he said softly. "The house is going to be damn hollow without you."

She was choking, dying from the bitter loss washing over her. "I'm—sorry, Marshall," she spoke through a veil of tears. "I didn't want the evening to end like this, either."

"You can't help it if you're sick, honey. Try to get some sleep and I'll check on you in the morning."

Relieved that he'd accepted her excuse, Mia quickly told him goodbye. But once she'd pushed the button to end the call, she broke into racking sobs that continued until she'd cried herself to sleep on the sofa.

When Mia woke the next morning, her heart was so heavy she could hardly push herself into the kitchen to make coffee. For all she noticed, the bright sunshine pounding against the windowpanes of the cabin might as well have been fierce raindrops. The first real joy she'd found since Nina passed away was over. The first real love she'd ever felt for a man couldn't be continued. She couldn't hold on to the happiness that love should bring to a young woman's life. And all because she'd made horrible choices in the past. Choices that painted her as a selfish gold-digger and someone that a good man like Marshall could never love.

After a quick cup of coffee, Mia decided the best thing she could do this morning would be to leave the cabin and go for a walk in the forest. That way when Marshall called or dropped by to check on her, she'd be gone. It was a cowardly way for her to behave, but she wasn't sure she could face him just yet without breaking down in tears.

She had changed into clean jeans and a white peasant blouse and was walking swiftly away from the cabin when she heard a vehicle approaching her from behind.

Her whole body heavy with dread, she turned to see Marshall's Jeep bearing down on her. He skidded to a stop beside her and hopped out with the athletic ease she'd come to associate with him.

"Good morning," she greeted, tilting her chin, bracing herself for what had to be.

"Good morning, yourself," he said, his stunned gaze whipping over her face. "What are you doing out here? I thought you were sick?"

Her heart was pounding so hard she thought she might lose her coffee right there in front of him. "I—was going out for a little hike this morning."

"After being bedridden with a migraine? Don't you think that's a little much?"

Of course he would view it that way. He was a doctor. Oh, God, help her, she prayed.

Clearing her throat, she glanced away from him and continued to pray for strength. "Okay, Marshall. I confess. I didn't really have a headache last night. I…knew if I didn't tell you something like that…you would…well, the two of us would end up in bed together again."

Looking even more stunned, he closed the distance between them and put a hand on her arm. The contact sent shivers of excitement and aching regret through her rigid body.

Bemused, he shook his head. "I don't understand, Mia. I thought you *wanted* us to be together—to make love."

Tightening her jaw to prevent her lips from trembling, she said, "I did. But I've been thinking it all through. And I— Well, this thing between us is going too fast. Way too fast." She forced herself to look at him and quickly wished she hadn't. Pain was clouding his brown eyes and the idea that she'd put it there made her even sicker. "I believe that we…need to cool things between us for a while."

He sucked in a deep breath then slowly blew it out and as he did, his eyes narrowed to two angry slits. "Why don't you just come out and say what you really mean, Mia. You jumped into bed with me. You've had your fun. And now you want out. Well, it looks like I was wrong about you. Dead wrong."

She froze inside. "What do you mean?" she asked tightly.

His face like a piece of granite, he said, "I didn't believe you were just one of those rich little teases out for your own enjoyment. I thought you were different— sincere. But it looks like the joke is on me, isn't it? I've got to admit, Mia, you really had me fooled. I thought— Oh, to hell with what I thought. You obviously don't give a damn what I think anyway!"

He turned and climbed back into his Jeep and though everything inside Mia was screaming at her to call him back, to explain that she hadn't been teasing him, using him, all she could do was stand there, her gaze frozen on the vehicle as he drove away.

Once his Jeep rounded a stand of trees and disappeared from view, finality set in and washed over her heart like a crushing wave. Everything between them was over. She'd accomplished what she'd set out to do. Now all she had to do was get over the only love of her life.

Chapter Thirteen

Two days later the weather turned wet and unusually cool for late August. For the most part, the guests at the resort were whiling away their time with indoor games and rounds of warm drinks from the bar and the coffee shop.

Marshall's patients had dwindled down to none and by late afternoon, he told Ruthie to close up shop and let the answering service deal with any oncoming calls. The idle day was driving him crazy. With too much time to dwell on Mia, his office felt like a cage.

He left the building by way of the back entrance and once in his Jeep, automatically turned the vehicle toward his home. But halfway there, he muttered a disgusted curse and made a U-turn in the middle of the dirt road.

There was no use in going home. The place was hauntingly empty without Mia.

That's what you get, Marshall, for letting the woman get close, for letting her into your home as though she were someone who'd be around for the rest of your life.

The accusing voice in his head was right. He'd been a fool to think an heiress would fit into his life on a permanent basis. What the hell had he been thinking? He hadn't been thinking. He'd been feeling. Only feeling.

Moments later, he passed the turn off to Mia's cabin and continued barreling on out of the resort. He'd not tried to contact her since their brief encounter the other morning. He wasn't a glutton for self-punishment and though he'd finally let his guard down and allowed a woman to get under his skin, that didn't mean he was a naive fool. She'd made it clear that she wanted to end things between them. There wasn't any sense in going back for more pain, to give her another chance to pour salt into his wounds.

By the time he reached town, he realized his misery was leading him to the one person he could really talk to. At this hour of the day, his brother Mitchell would be at work, but he wouldn't mind if Marshall showed up unexpectedly. With all of the Cates, family always came first.

Cates International, Mitchell's successful company, was located on the edge of town. The large metal warehouse's light green exterior was trimmed in a darker green and surrounded by a huge paved parking lot that was partially filled with displays of planting and harvesting equipment.

A fancy showroom was attached to one side of the building, along with Mitch's luxurious office, but Marshall ignored the double glass door entrance gilded with gold lettering and walked on to a simple side door that accessed the warehouse. If he wasn't swamped with customers, Mitch would most likely be inside, tinkering around in his workshop.

Having guessed correctly, Marshall found his brother working at a computer and from the look of deep concentration on his face he was in his creative mood.

Walking around the desk, Marshall stood behind his brother and peered over his shoulder. "Is that some new design you're drafting, or are you just trying to draw an ice cream cone?"

His concentration broken, Mitchell looked over his shoulder. "Hey, brother. What's up?"

Unable to summon a smile to his face, Marshall shrugged. "Nothing. The weather has everybody on the resort playing safely inside. I don't have a thing to do. And I thought…I'd come out and see what you're up to."

Mitchell pointed to the small object on the computer screen. "Nothing much, just working on a little toy that might eventually make me millions."

"What the hell is that? Looks like a dunce cap for a mouse."

Mitchell grimaced. "That's why you're the doctor and I'm the inventor. I'm trying to come up with a seed broadcaster that will work on a smaller implement but cover more ground. It would save hours of labor and gallons of diesel for farmers."

"Good luck. It might be nice to have one millionaire in the family," he said dryly.

Mitchell turned off the computer and rose to his feet, motioning for Marshall to follow him over to a little nook in the room where a coffee machine was located.

"You look like you need something to perk you up, big brother. I don't think I've ever seen you looking so grim."

Mitchell poured two cups full of coffee and handed one of them to Marshall. "I'd offer you a sandwich to go with it, but the crew ate them all."

"No matter. I'm not hungry," Marshall told him. "And I should leave. I'm interrupting your work."

Shaking his head, Mitchell walked over to a comfortable couch. After taking a seat, he patted the empty cushion next to him. "I needed a break anyway. Come on. Sit. I can see something is on your mind. Tell me about it."

Raking a weary hand through his windblown hair, Marshall took a seat. "I always thought the big brother was supposed to be the listener. I'm the big brother."

Mitchell grinned at that observation. "Then who's supposed to listen to you?"

Marshall lifted his gaze to the ceiling far above them. His brother was smart, successful and smart enough to avoid the snaring arms of a woman. Too bad he hadn't been more like Mitchell, he thought. Instead, he'd gone through women like a stack of cotton socks. Just as Ruthie had said. Only this time, the tables had turned and he was the one doing the hurting. Maybe he deserved this misery.

"I don't know. Dad, I suppose. But I can't talk to him

about this. He'd only remind me that I'd wasted years of my life regarding women as playthings when I should have been looking for a wife."

Sudden dawning crossed Mitchell's face. "Ah. A woman. So that's what this mopey look of yours is all about. I should have known. So the heiress has dumped you already?"

Marshall glared at him. "You don't have to be so flip about it."

This time Mitchell frowned. "Well, what do you expect, brother? The woman isn't your style. I don't know why you're bothering with her anyway."

His jaw tightened and then he answered in a low voice, "Maybe because I loved her. Because I…still love her."

Mitchell was suddenly regarding him in a different light. "I've never heard you talk this way. You're scaring me."

"I'm scaring myself. Especially now that Mia doesn't want to see me anymore."

"Why?"

Bending his head, Marshall stared at the concrete floor. "How the hell should I know! One day she was all warm and loving and the next she says she thinks we should cool it. I can't figure what's going on with her."

Mitchell studied him thoughtfully. "Hmm. Well, she seemed nice enough at the family dinner. A little introverted, but nice."

His heart was suddenly aching as he recalled the tears on Mia's face as she'd talked about losing her mother. He'd wanted so much to help her and he'd thought loving her would give her the support she needed. He'd been wrong. Painfully wrong. "She has reason to be. She's lost her family—her mother more recently."

Mitchell blew out a long breath. "Forget her, Marshall. She's trouble. You don't need a woman carrying around a trunk of emotional issues. Put Mia Smith out of your mind and find someone new."

Marshall groaned with frustration. "I don't want another woman, Mitch. I want Mia. That's the whole problem."

Mitchell laid a comforting hand on his brother's shoulder. "If that's the way you feel, then my advice is to go confront her. Make her tell you what's wrong."

Marshall regarded his brother for a long thoughtful moment before he finally gave him a jerky nod. "You're right. If Mia wants to dump me, she's going to have to tell me why."

At the same time Marshall was visiting with his brother, Mia had finally ventured out of the cabin and walked over to the lodge. The cold weather had made the past two days even gloomier for her and though she didn't want to risk running into Marshall, she couldn't continue to hide in her cabin. She had two choices, she thought grimly, face him with the truth or leave Thunder Canyon once and for all. Either way, she was bound to lose him.

Thankfully, there was a cheery fire burning in the enormous rock fireplace in the lounge and several guests were sitting around reading, talking and playing board games. Mia purchased a cup of hot cocoa from the coffee shop and carried it over to one of the couches facing the crackling flames.

She'd just made herself comfortable and was sipping at her drink when she looked around to see Lizbeth Stanton, the lounge bartender, easing down on the cushion next to her.

"Hi," she said. "Mind if I sit down?"

Since the woman was already sitting, the question seemed inane. Mia shrugged, while wondering what could have prompted Lizbeth to join her. Even though she was acquainted with the sexy bartender and had chatted with her during her stay here at the resort, the two of them weren't what you'd called bosom buddies.

"Not at all. Are you on a break from the bar?"

Lizbeth shook her head. "No. I don't go on for another thirty minutes. I saw you sitting here and thought I'd stop by. I—uh, there's something I've been wanting to say to you and you're probably going to take offense at my being so frank, but I don't know of any other way to approach you about this."

Piqued with curiosity now, Mia turned slightly toward the bartender. "Oh?"

Frowning prettily, the auburn-haired siren folded her arms against her breasts. "Yeah. I think you're making a big mistake. No, more like a *huge* mistake. Marshall is a great guy. Everyone around Thunder Canyon will tell you so. I don't know what your game is, but he doesn't deserve to be dumped."

Mia stiffened. Is that what all of Marshall's friends here on the resort were thinking? God, she couldn't bear it. "Where did you hear such a thing—that I dumped Marshall?"

"That's not important. News travels fast here on the resort. Although all of his friends didn't have to ask what happened. They can see he's miserable thanks to you." Her accusing gaze was practically boring into Mia's eyes. "It's beyond me how any woman could throw away a man like Marshall. But you seem to be doing it quite easily."

Mia drew in a bracing breath and tried to remember she was supposed to be an heiress with class and manners. She couldn't fire back at the bartender. She couldn't scream out that good men like her father died and left grieving widows and lost daughters. That there were no guarantees for lasting love.

"Look, Lizbeth, I think you're making a mistake by putting Marshall, or any man for that matter, on a pedestal. They're fallible. They don't always stick around. Or haven't you noticed?"

Lizbeth sneered. "What's the matter with you anyway? Are you jealous because Marshall dated me first?"

As Mia looked at her in stunned disbelief, she suddenly realized that her stay here at Thunder Canyon Resort was well and truly over. Tonight she would pack and in the morning she would put Marshall and his friends behind her.

"No. Marshall doesn't belong to me."

Lizbeth rolled her eyes. "Can't you see that Marshall is crazy about you?"

Maybe he was in love with her right now, Mia

thought painfully. But if he ever met Mia Hanover that love would dissolve like a sugar cube tossed into a cup of hot coffee. Swallowing away the burning tears in her throat, Mia muttered, "Marshall never has been a one-woman man. I think you know that, Lizbeth. Most love doesn't last forever and a woman needs to learn to lean on herself and cope with life on her own."

Pity suddenly filled Lizbeth's eyes. "You know, I think I'm actually starting to feel sorry for you. You're lacking something in here."

Lizbeth pressed fingertips to her heart and it was all Mia could do to keep from bursting into tears. Apparently this woman hadn't watched her father die. Hadn't watched her mother fall apart and turn to alcohol because she'd lost the love of her life. Mia wasn't blind or crazy; she understood that Lizbeth saw her as a hardhearted woman.

Oh, if only that were true, Mia thought. If only her heart were made of steel, or anything that couldn't ache. Then walking away from Marshall wouldn't be tearing her apart.

Rising to her feet, she stared down at Lizbeth. "You're probably right," she said coldly. "You're a far better woman to nurse Marshall's wounds. Maybe with all your virtues you'll be able to persuade him to walk down the aisle with you!"

By the time Mia reached the last words her voice had risen to a trembling shriek. She sensed the guests around them were all turning their heads to take notice, but for once she didn't care. She raced out of the lounge and didn't stop running until she was completely away from the lodge and halfway to her cabin.

Two hours later, her bed was covered with open suit-cases and she was blindly but methodically filling them with all her belongings.

The tears that had threatened to pour from her during her confrontation with Lizbeth had flowed like a river once she'd reached her cabin, but now they were dried tracks upon her cheeks. She felt dead inside.

She was pulling the zipper closed on a leather duffle bag when a knock sounded on the front door of the cabin. Frozen by the unexpected sound, she stared at the open door of her bedroom. Could that be Lizbeth wanting to go another round? If so, she was going to use a few choice words to send the woman on her way.

Leaving the bag, she walked out to the living room and peered through the peephole on the door. The moment she spotted Marshall standing on the other side, her heart stopped as though all the blood had drained from it.

He must have heard her approaching footsteps because he suddenly shouted through the door, "Mia, it's me. Let me in. I'm not going away until you do."

Marshall. In her wildest dreams she'd never expected him to speak to her again. Why was he here? To tell her that he didn't appreciate everyone on the resort knowing that she'd embarrassed and demeaned him?

Her hand trembling almost violently, she pushed back the bolt and opened the door. He didn't bother with a greeting or invitation. Instead, he strode across the thres-hold and came to a stop in the middle of the room.

Mia shut the door behind her and forced herself to turn and face him. He was dressed casually in jeans and boots and a navy-blue hooded sweatshirt. His cheeks were burnished to a ruddy color from the cool wind and his coffee-brown hair was tousled across his forehead. He looked so handsome, so endearing that it was all she could do to keep from running to him and flinging herself against his broad chest.

"I—" She swallowed hard and tried again. "I—never expected to see you here."

Anguish twisted his lips. "What were you thinking, Mia? That I'd simply keep my distance? Let everything between us end as though it had never happened at all?"

Fear rippled through her, making her insides quiver. She turned her back to him and bit down hard on her lip. "It would have been better if you had," she whispered starkly. "I'm a person that you need to forget, Marshall. I'm—no good. Not for you."

"What are you talking about?" he muttered roughly.

"Haven't you talked to Lizbeth?"

He walked up behind her but stopped short of putting his hands on her shoulders.

"No. What about Lizbeth? Has she been saying things about me to you?"

Mia bent her head, then shook it. "Don't worry. Only that you're Dr. Perfect and I'm stupid for throwing you away."

Moments passed in silence and to Mia's complete horror she felt more tears rush to her eyes. Dear God, where was this endless waterworks coming from? Why couldn't she gather herself together and stop her tears once and for all?

"Is that what you're doing?" he asked quietly. "Throwing me away?"

She squeezed her eyes, yet she couldn't hide the raw emotion in her voice. "No," she whispered. "I—I'm leaving…for your own sake."

Quickly, before he could stop her, she stepped around him and raced to the bedroom. Once there, she frantically began slinging the last of her clothes into an open suitcase.

Marshall hurried after her. "Mia? What—"

Glancing to see he'd followed her into the bedroom, she cried at him, "Don't try to stop me, Marshall! Don't ask me anything! It's useless. Totally useless!"

She was lashing out at him like a frightened kitten; hissing and pawing, when all she really wanted was to curl up in his arms.

Sensing that nothing was really as it had first seemed, Marshall went to her and folded his fingers around her shoulders. "Nothing is useless. Not when you love someone, Mia. And I love you. Don't you understand? Don't you care?"

I love you. How many times had she dreamed of hearing Marshall say those words to her? Too many. And now she had to rip them all away, to smear and mar the most precious thing he could possibly give her.

"I care. More than you could ever dream, Marshall. But—"

His hands came up to tenderly cup her tear-stained face and as the warmth of his fingers flooded through her, she suddenly realized she couldn't pretend anymore. Not with him. Not with anyone.

"Then what is it? Tell me," he softly urged.

She drew in a shaky breath, but it did little to brace her composure.

"I'm a phony, Marshall. I'm not really Mia Smith. I'm Mia Hanover. I—I've been using the name Smith in order to keep someone from trailing me."

Stunned, he dropped his hands from her face and she used the opportunity to turn away from his searching gaze.

"Someone," he repeated blankly. "Someone like a man? A lover? A stalker?"

With a shake of her head, she slowing began folding the last pieces of clothing lying atop the mounded suitcase.

"No, the only man I've ever been seriously involved with was so disgusted with me he left—walked away. He didn't care enough to come after me and try again. This person is a woman. She's—uh—my birth mother. Her name is Janelle Josephson."

Marshall looked confused. "You said your mother was killed in a car accident."

"That's right. Nina Hanover. She was my adoptive mother. She's the one who raised me since I was a baby, the one who nurtured me as I grew up, sacrificed to give me food, clothing and a roof over my head." Groaning with pain, she squeezed the fragile silk blouse in her hands. "You see, Marshall, when my father—my adoptive father—died, I was about to enter college. Up until then my family—my *life*—had been so nice. My parents loved me and although we didn't have lots of money, I had all the necessities. Daddy saw to that. But then he developed lung cancer and it seemed to take him almost overnight. Mom—Nina—was devastated. For more than twenty years, he'd been her whole life, the only man she'd ever loved. Losing him so suddenly broke her, Marshall. She couldn't deal with the grief and at some point—I can't even remember exactly when— she started drinking."

Marshall's head swung back and forth with complete dismay. "Oh, Mia. I'm so sorry."

"You won't say that. Not when I tell you the rest."

Putting a hand on her arm, he slowly turned her back to him. "Mia, nothing you say will change my love for you. Believe that."

As she met his loving gaze a sob choked her to the point that she could scarcely get any words past her throat. "You don't understand, Marshall. I caused my mother's death! I caused Nina to get behind the wheel of her car and drive. She was driving to see me—to meet with me because…because I'd been avoiding her— moving on with a life away from her."

Marshall didn't make any sort of reply. Instead he cleared an area on the side of the bed and sat Mia down, easing himself down next to her. "I want you to slow down, Mia," he said gently. "Tell me what happened from the very start."

She wiped a shaky hand over her face and sniffed back her tears. "Maybe I'd better go back to after my father died. That's when everything started going downhill."

Nodding, he reached for her hand and clasped it tightly. "Your father died and your mother started to drink. Did she become an alcoholic then?"

Mia considered his question for a moment, then shook her head. "No. I don't think she was dependent on the stuff at that time. She didn't have the opportunity to drink too much, she was always working. But no matter how many jobs she had, we could barely afford rent and utilities."

"What about the farm? You didn't try to keep it?"

Regret twisted her features. "We were forced to sell it to pay off the astronomical medical bills. There wasn't much left after that and it went quickly. During that time I began to think that if Mom and I only had money it would fix everything. It would make her happy. She wouldn't have to work all the time and it would give us both security and all the things we needed. She wouldn't want to drink anymore and everything would be wonderful again. I thought it was the answer for everything. And then I began to wonder about my real mother. I kept thinking that if I could only find her she might want to help me."

The desperate picture she was painting struck Marshall like the blade of a knife. It was so far removed from the born-into-riches-heiress he'd first believed her to be and he could only wonder at the suffering she'd gone through.

"You didn't know the circumstances of your birth?"

Shaking her head, she looked down at his hand closed tightly over hers. "No. Not a clue. Nina didn't know, either. And she didn't want me to know. She feared that if I did find my birth mother I might learn something that would haunt me for the rest of my life.

But I wouldn't listen. The image of finding my birth mother had become a beautiful dream to me. One that I wasn't about to let go."

"How on earth did you find her? Adoption information is carefully guarded."

"It took years. I used the Internet and newspapers to ask questions and put out information. I met with any- and everyone associated with my parents back around the time I was born and tried to gather any sort of leads from what they recalled about my adoption."

"Were any of them able to help you?"

"In a roundabout way," Mia answered. "One man who'd lived next to our farm, but later moved from the area, remembered that my parents had traveled up to Denver to get me. And he thought that was where the adoption had taken place. With that information, it was logical to assume the records would be there and I was determined to get my hands on them somehow. But that was like butting my head against a brick wall. I begged, cajoled, even tried to con my way into getting a glimpse at my adoption papers. Security eventually threatened to have me arrested if I didn't quit badgering the filing clerks. Then I finally happened on to a young woman working in the capital building in another department who empathized with my predicament. She was also adopted and she understood this driving need I had to know about my family. She managed to acquire a copy of my papers and mail them to me. After that it was fairly easy to trace Janelle's maiden name of Laughlin to her married name of Janelle Josephson."

Marshall tried to imagine what it would be like not knowing the woman who'd given birth to him, not knowing why she'd given him away. The anguish would haunt him, eat at him until he would probably do just as Mia had done. He would search for her and the answers he hungered for.

"That must have been like finding a rainbow in a hurricane," he murmured.

Mia nodded grimly. "Literally. Complete with the pot of gold beneath it. Janelle had come from a very rich family. Her father was a real-estate mogul in and around Denver. They were worth millions and too prominent a part of the community to allow their teenage daughter to raise a child out of wedlock. They tried to pressure her into an abortion but Janelle fought them all the way. Finally they appeared to give in to letting her have the baby, just as long as she would agree to stay with relatives living in another state until I was born."

"Sounds like a pair of real loving parents," Marshall said sarcastically. "She must have been underage and unable to reach out to anyone else for help. So how did they talk her into putting you up for adoption?"

"They didn't. After she gave birth they told her that I'd been stillborn and they didn't want her to go through the trauma of seeing me. They even held a mock funeral to make things look real to Janelle."

"Incredible," he muttered with amazement. "So what happened when she discovered that you were really alive and a grown woman?"

Mia closed her eyes and drew in a ragged breath.

"She was shocked, but ecstatic. She immediately took me into her home and began lavishing me with everything, clinging to me as though she couldn't bear for me to get out of her sight."

"What about her husband? What did he think about all this? And her parents—your grandparents—are they still around?"

"Her father died a few years after I was born. Later on, Janelle's mother became debilitated from a stroke and she now resides in a nursing home. As for her husband, he died a few years ago of a heart attack and since then Janelle has remained a widow."

Frowning now with confusion, Marshall studied her rueful expression. "So you came along and filled Janelle's life up again. That's good. Good for both of you. Wasn't it? *Isn't* it?"

"In many ways, yes. But on the other hand there was Nina—the only mother I'd ever known. It wasn't long before the two women were pushing and pulling me between them. Janelle was offering me a secure home, riches beyond my wildest imaginings. Nina accused me of turning my back on her and ignoring her because she was poor." Her pleading eyes lifted to Marshall's. "That wasn't true, Marshall. But I'm sure it must have seemed that way to Mom."

His hand left hers and lifted to gently touch her cheek. "What was the truth, Mia?"

"The truth?" She let out a mocking laugh. "God, Marshall, I've tried to hide and pretend for so long now I often have to ask myself who I am and what I'm supposed to be doing. But the truth was that I grew to care about Janelle. How could I not? She loves me and she wants to care for me. Nina loved me, too, but the more I tried to reason with her the more she wanted to drink. She began to cling and whine and tell me that it was all my fault that she couldn't leave the bottle alone. She kept insisting that if I'd come home to her she'd get sober and stay that way."

Marshall's head swung back and forth. "You didn't believe her, did you?"

"Not really," Mia said sadly. "But I didn't want to give up on her completely. I gave her money. Helped her buy a nice home and a car. I thought lifting her out of poverty would help her see that she had every reason to quit drinking. It didn't. She wanted me to come home. One day I agreed to meet with her for lunch—to talk things over and try to reassure her that I would always love her no matter where I lived. I had hopes that I could talk her into entering rehab." She looked away from him and when she spoke again her voice was as hollow as a drained barrel. "She crashed her car on the way to meet me. Later, the toxicology report in the autopsy revealed that she was driving drunk. So now you know. I killed my mother…she died trying to… reach me."

Her chin suddenly dropped to her chest and silent sobs shook her shoulders. Crushed by the sight of her pain, Marshall moved closer and put his arm around her.

"Mia, don't keep punishing yourself like this. Nina's death wasn't your fault."

Mia lifted her head and stared at him in stunned fascination. "You mean—you don't think I'm a greedy gold digger? That I caused my own mother to kill herself?"

Her questions amazed him. "Is that what you've been afraid of all this time? That if I knew about your past that I wouldn't want anything to do with you? Oh, Mia, can't you see that you didn't cause Nina's death? She was the one who chose to drink. She was the one who climbed behind the wheel."

A sob caught in her throat. "Yes. But I made her unhappy. Because I started making a new life with Janelle."

Groaning, he slipped a hand behind the back of her head and pulled her forward until her cheek was resting against his shoulder. "I've gathered enough from all you've told me that Nina chose to be unhappy long before you found Janelle. She had issues that you weren't qualified to deal with, Mia. She needed professional help. Alcoholism is a horrible disease—you couldn't have cured her just by staying away from Janelle."

Sobbing now with relief, Mia held on to him tightly. "I came here to Thunder Canyon to hide from Janelle. In lots of ways I guess I thought of her as a coconspirator in Nina's death and I resented the love she was trying to give me. I suppose it made me feel even guiltier about Nina. But now I can see that I was wrong about that, too." Lifting her face up to his, she tried to smile. "You've opened my eyes, Marshall. In so many ways."

"I think you should call Janelle. I'm sure she's worried sick about you." He stroked her long black hair with slow, steady movements. "And now that your eyes are open, I hope you can now see that I love you. More than anything, Mia."

She groaned with disbelief. "I don't know why. I'm a bundle of trouble."

"A beautiful bundle," he crooned. He brought his lips over hers in a long, tender kiss. Once it ended, he looked at her pointedly, expectantly. "This means you're going to stay here in Thunder Canyon, doesn't it? With me?"

Slowly, thoughtfully, she eased out of his arms and he watched with a sense of dread as she folded the last of her clothes and placed them in the open suitcase.

"I've got to leave, Marshall. There're so many unsettled things in my life that I need to deal with right now. It wouldn't be right for me to make promises to you. Not when I need to straighten up my head and my heart." With a tiny flame of hope flickering in her eyes, she glanced at him. "Can you understand that, Marshall? Really understand?"

Rising to his feet, he placed his hands on her shoulders and gave her an affectionate squeeze. "A month ago I probably wouldn't have been able to appreciate what you're feeling. I was so full of myself that I never stopped to really look at my patient's needs or count the blessings that I'd been given. You've changed me, Mia. I'd rather you stay here and not leave my sight." A wry smile touched his lips. "But you've already had enough people pulling and pushing you. I don't want you here with me because you're under duress. If you come back to me I want it to be because you love me, because it's where you want to be."

Turning toward him, she pressed her cheek gratefully against his heart. "Thank you, Marshall, for understanding."

Chapter Fourteen

A week later, in a small cemetery on the outskirts of Alamosa, Colorado, Mia carried bunches of yellow and bronze chrysanthemums as she worked her way to the small patch of ground where her parents lay in rest.

A cool wind was blowing across the graveyard, but a bright sun was shining overhead, glinting off the double granite headstone shared by her parents.

Bending on one knee, Mia brushed away the fallen autumn leaves, then carefully propped the bright cheerful mums against the sparkly black rock. After a moment, she spoke to her mother.

"It's me, Mom. I've come back. Finally. I realize I'm too late to feel your arms wrap around me or to tell you how very much I love you. But I pray that you can somehow hear me now, that you understand I never, ever once stopped loving you.

"After Daddy died we went through so much together. So many hard times. So much sadness. I didn't know how to help you deal with your disease and you didn't know how to fight your way out of it. In the end I guess we were both guilty of not trying hard enough. But I'm positive you've gone on to a better place. And now when I think of you, Mom, I'm going to think of all the good and happy times we had together. I'm going to smile and remember how lucky I was that you chose me to be your daughter."

With a whispered goodbye, Mia rose to her full height and wiped away the single tear on her cheek.

The walk back to her car was short, yet as she lifted her gaze toward the sky, she was certain it had become brighter and there in the vivid blue she could almost envision Nina's smiling face.

Sweet release poured over her like warm sunshine as she pulled a cell phone from her coat pocket and punched in Janelle's number.

Several days later, Marshall was in his office, using the last of his lunch break to make a long distance call to his old friend DJ Traub down in Georgia. For weeks now he'd been trying to talk the other man into coming home once and for all. And today, for the first time, Marshall caught a hint that DJ was seriously considering a return to Montana.

As their conversation reached the end, Marshall made one last pitch to his friend. "All right, buddy, I hope we see you soon. Everybody here misses you. And Thunder Canyon could use some of that good barbecue. There's plenty of space for a Rib Shack here on the resort. Get yourself on a plane and get back here, DJ. No excuses."

Marshall added a quick goodbye and was hanging up the phone when Ruthann paused at the corner of his desk.

"Who was that? I thought I heard you say something about barbecue," she said nosily.

"Sure did. That was DJ Traub. Remember him?"

The nurse thoughtfully tapped a finger against her chin. "I think I do. He's Dax's brother, isn't he?"

"You're right."

"And isn't he the one who made all that money with some sort of barbecue sauce?"

Marshall smiled. "Give the woman a prize. Right on both counts. Besides the sauce he now has a chain of restaurants called DJ's Rib Shack. I'm trying to talk him into putting one here on the resort."

"Oh, now that would be my style of eating," Ruthann told him. "Elbows on the table, paper towels for napkins. The next time you talk to him, tell him he's got one waiting customer for sure."

"I'll be happy to." Marshall reached around to his hip and pulled out his billfold. As he pulled out several large bills and tossed them toward his nurse, he said, "There. Go buy yourself a fancy dress. You and I are going to the Gallatin Room tonight. I promised and now I'm following through. And I don't want to hear any arguments from you, Ruthie."

Frowning, she picked up the bills, counted them, then shook her head in dismay. "I'm not about to waste this money. Like I just told you, I'm not fancy. You need to save this—" she waved the money at him "—and take the heiress to the Gallatin Room."

A shadow crossed Marshall's face. "Have you forgotten, Ruthie? Mia isn't here at the resort anymore."

Her expression was suddenly apologetic as she sunk into one of the chairs in front of Marshall's desk. "I'm sorry, Marshall. I guess I got so used to you talking about the woman that I forgot she isn't here anymore. Have you heard from her since she left?"

Picking up a pen, he doodled senselessly on a prescription pad. "No. Not yet. But I will. At least, I'm praying that I will."

The nurse studied his glum face. "You got it bad for her, huh?"

He drew in a long breath and released it. For days now, he'd been trying to convince himself that Mia loved him, that one of these days he would look up and see her smiling face. But as each day slipped by without her, he was beginning to worry that she had moved on to a life without him.

"I love her very much, Ruthie. She's changed me. Now I can see that life isn't just a game to be enjoyed. It's a precious gift."

Her expression perceptive, Ruthann leaned forward and touched his hand. "I can see the change in you, Marshall. I'd almost bet that when the snow comes this winter you'll be spending more time here in your office than out on the slopes."

A sheepish smile crossed his face. "I guess I did do a lot of playing last year. It annoyed the hell out of me when I'd have to come in and tend to a patient. I was a real dedicated doctor," he said with sarcasm, then shook his head with a hefty measure of self-disgust. "You know, Ruthie, when the Queen of Hearts struck it rich and the town started going crazy making money, I thought it was the best thing that could have ever happened to this place. I still do think it's helped many people, but it wasn't the right thing for me. I got this cushy job and forgot why I'd become a doctor in the first place."

Ruthann tossed him a look that said she'd watched the circle he'd made and she couldn't be happier that he was back to treating his patients with real care and concern.

"Even if the heiress never comes back, she's been good for you, Marshall. You're back to being a doctor I'm proud to work for."

He wasn't going to even contemplate the idea that Mia would never come back. She had to. She'd become everything to him. "Oh, hell, Ruthie, you're getting maudlin on me now. Get out of here. Go buy that dress. I'm picking you up at seven. So be ready."

The nurse started to toss the money at him, but he grabbed her hand and folded it over the wad of bills.

"Don't argue, Ruthie," he said firmly. "Just do as I say."

"But, Marshall—"

A knock on the office door caused both doctor and nurse to pause and exchange a look of surprise.

"A patient probably took a wrong turn and can't find the exit out of here," Ruthie finally said. "I'll go see."

While Ruthann went to the door, Marshall closed the last chart he'd been updating and flipped off the lamp on his desk.

Rising from the chair, he glanced over to see his nurse was still speaking to someone on the other side of the door. It never failed that a patient would show up when the clinic was closing, but Marshall no longer minded being detained. Not if he could truly help someone.

"There's no need to dawdle around, Ruthie. If someone is sick or injured take the person back to an examining room. I'll be right there."

Ruthann tossed over her shoulder, "This is a patient I'm certain you'll want to see. I'll put her in examining room one."

"Fine. I'll be right there."

Picking up his stethoscope, he hung it around his neck and quickly strode out of his office. When he started down the hallway toward the examination rooms, Ruthann was nowhere in sight. Figuring she'd stayed with the patient, he rapped lightly on the first door he came to and stepped inside.

The moment he spotted Mia sitting on the end of the examining table, he stopped in his tracks and simply stared at her.

Smiling broadly, she said, "I hope you can fix me, doc. I'm really hurting."

"Mia!"

Her name was all he could manage to get out as he rushed forward and enfolded her in his arms.

Mia held him tightly and as the warmth of his body seeped into hers, she knew without a doubt that she had finally come home.

"There's no other place I could be. Except here with you."

Thrilled by her words, he eased his head back far enough to search her smiling face. "You look happy, Mia. Really happy. Are you?"

Her hand lifted to his face and he turned his lips into her palm and pressed a kiss on the soft skin.

"Thanks to you, Marshall. If you hadn't made me face my past I think I would still be running, hiding, trying to forget all the mistakes I have made. Facing them has been more therapeutic than you could ever imagine. Or maybe you can," she added, her eyes twinkling. "You're a doctor. A very special one, too."

He rubbed his cheek next to hers and she closed her eyes and savored the sense of contentment sweeping through her.

"What about your mother—Janelle? I hope you're getting things settled with her."

"Very much so. I think she finally understands that she doesn't have to make demands or smother me to have my love. I've assured her that I'll see her on a regular basis and she can contact me anytime on the phone."

"If you'll answer it, that is," he said wryly.

Her blush was compounded with a guilty smile. "I confess. I had reached the point where I couldn't deal with her, Marshall. But then I met you and fell in love and everything started changing. When I finally saw that you could actually love me for the person I really was—that gave me the courage and strength to face my problems. *You* did all that for me."

His hands cradled the sides of her face as his gaze delved deeply into hers. "Did I hear right? You—fell in love with me?"

The shy smile on her face turned seductive and with a groan of desire, she rested her forehead against his. "I tried hard not to. But you're irresistible, Dr. Cates. Now you're stuck with me. I'm making my home here in Thunder Canyon. And I'm going back to school to finish my nursing studies—especially in counseling. Eventually, I'd like to use my inheritance to create The Nina Hanover Center, a place where women experiencing grief and emotional problems can come to get the help they need. What do you think about that?"

Smiling broadly, he closed the last small space between their lips. "I think it's the grandest thing I've heard since gold was found in the Queen of Hearts. And I just happen to know a good doctor with plenty of strings to help you. We'll build that center together, honey."

Mia's heart sang as she curled her arms around his neck and met the sweet promise of his kiss.

When he finally lifted his head, he shouted with sheer joy and plucked her down from the examining table. "C'mon! Let's go find Ruthie. I promised to take her to dinner tonight at the Gallatin Room. I've got to tell her it's going to be a threesome now." He tugged her toward the door, but before he jerked it open, he snapped his fingers with afterthought. "Hell, let's make it more than a threesome! I'm going to call my family and friends. We'll make tonight a big celebration."

Laughing, Mia followed him down the hallway and knew in her heart that life with Marshall would always be a celebration.

* * * * *

Next month, don't miss
HER BEST MAN
by reader favorite Crystal Green

The third book in the new
Special Edition continuity
MONTANA MAVERICKS: STRIKING IT RICH
Years ago, DJ Traub left home
to escape a broken heart.
Now he's back and he's got a second chance
with the woman he's never stopped wanting…

On sale September 2007
wherever Silhouette books are sold.

Welcome to cowboy country...

Turn the page for a sneak preview of
TEXAS BABY
by Kathleen O'Brien
An exciting new title from
Harlequin Superromance for everyone
who loves stories about the West.

Harlequin Superromance—
Where life and love weave together in emotional
and unforgettable ways.

CHAPTER ONE

CHASE TRANSFERRED his gaze to the road and identified a foreign spot on the horizon. A car. Almost half a mile away, where the straight, tree-lined drive met the public road. He could tell it was coming too fast, but judging the speed of a vehicle moving straight toward you was tricky.

It wasn't until it was about two hundred yards away that he realized the driver must be drunk...or crazy. Or both.

The guy was going maybe sixty. On a private drive, out here in ranch country, where kids or horses or tractors or stupid chickens might come darting out any minute, that was criminal. Chase straightened from his comfortable slouch and waved his hands.

"Slow down, you fool," he called out. He took the porch steps quickly and began walking fast down the driveway.

The car veered oddly, from one lane to another, then up onto the slight rise of the thick green spring grass. It just barely missed the fence.

"Slow down, damn it!"

He couldn't see the driver, and he didn't recognize this automobile. It was small and old, and couldn't have cost much even when it was new. It was probably white, but now it needed either a wash or a new paint job or both.

"Damn it, what's wrong with you?"

At the last minute, he had to jump away, because the idiot behind the wheel clearly wasn't going to turn to avoid a collision. He couldn't believe it. The car kept coming, finally slowing a little, but it was too late.

Still going about thirty miles an hour, it slammed into the large, white-brick pillar that marked the front boundaries of the house. The pillar wasn't going to give an inch, so the car had to. The front end folded up like a paper fan.

It seemed to take forever for the car to settle, as if the trauma happened in slow motion, reverberating from the front to the back of the car in ripples of destruction. The front windshield suddenly seemed to ice over with lethal bits of glassy frost. Then the side windows exploded.

The front driver's door wrenched open, as if the car wanted to expel its contents. Metal buckled hideously. Small pieces, like hubcaps and mirrors, skipped and ricocheted insanely across the oyster-shell driveway.

Finally, everything was still. Into the silence, a plume of steam shot up like a geyser, smelling of rust and heat. Its snake-like hiss almost smothered the low, agonized moan of the driver.

Chase's anger had disappeared. He didn't feel anything but a dull sense of disbelief. Things like this didn't happen in real life. Not in his life. Maybe the sun had actually put him to sleep....

But he was already kneeling beside the car. The driver was a woman. The frosty glass-ice of the windshield was dotted with small flecks of blood. She must have hit it with her head, because just below her hairline a red liquid was seeping out. He touched it. He tried to wipe it away before it reached her eyebrow, though, of course that made no sense at all. Her eyes were shut.

Was she conscious? Did he dare move her? Her dress was covered in glass, and the metal of the car was sticking out lethally in all the wrong places.

Then he remembered, with an intense relief, that every good medical man in the county was here, just behind the house, drinking his champagne. He found his phone and paged Trent.

The woman moaned again.

Alive, then. Thank God for that.

He saw Trent coming toward him, starting out at a lope, but quickly switching to a full run.

"Get Dr. Marchant," Chase called. "Don't bother with 911."

Trent didn't take long to assess the situation. A fraction of a second, and he began pulling out his cell phone and running toward the house.

The yelling seemed to have roused the woman. She opened her eyes. They were blue and clouded with pain and confusion.

"Chase," she said.

His breath stalled. His head pulled back. "What?"

Her only answer was another moan, and he wondered if he had imagined the word. He reached around her and put his arm behind her shoulders. She was tiny. Probably petite by nature, but surely way too thin. He could feel her shoulder blades pushing against her skin, as fragile as the wishbone in a turkey.

She seemed to have passed out, so he put his other arm under her knees and lifted her out. He tried to avoid the jagged metal, but her skirt caught on a piece and the tearing sound seemed to wake her again.

"No," she said. "Please."

"I'm just trying to help," he said. "It's going to be all right."

She seemed profoundly distressed. She wriggled in his arms, and she was so weak, like a broken bird. It made him feel too big and brutish. And intrusive. As if touching her this way, his bare hands against the warm skin behind her knees, were somehow a transgression.

He wished he could be more delicate. But he smelled gasoline, and he knew it wasn't safe to leave her here.

Finally he heard the sound of voices, as guests began to run around the side of the house, alerted by Trent. Dr. Marchant was at the front, racing toward them as if he were forty instead of seventy. Susannah was right behind him, her green dress floating around her trim legs.

"Please," the woman in his arms murmured again. She looked at him, the expression in her blue eyes lost and bewildered. He wondered if she might be on drugs.

Hitting her head on the windshield might account for this unfocused, glazed look, but it couldn't explain the crazy driving.

"Please, put me down. Susannah... The wedding..."

Chase's arms tightened instinctively, and he froze in his tracks. She whimpered, and he realized he might be hurting her. "Say that again?"

"The wedding. I have to stop it."

* * * * *

Be sure to look for TEXAS BABY,
available September 11, 2007,
as well as other fantastic Superromance titles
available in September.

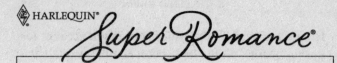

Bailey DelMonico has finally
gotten her life on track, and is
passionate about her recent career
change. Nothing will stand in the way
of her becoming a doctor...that is,
until she's paired with the sharp-tongued
Dr. Ivan Munro.

Watch the sparks fly in

Doctor in
the House

by *USA TODAY* Bestselling Author

Marie Ferrarella

Available September 2007

Intrigued? Read more at
TheNextNovel.com

REQUEST YOUR FREE BOOKS!
2 FREE NOVELS PLUS 2 FREE GIFTS!

Silhouette®

SPECIAL EDITION®

Life, Love and Family!

YES! Please send me 2 FREE Silhouette Special Edition® novels and my 2 FREE gifts. After receiving them, if I don't wish to receive any more books, I can return the shipping statement marked "cancel." If I don't cancel, I will receive 6 brand-new novels every month and be billed just $4.24 per book in the U.S., or $4.99 per book in Canada, plus 25¢ shipping and handling per book and applicable taxes, if any*. That's a savings of at least 15% off the cover price! I understand that accepting the 2 free books and gifts places me under no obligation to buy anything. I can always return a shipment and cancel at any time. Even if I never buy another book from Silhouette, the two free books and gifts are mine to keep forever.

235 SDN EEYU   335 SDN EEY6

Name	(PLEASE PRINT)

Address	Apt.

City	State/Prov.	Zip/Postal Code

Signature (if under 18, a parent or guardian must sign)

Mail to the **Silhouette Reader Service™:**
IN U.S.A.: P.O. Box 1867, Buffalo, NY 14240-1867
IN CANADA: P.O. Box 609, Fort Erie, Ontario L2A 5X3

Not valid to current Silhouette Special Edition subscribers.

Want to try two free books from another line?
Call 1-800-873-8635 or visit www.morefreebooks.com.

* Terms and prices subject to change without notice. NY residents add applicable sales tax. Canadian residents will be charged applicable provincial taxes and GST. This offer is limited to one order per household. All orders subject to approval. Credit or debit balances in a customer's account(s) may be offset by any other outstanding balance owed by or to the customer. Please allow 4 to 6 weeks for delivery.

Your Privacy: Silhouette is committed to protecting your privacy. Our Privacy Policy is available online at www.eHarlequin.com or upon request from the Reader Service. From time to time we make our lists of customers available to reputable firms who may have a product or service of interest to you. If you would prefer we not share your name and address, please check here. ☐

SSE07

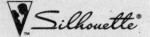

COMING NEXT MONTH

#1849 BACHELOR NO MORE—Victoria Pade
Northbridge Nuptials
Shock #1: Mara Pratt's sweet, elderly coworker led a double life—
decades ago, she'd run off with a bank robber and was now facing hard
time! Shock #2: The woman's grandson, corporate raider Jared Perry,
was back in Northbridge to help Grandma, and he saw Mara as a
tempting takeover target—trying to steal her heart at every turn!

#1850 HER BEST MAN—Crystal Green
Montana Mavericks: Striking It Rich
Years ago, DJ Traub had been best man at his brother's wedding to
Allaire Buckman—but secretly DJ had wanted to be the groom, so he'd
left town to avoid further heartbreak. Now the rich restaurateur had returned
to Thunder Canyon and into the orbit of the still alluring, long-divorced
Allaire. Had he become the best man…to share Allaire's life?

#1851 THE OTHER SISTER—Lynda Sandoval
Return to Troublesome Gulch
Long after tragedy had taken his best friend in high school, paramedic
Brody Austin was finally ready to work through his own feelings of guilt.
That's when he ran into his best friend's kid sister, Faith Montesantos.
All grown up, the pretty, vivacious high school counselor helped him
reconcile with the past and move on…to a future in her arms.

#1852 DAD IN DISGUISE—Kate Little
Baby Daze
When wealthy architect Jack Sawyer tried to "cancel" his sperm
donation, he discovered his baby had already been born to single
mother Rachel Reilly. So Jack went undercover as a handyman at her
house to make sure his son was all right. Jack fell for the boy…and fell
for Rachel—hard. But when daddy took off his disguise, would
all hell break loose?

#1853 WHAT MAKES A FAMILY?—Nicole Foster
Past betrayal and loss made teacher Laurel Tanner shy away from love
at every turn. And Cort Morente was hardly an eligible bachelor—he
was focused on rebuilding his own life, not on romance. But their
shared concern for a troubled child was about to bring them together in
ways they'd never dreamed possible.…

**#1854 THE DEBUTANTE'S SECOND CHANCE—
Liz Flaherty**
When journalist Micah Walker took over his hometown paper, the
top local story was former debutante Landy Wisdom. Domestic abuse
had left Landy broken—her selfless help for other victims had left her
unbowed. Could Micah give her a second chance at love…or would she
turn the tables and give *him* a chance—to finally find true happiness?

"Dr. Becca Talbert?"

Becca recognized that voice. For the past year and at the oddest times, she'd seen his face and the sadness in his eyes. "Yes," she answered readily.

"This is Cord Prescott."

She already knew that. But why was he calling her after a whole year without a word? She hadn't seen him since his wife's funeral.

"You may not remember me," he said. "I'm Colton's brother."

"Yes, I remember you, Cord, and your little girl. How are you?" Over the past year she'd often asked Colton about Cord and his daughter. He always said they were "trying to adjust."

"Not good," he answered. "But I know you're a pediatrician and I thought you might be able to help me with Nicki." He paused and she could hear him drag in a deep breath. "I've taken her to several doctors, even a child psychologist, but she won't talk to them. She insists on staying in her room, and she's hardly eating. She's lost so much weight I can't stand it. She won't talk about her mother. I think she's making herself physically ill with grief. I'd really like to get your professional opinion."

"Of course. I'd be glad to help any way I can," Becca said instantly, her heart heavy at the thought of what Cord was going through.

There was another long pause. "Nicki doesn't do well in an office setting. I was hoping I could persuade you to come out to the ranch and see her."

Dear Reader,

Cowboy at the Crossroads is about Becca Talbert who first
appeared in *Emily's Daughter*. I've been asked so many times
when Becca's story is coming out. This is it. The wait is over.

Plotting Becca's life wasn't easy. She has this marching-in-
where-angels-fear-to-tread personality. So how would the
trauma of finding out about her birth affect her? Would she
continue to feel angry and resentful or would she accept her
life and make the most of it? And—equally important—what
type of man would steal her heart? Those questions took
me some time to sort through, and *Cowboy at the Crossroads* will
give you the answers. It may not be what you expect, but I
hope you'll enjoy this journey with Becca as she finds love
and happiness—her way.

Thanks for reading my books.

Linda Warren

P.S. Your mail is always welcome. You can reach me at P.O.
Box 5182, Bryan, TX 77805 or e-mail at LW1508@aol.com.

Books by Linda Warren

HARLEQUIN SUPERROMANCE

893—THE TRUTH ABOUT JANE DOE
935—DEEP IN THE HEART OF TEXAS
991—STRAIGHT FROM THE HEART
1016—EMILY'S DAUGHTER
1049—ON THE TEXAS BORDER

Cowboy at the Crossroads
Linda Warren

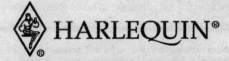

HARLEQUIN®

TORONTO • NEW YORK • LONDON
AMSTERDAM • PARIS • SYDNEY • HAMBURG
STOCKHOLM • ATHENS • TOKYO • MILAN • MADRID
PRAGUE • WARSAW • BUDAPEST • AUCKLAND

ISBN 0-373-71075-5

COWBOY AT THE CROSSROADS

Copyright © 2002 by Linda Warren.

This edition published by arrangement with Harlequin Books S.A.

® and TM are trademarks of the publisher. Trademarks indicated with
® are registered in the United States Patent and Trademark Office, the
Canadian Trade Marks Office and in other countries.

Visit us at www.eHarlequin.com

Printed in U.S.A.

To my sisters-in-law,
Sondra Siegert, LaVal Siegert, Melinda Siegert,
Sandra Lenz and Betty Patranella, who have supported me
wholeheartedly from the start. Thanks, ladies.

And thanks to
Dr. Mark Fuller, DVM,
and Randy Rychlik, paramedic,
who shared their expert knowledge.

Any errors are strictly mine.

PROLOGUE

WHAT SHOULD SHE SAY TO HIM?

Rebecca Talbert knew she had to say *something,* but when she looked at Cordell Prescott words eluded her. He sat on the sofa in a dark suit with his elbows on his knees and his hands clutching a glass of punch. That expression of loss and sadness twisted her stomach into a hard knot.

She hated funerals, especially when the person was so young and had died so needlessly. Anette Prescott's death from alcohol poisoning had left not only a grieving widower, but a motherless four-year-old girl. Becca had never met Anette; in fact, this was the first time she'd actually met Cord. She knew Clay and Colton, his brothers; they were business associates of her father. Her parents were in Europe and she'd attended the funeral in their place. But she would have come, anyway, because she and Colton were close friends. There'd been a time she'd thought their relationship would develop into more, but the passion just wasn't there. And she wanted that passion, the kind of deep, lasting love her parents shared. Based on her relationships to date, she had a feeling she was going to grow old looking for it.

Becca took a sip of her punch and glanced around. They were in the large family room of the Prescott ranch house, a room that was attractively rustic with wood beams on the ceiling, a stone fireplace and hardwood floors. Colton had told her the ranch-style two-story house had been built by his great-grandfather in the 1800s and there'd been Prescotts here ever since. Cord was the rancher in the family; he'd continued to run Triple Creek, while his brothers had opted for another way of life in the city.

As the grandfather clock chimed, Becca realized she had to leave, and soon. She was on duty at the hospital in an hour, and it was a thirty-minute drive back to Houston. She set her glass on a table. It was now or never. She had to offer her condolences to Cord, then make her way out to where the cars were parked. A few family and friends had returned to the ranch after the funeral, and Colton had insisted she come, although Becca felt a bit out of place.

She took a deep breath and walked over to the sofa. When she sat beside Cord, he didn't move or acknowledge her presence.

"I'm so sorry about your wife," she said. It sounded lame even to her own ears. He'd probably heard those words a hundred times today.

He still hadn't responded, so she started to get up. She didn't want to cause him any more stress than necessary.

Then his voice came. "I just wish I understood. Why? Why did this happen? Anette never drank that much. I just don't understand it. And Nicki…" As he said his daughter's name, his voice cracked.

Becca did what she would have done with anyone who was in that much pain. She put her arms around him. He murmured something she didn't hear, and to her surprise, his arms locked tightly around her. She knew he had had a drink and she didn't know what he'd done with it. Nor did she care. She only wanted to comfort him.

As his arms tightened, she became aware of his strength and the tangy masculine scent that filled her nostrils. He was different from his brothers—in appearance, in manner, in aspiration. Clay and Colton had blond curly hair and blue eyes. Cord's hair was a darker blond with a slight curl and his eyes were brown. He also had a stylish mustache. Colton said that Cord took after their father with his love of the land. His brothers were businessmen and had never returned to the ranch after leaving for college, whereas Cord didn't want any other life. His manner, too, revealed a directness, a simple honesty that was quite removed from his brothers' more polished charm.

Becca didn't know how long they sat there with Cord holding on to her like a lifeline. She didn't mind. He needed to hold someone and he probably wasn't even aware of who she was. How could Anette Prescott do this to him? she found herself wondering. Cord seemed so family-oriented, and he obviously worshiped his little girl. From what Colton had told her, she knew Anette had been in a state of depression. She'd always wanted a child and had gone through several fertility procedures before she conceived Nicki. But once the baby was born, she sank into postpartum depression. Since it had continued for at least four years, it had obviously turned into a psychiatric disorder, maybe hormonal in cause, maybe not. She apparently functioned reasonably well, so it wasn't clinical, but she should have had some form of therapy. She could've gotten treatment, done something besides drink herself to death. Becca knew her opinion was tempered because of her medical training and because of the man trembling in her arms. But like Cord, she didn't understand.

"Mr. Prescott." A woman's voice interrupted them. "I can't find Nicki. I've looked everywhere."

Cord drew away and got to his feet. He stood at least six foot two, much taller than his brothers. "Don't worry, I'll find her," he said in a tired voice. "She's been hiding a lot since her mother…" He stopped, unable to finish the sentence.

Becca also stood, her heart aching for this man. "I'm sure she'll feel better when she sees you," she said softly.

He blinked distractedly at her. "Thank you, Becca," he murmured, walking away.

He knows who I am. It was silly, but she couldn't shake the warm feeling that gave her.

She hurried over to Colton. "I've got to get back to Houston," she told him.

"I know, and I appreciate your coming." Frowning, Colton ran one hand through his blond hair; until recently he'd worn it shoulder-length and she guessed he wasn't used to this newly short style. "I saw you talking to Cord. Did he say anything?"

"Just that he doesn't understand why this happened."

"Yeah, none of us do." He shrugged. "Cord keeps everything inside. Doesn't let his feelings out. We're worried about him."

"Cord will be fine." Blanche, Colton's mother, spoke up. Becca had never met Blanche before today. She'd heard Colton talk about her for years, and it was quite an experience meeting her in the flesh. In her sixties, she dressed as if she were much younger. She wore a tight-fitting black dress that ended four inches above her knees. The plunging neckline showed off her ample breasts and the diamonds around her neck. Her bleached blond hair was styled in a stiff pageboy, but no amount of artifice could hide the aging on her face.

"Anette was never right for him, anyway," Blanche was saying. "She hated the ranch and the cows and horses. I never figured she'd take the easy way out, though. I wonder who she thought was gonna take care of that kid upstairs. It certainly isn't gonna be me."

As Blanche walked off, hips swaying, Colton remarked with raised eyebrows, "Charming, isn't she?"

Becca didn't say anything. She could only stare after the woman in stunned silence. Blanche was crude and unbelievably hard-hearted. Still, Becca didn't know why she was surprised; she knew the story of Blanche Duffy and Claybourne Prescott. Blanche had married Claybourne when she was eighteen. He'd been sixty. It wasn't a love match—she'd wanted security and he'd wanted a son. His first wife and eldest daughter had died in a car accident. His second daughter, Edith, was still alive and in her seventies. She lived on the ranch, and Colton had mentioned that the relationship between Blanche and Edith was strained. Having met both ladies, Becca had no problem imagining the situation. Edith was a quiet, demure person, and Becca was sure that Blanche made her life a living hell. The Prescott family was an eccentric group, to say the least.

She kissed Colton's cheek. "Talk to you later."

"I'll call when I get back to Houston," he said.

Becca wished again that there was a spark between them. But they were just friends. Not for the first time, she wondered how Colton felt about her—whether he hoped for more than the easy companionship they now shared. They never discussed their relationship, but since Colton had opened a branch office of his computer company in Houston, they spent a lot of evenings and weekends together. Colton was almost forty, and if he harbored feelings for her, they had to talk about it. Why was she thinking about this today? she asked herself as she went into the foyer to get her purse. She and Colton had a good friendship and they were both adult enough to accept that. She glanced at her watch—three-ten. She'd better get moving.

Before she could reach the front door, she saw a small bare foot sticking out of a partially opened closet. It had to be Nicki. Becca opened the door and found a little blond girl sitting on the floor. Her curls were everywhere and her pink nightgown was wrinkled. She clung to a doll that was as big as she was.

"Hi," Becca said.

Nicki didn't answer. She buried her face in the doll's hair.

"Your daddy's looking for you."

At the mention of her father, Nicki raised her head. Her eyes were brown and filled with the same sadness Becca had seen in Cord's.

"I can't find my mommy," Nicki said in a tiny voice. "Daddy said she went to heaven, but I can't find her."

Becca's heart crumbled inside her, and she dropped to the floor and gathered the child into her arms, just as she'd done with her father. Nicki nestled against her.

"My mommy tells me a story," Nicki whimpered. "I can't sleep until Mommy tells me a story."

"I can tell you a story," Becca murmured, gently brushing blond curls away from Nicki's face. "I have a brother who's seven and I tell him stories. He likes the ones about monsters and dragons."

Nicki shook her head. "I don't like monsters. They 'care me."

"What kind of stories do you like?"

"The princess one" was her quick answer. "The princess with the fairy godmother."

Why did every little girl love that story? *Just wait, little princess, life will change your mind. There are no fairy godmothers in this world. And as for princes, forget it. They're all frogs.* God, was that cynical or what? She didn't actually feel that way, did she?

She searched her mind, trying to remember the story. "Once upon a time there was a girl named Cinderella. She lived with her wicked stepmom and mean stepsisters. They made her scrub the floors and do the laundry, and they were very unkind to her.''

"That was bad,'' Nicki said.

"Very bad,'' Becca agreed. "Then one day her fairy godmother changed Cinderella's rags into a beautiful dress, and a handsome prince came and saved her from the wicked stepmother. They rode off into the sunset on his big horse and lived happily ever after.'' That was a drastically shortened version, but it seemed to satisfy Nicki.

Nicki stared at her with wide eyes. "My daddy rides a horse. Is he the prince?''

Before Becca could form a response, Cord appeared in the doorway. "Nicki, baby, I've been looking all over for you.'' He reached down and drew Nicki out of Becca's arms. As he did, his hand brushed against her breast, and a current of warmth shot through her whole body. This was crazy! His touch was innocent and unintentional and didn't mean a thing. Her emotions were just highly charged.

Nicki hid her face against Cord's shoulder, still clutching the doll. Cord stretched out his hand to Becca. She placed her hand in his and he pulled her to her feet. As soon as he released her, she straightened her black dress with as much dignity as she could and picked up her purse.

"I can't find Mommy,'' Nicki whimpered.

Cord winced, and Becca could see that he was trying to maintain his own composure. "I know, baby, I know,'' he whispered, dropping a kiss on Nicki's head.

Becca had a hard time controlling her own emotions.

"Thanks, Becca,'' Cord said. "I've got to get this one to bed.'' He kissed Nicki's cheek and headed for the staircase.

Becca stared after him with one thought on her mind. *Yes, Cordell Prescott is a prince.*

CHAPTER ONE

One year later

"I WANT BABIES AND A HUSBAND, and preferably not in that order," Rebecca said as she took a swallow of champagne.

"You've had too much to drink," her friend Ginger replied, studying the bubbles in her own glass. "Or maybe not enough," she added reaching for the bottle on the coffee table. They were in Becca's apartment after a big night of celebrating.

"Why aren't I happy, Gin?" Becca asked woefully. "I just finished my residency in pediatrics. I should be happy, ecstatic. All the hard work's behind me and now I can treat children like I've always planned. I don't understand why I'm not happier."

"Maybe you didn't do it for yourself," Ginger muttered. "Go to medical school, I mean."

Becca's head jerked up. "What are you talking about?"

"Maybe you did it for Emily and Jackson. Ever since you found out they're your real parents, you've been trying to be the perfect daughter—doing everything to be the daughter they wanted. But hell, Bec, no one's perfect. Not even you."

"You're drunk," Becca said, refusing to believe a word Gin was saying. At seventeen, she'd found out that Emily, the sister she adored, was really her mother and that Rose, her grandmother and the woman she'd believed to be her mother, was not. It had been a traumatic time, but she'd adjusted.

"Maybe." Gin hiccuped. "But the truth is a hard pill to swallow."

"I've wanted to be a doctor ever since I can remember," Becca said defiantly. "Finding out about my birth had nothing to do with it."

"Yeah, you started saying that in first grade. *I want to be a doctor like my sister.* Then *bam,* you find out your sister's really your mother and you *have* to be a doctor. There wasn't any other choice for you."

Becca stared at Gin with a mutinous expression. They'd been best friends since kindergarten and they knew each other better than anyone. Gin always spoke her mind, and that sometimes got on Becca's nerves—as it did now. She hadn't gone to medical school to please her parents. Or had she? God, she needed more champagne. She grabbed the bottle and refilled her glass.

"You're wrong, Gin," she murmured under her breath.

"Let me ask you a question," Gin said as she twisted her glass. "You have a month off before you join Dr. Arnold's practice in July. What do you plan to do with that time?"

Becca's eyes darkened, but Ginger didn't give her a chance to speak. She answered her own question. "I'll tell you exactly what you're going to do. You'll spend that month with your parents and Scotty, like you always do. You want babies? Well, doctor or not, you don't seem to realize you need a man to accomplish that. And you haven't had much of a social life in the past ten years, except for Colton who's always hanging around—like a little puppy waiting for your attention."

"Colton and I are friends," Becca said in a cool tone.

"I bet you haven't even slept with him."

"We don't have that kind of relationship."

"The man is forty years old, Becca. If he doesn't want that kind of relationship, there's something wrong with him."

"Shut up! You're making me angry."

Ginger took a long swig of champagne and set the glass on the table. "Damn, that was good. Your dad doesn't spare the bucks when he buys the bubbly."

Becca knew what Gin was doing—changing the subject—but Becca wasn't letting her get away with that. They had started this and they were going to finish it.

"My relationship with Colton is my business," she snapped.

Ginger lifted an eyebrow. "Did I say it wasn't?"

"You're making snide remarks and I don't like it."

"Okay, I'll keep my mouth shut."

Becca sighed. "I don't want to argue with you."

"Me, neither," Ginger agreed, and stretched out on the sofa. "All I'm saying is if you want those babies, you have to do something about it. You have to have a life of your own."

Becca settled back in her chair and didn't say anything. She hoped she wouldn't remember any of this in the morning, but she couldn't shake the discontent inside her. She should be so happy. She'd finally graduated from medical school with a specialty in pediatrics, and her parents had thrown a big party to celebrate her achievement. They were proud of her and had invited all her friends and family—including Colton. When she'd first met him, she had disliked him on sight. He was intelligent, good-looking and far too sure of himself. But as she got to know him, her opinion changed, and she found that he had a softer, more vulnerable side. It was an appealing quality in such a driven businessman.

Because of Colton's connection to her father, he spent a lot of time with her family. Did Colton think their relationship was more than friendship? Surely not. But after talking with Gin, she realized it was time to clear things up with Colton. She'd been saying that for over a year now and still hadn't done anything about it. They'd both been so busy and…

Damn, what was wrong with her? Why was she finding fault with everything in her life? She glanced at Gin, who was now snoring into a cushion. Becca smiled. She treasured her bond with Gin and was glad they hadn't lost touch after high school. Becca had come to Houston to live with Emily and Jackson after she'd found out they were her real parents, while Ginger had gone to secretarial school and had become a secretary to the CEO of an insurance company in Houston. They talked often, and Becca valued her opinion. That was why Gin's words weighed so heavily.

Maybe Gin was right. She'd spent the past ten years being Emily and Jackson's little girl. Even though she now had a medical degree, she still felt like that little girl. She had to find the woman inside, and maybe that meant leaving Houston…and her family.

How did she do that? She loved her family. As she yawned and stretched, she knew it would be one of the hardest things she'd ever have to do. But she also knew it was the only way to release this restlessness inside her— to find true happiness and all that crap. God, she'd had too much champagne. There was nothing wrong with her life. Oh, yes, there was. She wanted babies—babies with big brown eyes and…

IT TOOK BECCA TWO DAYS to recover from the hangover. She'd never drunk that much in her life, but she and Gin had really tied one on that night. It was a kind of release, she supposed. She'd worked so hard for so many years; she was exhausted, physically and mentally. A long rest and she'd be as good as new.

Gin was right about one thing, though. For a twenty-eight-year-old woman, soon to be twenty-nine, she spent too much time with her family. But she'd needed those years with Emily and Jackson and Scotty. They had connected as a family, and that was important to her. Leaving seventeen years behind hadn't been easy, and in retrospect she realized she hadn't. She had merged the two parts of her life, and she was happy with her relationship with Rose and Owen, her grandparents, the people who had raised her, as well as her relationship with Emily and Jackson. Then why…?

No, she wouldn't do this. It was Monday morning and she didn't have to go to work. It was her time off and she could do anything she wanted. Anything at all. Analyzing her life wasn't on that list. Carrying her coffee cup, she went into the living room and sat down in her favorite chair. She started to call Gin, but realized she'd be getting ready for work. Becca would call her later.

Try as she might, she couldn't keep her thoughts from drifting to her mother and the twists and turns in their lives. At seventeen, Emily Cooper had fallen in love with Jackson Talbert. Jackson and his father had come to Rockport, Texas, for a fishing trip. Rose and Owen, Emily's parents, rented cottages to tourists. Since it was November, the cottages were closed for the winter months, so Owen rented them the spare room. At the time, Rose, who was forty, had just found out she was pregnant. Emily was very upset by the news. She was in high school and embarrassed by the whole situation. That was why she'd done things with

Jackson she wouldn't normally do. She'd wanted to get back at her parents. Well, that wasn't the whole situation, of course. She'd fallen for Jackson, and fallen hard.

Soon after the Talberts left, Emily found out she was pregnant. It was devastating news, and Rose had berated Emily for her stupidity. After several attempts to reach the Talbert family without success, Rose insisted Emily give up the baby for adoption. Emily fought it, resisted, to no avail. Rose and Owen had their own child on the way and couldn't help her. Besides, all her life Emily had planned to be a doctor, and Rose wasn't letting anything interfere with that. In the end, Emily did what her parents wanted. After graduation, Owen took Emily to San Antonio, where the adoption had been arranged.

At the same time, Rose gave birth to a baby girl, who died after a few weeks. In a depressed and disturbed state of mind, Rose cancelled Emily's adoption, and when Emily's baby was born, Rose took her home and raised Rebecca as her own. Emily never knew. She went to college, then to medical school, never knowing the truth. Everyone thought Becca was Rose's—even Emily.

For years, Emily had nightmares about giving her baby away, and when Jackson came back into her life, she told him about the pregnancy. He was angry at first, and then they set out to find their daughter—neither of them dreaming that she was so close.

Becca took a sip of coffee as she relived the heartache of that time. She'd felt so angry when she found out what Rose had done. She'd been furious with everyone, including Emily. Especially Emily. The mother who'd let her go. But eventually they had gotten through all the pain, and Emily and Jackson were more deeply in love than ever. Now they had Scotty, too. Rose and Owen still lived in Rockport, and Becca saw them as often as she could.

Forgiving was easy, but forgetting was sometimes hard.

Someone had once asked her what you do when you discover you're not really who you thought you were. The answer was that you fall apart, then you pick yourself up and get on with your life. Now Becca was wondering if she should be making bigger changes in that orderly life of hers and—

The ringing of the phone stopped her thoughts. She put her cup down and picked up the receiver. "Hello."

"Dr. Becca Talbert?"

Becca recognized that voice. For the past year and at the oddest times she'd seen his face and the sadness in his eyes.

"Yes," she answered readily.

"This is Cord Prescott."

Becca already knew that. But why was he calling her after a whole year without a word? Why was he calling when they were practically strangers?

"You may not remember me," he said, "but I'm Colton's brother."

"Yes, I remember you, Cord, and your little girl. How are you?" Over the past year, she'd often asked Colton about Cord and his daughter. He always said they were "trying to adjust."

"Not good," he answered. "Colton said you're a pediatrician and I thought you might be able to help me."

"With Nicki, you mean?"

"Yes," he replied. "I know you're busy, but I'm not sure what to do anymore."

Becca curled her feet beneath her, settling more comfortably into the chair. "Tell me about Nicki."

"I've taken her to several doctors, even a child psychologist, but she won't talk to them. She just clings to me, and if I leave the room she screams and cries."

"Then she hasn't adjusted to her mother's death?"

"Not at all," he said. "She insists on staying in her room and she's hardly eating. She's lost so much weight I can hardly stand it. She used to love the outdoors, but she won't even ride her horse. She won't talk about her mother, and I'm at my wits' end. I think she's making herself physically ill with grief. I'd really like to get your professional opinion."

"Of course. I'd be glad to help any way I can," Becca said instantly, her heart heavy at the thought of what Cord was going through.

"Thanks, Becca. I'd appreciate it."

"But I'm not seeing patients until July."

"Oh."

There was a long pause. "Nicki doesn't do well in an office environment. I was hoping I could persuade you to come out to the ranch and see her."

This time Becca was the one who was startled, but it didn't take her long to decide. "I can do that. As a matter of fact, I have the afternoon free. Why don't I drive out there today."

"Thank you so much," he said earnestly. "Do you remember where we are?"

"Yes. But Cord...you have to understand that I treat the body. Nicki may need a psychologist. I've had courses, but it's not my specialty."

"Just see her, that's all I ask. Colton says you're a very good doctor—and I trust his judgment."

"Fine. I'll be there around four o'clock."

As Becca hung up the phone, she wondered what else Colton had told him about her. She shook her head. What did that matter? Nicki Prescott needed help, and she had to do everything she could.

CORD REPLACED THE RECEIVER with a long sigh. He remembered how comforting Becca had been the day of the funeral. He'd been so overwhelmed by anger, disillusionment and pain that he didn't remember much, but he remembered Becca. And she would help his baby. She had to.

He hurried down the hall to the kitchen. Della, the housekeeper, was sitting on a stool, peeling potatoes. At sixty-five, Della was a high-strung woman who never seemed to tire or lose energy. She'd been with the Prescott family since Cord was a young boy. Her hair was now gray and her blue eyes not as sharp, but in other ways she was unchanged.

"What are we having for supper?" he asked.

"Roast. Why?" She didn't look up, just kept on peeling potatoes.

"Because Dr. Talbert's coming to see Nicki, and I'm going to invite her to eat with us."

"Dr. Talbert?" Della raised her head, frowning. "Isn't that Colton's...friend? Becca, right?"

"Yes."

"Does Colton know she's coming?"

"No, and what difference does it make?" There was a note of exasperation in his voice that he couldn't hide. He hadn't called Colton because he didn't want a lot of people around. He wanted to keep this as private as possible, for Nicki's sake.

"None whatsoever," Della replied, returning to her potatoes.

"Becca will be here to see Nicki, that's all."

"It's time someone helped that child. She can't go on like this much longer."

"I know. That's why I want this evening to be special—calm and quiet—so Becca can interact with Nicki."

"Does the queen of the house know you're having a guest for supper?"

"I don't give a damn what Blanche thinks."

"Your mother doesn't like it when things are done without her knowledge."

"You can tell Blanche—" He stopped and took a breath. "Never mind, I'll handle Blanche. Just prepare an extra-special meal."

Della glanced at him. "You're very excited about this."

"I am. My daughter's life depends on it."

As BECCA WAS TRYING TO DECIDE what to wear, she thought about Nicki. The child should have adjusted to her mother's death by now, but it was hard to judge with children. Trauma affected them differently. Becca could still hear her saying in that pitiful little voice, *"I can't find my mommy."* Death was so hard to explain to children, and Becca wasn't convinced she could help Nicki. However, she'd certainly try.

She dressed in a tan pantsuit and brown blouse, then brushed her long brown hair and let it hang loose down her back. Working or at school, she always wore it pinned up or clipped at the nape of her neck. As a teenager, her hair was much longer, an unruly mane that used to drive Emily crazy. But these days Emily never complained about Becca's hair. Considering everything that had happened in their lives, they got along exceptionally well.

Becca stared at her brown eyes and olive complexion in the mirror. Everyone said she was looking more and more like her mother. Becca had always thought Emily was beautiful, but she didn't feel *she* was. Emily had a grace and sophistication that Becca felt she lacked. Becca was more down-to-earth in both temperament and appearance. She had far less patience than Emily and often lost her temper.

Emily never did, and Becca envied that about her. Becca envied everything about her wonderful mother; maybe that was her problem.

She applied lipstick and forced herself to stop thinking. All this free time, all this soul-searching, was making her feel confused. And she *wasn't* confused—she just needed to get her life and goals in perspective and then everything else would fall into place. Like her social life. Gin said she didn't have one, but Gin was wrong. She'd dated several interns, and each occasion had proved to be an exercise in restraint. They thought sex was the normal conclusion to a date. She didn't. She wanted love and passion—not just sex. Emily had told her when she was a teenager that sex without love was just an act and she would know when the time was right. So far, that time hadn't happened for her. In high school, her boyfriend Tommy had pressed her continually for sex, but she'd never taken that step. Not with him or with any other man.

When she'd found out about her birth, her world had been turned upside down and she rebelled, dating guys Rose and Emily disapproved of. Still, she couldn't degrade herself by sleeping with boys she didn't care about merely to punish her family. Later she was so busy with her studies that love eluded her, and she refused to have sex without it. Her feelings on the matter had to do with her upbringing and with Emily's influence. Now she was older and knew more about sex and life, but her standards hadn't changed. She was waiting for the right man…and love. Any nice guys left out there? One came to mind and she quickly grabbed her purse. She didn't want to keep a nice guy waiting.

BECCA HEADED FOR INTERSTATE 10 and drove out of Houston toward Beaumont. The city gave way to farmland and ranchland. Soon she saw the stone and wrought-iron entrance. The sign—Triple Creek. Prescott Ranch—appeared on a high arc above the cattle guard. She drove through, between wood rail fences, watching the grass sway gently in the breeze and the cows and horses grazing. The land was mostly flat with creeks and valleys; here and there she noticed some beautiful old oak trees.

The white stone ranch house came into view. Sprawling and roomy, it had a long front veranda with stone pillars and a wrought-iron fence that enclosed the backyard. She parked in front, grabbed her medical bag and walked to the door. She rang the bell, which she heard resounding throughout the house.

Cord opened the door, and for a moment Becca was speechless. He had on worn boots and jeans with a blue cotton shirt, the sleeves rolled up. His dark blond hair was combed neatly and curled onto his collar. His mustache and honed masculine features told Becca that here was a true Texas cowboy. That wasn't an idle impression. She knew from what Colton had said that Cord's appearance was a true reflection of his personality and his calling.

His mustache moved slightly as he said, "Come in, please. Sit down."

Becca walked past him through the large foyer and into the den. She took a seat on a leather sofa.

Cord watched her for a second, then sat opposite her in a matching leather chair. A saying he'd heard many times from Gus, his ranch foreman and Della's husband, came to mind. *That gal's been spit and polished until she shines.* Cord never paid much attention to Gus's sayings, but looking at Becca, he knew what it meant. Becca with her bright smile and sophisticated manner caught his eye like a shining star. No wonder Colton was so enamored of her.

"Thank you for coming. I'm really grateful," he said before he got completely sidetracked.

"You're welcome," Becca answered, glancing around. "Where's Nicki?"

"Upstairs in her room. As always."

"She's been in her room all day?"

"Yes. The only time she comes out is when I force her, and it's getting increasingly hard to do that since she cries most of the time."

"That's not good, Cord," she said in a solemn voice.

"I know—and I'm hoping you can figure out what to do," he replied.

She saw a familiar sadness in his brown eyes, but it was much more intense than the last time, and something in her reacted strongly to that—just as before.

"Can I see her?" she asked with a catch in her voice. "I'd like to examine her."

"Sure." He got up and led the way toward the stairs. At the bottom, he stepped aside to let her go first. She wore medium heels and felt dwarfed by his height. But it wasn't only that. She was very aware of Cord Prescott—as a man. Maybe it was the cowboy thing. That persona intrigued her, as it did most women. Or maybe she just empathized with him because of what he was suffering, because of his grief and his fear for his daughter.

"Second door on the left," Cord said as they reached the landing. There were hardwood floors throughout the house and beautiful area rugs. A lot of the furniture was antique, probably dating from when the house was first built. Portraits of Prescott men were displayed on the wall of the staircase. Becca remembered Colton telling her that all the Prescott men's names began with the letter *C;* it was a tradition kept alive from generation to generation. She wondered why there were no pictures of Prescott women or wives. They could be in another area of the house, she supposed, and she would definitely ask Colton about it.

Cord opened the door and they went inside. Nicki sat in a children's rocker clutching the same doll she had a year ago. Becca was dismayed by what she saw. The child's blond curly hair was neatly combed and in pigtails, and she wore pink shorts, a matching top and sandals—but her cheeks were hollow and her little arms and legs were so thin. She reminded Becca of anorexic teenagers she'd seen. What had happened to this child?

Cord squatted beside her. "Baby, we have company. Do you remember Becca?"

Nicki hid her face in the doll's hair. Just as she had a year ago.

Becca knelt on the floor. "It was a long time ago, but I told you the story about Cinderella and the prince. The prince who rode a horse like your daddy. Do you remember?"

Nicki shook her head and didn't look at her.

"Would you like me to tell you another story?"

Nicki shook her head again, but Becca wasn't giving up.

"I know lots of stories," Becca said. "Of course, most of them are about monsters or scary stuff that my brother, Scotty, likes. But we're girls and we don't care for that kind of nonsense, do we."

Nicki still didn't answer and seemed to burrow into the chair.

"Baby, Becca asked you a question," Cord said softly. Nicki still didn't respond. "Look at me, baby," Cord added in that same soft tone.

Nicki slowly raised her head and stared at Cord. "I'm tired, Daddy. Make her go 'way."

Becca's heart sank, although she didn't know why, since

she hadn't expected any miracles. It was just so painful seeing the child in this condition.

"I'm a doctor, Nicki," she told her. "I'm going to check your vital signs. Is that okay?"

Nicki didn't answer, but Cord nodded. Becca opened her bag and took out her stethoscope. Nicki's signs were weak, and Becca knew she was in a danger zone. Her first reaction was to get her to a hospital immediately, but something held her back. The hospital would only frighten Nicki, and she wanted to try a different approach first.

"Daddy, make her go 'way," Nicki whimpered, when Becca had finished her exam.

"Okay, baby," Cord said, smoothing Nicki's hair. Becca noticed that his hand shook slightly. "Della made some chocolate chip cookies. Why don't I get you one."

"Not hungry."

"Please eat something, baby." The ache in Cord's voice squeezed Becca's heart until she had trouble breathing.

"I'm not hungry, Daddy."

"Okay, baby," Cord said, and kissed her cheek. He got up, and they walked back down the stairs and into the den.

Cord started to pace; she could see he was terribly upset. "I can't take much more of this. I can't stand to see her in this state."

"Yes, she has deteriorated. Her body's starved for nourishment, she's dehydrated and her heart is weak."

"I don't know what else to do!"

Becca knew it was time for some hard truths, and Cord wasn't going to like what she had to say. But in the few minutes she'd been with them, she could see what part of the problem was.

"Are you familiar with the term *enabler?*"

He stopped pacing and stared at her. "What?"

"An enabler, Cord. That's what you are. You're enabling

Nicki to stay in that room. You're enabling her not to eat. You're enabling her to do whatever she wants.''

His eyes darkened. ''What the *hell* are you talking about?''

''If Nicki doesn't want to eat, you don't make her. If she wants to stay in her room, you let her. You're giving in to her every whim—and it has to stop.''

His eyes became blacker, if that was possible. ''My God, you want me to force her to eat and to drag her out of her room?''

''I'm afraid so,'' Becca admitted.

''After what my daughter's been through, I would *never* do that to her.''

Becca swallowed the constriction in her throat. ''It's called tough love, and you have to do something, or Nicki will not survive this. Can't you see that?''

Cord swung away in anger, then swung back. ''I think you should leave,'' he said in the coldest voice she'd ever heard. ''You're not the doctor or the woman I thought you were.''

CHAPTER TWO

"No," BECCA SAID without blinking.

"Excuse me?" Cord said, and she was chilled by his scorn.

"You asked me to help Nicki, and I'm not leaving until I get that chance."

"I've changed my mind."

She watched the stubborn look on his face and knew he was struggling with his own emotions. He didn't want anyone to hurt Nicki—ever again. He wanted what was best for his child, but he was blinded by love.

"Sorry, it doesn't work that way," she told him. "I'm here and I'm staying. You can clearly see that Nicki needs help. That's why you called me. At her age, her muscles and bones are developing, but without nourishment, that growth is being hindered. You may not like my methods, but for Nicki's sake, you *have* to give me a chance."

"I won't allow her to be upset."

His voice wasn't as angry or cold as before, and Becca felt a glimmer of hope. "Is being upset worse than the almost catatonic state she's in now?"

He didn't answer, just stared at her with brooding eyes.

Becca kept on. "She's going to get upset, Cord. You might as well resign yourself to that. She'll be reacting to external stimuli, and that's what she needs instead of this inert passivity."

He ran both hands through his hair in a weary gesture and sank into a chair. "I just can't take it when she cries."

At the pain in his voice, she took a deep breath. "Why don't you go outside and let me spend some time with her," she suggested, knowing she would get nowhere with Nicki if Cord was around.

His eyes met hers. "I don't know if I can do that."

"You have to," she said, her eyes not wavering from his. "I have to reach Nicki on some level, and I can't do that with you present."

He didn't say anything and Becca added, "At this point she needs to be in a hospital unless I can do something with her right now. You can either let me try, or call for an ambulance. It's your choice."

His face turned white and he drew in a long, shuddering breath. "Fine, you have until eight o'clock. Just be very careful, Becca. There is just so much I'll allow."

"I will not do anything that will harm her physically or mentally."

"That's all I need to know," he said as he moved past her.

"Cord," she said, and he turned back. "If you hear Nicki crying, please don't come inside."

There was a moment of indecision in his eyes, then he walked out the door.

Becca removed her jacket as she went into the kitchen. She had a plan in mind and it started with dinner. A gray-haired woman was putting meringue on a pie.

"Hi." Becca smiled. "I'm Becca Talbert and I'm hoping you're the housekeeper."

The woman glanced up. "That's me. My name is Della. What can I do for you?"

"What time does Nicki usually have dinner?"

"Dinnertime is six o'clock, but with the way that child eats, it's anybody's guess."

"I'm not trying to be nosy, but could you tell me how many people will be here for dinner?"

"Edie eats in her room and Blanche is out, as usual, so there'll be you and Cord."

"I see," Becca murmured. "Do you mind if I ask what you're preparing?"

Della lifted an eyebrow. "That's a popular question today, but we're having roast, new potatoes, carrots and fresh green beans." She pointed to a pan of rolls. "Homemade rolls are rising, and I just finished making a chocolate pie."

"Does Nicki like any of these things?"

Della shrugged. "When Anette was alive, Nicki ate almost anything. She loved chocolate pie. Used to stick her finger in the chocolate and lick it off and Anette would get mad. She wanted Nicki to be a proper lady and act like a grown-up." Della shook her head. "The woman was very peculiar."

"Sounds as if you didn't like her."

"Like?" Della seemed to study the word for a moment. "Can't really say. All I know is she got on my nerves. Too damn picky. All the food for Nicki had to be cooked at a certain temperature and it couldn't stay out too long and she wanted everything made from scratch. She also insisted that Nicki eat at certain times, never mind the rest of the household. In that case, I told her, she needed to cook the food herself, but she never did. I don't think she knew how to cook. She was a city girl with city ways and she hated this ranch."

"But she loved Cord and Nicki?" Becca knew she was gossiping but she couldn't resist. Besides, she told herself, she might learn some valuable piece of information, some fact that might help her.

"Oh yeah, that's why she stayed." Della put the meringue bowl in the sink. "I never knew she was drinking so much and neither did Cord. She hid it well. Such a tragedy." Della shook her head again. "Cord locked up her room and nothing in there's been touched since."

It *was* a tragedy, Becca thought, and now it was time to heal—for the whole Prescott family. "Colton mentioned that she'd been on antidepressants, too."

"That's right. After Nicki was born, she just seemed to hit rock bottom. On the days she felt really bad, Edie or I would watch the baby. Cord wanted to hire a nurse, but Anette wouldn't have it. She wanted to care for her child. She really did."

"Then, Anette was a good mother."

"Yes, even I will admit that. Nicki was never out of her sight for long. I guess that's why the little one's taking this so hard."

Becca brought her concentration back to the present and Nicki. She'd been gossiping too long with Della. Something she didn't normally do, but she was very curious about Anette. And Della had definitely filled in some of the background facts.

"Would you please set a place for Nicki at dinner?" Becca asked.

Della turned from the sink with a startled expression. "She's coming down to eat?"

"Yes," Becca said with more confidence than she was feeling. "I'm going up to see her now, and Della, if you hear her crying or complaining, please don't interfere."

"Does Cord know about this?" Della inquired, wiping her hands on her apron.

"Yes," Becca answered, heading for the stairs. As she walked up, she silently prayed that she could get through to Nicki. She opened the door and found Nicki sitting exactly as they'd left her—and Becca knew she had to use drastic measures to shock Nicki back into the real world. To do that, she had to be strong and keep her emotions in check.

She knelt in front of the rocker. "Hi, Nicki," she said cheerfully. "My name is Becca. I told you that before, remember?"

No response, as she had expected.

"I'm a doctor and I take care of girls and boys. If they don't feel well, I try to make them feel better. Do you feel bad?"

No response.

In Becca's experience, it was sometimes easier for a child to talk through an object like a toy. She focused on the doll in Nicki's arms. "What's your doll's name?"

Again no response.

She sat on the floor in a comfortable position. "I had a doll similar to that when I was your age. My sis—" She stopped as she realized she was about to say *sister*—a minor slip of the tongue. It was so hard to think of Emily as her mother when she remembered herself at that age. Lord, she was getting sidetracked and it was a weird feeling, but one she could handle. "Actually, my mother bought me the doll. She bought me lots of dolls, but I liked that one best. I named her Chocolate because I love chocolate, and I called her Coco for short. Does your doll have a name?" Becca held her breath as she waited.

Nothing.

"It's important for a doll to have a name, don't you think?"

Still nothing.

"She has blond hair like you, so is her name Nicki?"

Nicki rubbed her head against the doll's. "Dolly," she murmured.

"That's nice," Becca said, grateful for a response. She knew that if she kept talking, kept pushing, Nicki would respond in some way. She was hoping for a positive reaction, but she'd take anything at this point. "Does Dolly like to eat?"

Nicki shook her head.

"That's a shame, because Della's prepared this wonderful meal. I was just down in the kitchen and the smell alone was a real treat. She's made this chocolate pie that has a fluffy meringue about three inches thick. Do you like chocolate pie?"

"No. Go 'way. I don't like you," Nicki said in a defiant tone.

Good, Becca thought. Now they were getting somewhere. She had to keep pushing.

"You don't have to like me, but I've come all this way to see you and I expect you to eat dinner with me."

"I'm not hungry. Go 'way."

Becca reached up, and caught Nicki's face with both hands and forced the child to look at her. "I'm not going away and you're coming downstairs to eat."

"No." Nicki spat the word. "Daddy says I don't have to and you can't make me."

Becca still held her face and looked into those angry eyes. "I'm going to pick you up and we're going downstairs." As she said the words, she got to her feet and gathered Nicki in her arms. This action was met with resistance. Nicki began to cry "No, no, no" and hit at Becca with her free hand and her feet. Becca kept walking; the blows to her face, neck and legs didn't stop her. Halfway down the stairs, Nicki began to scream, blood-curdling screams. Becca still didn't stop.

CORD JUMPED TO HIS FEET when he heard the screams. He ran for the patio door, then halted abruptly when he heard

Becca's words. *"Please don't come inside."* He turned and went back to his chair, but the screams continued. What was she doing to his baby? He marched back to the door and stopped again. God, how was he supposed to handle this? He wanted his child to get better, but he couldn't take this. Each scream was tearing his heart out. He grasped the doorknob.

WHEN BECCA REACHED the bottom step she sat down, with Nicki still fighting and screaming in her arms. Suddenly Becca screamed as loudly as Nicki. Nicki stopped and stared at her with tear-filled eyes.

"I can scream as loudly as you," Becca informed her in a calm voice. "So are we going to scream or eat dinner?"

"I don't like you," Nicki muttered, rubbing her eyes.

"I don't like you too much right now, either," Becca replied.

"You're mean," Nicki said crossly.

"I don't want to be mean," Becca told her.

Nicki didn't answer. She still had a death grip on Dolly, who was looking a little worn and tattered. Now was the time for a softer approach.

"Dolly seems so sad," Becca said.

"She is," Nicki told her.

"Oh, that's too bad. What do you think will make her feel better?"

Nicki shrugged.

"Chocolate always makes *me* feel better."

"Candy?" Nicki's eyes opened wide. She was talking, asking questions. That was good—very good.

"Yes, when I've had a long day and I'm tired, a chocolate bar perks me right up."

"It does?"

"Sure does, but even though I love chocolate, chocolate doesn't love me."

"Why?"

"Because when you get to be a woman my age, you have to watch your weight and if I eat a lot of chocolate, my butt gets bigger and bigger."

"You got a big butt?"

Becca laughed out loud. She couldn't help it. Why in the world had she said that? She just wanted to keep Nicki talking, and the words seemed to come of their own volition. How could she correct this?

Before she could gather her wits, Cord came charging in, Della right behind him. Nicki immediately crawled off Becca's lap and ran to her father. He picked her up and held her tight.

"How's my baby?" he whispered.

Nicki pointed a finger at Becca. "She's mean. I wanna go to my room."

Just like that, Nicki had reverted to her old self. Becca got to her feet. Her eyes locked with Cord's. *Don't you dare* was flashing in their depths, and she hoped he got the message.

Cord received the message loud and clear. Thirty minutes ago he would've taken Nicki back upstairs. When he heard her scream, it was a certainty. Then he'd gone into the den and heard Nicki talking to Becca in a normal tone of voice. He couldn't make out what she was saying, but she was interacting with Becca—something she hadn't done with anyone in a long time. Now he had to look at himself. Was he an enabler, as Becca had said? Was he enabling Nicki to be the way she was because he didn't have the strength or the courage to do anything else? Yes, he was. He could see that. Now he had to try some of that tough love Becca had talked about. Nicki's future depended on it.

"No, baby," Cord said with every bit of strength he possessed. "We're eating dinner in the dining room. Della has the table all set." Without another word, he moved toward the door.

"'Kay, Daddy," Nicki said meekly, and laid her head on his shoulder.

Cord let out a long breath. If she'd started crying, he still would have made her, but this was so much easier. Becca was right; he had to be firm.

Becca followed them into the large dining room. As Cord settled Nicki in her chair, Becca glanced around. The furniture was exquisite and definitely antique. She guessed the late 1800s. The table could easily seat twenty people. There was also a hutch and a china cabinet. The entire set was made of dark wood and decorated with an ornate design that was unlike anything she'd ever seen. The carving had to have been done by hand. She also noticed the china in the cabinet, which was old and very beautiful. She'd bet it wasn't used anymore because of its fragility, but it was a pleasure just to look at.

Becca took her seat next to Nicki, and Cord sat at the head of the table. Della brought the food to the table without a word. Afterward she said, "If you need anything, I'll be in the kitchen."

"Thanks, Della," Cord said, and began to fill his plate and Nicki's.

"I'm not hungry," Nicki said with her arms tight around Dolly.

The silence became strained, and Becca could see that Cord was struggling with himself again. She had to do something, and fast. She did what came naturally—she talked.

"My, this looks wonderful," she said as she dished roast and potatoes onto her plate. "In the hospital, I eat in the cafeteria and it's not the most appetizing food. The vending machine and I are best friends. Of course, it's not very healthy so I try not to indulge too often. But sometimes the mind and the stomach aren't in agreement." As she talked, she mashed Nicki's potatoes with her fork and dipped gravy onto them. Then she lavishly buttered a roll and placed it beside the potatoes.

As Cord watched her, he thought, *Anette used to do that.* She'd make the food appealing so Nicki would eat. Maybe he should've been doing that.

"These potatoes are delicious, don't you think so, Cord?"

He blinked and realized Becca was talking to him. She stared pointedly at his fork, and he realized she wanted him to start eating. He recovered himself and began to do just that.

"Yes, yes, the potatoes are great," he said, following Becca's lead.

"Della said they were new potatoes. Does that mean she grows them?"

"Gus does," Nicki chimed in. Until that moment, she hadn't said a word or even attempted to pick up her fork, but she was avidly watching Becca.

"Gus?"

"That's my ranch foreman," Cord answered, as Nicki didn't say anything else. "He and Della have been here since I was a kid. They live in a small house not far from this one."

"Well, Della can certainly cook. I've never tasted food so good. And this roll—" she took a bite and purposefully swallowed "—is about the best thing I've put in my mouth. I remember one time, my friend Ginger and I decided to make cinnamon rolls. The concept of yeast rising clearly escaped us and our rolls were like pancakes with cinnamon.

So I admire anyone who can make rolls like this. It definitely takes talent and patience."

Becca's voice drummed on inside Cord's head. The woman had one button—On—and she rattled incessantly about anything and everything. He was almost ready to scream *stop,* when he saw Nicki reach for her fork. Slowly she began to eat the potatoes, then she picked up the roll and took several bites. Cord kept eating, watching this miracle out of the corner of his eye. Becca's voice hummed on, and it was the most beautiful voice he'd ever heard. He now knew what she was doing—distracting Nicki so she wouldn't feel forced to eat…and it was working. His baby started eating, and before he knew it almost all the food on her plate was gone.

Becca was also watching Nicki closely. She leaned back in her chair. "My, that was the best meal I've ever eaten."

Nicki also leaned back. "Me, too," she said.

Della brought the pie out and set it on the table with a knife and plates. Then she began to collect the dinner plates.

"I'll help you, Della," Becca offered.

"No, you won't," Della was quick to say. "That's my job. You can cut the pie and serve it."

Becca didn't argue. She picked up the knife and cut three pieces. She handed one plate to Cord, placed one in front of Nicki and took the third for herself. She stuck her forefinger in the chocolate and tasted it. "Mmm. That's delicious."

Nicki scrambled to her knees and Dolly fell to the floor. Nicki stuck her finger in the chocolate as Becca had done. "Mmm, it's good," she said.

"Oh, I love chocolate," Becca said as she reached for her fork. "I could eat this whole pie myself."

"It's gonna make your butt bigger," Nicki said as she put a spoonful in her mouth.

Becca almost spit the chocolate onto the table.

"Nicki!" Cord admonished.

"What?" Nicki looked at Cord with big, innocent eyes.

Becca swallowed quickly. "It's okay, Cord. Nicki and I were talking about this earlier. It's really okay." It was an effort to keep her face from turning red, but she managed.

Cord couldn't figure out why Becca was talking to Nicki about big butts. That made no sense. Besides, Becca didn't have a big butt. She was very slim with curves in all the right places and—he put skids on that thought. She was Colton's girlfriend and he'd do well to remember it.

After they finished their pie, Becca smiled at Nicki. "You have chocolate all over your face."

A look as if she'd done something wrong came over Nicki, and Becca wanted to quickly dispel it. "But that's okay because I'll just lick it off." Becca tasted chocolate from Nicki's cheeks with her tongue, and Nicki giggled. "You're like one big chocolate bar and I could eat you up."

"No, don't eat me." Nicki giggled more loudly and it was a delight to Becca's ears. A hospital wasn't going to be necessary; Nicki just needed some tough love. Now she had to make Cord understand that. Finally she reached for a napkin, dipped it in water and wiped Nicki's face.

Anette used to do that, Cord thought again. She always wiped Nicki's chin and cheeks with a napkin—but she'd never lick food from Nicki's face. That was too undignified. And she would never permit Nicki to laugh at the dinner table. Anette had all kinds of ridiculous rules. They had argued about them all the time. He believed children should be allowed to be children, and Anette—

Cord got to his feet. "Let's go into the den so Della can clean up."

"'Kay, Daddy," Nicki said, crawling out of her chair and scooping up her doll. Becca followed them, trying to think of something to occupy Nicki. She didn't want her going to her room just yet. Cord sat in his chair and Nicki climbed onto his lap.

"Let's play a game," Becca suggested.

Nicki frowned at her and that same frown was echoed on Cord's face, but it didn't bother Becca. Nicki needed to act like a normal child.

"I know," she said, a game they often played in the hospital coming to mind. "I'll mention an animal, and you have to act and sound like that animal. The one who's the best animal wins."

Two pairs of brown eyes stared blankly at her. The Prescotts were not cooperating.

"Okay, I'll go first." She thought for a second. "A chicken. I'll do a chicken."

She tucked her hands under her armpits and flapped her elbows like wings, then pranced around the room squawking.

Nicki laughed out loud and pointed a finger at Becca. "You're funny."

Cord was hypnotized by the sound. Nicki had giggled earlier, but he hadn't heard her laugh outright in so long that for a moment he felt winded by the pleasure.

"Okay, funny pants." Becca grinned. "It's your turn. Let's see. A cow. You have to do a cow."

Nicki jumped out of Cord's lap, the doll falling to the floor again. "I can do a cow. I can," she said as she got on all fours and trudged around the den going "Moo, moo, moo."

"That's about the best cow I've ever seen. What do you think, Cord?"

"The very best," he agreed. "Better than any of the cows I have in my pastures."

His eyes met Becca's, and for an instant something seemed to pass between them, but Becca was sure she'd only imagined it.

"It's Daddy's turn," Nicki called, interrupting the moment. "Daddy has to do one. What can Daddy be, Becca?"

Becca eyes gleamed because Cord was clearly resisting the idea. "A horse. I think Daddy should be a horse."

"Me, too," Nicki agreed brightly, and pulled Cord to his feet. He had that *I'll get even with you* look in his eyes, but he got down on his hands and knees and crawled around the room with an occasional "Neigh."

Nicki crawled onto his back and shouted, "Giddyup, giddyup, horsey."

Cord laughed, a sound that came from his heart, and rolled over and held Nicki in the air as her delightful giggles filled the room.

"What the hell's going on here?" Blanche demanded from the doorway, then glanced at Becca. "And who the hell are you?"

"Becca Talbert," she answered stiffly, taking in Blanche's tight-fitting red dress and heels.

"Colton's girfriend? Is Colton here?"

Cord swung to his feet in one easy movement, Nicki held tight in his arms. "No, he isn't."

"Then, what's she doing here?"

Becca bit her tongue to keep a retort from tumbling out.

"I invited her," Cord said woodenly.

"You're fooling around with Colton's girl? I won't have this, Cord."

"Please, Blanche, acting like a mother is out of your

league, so give it a rest. I've got to get Nicki to bed.'' Exhausted from the unaccustomed exertion, Nicki was falling asleep on his shoulder.

"Cord," Becca called after him. "It's getting late, so I'll be going."

He looked back at her. "Could you wait for just a minute? I'd like to talk to you. This won't take long."

"Sure," she said unenthusiastically. Spending time with Blanche was like spending time in a room full of red wasps. Didn't matter what you said or did, you were gonna get stung.

As Cord left, Blanche went over to the built-in bar and poured a glass of scotch. She raised the glass to Becca. "What're you up to, sugar?"

"I don't know what you're talking about," Becca said, reaching for her jacket.

"Sure you do," Blanche muttered. "You're playing my boys against each other."

Becca opened her mouth, but quickly closed it. She wouldn't dignify that statement with an answer. It wasn't any of Blanche's business, anyway. This was between her and Cord.

"Let me give you some advice, sugar," Blanche said, when Becca remained silent. "Stick with Colton. He has the money. Cord's a rancher and always will be. It's in his blood. That stupid Anette tried to change him and get him away from here, but it didn't work." She paused for a second and took a big swallow of scotch. "Aren't you a doctor or something?"

"Yes, I'm a doctor."

"Then, you're not stupid and I'm sure you can see the writing on the wall. Cord has that rugged handsomeness that appeals to women, but sugar, in the dark it don't make no never mind, as my dearly departed husband used to say. So stick with Colton. He has the big bucks."

"Is that what you did, Blanche? Stick with the big bucks?"

A sly smile played across her red lips. "I see you've heard my story. But until you've walked a mile in my shoes, sugar, you don't have the right to judge me."

"I'm not judging you," Becca said, but knew she was. She couldn't imagine why an eighteen-year-old girl would marry a sixty-year-old man—other than the obvious reason. Money.

"Claybourne was a lot like Cord—very handsome even at sixty. I wouldn't have married him, otherwise."

"I'm sure that's a matter of opinion." Becca couldn't keep the words from slipping out.

Blanche was angry. Becca could see it in her glittering blue eyes.

She finished off the scotch and walked over to Becca. "Let me tell you something, sugar. Get your ass back to the city where you belong before the same thing happens to you that happened to Anette."

"Is that a threat?" Becca asked in a barely controlled voice.

"Take it any way you like, sugar, but stay away from my boys." With that, she swept from the room.

CHAPTER THREE

Becca picked up her purse and slid it over her shoulder. She would really prefer to leave, but she'd promised Cord she'd wait.

He soon returned. "I'm sorry," he said. "I hope Blanche wasn't rude to you."

Becca wasn't sure how to answer that or how to tell a man that his mother was obnoxious and vile, so she said, "I'm sure Blanche is always the same."

"Yeah." He sighed. "She's hard to take on a good day."

Becca retrieved her medical bag thinking the Prescott men had a strange relationship with their mother. "You said you wanted to talk to me."

"It's about Nicki."

Becca had expected as much. That was why she'd stayed, even though Blanche had made her temperature rise. "She's at a critical stage. In the morning it'll start all over again. She won't want to leave her room or eat, but you have to make her."

"I'm not very good at that."

"You have to be, for Nicki's sake."

He gazed directly at her. "I was hoping to persuade you to come here for a couple of days so Nicki can keep progressing. I know that's asking a lot, but I'm desperate. Della and Edie have tried to coax her out of that room with no results. You did it, though, and you had her talking and laughing. I want my little girl back. Please, Becca.''

Her stomach turned over at the sound of his saying her name. She hadn't anticipated this, and found herself grappling for the right answer. She knew there was only one— but, still, she hesitated.

''Does Nicki go to school?''

''Anette had enrolled her in a private school in Houston. She started pre-kindergarten, but it didn't last long. After Anette's death, she cried all the time, and the teacher suggested maybe it would be best for her to be at home with a private teacher.''

''Did you do that?''

''Yes, I hired Mrs. Witherspoon, who's also a nanny, but she can't get anything out of Nicki, either. Nicki's enrolled for kindergarten in the fall, but I'm not sure how that's going to go.''

''Nicki's health is at stake here,'' she told him. ''Nicki has to start acting like a normal child and the adults in her life have to be strong. They—and not Nicki—have to call the shots.''

''That's not easy.''

''You don't have a choice.''

''She responds to you like nothing I've ever seen. I'm just asking for a little of your time.''

Becca took a long breath and tried to explain. She didn't want to seem insensitive, but she had to be practical. ''Nicki needs to start interacting with the people in her own environment. If she becomes attached to me, it'll only make things worse.''

''Okay, Becca, I think you've made your position clear. I'm sorry I asked.''

Oh God, this wasn't what she wanted at all! For the first time in her life, she was afraid of becoming too attached to a child—and to the child's father. But Nicki needed help, and Becca had started a course of treatment and she had to see it through…to see Nicki happy again. That was the one thing, the only thing, that mattered. This wasn't about Becca or her feelings. Besides, Cord wasn't interested in her as a woman. He was still dealing with a lot of emotion over his wife's death.

She'd wanted a change, an opportunity to get away from Houston for a while. The ranch wasn't far, but it could be perfect. She'd have the time and peace to sort through all her own discontent.

"What's it like living on a ranch?"

His eyes narrowed. "Pardon?"

"I was raised on the coast and I don't know a thing about cows or horses or the ranching life."

He blinked. "Does this mean you'd consider coming here to help Nicki?"

"If the offer's still open." She smiled. "I'm a sucker for a child in need."

His face relaxed. "Thank you. Oh, Becca, thank you. I know you probably have a hectic schedule, but if you can just fit us in for a couple of hours, I'd really appreciate it."

"Actually, my schedule's open. I have some free time before I begin my practice in July."

"Oh." He seemed shocked. "Then, you'd be willing to stay here and help Nicki?"

She nodded. "Yes, but the nanny stays, too. I want Nicki to realize that I'll only be here for a short time."

"Sure, no problem." He watched her for a moment. "I can't believe you've actually agreed to do this."

"I have an ulterior motive."

He raised an eyebrow. "Really?"

"I've had an exhausting schedule for the past few years

and I need a break. A break from city life.'' *And so many other things.*

''Well, then, I hope this works out for both of us,'' he said. ''There's a pool in the backyard, horses to ride, wide-open spaces, and more cows than you'll ever want to see. You won't be bored.''

That was one thing she couldn't possibly be around Cord. For some reason, whenever she was near him her senses seemed magnified.

''I hope Blanche won't mind my being here.'' One encounter with the woman was one too many, but Becca wasn't going to let her interfere with Nicki's health.

''Don't worry about Blanche. I'll take care of her.''

She was sure he would. The relationship between the Prescott men and their mother was an odd one. And she intended to keep out of it.

''I'll be back sometime tomorrow morning,'' she said as she moved toward the door.

''I'll have Della prepare a room for you—and thanks again for doing this.''

She turned in the doorway. ''Nicki just needs someone to push her, and I can see you're hopeless in that area.''

''Yeah.''

''I'll see you tomorrow,'' she said, forcing herself to walk to her car. She wanted to continue talking to him, to continue… There was something about Cord that touched a place deep within—a place no man had ever reached. Maybe it was the sadness she saw in his eyes or the struggle to help his little girl. Whatever it was, it had made her do an impulsive thing. Staying at the ranch was not in her plans, and yet she'd suddenly found herself volunteering. She didn't regret that impulsiveness. In all honesty, she was looking forward to living at Triple Creek for a few days.

Or even a few weeks. Now she had to tell her parents—and Colton.

CORD WATCHED until her taillights disappeared down the driveway. He couldn't believe his luck. She was coming back and she'd be staying here. That was far more than he'd ever hoped for. This was exactly what Nicki needed—someone to help her deal with Anette's death. Lord knows he hadn't been able to do it.

She's coming back was all he could think as he went in search of Della. As usual, he found her in the kitchen.

"Becca gone?" Della asked as she wiped off the counters.

"Yeah," he answered.

"She sure has a way with that child. Lordy, lordy, that was wonderful to see."

"It was," Cord agreed. "Please get the room across from Nicki's ready. Becca is coming back to stay for a while." Was he smiling? He couldn't seem to stop.

"Wow, that's good news! But you're in the room across from Nicki."

"Damn, what was I thinking?"

"Yeah, what were you thinking?" Della repeated with a sly smile.

He'd moved into that room after Anette's death because their old room held too many painful memories.

He looked at Della, not rising to the gleam in her eyes. "How about the room at the end of hall? That's not far from Nicki."

"What *about* the room at the end of the hall?" Blanche asked as she strolled into the kitchen wearing a short black silk robe.

Cord turned to face his mother. "I'm having the room

prepared for Becca. She's going to be visiting for a while to help Nicki.''

"Really." Blanche placed her hands on her hips. "I don't recall being consulted, and I own this house and this ranch. No one stays here unless I say so."

Cord's eyes darkened. "Becca is staying."

"Don't push me, Cord." Her tone was threatening, and Cord reacted to it.

He stepped closer to her. "You may own this place, but I run it and at a profit that you enjoy. So if you have a problem with my decision, then you have a problem—because my baby needs help and I'll fight you tooth and nail to ensure her well-being."

"Okay, okay." Blanche changed her tone. "Don't work yourself into a lather." She walked over to the refrigerator and got a bottle of water. "This Becca is Colton's girl-friend. Have you forgotten that?"

"Of course not, and I don't see what difference it makes."

"Because you have the hots for her," she answered crudely.

Cord felt the blood rush through his system in raging anger, but he forced himself to remain calm. He wouldn't let her get to him.

"You haven't looked at a woman since Anette died, and your brother's girl is not the woman to start with."

Cord whirled toward the door. "I'm checking on Nicki." He stopped, unable to leave without setting this straight. "Becca is staying here for *Nicki*. That's it. And I don't want you telling her these lies. I'll speak with Colton to make sure he's okay with the arrangement. Other than that, I'd appreciate it if you'd keep out of my business."

"I tried to tell you about Anette. You wouldn't listen to me then, either, and look how that turned out."

Cord ran his hands through his hair in a weary gesture. "Blanche, leave it alone. For God's sake, just leave it alone." He sighed deeply and hurried through the door.

Blanche glanced at Della. "I don't care how old they get, kids never grow up."

"Cord's been grown-up most of his life," Della remarked.

"Don't take that haughty tone with me, Della."

Della's blue eyes became sharp. "Cord's in pain. He's lost his wife and now he's fighting to save his child. Give him a break. Give us all a break." Without a backward look, she followed Cord.

BECCA DROVE TO HER PARENTS' HOME in Bellaire. She parked by the garages and went in through the kitchen, where she came upon Emily and Jackson putting dishes in the dishwasher. Scotty ran through from the den, shouting, "Sissy!" and hurled himself into her arms. She hugged him tight. At eight years of age, he was getting so tall. She could hardly believe he wasn't a baby anymore.

"I got a new computer game. Wanna play?" Scotty asked, his green eyes shining. Like his father, Scotty loved computers, and spent as many hours as he could at a keyboard, or at least until Emily made him go outside and play.

"In a minute, tiger," she answered. "I want to talk to Mom and Dad first."

"Okay, I'll be in my room." He dashed out the door.

Emily hugged her. "This is a nice surprise."

Every time Becca looked at Emily or heard her voice, she felt a surge of love and warmth. They had a strong bond that pain and heartache had not diminished.

Jackson planted a big kiss on her cheek. "How's my girl? Hope you've been getting some rest."

All this love had kept her sane during that dark time, but

she sometimes wondered if Emily and Jackson saw her as an adult or only as their little girl. For a parent she was sure that feeling never changed, but Becca knew she had to be more than their daughter. And she didn't know how to explain that. She would just try to be honest and hope they understand.

They sat at the kitchen table. "What do you want to talk about, angel?" Jackson asked.

Becca made an effort not to squirm in her chair. "I just wanted to let you know that I'll be going away for a little while."

"Oh?" Emily raised an eyebrow. "When did this come about?"

"Cordell Prescott called me today," she said slowly. "His daughter, Nicki, still hasn't adjusted to her mother's death. I went out to the ranch to check her over, and she's not doing well. Grief is making her physically ill."

"I'm so sorry to hear that," Emily murmured.

"Colton never mentioned a thing," Jackson said.

"I'll be staying at the ranch, trying to help her."

Emily frowned. "Becca, angel, that's not your field. Cord needs to get her to a psychologist."

"He has, and it didn't work. If I see things aren't improving, then I'll suggest it again. But I feel I can help her."

Jackson patted her hand. "You're very good with kids."

"Thanks, Dad. I'm a pediatrician. I'd better be."

"Becca—"

"I know what I'm doing," she said emphatically, before Emily could say anything else.

"Sure you do," Emily agreed. "I was just hoping that…"

"I'd rest and have fun," Becca finished for her. "Getting away to the ranch will be good for *me,* too, and I need that.

A different environment, different kinds of activities...
Please try to understand.''

"Of course," Jackson said.

"And I'm very fond of Nicki and I want to help her."
She got to her feet. "Now I'll go and let Scotty beat me
at this new game, which won't take much letting on my
part."

EMILY AND JACKSON STARED at each other as Becca left
the room. "Do you think Colton knows about this?" Emily
asked.

"I don't think so."

"This is so sudden and I—"

Jackson leaned over and kissed her. "Stop worrying."

"It's so hard."

"I know," he whispered. "But I think Becca's feeling
the constraints of our love. She's not our little girl anymore.
She's our grown-up daughter who can make her own decisions."

"I just want to protect her."

"Me, too, but we've had her for ten wonderful years. I
consider that a blessing. Now we have to support her in
whatever she chooses to do."

Emily smiled. "You're so wise."

He kissed her again. "And don't forget it."

WHEN BECCA GOT BACK to the apartment, she called Colton and asked him to stop by on his way to work in the
morning. He'd been in Dallas and she was glad he was
back; she needed to talk to him.

Sleep didn't come easily. Explaining her life to everyone
was starting to get on her nerves. She sensed that her parents disapproved, especially Emily, but this was *her* decision, and she hoped it was the right one. Minutes later, it

seemed, the doorbell woke her. God, she'd overslept! She grabbed a terry-cloth robe and headed for the door.

Colton stood on the doorstep, wearing an impeccable tailored gray suit and holding two takeout cups of coffee. "Hi, gorgeous," he said with a smile.

"I'm not gorgeous," she muttered grumpily, as she ran her hands through her tangled hair. "I look like hell."

"That's a matter of opinion," he said, as she accepted one of the coffees, mumbling her thanks.

She led the way into her living room. Colton took a seat on the sofa beside her.

"How's the time off going?"

"Pretty good," she answered, sipping her coffee. Cream, no sugar, exactly as she liked it. She told him about her visit to the ranch.

"Damn, I feel terrible," he said. "I haven't talked to Cord in over two weeks. I've been so busy I never seem to have time for anything except work. I knew Nicki wasn't doing well, and I told Cord weeks ago that he should consult you. I never dreamed he'd take my advice."

The Prescotts were not a close family, and Becca knew Blanche was the primary reason for that. She took a deep breath. "I'm planning to spend some time at the ranch, so I can try to help Nicki."

"You are? That's wonderful," Colton said. "If anyone can help her, it's you."

"Thanks." They talked about Nicki and about Colton's business trip, but she was well aware that there was another conversation they had to have. She wasn't quite sure how to bring it up.

"Colton?"

"Hmm?"

"We're good friends, aren't we?"

"The best."

"Have you ever wished that our relationship had turned into...more?"

He moved uncomfortably. "Yeah, but I've always realized that you don't have those feelings for me."

"Oh, Colton." She felt like crying.

"Don't worry about it. Besides, I'm too old for you, anyway." His eyes narrowed. "Why are you mentioning it now? Oh." He answered his own question. "You've been listening to that crazy redhead."

"Don't call Ginger that!"

"She's loony as a bat and always making nasty comments about our relationship."

"She's very outspoken," Becca said in Ginger's defense.

"Yeah." He laughed sarcastically. "But our relationship is none of her business and she'd better keep her opinions to herself."

"You're getting angry for nothing," Becca told him. "I just didn't want you hoping that something was going to happen between us, because I'm not sure what I want and you're too nice a person to keep baby-sitting me. You deserve a—" The doorbell interrupted her.

"Excuse me," she said, and got up to open the door.

Ginger brushed past her. "Look at this," she cried agitatedly. "Look at my hair! It's one big fuzz ball. I can't go to work like this."

Ginger had naturally curly red hair, and on humid days it sprang into a mass of tight ringlets. During the sweltering Houston summers, Ginger was always in a panic about her hair.

"I looked in the car mirror and I couldn't believe it! I just fixed it, and now I resemble the bride of Frankenstein. Your place is close to work, so I came here for emergency repairs. Can I use your curling iron?" Ginger turned and saw Colton. "*You're* here awfully early."

"Got something to say about it?" Colton asked in a hard tone.

"Had nails with your coffee, Prescott?" Ginger returned without skipping a beat, then swung toward the bathroom.

Becca shrugged. "That's Ginger."

Colton stood up, shaking his head. "I don't know how you put up with her."

"We've been friends for a very long time."

Colton looked into her eyes. "Don't worry about us. Don't worry about anything."

"Colton…"

He placed a finger over her lips. "I've got to get to work. I'll call you later, and I'll call Cord as soon as I get to the office." He started for the door. "Thanks for doing this for my family. I know Cord will appreciate it." Becca stared after him.

Ginger came back with her hair looking much better. "Stuffed Shirt gone?"

"Ginger, don't."

"I have to run, anyway."

"Can you wait just a second?"

Ginger glanced at her watch. "That's about all I've got."

Becca told her about the visit to Triple Creek, about motherless Nicki and her father.

"Wow. What's this Cord like?"

Becca groaned. "It's not about Cord. It's about Nicki."

"If you say so." Ginger sighed. "Now, I've *really* got to go."

"Can you water my plants while I'm gone?"

"Sure," Ginger called, hurrying out the door. "Phone me when you're back in town."

As Ginger left, Becca tried to ignore her words. Was she doing this for Nicki—or Cord? *For both of them* was her instant response, and she was getting tired of justifying her actions to everyone. She let out a long breath and went to make fresh coffee.

Fueled by the additional caffeine and new resolve, she called the Prescott ranch. Cord answered it on the second ring.

"Cord, it's Becca."

"Hi, how are you this morning?"

Her stomach trembled at the undertones in his voice, and she wondered why he had this effect on her and Colton didn't. She swallowed.

"Fine. Where's Nicki?"

"In her room."

"Cord." She couldn't keep the frustration out of her voice.

"Della's fixing her breakfast and I was about to go upstairs and get her. I'm not looking forward to this."

"Crying and screaming won't hurt her. Not eating *will*."

There was a pause, then he asked, "When are you coming?"

"In about two hours."

"Well, maybe I'll wait and let you work your magic."

"Oh, no, Cordell Prescott. You go upstairs and bring her down for breakfast. Today is the day she starts to get better, and you have to be strong."

"All right, but if I'm a wreck when you get here, you'll know why."

"Yes, I'll know why. I'll also know you're the biggest softie I've ever met."

"I've been told that."

Another pause. Then he asked, "Do you know where Colton is? I tried his apartment but he wasn't there."

"He was here, and he just left. You should be able to catch him at his office."

All the warm feelings inside him dissipated and he didn't

understand why. He knew Becca and Colton were seeing each other. That had been for years, so why, all of a sudden, was he feeling so discouraged by this evidence that they were sleeping together? Could Blanche be right? No, Blanche was never right about anything. His interest in Becca was strictly for Nicki's sake. He would never covet his brother's lover.

"Cord."

He jerked himself to attention as he realized she was saying his name. "Yes."

"I'll be there as soon as I can."

He hung up the phone with a frown on his face. What was wrong with him? Nothing, he told himself. He just felt like this because of Blanche and her crude suggestion. He wasn't attracted to Dr. Becca Talbert. Not at all.

CHAPTER FOUR

BECCA WASN'T SURE what to pack, so she took a few of everything, but mostly jeans and tops. With her suitcases in the living room, she stopped to call Grandpa George—Jackson's father—as well as Rose and Owen. Then she called Dr. Arnold's office to let them know her whereabouts in case they needed to contact her. Hanging up the phone, she decided that part of her problem was the fact that she had to justify her whereabouts to so many people. At her age, she shouldn't have to do that. Their love was overwhelming her. Was that ungrateful? She hoped not. She loved her family, but she needed to be free, to experience life on her own. And that was exactly what she was going to do.

With her bags loaded in the car, she drove toward Triple Creek Ranch. Once she left Houston proper, the scenery along the route was serene and peaceful, so unlike the busyness of the city. Again she parked in the drive near the house and walked to the front door. It swung open before she could ring the bell. A frantic Cord stood there, holding Nicki in his arms. The child's face was buried in his shoulder and she was crying. Cord stared helplessly at Becca.

"Good morning," she said brightly as if everything was normal. "My bags are in the car. Do you mind getting them?"

Cord seemed dumbfounded. "Sure," he answered distractedly, and slowly set Nicki on her feet.

Nicki wrapped her arms around his leg and began to cry louder. "I wanna go to my room. I wanna go to my room."

"Becca's here, baby. Don't you want to say hi to Becca?"

Nicki rubbed her head against his leg. "No. Don't like her."

"You liked her yesterday."

"No, I didn't. I wanna go to my room. Daddy, please."

Becca could see Cord weakening. "Would you get my bags, Cord?"

Didn't she notice he had a child attached to his leg? Then Cord realized this had to be one of her maneuvers to get him out of the way. He disentangled himself from Nicki, but she ran after him crying, "Daddy! Daddy!"

Becca caught her before she could follow him to the car. She carried Nicki, kicking and sobbing, into the house and sat her firmly on the sofa.

"Leave me 'lone," she whimpered, and reached for Dolly.

Becca held her face between both hands, rubbing her thumbs over the girl's wet cheeks. "No, I'm not leaving you alone. I've come to spend some time with you and that's what we're going to do."

"Don't want to."

"Why?"

"'Cause."

"'Cause why?"

"'Cause you're mean."

"We had fun last night. I was a chicken, you were a cow and Daddy was a horse. Remember?"

"Yeah." She hiccuped.

Cord came into the room and set down her bags. As soon as she saw him, Nicki threw out her hands and started to cry again. "Daddy, I wanna go to my room."

Cord took a ragged breath. "Baby, we're not going to your room."

She drummed her legs on the sofa in a temper tantrum. "Daddy, please! Daddy, please!" she wailed.

Becca stood and walked over to Cord, whose face had turned a grayish white. "Just leave, Cord. I'll handle her."

"Becca." Her name sounded more like a groan.

"It'll be all right. I promise." She gently pushed him toward the door. As she did she noticed that two women had come to stand in the doorway, one tall and thin with gray hair, the other short and on the plump side.

Cord looked back at Becca. "This is Mrs. Witherspoon, the nanny."

The plump lady stepped forward and shook Becca's hand. "Nice to meet you, Dr. Talbert."

"And I think you've met my sister, Edith," Cord said. "We call her Edie."

Becca smiled at the older woman. "Yes, it's good to see you again, Edie."

Nicki's wails drowned out her words.

Becca gave Cord a knowing look, and he slowly made his way out the door, preceded by the two women.

Nicki's cries continued and Becca sat beside her. She could understand now why everyone was so reluctant to make Nicki leave her room. This type of behavior was hard on the nerves. She waited for a moment, trying to figure out the best approach to this situation. Her attention was drawn to the doll clutched in Nicki's arms, and she started to talk.

"Dolly, do you know what you and I are going to do today? No? Well, I'll tell you. We're going outside. The sun is shining. The birds are singing. It's a beautiful day. Of course, I'll have to put some sunscreen on you. Your skin's so light and we have to protect it. My skin, I don't have to worry too much about. I just get brown. Still, it never hurts to be careful with the sun. When I was little, I was in the sun all the time. My mother called me a brown-eyed Susan. I never knew what that was, and it confused me. My name's Becca, not Susan. What do you think of that, Dolly?''

The wails stopped, and Nicki opened one eye and stared at Becca. ''Dolly can't talk.''

''That's a pity because I like Dolly.''

''She don't like you.''

Becca brought one hand to her chest. ''That breaks my heart.''

Nicki opened her other eye. ''It does?''

''Yes.''

''What does that feel like?''

''It feels sad. Does Dolly feel sad?''

''Yes.''

''Everybody's sad sometimes, but it's not good to feel sad for too long.''

Nicki smoothed Dolly's hair. ''No.''

Becca knew it wasn't the right moment to delve further, so she got to her feet. ''Tell you what. Why don't you and Dolly show me to my room and help me unpack?''

Nicki's eyes narrowed, and Becca was waiting for an *I don't want to,* but instead Nicki scooted to the edge of the sofa. ''‘Kay.''

Becca picked up a suitcase just as Edie returned to the room.

''Let me help you with those.'' Edie had to be in her seventies, but she was still agile, her posture as straight as that of a younger woman.

''Thank you,'' Becca said, pretending she couldn't lift the other case. ''I think I need help with this one.''

''I'll help,'' Nicki piped up and ran over to Becca. It was

the response Becca had wanted. Together, the trio clambered up the stairs.

On the landing, Becca looked around. There was a long hall with half a dozen doors. She remembered Della's saying that Cord had locked up Anette's room. She wondered which room it was. She shook her head; it didn't matter. Still, Anette had died over a year ago, and Becca felt that Cord should have disposed of her things, kept some for his daughter, perhaps given the rest away. Maybe the task was still too painful for him.

"Which room is mine?" she asked to divert her thoughts.

Nicki shrugged.

"The one at the end of the hall," Edie said. "Mine's at the other end, and—" she pointed to a door on the right "—that's Cord's. Blanche has the big suite downstairs."

"Thanks," Becca replied, entering the room. It was elegant with dark furniture and a four-poster bed. The decor was in peach and pale green, and very soothing. She was going to like it here.

"If you don't need anything else, I've got a function at the church I need to attend."

"No, and thanks for helping, Edie."

"Sure." Edie glanced at Nicki, who had crawled onto the bed. "Good luck. Bye, Nicki."

"Bye, Edie."

That was all very polite, but Becca knew it wouldn't last. Nicki had been allowed to do whatever she wanted for too long. When she couldn't get her way, she became angry and defiant. Becca would try to change all that because she knew it stemmed from Anette's death. Inside Nicki was still hurting…and so was Cord.

Becca opened her suitcase and began to put her clothes

away in an old-fashioned wardrobe that looked priceless. She loved the antique furniture in this house.

Nicki sat, still on the bed, watching her. When Becca opened her makeup bag and set out the contents on the dresser, Nicki's eyes grew big.

"My mommy had thin…" Her voice trailed off as she realized what she was saying.

Becca sat beside her. "It's all right to talk about your mother."

"No, I don't want to." Nicki hung her head.

"Are you mad at your mother?"

Nicki didn't answer.

"I used to be mad at my mother."

Nicki glanced at her. "Why?"

Becca wasn't sure how much to say, but she went with her gut instincts. "Because she gave me away when I was a baby and I didn't know she was my mother until I was seventeen years old. I did mean and bad things because I thought she didn't love me."

"Did she?"

"Oh yeah."

"How you know?"

Becca placed a hand over her heart. "I know in here. Just like you know in there—" she put her hand on Nicki's chest "—that your mother loved you."

Nicki's eyes widened as she tried to understand what Becca was saying. Becca waited a minute, then said, "It's almost lunchtime. Why don't we go and see what Della's fixing?"

"I'm not hungry."

"Well, I am. I only had coffee this morning."

"I wanna go to my room."

Becca took a deep breath. "Nicki, sweetie, we're not going to your room. Please try to understand that. We'll do anything else that you want—swim, play dolls, swing... anything.''

''No, I'm going to my room.''

Before Becca could stop her, she jumped off the bed and ran for the door. Becca caught her halfway down the hall and swung her up. Nicki kicked and screamed, and Becca joined in as before.

CORD CAME THROUGH the back door, wiped his boots on the mat and stopped in his tracks. Screams. Oh God, how did he deal with this? He walked into the kitchen and asked Della, ''Has this been going on since I left?''

Della looked up from the stove. ''No, it just started.''

Suddenly the screams stopped, and Cord wondered if he should interfere. He'd wait, he decided; he had to give Becca a chance. He felt sure she knew what she was doing. But it wasn't easy to hear his child in torment.

BECCA AND NICKI EYED each other. Nicki rubbed her eyes with one hand, still clutching Dolly with the other. ''Why you do that?''

''Because I don't like it when you scream.''

''I don't like it when you scream, either,'' Nicki muttered crossly.

''Well, then, let's not scream.''

Nicki gave her an assessing look. '''Kay.''

Becca smiled. It was a very tiny step, and there were so many more. ''Ready to go downstairs and have lunch?''

Nicki shook her head. ''I'm not hungry.''

Another step to take, Becca thought. ''That's okay. You can watch me eat.'' She set Nicki on her feet and they walked downstairs.

When they entered the kitchen and Nicki saw Cord, she

ran to him, crying, "Daddy, Daddy, I wanna go to my room!"

It seemed to be a statement Nicki routinely used to get her way. Her room was where she could grieve in peace—but that wasn't happening anymore. Becca would insist on it.

They ate at the kitchen table. Della had prepared hamburgers, homemade French fries and cut-up fruit. Just like last night, Becca didn't force Nicki to eat; she filled Nicki's plate and cut the hamburger into four pieces so she could eat it easily. She poured lots of ketchup on her plate, then left Nicki alone and started on her own food.

"This burger is absolutely delicious," she said as she took a bite.

"Triple Creek beef. It's the best," Della told her.

"It certainly is," Becca agreed. "So you eat the beef raised here on the ranch?"

"Sure do," Cord said. "I won't sell something to a consumer that I won't eat myself."

Beef was something Becca got at the supermarket, not something in her yard. Or was that *pasture?* She didn't think she could possibly eat a cow she was personally acquainted with. But if she said that, Cord would laugh. She was a city girl, not used to country ways. Didn't mean she couldn't learn, though.

"Do you have a lot of cows?"

"Sometimes more than I want."

"I've never even touched a cow."

Cord raised his head. "You're kidding."

"No, like I said, I was raised on the coast. I've touched plenty of fish, but I've never even been near a cow."

A smile curved his lips. "We'll have to change that—give you a close-up view."

As they talked, Nicki started to eat her burger and nibble

on the fruit. Cord looked at Becca and smiled. They were making progress, and she was warmed by that light in his eyes.

Della placed a bowl of chocolate pudding on the table.

"Look, Becca, it's chocolate," Nicki said with her mouth full of fruit.

"So I see." Becca grinned and spooned some into their bowls.

Nicki stuck her finger in hers, then glanced guiltily at Cord.

"It's okay, baby, you can eat it any way you want," he assured her.

Which she did. She got it on her face, her clothes and the table. Finally Becca took Nicki upstairs to wash her and change her outfit. The child was falling asleep. Staying up had taken its toll, and now she needed a nap. Becca carefully laid her in bed, covering her with a sheet.

Cord was waiting for her outside the door. Her stomach tightened as she encountered him—his tall lean frame, his rugged features and dark eyes. Funny how her body reacted to him.

"Thanks, Becca. I didn't think I was gonna survive after this morning. She fought me every step of the way. She doesn't seem to do that with you."

"She knows you'll give in," Becca said as they walked downstairs to the den.

"Yeah, but it's so hard to discipline a child when you know she's hurting."

"It'll get better."

"With you here, I know it will. You have a magic touch with her."

"Thank you" was all she could say.

They gazed at each other for a few seconds, then Cord said, "I'd better get back to work. I've got hay being baled and calves that need vaccinating. I'll see you later.'' He turned, then stopped. "Oh, Mrs. Witherspoon asked if she could have some time off to go see her sister, who's not feeling well. I said I'd have to ask you."

Becca shrugged, amazed that he was clearing this with her. "Sure, as long as Nicki knows she's coming back."

"Good." He nodded and left the room.

BECCA WAS ABOUT TO SIT DOWN in the den, when Blanche breezed in, wearing yet another skintight knit dress.

"I see you've arrived, sugar."

"Yes," Becca said curtly, not wanting a scene with Blanche.

Blanche looked at herself in a mirror on the wall and fluffed her hair, then she turned to Becca. "Let's get one thing straight," she said coolly. "This is *my* house and I've agreed to let you stay here for Nicki's sake. Cord seems to think you can help her, but at the first sign of trouble, your ass is out of here."

"Okay, Blanche," Becca replied in an equally cool voice. "You want to be straight? I will, too. First of all, I do not need a place to stay. I have my own apartment. I'm at the ranch to help Nicki—that's it. You keep referring to trouble, but I have no idea what you're talking about."

"I'm talking about my boys, sugar. Cord and Colton."

"So?"

"You have to be incredibility naive or just plain stupid. Colton's has been seeing you for years and now you're here with Cord."

Becca drew a patient breath. "I am not here with Cord, and Colton and I are just friends."

"Sugar, if I know anything, it's men and women, and they can never be friends. There isn't any such animal when it comes to the sexes."

"Then, you don't know your son because—"

"Oh, please," Blanche interrupted sarcastically. "Colton's been hanging around you all these years for one reason and one reason only. He wants you."

Was that true? She remembered how uncomfortable Colton had been when she'd brought the subject up this morning. She also remembered that he'd said he knew she didn't have "those feelings" for him. Oh God, that meant he *did* have "those feelings"—for her. All these years, and they'd never talked about it until today. They'd always been thrown together at family events, gone to movies and out for dinner, enjoyed each other's company. Maybe she *was* naive, because Gin saw Colton's attraction to her, and so did Blanche. Why hadn't she done something about it? Because they were friends and she didn't want to lose that friendship. Now what? She didn't know. Well…yes, she did. She simply had to let go of Colton so he could find the woman of his dreams. That woman was out there; it just wasn't her.

"I can see you know what I'm talking about," Blanche murmured.

Becca raised a hand to her throbbing head. "Blanche, it may be hard for you to believe, but Colton and I *are* friends. I met Cord at the funeral, and I saw him yesterday for the first time in a year. There's nothing going on between us. I hardly know him. As I already told you, I'm here to help his daughter. Nothing else."

"You're lying to me, sugar, and you're lying to yourself. And I don't think you even know it."

"What are you talking about?"

"Last night when I walked into this room, I saw the way you were looking at Cord and the way he was looking at you. There was enough electricity to jump-start Hoover Dam."

"Don't—"

"No, you listen to me," Blanche cut in. "Cord hasn't looked at a woman in over a year, so don't take those glances seriously. He just needs what all men need, and it has nothing to do with those fairy tales in your head."

Becca's eyes narowed. "You're a very crude person."

"I'm also realistic. You're a doctor with a medical practice, and here you are baby-sitting a five-year-old girl who throws temper tantrums."

"It's much more than that," Becca insisted.

"I don't think so. Cord and that witch, Edie, have just pampered Nicki since Anette's death. They haven't even tried to address the real issue, but I'm staying out of it. I've got better things to do."

Becca frowned. "I can see you love your granddaughter as much as you love everyone else."

Blanche peered at the diamond watch on her arm. "Damn, I've got to run. I'm gonna be late for my luncheon." She whirled toward the door. "Help yourself to my house, sugar, and anything in it, even my son." She threw the words over her shoulder in a baiting tone.

Becca felt the urge to stomp her feet and scream like Nicki. Blanche had that effect on her. She probably had that effect on most women. Becca wondered about her relationship with Anette; from the remarks Blanche had made, it didn't sound like a good one. And how did Nicki fit into the picture? Blanche didn't seem to care for her at all. Becca ran both hands through her hair and sank onto the sofa. The Prescotts were hard to take. She'd only been here a few hours and she was already yearning for the love and closeness of her own family. Maybe you had to leave something before you could truly appreciate it.

Becca leaned against the sofa and tried not to think about the things Blanche had said, but they were pounding through her head. She wasn't attracted to Colton in a sexual way, and Colton knew it. Then, why had he hung around all these years? *Oh, Colton,* she prayed, *please don't love me.* She couldn't bear the thought of hurting him. Colton had told her not to worry, but she did. They had to talk again, and soon.

Enough electricity to jump-start Hoover Dam.

Blanche was right about that. Becca couldn't deny that she was attracted to Cord; it was there every time she looked at him. She couldn't explain it and she sure didn't understand it. He had done nothing to encourage her, except love his little girl. She admired that in him. She'd noticed it the very first time she'd met him—his love, his heartfelt pain and his strength. She genuinely liked Cord Prescott, and beyond that she didn't want to think. Her goal was to guide Nicki through this rough time, then go back to Houston to begin her new life. She'd finally achieved the goal she'd been working toward for almost ten years.

Why wasn't she more excited about it? Why, instead, did she keep seeing two pairs of brown eyes? She was so afraid that Nicki might become attached to her, but what if Becca became attached to Nicki—and to Cord? Oh God, what was she going to do?

CHAPTER FIVE

BECCA RESOLVED to stop thinking about the negatives and do what she'd come here to do. As soon as Nicki opened her eyes, Becca didn't give her time to start crying or begging to stay in her room. She brushed the child's blond curls and put them in pigtails. She grabbed some children's books off the shelves, then carried Nicki—Dolly and all—downstairs, even though the child should walk on her own. When they reached the bottom of the stairs, she set Nicki on her feet, waiting for a temper tantrum. None came. Mainly, Becca suspected, because Nicki was still half-asleep. She took her hand and they walked into the kitchen.

Della glanced up from snapping green beans. "Well, ain't this something," she remarked.

"Could you tell me how to get to the backyard?" Becca asked. "Nicki and I are going outside for a while."

"You can go out this back door or through the French doors in the den."

"Thank you, Della," Becca replied. "We'll go out this door."

"Amazing," Della muttered, as Nicki followed Becca without a word of protest.

Outside, Becca caught her breath. To the right were garages, but to the left was a beautifully landscaped yard. The swimming pool had a cascading waterfall. At the shallow end was a kiddie pool, probably built for Nicki. The large swing set and sandbox, she knew, were also for Nicki. A decorative wrought-iron fence enclosed the yard, and green shrubs and flower beds surrounded it. Through the fence, Becca got a view of the ranch. Nearby were numerous barns and sheds, but her eyes were riveted on the valley below. Cattle dotted the landscape, so many that she couldn't even count them. Two tractors and a truck were moving toward the barns, and in the distance, several riders on horseback meandered among the cattle. It was like something out of a movie, an old western with John Wayne or Gary Cooper. She wondered if Cord was on horseback or in the truck or tractor.

She shook her head and walked to the covered patio. Placing the books on a table, she turned to Nicki, who stood there staring at her with sad eyes. Becca tried to get her to swing, to play ball, to run, to laugh, but nothing worked. This was going to be a long afternoon.

Finally they went in for a snack. Della had milk and cookies waiting. Nicki took a bite and drank half her milk, but that was it. When they went back outside, Becca noticed the books she'd put on the table.

She sat in a lounge chair and reached for one. "How about a story?"

Nicki shook her head. "No, I don't want to."

Becca opened the book, and on the title page was inscribed "To my precious baby, Nicki. I love you. Mommy." She saw that each book had a similar inscription. She wondered if Nicki even knew about it.

Becca opened the first book a little wider. "Do you want me to read this to you?"

"No," Nicki shouted, jerking it out of her hands.

Nicki knew what was written in the book—that was obvious. It was time to talk about Anette. "Your mommy wrote something on one of the pages."

Nicki's eyes grew stormy.

"She wrote that she loved you."

"No, she didn't," Nicki shouted, then added in a pitiful voice, "She went away."

Becca pulled the child onto her lap. She just held her for a moment, suddenly understanding the source of Nicki's pain. Nicki thought her mother didn't love her and that was why she'd left.

She kissed her forehead. "Sweetie, listen to me. Your mother didn't leave you. She was sick and she died."

"She didn't feel good," Nicki mumbled.

Evidently Anette had a lot of those days and Nicki was aware of that, which Becca hoped would make her mother's death easier for Nicki to grasp. "Yes," she said, opening the book, "but she loved you. It says so right here and you feel it in your heart " she placed her hand on Nicki's chest "—don't you?"

Nicki nodded, then abruptly jumped up, dropping Dolly and running to where some crows were scratching in the flower beds. "No, no, no!" she screamed, shooing the birds away.

Becca didn't know what to think, but she quickly followed. Nicki knelt in the dirt and carefully spread leaves into a neat pile.

"Nicki, what's wrong?"

"They were bothering Goldie."

"Goldie?"

"That's my goldfish. He died, and Daddy and me buried him here. See?" She pointed to a pole in the fence. "Daddy marked a X on the fence so I'd know where Goldie was."

"I see," Becca said, thinking this over. Did Nicki know where her mother was buried? That sense of not knowing where her mother was could result from never having seen her grave. Becca would have to find out about this.

She took Nicki's hand. ''Goldie's fine. Come, let's sit on the swings.''

Nicki trudged obediently to the swings and sat there with her head down. Becca could only imagine what she was thinking.

''Nicki, have you ever been to your mother's grave?''

Nicki looked at her with big eyes, then shook her head. Becca had thought as much. Cord was trying to protect her, but Nicki needed to see the place where her mother was buried.

''Would you like to go?''

Her eyes grew even bigger. ''Can I?''

''Sure, and we'll take some flowers.'' She made that decision without thinking. Cord wasn't going to like this, she felt sure. Maybe she should've tried to explain it to him first, but it was too late.

''Roses!'' Nicki clapped her hands together. ''Mommy loves red roses.''

Before Becca could curb her excitement, Cord came through the back gate. Nicki immediately ran to him. ''Daddy, Daddy,'' she cried, and he swung her up in his arms.

''How's my baby?'' Cord asked.

''Becca and me, we…we…'' She twisted her hands in her excitement.

''Slow down so you can tell me,'' he instructed gently.

''Becca and me, we…we gonna go to Mommy's grave.''

''What!'' The blood drained from his face and he pinned Becca with a cold stare.

''Yeah, Daddy, and we gonna takes roses 'cause Mommy likes them.''

''Nicki, sweetie, you'd better go get Dolly.'' Becca intervened, knowing she had to get Cord alone. ''She looks awfully lonely.''

"'Kay," she said, and ran to the patio.

"How could you?" Cord demanded as soon as Nicki was out of earshot. "I never expected you'd do something like *this*. Go to Anette's grave? That's insane!"

"Would you listen to me for just a second?"

"No, I don't think so. I told you there're just so many things I'll tolerate, and this isn't one of them."

Becca brushed back her hair with an angry gesture. "That's too bad, Cord, because Nicki needs to know where her mother is."

"What are you talking about?"

She told him about the books and Goldie, and she could see him calming down. "She thinks her mother left because she didn't love her. She doesn't understand that she's in a grave—like Goldie. She *needs* to see that."

He pulled off his hat and shoved a hand through his hair. "Becca, I—"

"Look at her. She's excited at the prospect."

His eyes caught hers. "The cemetery is such a depressing place."

"It's part of life and you can't shield her from that. Besides, we'll be with her."

The word *we'll* sounded so good to him. What would she say if he told her he needed someone with him when he went there, too? He hadn't been to the cemetery since Anette's headstone was set. After the sadness and loss had worn off, he'd felt angry. He still did. So angry that she'd hurt him and Nicki like this. It seemed impossible to get through those emotions, and he had no real desire to visit Anette's grave. Now Becca wanted him to take Nicki. He didn't know if he could do it.

At his hesitation, Becca said, "I can't take her without your permission."

They continued to stare at each other, and Cord suddenly

realized he didn't have much of a choice. For his daughter, he would do anything—even visit her mother's grave. One thought kept running through his mind: *Becca will make it easier for both of us.*

"Let me go inside and get cleaned up, then we'll go."

Becca smiled, and his chest tightened. God, she was beautiful.

"Thank you, Cord. I know this is hard, but I believe it's what Nicki needs."

"You're the doctor," he said, moving toward the house. "Daddy will be right back," he called to Nicki.

"'Kay," she answered.

Inside, he took a long breath. He'd never realized that having Becca here would be so difficult for him. He hadn't felt the inclination to be with a woman in over a year. At forty-two, he'd thought those urges were gone; looking at Becca, he knew they weren't. But he could control them, and he would. Being Colton's girlfriend put her way off-limits. Not to mention the fact that she was too young. He wouldn't be foolish like his father. Becca was here for Nicki and that was the only interest he had in her. He had to keep telling himself that.

SOON THEY WERE IN CORD'S TRUCK and traveling toward Houston. The truck was a four-door cab with leather seats and every feature available. To Becca's astonishment it rode like a car. Becca sat in the passenger seat, with Nicki in the back.

"We have to get flowers, Daddy," Nicki reminded him.

"Okay, baby," Cord said, pulling into a small flower shop.

Before they could stop her, Nicki crawled out of the truck, leaving Dolly on the seat. "I have to pick them out. I know what Mommy likes."

Cord glanced at Becca, and they slowly followed.

In the flower shop Nicki became shy and didn't say a word.

"We'd like to see some red roses, please," Cord said.

The florist brought out a huge vase of red roses.

Cord looked at Nicki. "What do you think?"

Nicki held up three fingers. "We need three."

Cord didn't know why they needed three, but he paid the lady and she put them in a box. Nicki carried the box to the truck and sat with the roses on her lap.

A few minutes later, Cord drove through the gates of the cemetery, parking near Anette's grave. He gulped a couple of deep breaths, then got out of the truck. Taking Nicki's hand, he made his way to the grave. They stood for a while, staring at the headstone. *ANETTE PRESCOTT* was written in bold letters.

Pain and memories overwhelmed Cord, and he tried to dredge up Anette's face, but he couldn't. It was shadowy; he couldn't make it out. God, what was wrong with him? he thought, panicking a little. He should be able to see his wife's face.

Cord was lost in his own inner pain, so Becca led Nicki to the gravestone. Nicki pointed to the lettering. "That's my mommy's name," she whispered.

Becca knelt down. "Yes, it is. This is where your mommy's buried."

"Oh," she whispered again, her little arms locked tightly around the box of roses.

"You want to put the roses on the grave?"

"'Kay."

Becca opened the box. Nicki removed the roses and placed them, one by one, on the grave.

"You can talk to her if you want," Becca said.

Nicki twisted her hands. "Will she hear me?"

"Yes, she'll hear you."

Nicki stared at the roses, and Becca knew she was nervous, so she pulled the child into her arms. "Go ahead, say what you want to."

"I brought you flowers, Mommy," Nicki said in a breathless voice. She glanced at Becca. Becca nodded and Nicki continued. "Red roses that you like. One's from me, one's from Daddy and one's from Becca."

Again Nicki turned to Becca. "Anything else you want to say?" Becca asked.

Nicki was still twisting her hands, and Becca sensed that now was the time to get everything out in the open. "If you're mad at your mother, tell her."

Nicki shook her head. "I'm not mad at her." She looked at the grave. "I'm not mad at you, Mommy. You didn't feel good. Do you feel better now?"

A lump formed in Becca's throat, and her arms tightened around Nicki. "Oh, yes, she feels much better because you're here."

She held her for a little while longer, then got to her feet. "Ready to go?"

"Uh-huh."

Becca stopped when she saw Cord's shattered expression. He held his hat in his hands, his fingers crushing the Stetson. It was painful to watch. She wondered how many times he'd been to Anette's grave. From his reaction, not often.

"Cord," she said tentatively.

His head jerked in the direction of her voice, but all he could hear was Nicki's words. *I'm not mad at you, Mommy. You didn't feel good.* He heard the awe and joy she felt at being near her mother again. Why hadn't he brought her here? Why hadn't he seen that his child needed to visit her mother's grave? He felt like a failure as a father because he'd let his hurt and pride get in the way. He had failed Nicki.

"Cord."

He made an effort to collect himself. "Yes."

"Are you ready?"

"Sure."

The drive from the cemetery was quiet, until Nicki started asking questions.

"Becca?"

"Hmm?"

"Is my Mommy 'cared?"

"No, sweetie, she's at peace and she's in heaven." She looked surreptitiously over at Cord, to make sure he approved of that answer. He nodded.

"Becca?"

"Hmm?"

"Is heaven a nice place?"

"Very nice, and no one feels bad in heaven."

"Oh."

On and on it went. Nicki kept asking questions. Cord noticed that she never asked him, just Becca, and he was beginning to feel left out, which was patently ridiculous. But he wanted Nicki to turn to *him*. He wanted to be the one to help her, even though he'd realized months ago that he couldn't. He was too emotionally involved. It took someone like Becca to free Nicki from the doubts and fears caused by Anette's death.

"Daddy."

Cord was so consumed by his own misery that he didn't hear Nicki the first time.

"Daddy!"

"Yes, baby. What is it?"

"Can I have an ice cream?"

He glanced at Becca and smiled. He couldn't help it. His

baby wanted to eat. Hallelujah. He didn't even care that it was close to supper.

"Sure," he replied happily.

"I want chocolate on mine. Becca does, too."

"Really?" Cord raised an eyebrow at Becca.

She shrugged. "I have a thing for chocolate."

"Yeah, I think I heard that before." The glint in his eyes made her stomach tense excitedly.

They each had a cone dipped in chocolate, and it was a joy to watch Nicki gobble hers. Cord got ice cream on his mustache, and Becca had the ludicrous urge to lick it off. As he wiped it away with a napkin, her fantasy dissolved into a pleasurable ache.

When they got back to the ranch, Della had supper waiting. As usual, Edie was eating in her room and Blanche was out. They sat at the kitchen table, just the three of them. Nicki hadn't stopped talking during their drive home or during the meal; finally her head started to bob and Becca saw that she was about to fall asleep.

Becca got to her feet. "I'll take her to bed."

"I can put my own child to bed," Cord snapped as he scooped Nicki up.

"Sure," Becca said, wondering what that was about. He seemed put out with her. Maybe he was still feeling emotional over the visit to the cemetery. Whatever it was, she didn't like the feeling that he was upset with her.

CORD STRIPPED NICKI OUT OF her clothes and pulled her nightgown over her head, then held her tightly in his arms. "I love you, baby," he whispered in her hair.

"Love you, Daddy," she answered sleepily.

His child was back. The process of healing had started. He knew there'd still be bad days, but he felt so much better about things. Yet he also felt helpless because he hadn't been able to do this for her, his own daughter. And he'd snapped at Becca for no reason. Oh God, he had to apologize for that.

He gently tucked Nicki in and removed the pigtail bands from her hair. He stood for a moment, staring at his precious child. He could finally see the light at the end of the long, dark tunnel. They were going to make it; he knew that with certainty.

Now he had to find Becca.

DELLA SAID SHE'D GONE to her room, so he went back upstairs. He knocked on her door.

She opened it with a hairbrush in her hand. "Cord," she said in surprise.

"Hi. Could I talk to you for a minute?"

"Sure." She moved aside to let him in.

"I'm sorry to bother you."

"It's okay. I was just brushing my hair before my shower. Something I do every night."

He'd love to watch that ritual, but shook his head to rid himself of those thoughts. "I have to apologize," he said quickly, sitting in a chair positioned near the door.

"For what?"

"For snapping at you and being in a disagreeable mood."

She sat on the bed facing him. "I know this isn't easy for you."

"No, it's not, but that's no reason to get angry at you."

"It's okay, Cord."

"But it isn't," he said earnestly. "I've tried everything I know to help my daughter deal with her mother's death, but nothing worked. Things just got worse and worse. You've been here two days, and she's almost back to normal.'' He sighed. ''I'm thrilled—and deeply grateful—but I don't feel like much of a father.''

She hated that look on his face. ''I've been trained to deal with children. Sometimes I can read them, other times I can't. I got lucky with Nicki.''

''I don't think luck has anything to do with it.''

''I'll take that as a compliment.''

His eyes met hers. ''It was meant as one.''

He was the first to glance away. He rested his elbows on his knees and clasped his hands. ''You see, I've only been to the cemetery once since Anette died, and that was when they installed the headstone. I've been so angry at her that…''

When he didn't say anything else, she asked, ''Is that why you locked her room?''

His eyes swung to hers again. ''How do you know that?''

''Della mentioned it.''

''Oh,'' he said in a quiet tone, staring down at his hands. ''Partly, I suppose. I didn't want to be reminded of those memories, and I didn't want Nicki going in there and re-membering, either.'' He paused, then added, ''I felt the same way about the cemetery. That was selfish on my part. I should have considered Nicki's feelings, but I thought it would just hurt her more.''

''Stop blaming yourself. You did the best you could un-der the circumstances.''

''No, I didn't. I never should have married Anette. Ranching life wasn't for her, but a man doesn't think too clearly with his head in the clouds.''

He loved his wife. She should be happy about that, but she wasn't. She didn't want him to love… Oh God, she was getting in too deep, too fast. She had to stop this.

''The main thing is that Nicki's getting better,'' she said to return to a subject she was comfortable with.

"Yes, thanks to you."

Their eyes met again, and for a moment she was lost in feelings she wanted to deny.

"Colton called this morning," Cord said abruptly.

"Oh." Her voice was low and detached.

"I invited him for the weekend. I thought you might like that."

She swallowed. "What did he say?"

"He said he had a lot to do, but he'd try."

"Colton's always busy."

"But he makes time for you, doesn't he?" If she was the woman in *his* life, he'd move heaven and earth to be with her.

She frowned. "My relationship with Colton is hard to explain."

"You don't have to explain it to me."

She didn't seem to hear him. "Colton and I have been friends for ages."

"I know. He's talked about you a lot."

Her eyes grew mischievous. "Don't believe everything you've heard."

"Oh, I think I will," he said, getting to his feet. "I'd better let you take your shower. And thanks for everything."

She stood, too. "You're very welcome."

They stared at each other, and then Cord started to move away, but he turned back. Almost in slow motion he took her in his arms. She wrapped her own arms around his waist and laid her head against his chest. Her heart was beating so fast that she couldn't hear or think. All she could do was feel his hard, lean body, the strength of his arms and the sadness that was such a part of him.

"Thank you, Becca," he whispered, then released her and walked out the door.

Becca felt empty and alone. She wanted his arms back. She wanted all of him. For years, she had waited for these feelings, but she'd never dreamed they'd happen with a man who didn't want her in the same way. She sank heavily onto the bed. Now what?

WHAT WAS HE DOING? Cord berated himself as he strolled to his room. He shouldn't have touched her. But he couldn't resist. He could still feel her softness, smell the scent of her hair. And she was Colton's lover. That truth jolted him and stiffened his resolve to stay away from her. He had to, no matter how he was beginning to feel about her. She belonged to Colton.

CHAPTER SIX

BECCA FOUND that the next few days were easy and difficult at the same time. Nicki was progressing. She was playing, laughing and learning to be a kid again. She didn't mention going to her mother's grave; she now knew where her mother was, and that seemed to satisfy her.

Dealing with Nicki was not a problem. Dealing with her father was. They discussed Nicki every night, and she was so drawn to him, so aware of him, but he was creating a distance between them. He left early in the morning and didn't return until almost dark. He seemed to be avoiding her, and she didn't understand it. He'd been so considerate, even loving, that night in her room. She thought they'd reached a new level in their relationship, but evidently not. If he wanted to avoid *her,* that was fine, but he couldn't avoid his daughter. Things had to change. In fact, a *lot* of things had to change in the Prescott house.

Nicki needed a stable family environment. Becca didn't see any of that. She and Nicki were alone each and every day. When Edie wasn't at church functions, she stayed in her room. Blanche slept till almost noon, then left to go to her club in Houston and didn't get home until Nicki was in bed. Becca was the only person Nicki consistently interacted with, and she needed more than that. She needed grown-ups to guide her and she needed to be with children her own age. Becca planned to talk to Cord about this as soon as possible.

She had told Nicki she'd only be here for a few days and that Mrs. Witherspoon would be returning. Nicki seemed to understand, but Becca wasn't sure. If Becca became too attached to her, then her departure would be traumatic. It would destroy all the progress they'd made. She didn't want to think about her own feelings in the matter because they were irrelevant. Besides, she could handle them.

That night, Becca waited for Cord in the den. Every evening he bathed Nicki and put her to bed, then read her a story until she fell asleep. It was their little ritual, and Becca didn't intrude. Nicki needed all the time she could get with her father.

Deep in thought, Cord walked into the den—and stopped suddenly when he saw Becca sitting on the sofa. She was usually in her room by now. At the sight of her in jeans and a knit top, with her dark hair hanging loose around her shoulders, his body tightened with unbelievable need. That reaction seemed to be getting more frequent—which was why he was trying to stay away from her. She was beautiful, fresh, exciting and young, young, young—way too young for him. And she was Colton's. He had to keep saying that to himself, but somehow it wasn't working. God, he was in so much trouble.

"May I speak to you?" she asked when she saw him.

Cord moved to his chair and sat down. "Sure," he replied in a distant voice.

She frowned. "Cord, are you upset with me?"

"No, of course not," he answered in that same tone. "How can I be upset with someone who's given me back my daughter?"

"That's what I want to talk about—Nicki."

"Is something wrong?" he asked urgently.

"Yes, she needs more interaction with her family. Blanche and Edie are never here and you're gone all day."

"It's a busy time with roundup and baling hay."

"You're here on the ranch. Why can't you have lunch with her?"

"It's not that simple. When I have a pen full of calves to be tagged, vaccinated and branded, I can't just drop everything. Besides, I'm miles from the house."

"Don't you eat?"

"Gus always carries an ice chest full of cold cuts for the ranch hands. We have a quick bite and get back to work."

"Can Nicki and I join you?"

"Beg your pardon?"

"If you'll give me directions, I can drive us to where you'll be working."

"This is a ranch. We don't have highways."

Her eyes narrowed. "I didn't think you did."

"If I told you to drive due south for fifteen miles, would you know what I was talking about?"

"Yes, if you gave me a starting point."

God, she was serious—absolutely serious. Anette had lived here for years, and she'd never left the house or the backyard. The cows and horses frightened her, and she found the vastness of the property terrifying. Apparently Becca didn't have that problem.

She watched him for a moment. "Cord, you're acting like you'd rather I wasn't here anymore. If that's the case—"

"No," he interrupted. His emotions were contradictory. He was trying to stay away from her, but he didn't want her to leave or feel as if he didn't need her. "You're the only thing Nicki talks about, and now that she's better, I'm trying to catch up on the work I've put off to be with her. That's all, Becca. You're very welcome here."

Too welcome. That's the problem.

"And you can bring Nicki to where I'm working anytime you want." His eyes held hers. "Can you ride?"

"You mean, like a horse?"

He grinned. "Yeah, like a horse."

"No, I've never been near one."

Another city girl.

He shook off that thought. "We have a couple of Jeeps you can take. You'd ruin your car driving it in a pasture. Can you drive a standard shift?"

"Yes," she replied in a bright voice. "I learned in my dad's old—" She stopped as she realized what she was saying. "I mean, in my grandfather's old truck. Sometimes I have trouble keeping parents and grandparents straight."

She was trying to be lighthearted, but he saw the bewilderment and pain that flashed in her eyes. "Colton told me what happened. That must've been hard for you."

She linked her fingers. "Yes, it was."

Cord felt an overwhelming need to comfort her. He wanted to put his arms around her, the way she'd done to him the day of the funeral, but he couldn't touch her. He'd made a promise to himself.

"I'm sure that's why you're so good with Nicki. You can identify with her pain. You didn't actually lose a mother, but you…"

"Yes, I did," she said quietly. "I lost a mother and I gained my real one. I was confused, and I was angry, especially at Emily because she gave me away. But love has incredible healing powers." She smiled slightly.

"You're incredible." He meant it. Colton was the luckiest man on earth.

"I don't know about that," she said quietly. "I've rarely stayed angry for long. Once I tell the person I'm angry with how I feel, I'm able to deal with whatever's bothering me.

Back then, though, I didn't want to talk and I went through a destructive period. Emily was patient and understanding, even though she was hurting as much as I was, which I didn't understand until later. Luckily, we got through that rough time, and I'm grateful for the relationship I have with my parents *and* my grandparents.''

Becca couldn't believe she was telling him all this. Maybe it was because she knew he had a compassionate heart and she was consoled by the empathy in his eyes. She glanced down at her hands. "But sometimes I feel…''

"What?'' he prompted.

She looked up. "I feel as if they're smothering me. So many people love me and I love them. But I feel pulled in too many directions and I…'' She blinked away a tear as she tried to regain control of her emotions.

He got up to sit beside her. He'd said he wouldn't touch her, but he found himself reaching for her hand. Her fingers locked tightly around his.

"At times I still have difficulty figuring out who I am.''

His other hand touched her cheek. "You're Becca, a beautiful woman, inside and out.''

She smiled through the tears. "I think I've heard that line before.''

"From many eager guys, I'm sure.'' He was suddenly jealous of all those guys.

She took a quick breath. It was so easy to talk to him that she'd told him things she'd never shared with anyone, not even Gin.

"I'm sorry. I shouldn't have unloaded on you like that. I'm not usually so weepy.''

"Don't worry about it,'' he said softly. "After what you've done for Nicki, you can unload on me anytime you want.''

She removed her hand from his and brushed her hair

back in a nervous gesture. If he kept holding her hand, she was going to kiss him—to experience all those feeling that were about to overtake her. He didn't reciprocate her feelings, though, and that was the only thing that stopped her.

"Nicki," she said quickly to cover her embarrassment. "That's who we were talking about before I got sidetracked. As I started to say, I feel Nicki needs more interaction with her family, especially Blanche and Edie because they live here."

"We're not much of a family, Becca," he said in a regretful tone, "but I guess you've figured that out. Edie and Blanche have been at each other's throats since the day Pa married Blanche. That's been going on for over forty years, and it's not going to change, not even for Nicki."

"Has Edie always lived here? Has she never married or left home?" Becca thought that if she knew more about Edie and Blanche, she might be able to understand them— at least a little.

"She went to Texas A&M to become a veterinarian. She came home for a weekend to see her sister, who'd been married a couple of years and just found out she was pregnant. They went on a shopping trip to Houston with their mother and were involved in a bad car accident. Edie's mother and sister didn't survive. Edie was injured and spent months in the hospital. She was engaged at the time. Pa said the guy came around for a while, then eventually stopped coming. After Edie recovered from the accident, she never went back to school. She took care of the house and helped Pa. It was just the two of them for several years."

"Then he married Blanche," Becca murmured. "And things have never been the same for Edie."

"That about sums it up. And Pa didn't help matters. He was from the old school, where the man was the head of the household and his decisions were not to be questioned. The women were supposed to be pampered and taken care of. Pa never explained anything to them or tried to help with the transition. He just expected them to accept his decision.''

''That must've been difficult for both of them,'' Becca said.

''Yeah, Edie was twenty-seven at the time, and sharing the house and Pa with a younger woman didn't sit well with her.''

''How old was Mr. Prescott when he died?''

''Ninety-six, and he rode a horse until the day before his death. He got dizzy after riding and I had to carry him into the house. The next day he quietly passed away with Blanche and me by his side.''

She could hear the love for his father in his voice. ''So your parents were married for thirty-six years?''

''Yep.''

''He lived to see all his sons grown,'' Becca added.

''Sure did. I was thirty-two when he died.''

''And the apple of his eye,'' she said, smiling.

He glanced at her. ''Some people say that, and I have to admit Pa and I were close. We both enjoyed ranching, and he taught me everything I know. He argued a lot with Clay and Colton because he didn't understand either of them.''

''Did Blanche?''

''Blanche is Blanche and it's hard to explain her, but she's never had much interest in her sons.''

''But she was always there for your father.''

''Yep, I'd have to say she was.''

''Then, that has to count for something.''

''Becca, don't go looking for miracles,'' he told her shortly. ''There aren't any in this house.''

''Are you sure?''

"What do you mean?"

"I mean, have you asked Blanche or Edie to share in Nicki's life? Like having supper with her in the evenings or just spending time with her?"

Cord rubbed his jaw. "No, because I know it's a waste of my breath."

"Do you mind if I try?"

He shook his head in amusement. "If you can get my mother to take an interest in my daughter, hell will freeze over, as the saying goes. Blanche is interested in no one but herself. I learned that when I was a kid, but if you want to try, go ahead."

"I will," she said, determined to make some changes for Nicki's sake. "I'd also like to enroll Nicki in a play group. She needs to be around children her own age."

He frowned. "Do you think she's ready for that?"

"Yes."

"Then, I trust your judgment. It hasn't been wrong so far."

"Thank you," she said sincerely. "And tomorrow we'll pay you a visit on the ranch."

He shook his head. "Not tomorrow. It's Saturday and I have to take care of business in town. Besides, Colton will probably be coming for a visit. Don't you want to stay close to the house for that?"

"No. Anyway, if Colton was going to visit, he would've called me," she said, to his surprise.

"He hasn't called you?" He couldn't keep the shock out of his voice. "He's not coming to see you?"

She tucked a strand of hair behind her ear, deciding to set him straight about Colton. "No, we don't have that kind of relationship. Colton was there when I found out about my parents. I didn't like him at first, but he spent a lot of time at our house because of his business dealings with my father. Gradually, I began to like him and we became friends. When he opened an office in Houston, I saw more of him. He'd call and take me out to dinner, to a movie, whatever. Colton and I are friends, very good friends. That's all.''

She could see he didn't believe her. ''It's true. You can ask Colton.''

Cord still wasn't sure about that; however, it really didn't make a difference. Becca was too young for him, anyway. But, oh, she was so damn good to look at and to be with.

Becca got to her feet. ''Now, I expect you to be home in time to have supper with your daughter tomorrow. I'm going upstairs to speak with Edie, and I'll talk to Blanche when she gets in.''

''You're serious about this, aren't you?''

''Yes.''

''Becca, don't expect too much.''

''Oh, I do, Cordell Prescott,'' she said mischievously. ''And you'd better remember that.''

As he watched her leave the room, he had a feeling that hell was about to freeze over.

BECCA KNOCKED on Edie's door. There was no answer, so she knocked again. Suddenly the door swung open. Edie stood there in a blue cotton robe, her gray hair frizzed as if she'd been sleeping.

''I'm sorry. I didn't mean to wake you.''

''I was catnapping.'' She waved off Becca's apology and tried to tame her hair.

''I just wanted to talk to you for a second.''

''Okay,'' Edie said, and Becca followed her into the suite. There was a bedroom area, a sitting room that held a tiny refrigerator and microwave, and a small alcove complete with a computer and electronic sound equipment. Floor-to-ceiling bookshelves covered one wall.

No wonder Edie stayed in her room; this was her own little world away from her stepmother.

"I wanted to talk about Nicki."

"She's doing so well," Edie said. "I don't hear the crying or screaming anymore."

"Yes, she is, and I'd like that progress to continue."

"Of course, and if I can help I will."

"I'm glad to hear that, because Nicki needs to feel her family's love. And I was hoping you'd join us for supper tomorrow night."

Edie's calm face became hard. "Will the harlot be there?"

"If you mean Blanche, yes, I hope so. I'm asking her, too."

"Then, I won't be there. I'm happy having dinner in my room. I can't breathe the same air as that woman."

"Not even for Nicki?"

Edie remained silent, and Becca knew this was going to be as hard as Cord had predicted. Time to bring out the guilt.

"You love Nicki. I know you do."

"Yes, she's like a ray of sunshine, even though her mother was…" Edie shook her head as if to clear it. "But that has nothing to do with Blanche. She destroyed my life and she destroyed Pa's."

"How did she destroy your pa's? She gave him the sons he wanted."

Edie paled, and Becca knew she was hitting close to home. "And you love those sons. Actually, you raised them, didn't you?" Becca was basing this on what Colton had told her.

"The nanny was incompetent! I was the one who got up

with them in the middle of the night. I was the one who rocked them when they were sick. I was always here for them. Their mother wasn't.''

''So she gave you a great gift,''

Edie's face became rigid. ''What are you talking about?''

''I'm talking about Clay, Cord and Colton. She practically gave them to you.''

''Because *she* didn't want them.''

''But Mr. Prescott did.''

Edie's skin turned almost white. ''Pa always wanted sons and he let that harlot talk him into—''

''Come on, Edie, even you have to admit she probably didn't have to do much talking.''

''No, men that age aren't too discriminating.''

Becca wanted to laugh but didn't. She was just glad Edie had a sense of humor.

''Edie, it's time to let go of the resentment and hatred.''

''She's a vile woman.''

Becca had to admit that Blanche wasn't on her list of favorite people, either, but there had to be a way to pull this family together. ''Bottom line, Edie, I was hoping you'd do what's best for Nicki.''

There was no answer, so Becca pushed further. ''And by staying in your room, you're letting Blanche win.''

That got a reaction. ''I will *never* let her win!''

''Then, you'll be there for dinner?''

''I'll be there.''

Becca had to get one thing clear. ''I don't want this to turn into a scene, especially in front of Nicki.''

Edie straightened to her full height. ''I will behave like a lady, but a harlot is a harlot, no matter how much money is lavished on her.''

''Okay,'' Becca said slowly, thinking maybe she should've left well enough alone. ''Tomorrow at six, and thanks. I know you'll make this a wonderful evening for Nicki."

Yeah right, she thought as she left. A barroom brawl was more likely. Two women with strong points of view and neither willing to give in. This could turn out to be awful. Why had she started it? For Nicki. And she'd see it through. Now she had to talk to Blanche, which was going to be as much fun as stepping on a rattlesnake.

FROM HER ROOM, Becca had a view of the garages, and when she saw a flash of headlights she knew Blanche was home. After ten minutes, she went downstairs.

Becca tapped on her door. "Blanche, it's Becca."

"Come in," Blanche called.

Becca entered the room and stopped in her tracks. Blanche stood in front of a full-length mirror preening without a stitch of clothing on. And she made no move to cover herself.

"What do you want, sugar?"

"I…uh…I…" She was at a loss for words.

"What's the matter? Haven't you ever seen a naked woman before?"

"Plenty, but never one without any modesty." Becca replied shortly.

"Come on, Becca, you're a doctor," Blanche said, admiring herself in the mirror. "Have you ever seen a woman my age with a body like this?"

Becca shut the door and walked closer. She found it a little bizarre to be studying Blanche's naked form, but Blanche didn't mind. That was obvious. Her butt was too tight—butt tuck. Her stomach flat—tummy tuck. And her breasts were too pert for a woman of sixtyplus. Blanche had had a lot of work done.

''No, I haven't,'' she answered. ''Not without plastic surgery.''

Blanche swung to face her. ''How dare you,'' she spat, and quickly reached for her black silk robe.

''As you said, Blanche, I'm a doctor. I can tell.''

''You can't tell a thing. What do you want, anyway?''

''I want to talk about family unity.''

''What the hell is that and what business is it of yours?''

''It's about Nicki and the fact that she needs a loving family around her.''

''Cord's very loving, as I'm sure you've noticed, and this doesn't concern me. Cord's told me that many times.'' Blanche sat at her dressing table and began to remove her makeup.

''Don't you want to be involved in your granddaughter's life?''

Blanche met her eyes in the mirror. ''Sugar, I'm not the motherly type, nor am I interested in being a grandmother.''

Becca could only stare at her. Didn't this woman have any feelings at all? Or was she an expert at masking them?

Blanche didn't miss her disapproving expression. ''Is that too cold for you?''

''I just find your attitude hard to understand.''

''Let me tell you something, sugar. I grew up fast and hard. My mother ran a beer joint on the outskirts of Houston and we lived above it. I never knew who my father was. I don't think my mother did, either. There were so many 'uncles' and 'special friends' that I lost track. I guess I was about twelve when men started hitting on me. You know what my mother told me?''

Becca shook her head, afraid to even hazard a guess because she had a feeling the answer would taint everything she believed about youth and innocence.

"She said to enjoy it, but to make damn sure I got everything I could out of the man."

Becca tried to keep the shock from her face, but knew she'd failed. Gin's mother worked in a bar and was on husband number five, but she loved Gin and would never suggest she do such a thing. She'd protected Gin from that kind of behavior. Of course, Gin and her mom had problems, but nothing like this.

"So you see, I grew up with what you might call a different kind of love. I don't know the kind of love you're talking about. The only time I came close was with Claybourne. He used to come into the bar, and I could see the way he'd watch me. He never tried anything like the other men. We talked a lot. He told me that when I turned eighteen he was going to marry me. I laughed and said I'd be waiting. He kept his word. The day I had my eighteenth birthday, he came back and I left with him. I haven't seen the bar or my mother since. I've never regretted marrying Claybourne. He was my ticket out and he knew it. We were always honest with each other. He wanted a son. I wanted freedom. I didn't want to be a mother, but I had the boys for Claybourne. Doesn't mean I don't care about them. Just means I look at life a little differently than other people."

Becca hadn't dreamed she'd get such a glimpse into Blanche's life. She felt great sympathy for that young girl who had never known true love or happiness. But Becca was well aware that her sympathy was wasted on Blanche.

"If you care about Cord, then you must care for Nicki."

Blanche turned to face her. "What are you getting at?"

"Nicki's improved so much, and I think a show of unity from the family would benefit her. All I'm asking is for her grandmother and her aunt to have dinner with her a couple of times a week."

"You want me to sit down to a cozy family dinner with the witch of Triple Creek?"

"With Edie, yes."

"Forget it, sugar. She hates my guts and I despise the pompous twit."

Trying to play on Blanche's heartstrings was futile, since they didn't seem to exist; Blanche required a different strategy. Becca noticed the mirror and immediately knew how to reach her.

"Does Cord know about your many nips and tucks?" She was guessing he didn't.

"It's none of his business."

"Good, then you won't mind if I mention it to him—and Edie."

Blanche stood and tightened the belt on her robe. "Are you trying to blackmail me?"

"Oh, blackmail is such an offensive word. I care to think of it as gentle persuasion."

Blanche's eyes narrowed. "I don't think you know who you're dealing with, sugar."

"Oh, but I do," Becca assured her. "I'm dealing with a woman who's struggled all her life to survive in a world that hasn't been kind to her. She's tough, crude and unbelievably hard-hearted, but underneath I'm hoping she has a tiny glimmer of concern for her granddaughter."

Blanche's eyes didn't waver. "Your hope is in vain."

Becca didn't back down, even though her knees were beginning to feel weak. "Okay," she said. "At least we know where we stand." She moved toward the door and turned back. "Let's see, that's a tummy tuck, a butt lift, breast enhancement and—oh, the face. You've had so much done to the face, I hardly knew where to start. I'm just trying to get this straight. I'm sure Edie will want all the details."

"I don't care what that bitch thinks."

"Fine," Becca said, and continued to the door. She would've sworn that Blanche would do anything to keep Edie from finding out her secret. Maybe she'd been—

"You little bitch."

Becca looked back. "Are you talking to me?"

"You got spunk. I admire that," Blanche said, watching her closely.

"Then, we'll expect you tomorrow night at six. Cord and Nicki will be pleased."

Blanche walked over to her. "Don't let this little victory go to your head, sugar. I'm still keeping an eye on you. Cord's not too wise when it comes to women. He doesn't need another city girl in his life. The last one almost destroyed him."

"You mentioned Anette before. What do you know about her death?"

Blanche took a step closer. "She drank herself into oblivion because she was a weak simpering idiot. Now, get your ass out of my room before I really get upset."

Becca left. She'd pushed enough buttons for one night. But a series of questions followed her to her room. Why was Blanche so bitter about Anette? Was something going on that Cord didn't know about? Blanche had said she'd do anything to protect her sons. How far would she go to accomplish that?

CHAPTER SEVEN

CORD HAD BREAKFAST with Becca and Nicki before he left to take care of his business. Becca worked with Della to plan a special meal for the evening; Della clearly thought she was out of her mind. And maybe she was. She just wanted this family to feel some sort of togetherness instead of the constant tension that seemed to permeate the place.

She and Nicki picked flowers from the backyard for the table and then arranged them in a crystal vase. Nicki wasn't as excited as Becca had thought she'd be. She didn't seem to be looking forward to the evening so much as resigned to it, which Becca didn't understand. Maybe she'd been hoping for too much. She couldn't help remembering the occasions when she and Rose would prepare a special table for Emily. She was always so excited at the prospect of seeing Emily. But then, there was a simple difference between their family and the Prescotts. Love. That was what had gotten them through the difficult times.

Nicki didn't have anything that even resembled a loving relationship with Blanche. She'd probably witnessed more arguments than a five-year-old should. Becca prayed everyone would be on their best behavior tonight.

That afternoon she read to Nicki on the patio. The fresh air was intoxicating, and Nicki fell asleep in her arms. Becca stared at the inscription in the book. The woman who'd written those words loved her child. That was very clear. Then, why would she kill herself and leave that child

behind? What had driven her over the edge? Depression—
or something else? She shook her head. She had to stop
thinking about Anette.

CORD'S DAY WASN'T GOING WELL. He'd planned to pay his
feed bills and make sure he had enough corn and milo to
last for the month. There were several farmers who supplied
him. He just wanted to arrange for the trucks to be at his
ranch on specific days to dump the grain. But all the farmers wanted to talk, and then he had to have coffee with
them. It was after five by the time he headed back to the
ranch. Becca was going to be annoyed with him.

He could remember when he'd had those same feelings
about Anette. But this was different. Anette had started laying down rules and schedules she expected him to follow,
even though she knew he had ranching commitments; that
had made him angry. With Becca, he felt an eagerness to
see her again. He shouldn't, but he did. He tried to recall
Anette's face. It wasn't there anymore. Everything about
Anette was receding in his mind—except her death. That
was vivid and clear. So were the emotions that went with
it. Conflicting thoughts and feelings ran through his mind.

It was 5:45 when he walked into the kitchen. Becca
strolled in from the dining room with Nicki trailing behind
her. His breath caught in his throat at the sight of her. She
wore a brown knit top and brown print skirt that flowed
around her ankles. She looked gorgeous, and he couldn't
stop staring at her.

"Hi, you're home," she said with a smile. No anger, no
threats, no hurt feelings. Oh, he liked this. A woman who
understood.

"Daddy!" Nicki shouted, and ran into his arms.

He noticed the dress and socks and shoes. Her hair

wasn't in pigtails or a ponytail. It was hanging around her shoulders in bouncing curls.

"How's my baby?" He kissed her cheek.

"Fine." Nicki hugged his neck, then looked at him with wide eyes. "You should see what we did." She wriggled out of his arms and raced into the dining room. "Come on, Daddy."

It was so good to see his child like this again—full of excitement and life. He glanced at the woman who'd made it happen and his heart swelled with so many emotions that he had a hard time figuring out which were real and which were a result of his gratitude.

"Daddy, Daddy," Nicki called, diverting his attention. He made his way into the dining room, Becca walking right behind him.

Della was arranging chafing dishes on the sideboard and she wore a dress. Cord was disconcerted for a second. Della never wore dresses except to church. She noticed his startled expression.

"I don't know how Becca did it, but she talked Gus and me into having dinner with you." She moved past Cord. "I think I'm in the twilight zone."

Before Cord could assimilate this, Nicki shouted, "Look, Daddy, look."

He swung his gaze to the table, where Nicki was pointing. It was fully set with linen, flowers and candelabras he hadn't seen in years. They used to be on the table at special functions when his dad was alive.

"Becca and me picked the flowers and fixed 'em," Nicki was saying. "Aren't they pretty?"

"Very pretty," Cord murmured, but he wasn't looking at the flowers. He was looking at Becca.

"And we put the ca...ca...I don't know what they're

called, but they hold the candles. Della said they belonged to somebody, but I forget.''

''Your great-grandparents.''

''Oh, I don't know them.''

''No, baby, they—'' He didn't want to tell her they'd died. He didn't want her to think about Anette. ''They lived here a long time ago.''

''Oh, I'm glad they left the ca—''

''Candelabra,'' Becca whispered in her ear, glad that Nicki was now taking an interest in the dinner. Once they'd started putting things together, Nicki's excitement had grown.

''Yeah, candel-la-bra,'' Nicki said slowly. ''Becca and me put 'em on the table.''

Becca and me. Cord heard that a hundred times a day and he didn't think he'd ever grow tired of it. He glanced at the woman in question. ''I'm going upstairs to get cleaned up. Five minutes is all I need.''

''It's okay, Cord,'' she assured him, evidently hearing the anxiety in his voice.

Was she for real? Why wasn't she berating him for being late? Anette would have.

''I'm not sure everyone will show up. I'm just hoping,'' she added.

He hurried for the stairs. They'd better show up, he thought, or he was personally dragging them down to dinner. Becca had gone to a lot of trouble and he wasn't having her disappointed.

He showered and dressed in starched jeans and a white shirt. The grandfather clock chimed six as he entered the den. Gus was fixing a drink. With his weathered skin and legs bowed from spending years in the saddle, he looked out of place among the elegant furniture and the beautifully set table. Gus was a cowboy to the core.

"Hey, Gus," he said.

Gus took a swallow of whiskey. "Wondered where you were. If I have to be at this shindig, so do you. Don't know why I let that little filly talk me into this. I just came by this morning to tell Della something, and she introduced me to the doc. Nice woman—and man, can she talk. Before I knew it, I was agreeing to have dinner with the family." He shook his head.

"Becca's very persuasive."

"I'll say, and I hate these ironed clothes. I feel like I've been rode hard and put up wet."

"You'll survive."

Gus tipped his glass. "Not too sure about that. Having dinner with Blanche could be about as much fun as putting panty hose on a bobcat."

"Remember, no scenes tonight. I want this to be perfect for Nicki." *And Becca.*

Becca and Nicki came in at that moment. "I guess we might as well sit down," Becca said in a resigned voice.

Cord knew Edie was upstairs, and if she'd said she was eating with them, then she was. "I'll check on Edie," he said, but before he could make an exit, Edie walked in.

"I'm sorry. I'm running a little late."

"That's okay," Becca told her. "We're just glad you joined us."

"Hi, Edie," Nicki said.

"Hi, and don't you look pretty."

"Becca fixed my hair."

"I can see that."

"Want me to show you where to sit? I know where everyone sits."

"Yes, I'd like that."

"Okay." She took Edie's hand.

Becca glanced at the clock. Six-fifteen. Blanche wasn't coming. At least Becca had tried.

But as they filed into the dining room, Blanche breezed in wearing a cream silk dress with a silver belt fitted over her hips.

"You're not gonna eat without me, are you, sugar?"

"We were just taking our seats," Becca said. She should've known that Blanche would have to make a grand entrance.

"And I know where everyone sits," Nicki put in.

"Aren't you smart?" Blanche responded in a condescending tone.

"Yeah," Nicki answered, not noticing the condescension. "Daddy sits at the head of the table and you sit at the other end. Edie is next to Daddy, then Gus and Della. And me and Becca are by Daddy on this side."

"How sweet," Blanche said in the same tone as she took her seat. "Let me get this straight. Della and Gus are eating with us?"

"Yes, I invited them," Becca told her, trusting Blanche wasn't going to make an issue of it.

"I'm glad I was consulted."

Before Becca could reply, Cord spoke up. "If you were home more and took an interest in the family, maybe you would be. But we're not talking about that right now. We're going to enjoy this wonderful meal that Della and Becca have prepared."

"And me, too, Daddy," Nicki reminded him. "I helped."

"And you, too, baby." Cord smiled at his daughter, then stared at Blanche, warning her not to say one more insulting word.

Della brought out the prime rib, and conversation

stopped while all the food was put on the table, then Della took her seat.

"Would you like to say a prayer?" Becca asked Nicki. They had talked about this earlier and Nicki had said she wanted to.

Nicki folded her hands and bowed her head. "Thank you for the food and everyone here. Amen."

"That was very nice, Nicki," Edie said.

"Yeah, kid, you heard that from the mouth of a—"

"Cord would you slice the prime rib, please?" Becca intervened before Blanche could say something hateful.

Cord spared Blanche a glance before he stood to carve the roast. Becca filled Nicki's plate—cutting up her meat, buttering her roll and mashing her potatoes.

"You're just a regular little mother, aren't you, sugar?" Blanche remarked.

"Thank you," Becca said, not reacting to the obvious insult.

"You outdid yourself, Della girl," Gus said. "This meat is succulent."

"It sure is," Cord agreed.

After that, conversation was mundane and the tension seemed to ease, until Blanche asked, "What did you do today, kiddo?"

"I played, and Becca and me picked flowers and fixed 'em for the table."

"Becca's a jack-of-all-trades, isn't she?"

Nicki frowned. "What's that?"

There was silence for a moment, then Cord answered, "That's a person who can do anything."

"Yeah, Becca can do anything," Nicki said, nodding vigorously.

Gus laid his napkin on the table and smiled at Nicki.

"Well, little bit, Half Pint's been awful lonely in that pasture. She sure needs riding."

A change came over Nicki and she leaned back in her chair with a sullen expression. "Don't want to."

"But you love to ride, baby," Cord said.

"No, I don't. I wanna go to my room."

Becca was shocked. The child hadn't said that in days. She turned to her. "Nicki…"

"I wanna go to my room," Nicki repeated, and before Becca could stop her, she jumped out of her chair and ran for the stairs.

Blanche stood. "Well, sugar, looks like you've got a lot more work to do. This has been more fun than I really needed. Now I've got to get to a party at the club."

"To a man, you mean," Edie slipped in.

"Shut your trap," Blanche snapped.

Edie glared at her. "I can say what I want in this house."

"You dried-up old bitch." Blanche went on. "I should've kicked you out the day Claybourne died."

Cord threw his napkin on the table. "Enough! This dinner is over. Just get out of my sight." With that, he headed for the stairs, and Becca followed.

"Cord," Gus called. He looked back. "I'm sorry. I shouldn't have mentioned the horse. I didn't know she'd react like that."

"It's all right, Gus. She's still dealing with a lot of pain."

Not a word was said as they walked up the stairs and into Nicki's room. Nicki was sitting in the rocker with her arms around Dolly. She rarely clung to Dolly these days. Something had triggered a major upset and Becca had to find out what. She hitched up her skirt and sat on the floor in front of Nicki.

"What's the matter, sweetie?" she asked softly.

"Nothin'," Nicki muttered.

"Yes, it is, 'cause you're so sad and when you're sad, I'm sad and so is Daddy."

Nicki didn't say anything.

"Look at me, Nicki."

Nicki raised her head. "I don't want you to be sad, Becca," she cried, and threw herself into Becca's arms.

Becca held her tight, smoothing her curls. "Then, tell me what's hurting you."

Needing to be near them, Cord sat on the floor beside Becca. Nicki made a dive for him, locking her arms around his neck. "What is it, baby—?" His voice cracked, but he couldn't help it.

"Mommy said…Mommy said…"

Cord's chest tightened. "What did Mommy say?"

"Mommy said she didn't want me to ride. It's not ladylike."

"Oh, baby." Cord held her close, trying to find the right words. "Mommy was scared of horses. You're not. You remember that book we read about Annie Oakley? She rode a horse. And you've seen those old westerns Gus likes. Even in those days, ladies rode horses. There was Dale Evans, and she was a grand lady."

"Then, it's okay to ride a horse?"

"You betcha." He kissed her nose.

"And Mommy won't be mad at me?"

Cord swallowed. "No, baby. Mommy loved you and she could never be mad at you."

"Oh." Nicki thought about it for a second, then she went back to Becca. "Mommy's not mad at me," she told her.

Becca stroked her face and kissed her. "No, Mommy's not mad at you."

She settled back on Becca's lap. "Becca?"

"What, sweetie?"

"Can you...can you..."

"Can I what?"

"Can you ride?"

"No, I've never been on a horse, but I'd like to try."

"Daddy can teach you and...and...you can ride with me."

"I'd like that."

And Daddy would, too, Cord thought.

"Now, would you like to go have dessert?"

Nicki clamped a hand over her mouth. "I forgot." She glanced at Cord. "We fixed a special dessert."

"I'll bet it has something to do with chocolate."

Becca made a face at him. "Actually, it's cheesecake," she said, then added with a grin, "but it's got a caramel-chocolate topping."

Cord got to his feet. "Somehow I knew chocolate would not be left out." He swung Nicki into his arms and reached out a hand to Becca. She placed her hand in his and he helped her to her feet. Her touch was soft, tempting, blocking out everything but the feeling in his heart.

Together they went downstairs. Edie, Della and Gus were in the kitchen eating cheesecake; Blanche had evidently left. Nicki immediately ran to Gus.

"I can ride Half Pint, Gus. Let's go now."

Gus gave Cord a puzzled look.

"Baby, it's dark outside. We have to wait until tomorrow."

She turned back to Gus. "And Daddy's gonna teach Becca how to ride, so she can ride with me."

"Now, ain't that somethin'."

"I'll ride with you until Becca learns," Edie offered.

"'Kay, but I ride fast. Can you ride fast?"

"At my age, I don't do anything fast, but I'll try to keep up."

After that, they sat around the table and ate cheesecake and talked. Eventually Nicki started to nod, and Cord took her upstairs and put her to bed.

The evening hadn't turned out exactly as Becca had planned, but she couldn't help feeling Anette's ghost had finally been put to rest for Nicki. After her shower, she slipped on a big T-shirt and started to get into bed, but the cheesecake had made her thirsty so she went downstairs to get a glass of ice water.

Heading back to the stairs, she thought she saw someone in the den. She strolled in to see Cord sitting on the sofa, his head buried in his hands. There was no light on, but the moonlight streaming in through the large French windows illuminated him clearly.

She walked closer. "Cord, are you all right?"

His head jerked up. "Becca. I didn't realize you were still awake."

"I just came down to get some ice water."

His shirt was pulled from his jeans and open down the front. His boots were lying on the floor. She felt as though someone had punched her in her stomach, and she had a hard time breathing.

She sat on the coffee table facing him, setting the glass beside her. "She's fine," she said, knowing exactly what was bothering him.

"Is she?" he asked in an angry tone. "Anette put so much garbage in her head, and it makes me angry that I allowed it. I never did anything to control her phobias and insecurities. I should've made her get more treatment, for that and the depression. She always resisted...."

"But she loved Nicki. That's very obvious from the inscriptions in all the books."

"Do you think that's normal?"

"Well, I hadn't really thought about it, but I don't see anything wrong with it."

"It seems weird to me, but Anette wanted Nicki to know how much she loved her. I guess it's exactly what she'd do. You see, her mother died when she was a teenager and her father married a woman Anette didn't like. There were arguments all the time, and Anette left to live with an aunt. I met her in Fort Worth when I was there for a cattleman's convention. She was the manager of the hotel where I stayed. It was a wham-bam affair, and I found myself going back on weekends, which I got tired of so we decided to get married. She had no problem giving up her job at the time, but I heard plenty about it later. Anette was looking for a family, and when she found out the Prescotts weren't the ideal American family she became depressed, and then obsessed with having a baby. God, I hated all those tests, but I did everything because I thought it would make her happy. Nothing did, though, not even Nicki's birth."

There was silence for a while. He couldn't believe he was talking so much. "Go to bed, Becca. I'm not in a very good mood."

She knew that. Still, she was reluctant to leave him. "What kind of relationship did Anette have with Blanche?"

"Tense—just like Blanche has with everyone. Why?"

She started to tell him what Blanche had said, but decided he didn't need any more problems. "Just that living here couldn't have been easy for Anette."

"No, but it's not a reason to kill yourself, especially when you have a four-year-old daughter." His voice was full of pain. "God, I just can't get past that. I—"

Becca moved to sit next to him and, unable to resist, she put her arms around him. His reaction was instant and urgent. He pulled her to him and held her tight. For a moment it was just comfort, but slowly other emotions began to take over. His breath on her hair and his hands on her body awakened a deep need in her. One hand stroked the hair at his nape while her other slid to his bare chest.

"Cord," she whispered.

He turned his head and kissed her. His lips moved over hers with an expertise that her body recognized and welcomed. She opened her mouth, and then they were lost in the joy of exploring each other. He pushed her gently into the sofa, his hands caressing her body through the T-shirt. Her senses started to spin, and she knew she'd been waiting for this all her life.

Cord wasn't thinking. He was only feeling—warm and overpowering emotions he'd thought he'd forgotten. But he didn't think he'd ever felt exactly like this. Wanting someone so badly that he hurt—someone he couldn't have. It was hard to remind himself of that when her soft, tempting hands touched his skin. But he had to. Oh God, he had to.

He tore his mouth away and got to his feet. He ran both hands roughly through his hair. "I'm sorry. I shouldn't have done that."

Becca sat up and straightened her T-shirt. "Why not?" she asked in as steady a voice as she could manage. "We're both adults and if we want to—"

"You're my brother's girlfriend."

She took a deep breath. "I'm Colton's *friend*. I told you that." She was tired of having to explain her relationship with Colton, but she had to make Cord understand. "I've known Colton for ten years and he's never kissed me like that."

Her words didn't ring true. "That day you called from your apartment. It was early in the morning and you said he'd just left. Friends don't sleep together."

"We don't *sleep* together," she said patiently. "He

stopped by on his way to work. He was there maybe fifteen minutes.''

Cord was thrown. If Colton hadn't kissed her like that or slept with her, he was a fool. *Why?* was his next thought. Had he misread the situation? It didn't matter; he had no right to kiss her. There were too many issues standing between them.

''Becca, do you know how old I am?''

She shook her head.

''I'm older than Colton. I'm forty-two.''

''So?''

''I'm too old for you.''

''Really?'' she mused. ''Then isn't Colton too old for me, as well? You're close to the same age.''

Her question rattled him. There were only fourteen months between him and Colton, yet he'd never considered Colton too old for her. Why? Maybe it was because he just *felt* so much older. Or maybe…

''Age has nothing to do with it,'' she said stiffly. ''If you regret kissing me, just say so and stop using every excuse you can think of.'' She made to walk past him, and he caught her arm.

''My dad was sixty when he married Blanche. A girl young enough to be his granddaughter. I promised myself I would never be that foolish.''

''I'm hardly young enough to be your granddaughter or even your daughter. I'll be twenty-nine on my next birthday, which isn't far away. I'm a woman who can make up her own mind. I wanted to kiss you and I think you wanted to kiss me.''

Cord didn't say anything. He couldn't. She was getting to him in the worst way, and he had to put a stop to it. ''Don't read too much into my reaction, Becca. It's been a long time since I've been with a woman.'' With that, he walked briskly to the stairs.

Her mouth fell open and she quickly closed it. Of all the— She took another deep breath as anger overtook her. *I'll never kiss you again, Cordell Prescott.* But before the thought left her mind, she knew she was lying.

CHAPTER EIGHT

THE NEXT MORNING Nicki was so excited, Becca could hardly keep up with her. The little girl wore her boots and jeans and she'd found her cowboy hat. Nicki was going riding, and the whole household felt her enthusiasm. They all went out to the corral to watch the big event. Everyone except Blanche.

Cord treated Becca coolly—as if they'd never kissed. Well, if that was the way he wanted it, fine, or so she told herself. But she could still feel his mustache on her skin— provocative, tantalizing…. She harnessed her thoughts. She refused to let Cord hurt her, but she was afraid he already had.

Becca, Della and Edie stood outside the fence as Nicki rode around and around on a black horse Gus had saddled and ready to go. Becca could see why they called the horse Half Pint. She was small and gentle and seemed perfect for Nicki. Cord opened the gate, and Nicki rode out into the pasture. The horse galloped at an alarming speed, and Becca held her breath waiting for Cord to call a halt. But he didn't. He probably knew what Nicki could and couldn't handle. She was acting like a nervous city girl. Wincing, she turned toward the house, thinking Nicki was going to hit the ground at any moment. She saw a curtain fall into place. It was Blanche. She was watching but didn't want anyone to know.

Becca's eyes shifted to the old black truck driving up to

the barn. A big man got out, tall and heavyset, and staggered toward them.

"Cord Prescott," he shouted, his words slurred. The man was obviously drunk.

"Get off my property, Bates," Cord shouted back.

Gus immediately got between the two men. Luckily Nicki was busy riding. "You'd better get outta here, Joe," Gus said.

"Not until I say what I come to say," the man snarled. "I spent six months in jail because of you, Prescott, and it's time you got what's comin' to you."

Cord walked closer. "You spent time in jail because you rustled Triple Creek cattle. That was your decision, not mine."

"You didn't have to press charges. I'd have paid you back."

"With what?" Cord muttered. "You were down on your luck because of your gambling and drinking. Besides, a cattle rustler is a disease to ranchers and you got what you deserved. Now get off this property before I call the sheriff."

"You bastard," the man yelled, stumbling to his truck. "I'll get even, Cord. I swear. You'll get what *you* deserve. Just wait and see."

"Is that a threat?"

The man laughed as he got into the truck and fired the engine. In a second he was roaring away from the barn.

"Forget it," Gus said. "He's just drunk."

Cord gazed after the truck. "Maybe, but I'll still let the sheriff know he was here." He shrugged. "If nothing else, he should be taken off the road, drunk as he is."

"Daddy, Daddy, watch me," Nicki called then, and Cord turned back to his daughter.

"Who was that?" Becca asked Della.

"Joe Bates," Della replied. "He used to work here until Cord caught him stealing cattle at night. I didn't know he was out of jail."

"He seems...dangerous," Becca said, rubbing the goose bumps on her arms.

"He is, and I hope the sheriff keeps him away from here."

THE REST OF THE DAY was spent watching Nicki ride. Cord didn't offer to teach Becca, and when he and Nicki went farther into the pasture, she walked back to the house feeling oddly left out. She thought maybe it was time to go home to Houston. She'd done everything she could here; Nicki would be fine without her. That thought did not make her happy.

She called her parents and talked to them and Scotty. Then she called Rose and Owen and Grandpa George. Her parents were planning a family trip to Rockport and wanted her to go, but she hesitated. She needed more time. Time for what, she had no idea. But it felt good to talk to everyone. The conversations confirmed that this was what she needed—time away to appreciate everything she had.

Becca sat on the patio reading medical journals she'd put aside. Her eyes kept straying to the valley below hoping for a glimpse of Cord and Nicki. She was glad Nicki was spending this morning with Cord. She just wished she didn't feel so alone. She thought about Joe Bates and wondered if he meant to harm Cord. The mere possibility sent chills through her body, and she knew her feelings for Cord were getting stronger and stronger. She didn't understand it, since he rebuffed her at every turn.

That evening, they all had supper in the kitchen. It was the meal they should've had last night. Everyone was laughing and talking, and Nicki was the center of attention, chatting on and on about her day. No one seemed to care that Blanche wasn't with them. But Becca did. She was part of this family and needed to be there. Becca knew that was strictly her own opinion. Blanche would not thank her for interfering, so she decided to stay out of it. Besides, she planned to leave soon, and it didn't concern her.

Later, Cord and Gus retired to the den, and Becca could hear them talking about the price of cattle, the delivery of grain and a pasture of coastal that needed cutting. After she, Della and Edie had cleaned up the kitchen, they joined the men. Nicki was curled up in Cord's lap, listening as if she understood every word.

Cord tried to focus on what Gus was saying, but he was having a hard time, since all he wanted to do was turn to Becca and apologize. The day had been dreadful without her, especially since every other word out of Nicki's mouth was *Becca*. He should've saddled a horse for her and taught her the rudiments of riding. But he couldn't. That would mean he'd have to be close to her, and he *had* to keep his distance. He'd made that decision last night and he'd had no sleep as a result. No matter how he tried, he could still feel her hands on his body. And that look on her face— God, he couldn't get it out of his mind. But he had to remind himself that she didn't need someone like him in her life. She was intelligent and beautiful and she had a high-powered career in Houston.

A flash of light from the entry caught everyone's attention.

"Who could that be?" Della said.

Cord immediately thought of Joe Bates and his spine stiffened. The guns were in the gun cabinet, not far away. But he didn't want anything to happen with Nicki in the room. He had to get her upstairs, then he'd deal with Bates.

Before Cord could move, Colton strolled in from the kitchen. "Hey, I wondered where everyone was."

Cord relaxed. With all of today's events, he'd forgotten that he had invited Colton out for a visit.

Becca was surprised to see him, and she jumped up excitedly and hugged him. He kissed her cheek. "Hi, gorgeous."

Gus stood and shook his hand. "Glad to have you home, boy."

Everyone else said hi, but Becca noticed that no one made a move to hug or kiss him, not even Nicki. What was wrong with this family?

Edie patted him on the shoulder and said, "Good to see you. Now I'm off to bed."

Why didn't she stay and talk? She probably hadn't seen Colton in months.

On impulse, Becca hugged Edie. "'Night."

Edie was startled and it showed in her eyes. "Yes, well…good night, all." Nervously she left the room.

"Della and me are gonna mosey over to our house," Gus said. "My easy chair is calling me."

Becca hugged both of them and there was silence for a moment, then Della said, "See you in the morning."

As they left, Cord carefully got to his feet, holding his daughter. "This one's falling asleep, so I'd better get her to bed." If Becca hugged him, he didn't know what he'd do, but he knew there was no way he could get out of this room without her hugging Nicki. Nicki was half-asleep, so maybe he—

"Becca," Nicki whimpered, and that small hope died.

"Right here, sweetie," Becca said, and walked over to kiss her cheek. Nicki reached for her and they hugged tightly. Cord could smell the scent of her hair, and her breasts were pressed into his arm as he maintained a grip on Nicki. God, he had to get out of here.

"'Night," Becca and Nicki chorused.

"Talk to you later, Colton," Cord murmured, and quickly left.

Colton raised his eyebrows. "Do I know how to clear a room or what?"

Becca sat on the sofa and Colton followed. "What are you doing here?" she asked.

"Wanted to see how you were getting on?"

"Your family lives here. Didn't you want to see them, too?"

"We're not your typical family."

"So I gather. Still, aren't you glad to see them? As mad as I've been at Rose, I'm always glad to see her."

"That's because you have a strong family bond. We don't have that."

"Colton." She sighed.

"Let me tell you what it was like in the Prescott house at Christmas. Edie and Pa would wake us up, and we'd come downstairs and open our gifts. Then we'd have breakfast and play with our toys. Blanche made an appearance when dinner was served because Pa insisted. She always had on a fancy negligée and inquired what we'd gotten for Christmas. After that, she spent her time snapping at Edie until a full-blown argument erupted. Believe me, we were glad to get that day over with."

"Your mother is very…unconventional, but Edie was always there for you. Why don't you have any affection for her?"

"We do, but we just don't show it."

"Why not, for heaven's sake?"

"Because we weren't raised that way." He glanced at

her with blue eyes so like Blanche's. "What's this about, Becca?"

"It's about Nicki. She should be surrounded by a loving family. She needs that now."

"I'm hardly ever here."

"But just now, you didn't even hug her."

He squirmed uncomfortably. "You may have noticed, I'm not a demonstrative person."

"You hug me."

"Mainly because you hug me first. You've always been like that. You're not afraid to show your emotions."

She was completely dumbfounded. Over the years, had Colton taken her openness and friendliness as something more? No, she was sure he hadn't, but she had to be certain.

She curled her feet beneath her and turned to face him. "Your mother and Cord are under the impression that we have a sexual relationship."

"Really? Where would they get an idea like that?"

"Evidently when you see them you talk about me a lot."

He shifted again. "So? That doesn't mean anything."

"We talked about this in my apartment, and you told me not to worry, but I can't help it."

His eyes met hers. "I know you don't love me."

She touched his arm, still looking into his eyes. "But do you love *me*?"

"Becca," he sounded aggrieved.

"Tell me the truth."

"I could have," he admitted. "Probably very deeply, but do you remember that time we kissed under the mistletoe at your parents' house?"

"Yes," she replied, remembering it quite well. She'd thought that if Colton kissed her passionately, all the other feelings would follow, but it hadn't happened that way. There was only a comfortable warmth between them.

"That spark, the explosion of the senses, wasn't there, and I knew you didn't have those kinds of emotions for me, nor I for you." He leaned his head against the sofa. "Why *don't* we feel that way about each other?"

"Because we're not the half that makes the other whole. That's what true love is. When you can't stop thinking about the other person, when you want to be with him in the worst way, when your heart beats faster at just the sight of him and when you'd do anything to make him happy."

His eyes narrowed. "Sounds as if you've…" He sat up straight. "You haven't fallen for Cord, have you?"

"Colton, I—"

"Cord's not the man for you," he told her swiftly. "His life is so screwed up. Anette hurt him so much, he'll never be the same. I know you're helping Nicki, but leave it at that. Don't—"

"Don't tell me what to do." She stopped him, her voice sounding angry.

"I'm not. I just want you to be happy."

"I will, but I have to find that happiness on my own. I hope you understand."

"Sure," he said slowly.

"And I hope you find a woman who makes you so silly-giddy in love that you can't think straight."

He grunted. "I don't think that's gonna happen. I *always* think straight."

"About business, yeah, but you just wait."

"Luckily, I don't have the silly-giddy capability."

"Life is not all about business."

"I haven't found that out yet."

Becca realized why she and Colton had never worked as a couple. His mind was constantly on business. There wasn't room for anything else. He was right when he said he didn't have a silly-giddy side. He had a dead-serious personality. Someday the right woman would awaken the other part of him. But that woman wasn't her.

The silence stretched between them, and Becca tried to think of something to say to ease the tension. Her mind drifted to her apartment and her plants. She hadn't even thought about them and she wondered if Gin had.

"Have you seen Gin lately?" she asked suddenly.

"The crazy redhead? Of course not. I avoid her at all costs."

"I haven't talked to her since I got here. She's supposed to be watering my plants in the apartment."

"Consider those plants dead."

She tapped him on the shoulder. "Gin's not like that. She's very responsible."

"Yeah, right. This is the same woman who's lost her car keys four times that I know of and the same woman who—"

"Okay, she's a scatterbrain, but that's why she's so much fun."

"More like a nightmare."

"You should get to know her. You have a lot in common."

His eyebrows shot up. "Like what?"

"You both have very unconventional mothers."

"Yeah, now there's something I'd enjoy talking about on a regular basis," he said facetiously, then added, "but I'll check on your plants if you want me to."

"Gin has the key, so just call and remind her." Becca knew she could call Gin herself, but it wouldn't hurt them to get better acquainted. Maybe then they'd stop saying mean things about each other.

Colton groaned dramatically. "I'd rather buy you new plants."

She tapped him on the shoulder again, and they settled

into easy conversation like they always did. He told her how he and Scotty were working on a new computer game and how he was thinking of going to Rockport with her parents. Colton was so involved with *her* family. He needed to be involved with the Prescott family—or was that completely outside the realm of possibility?

CORD PACED in his room. He wouldn't go down. He wouldn't. Colton had come to see Becca, and he wouldn't interrupt. He'd give them some time alone. He sat on the bed. Becca said they didn't have that kind of relationship, but she seemed eager enough to see Colton. What were they doing? Kissing, touching… He stood, unable to tolerate the images in his head. It was what he wanted, wasn't it? For Becca and Colton to… Without even realizing what he was doing, he found himself opening the door and hurrying downstairs.

They were sitting on the sofa talking, and his heart slowed. He moved to go back upstairs, but Becca saw him.

"Is Nicki asleep?" she asked in a concerned voice that turned his insides into a quivering mass.

"Yeah, she's out for the night," he answered stiffly. "I was just on my way to the kitchen."

"Why don't you talk to Colton?" she said. "You two haven't seen each other in a while, and I'm sure you have a lot of catching up to do. I'm off to bed." She stood, stretching. "'Night."

Cord watched her leave with a confused look on his face.

"So how's the ranching business?" Colton asked.

Cord collected his thoughts and sat down. "Busy."

"Yeah, that's how the computer business is."

Silence.

"Computer working okay?"

"Yeah, thanks," Cord answered absently. "Keeps track

of everything, just like you said it would. It's difficult making time to feed it the information, though. There's so much work to be done on the ranch.''

''Have you ever thought of letting the cowboys handle the work and you take care of the business end?''

''The outdoor work is what I enjoy.''

''Pa used to say if you were on a horse and had a rope in your hand, you were in hog heaven. I guess that hasn't changed.''

''No.''

Silence again.

''Heard from Clay lately?'' Colton asked abruptly.

''No. Since he moved to Alaska, we don't get to talk much.''

''We're a pathetic family. I haven't even seen Clay's girls. They're seven and four, I think. He didn't even bring them to Anette's funeral.''

''I guess he felt it wasn't appropriate.''

''Hell, we're family. When *is* it appropriate?''

Cord wondered what this was about—and then he knew. Becca. Becca was working her magic. She just didn't understand that the Prescotts weren't like other families.

''Becca's been talking to you,'' he said quietly.

''Yes, and she's right. We need to be closer.''

''Easier said than done.''

''Yeah, what am I thinking? We have Blanche for a mother.''

They smiled at each other. Cord rested his forearms on his knees. ''Can I ask you a personal question?''

''Sure.''

''What kind of relationship do you have with Becca?''

Colton rubbed the palms of his hands over his slacks. ''That's hard to explain, but I can see it's important to you.'' He paused, then went on. ''Since I'm in the computer business with her father, I've gotten to know her quite well. I've seen her go through the depths of hell and come out smiling. She has that ability—to take what life shoves at her and make the best of it. I admire that in her. She's intelligent, beautiful and strong. From time to time, I've wished our relationship would deepen into something else—but we're just friends." His eyes pierced Cord. "And I don't want to see her get hurt."

"Sounds like a warning." Cord met his look squarely.

"It is. Don't hurt her. She doesn't deserve that."

"I will never hurt Becca," Cord said quietly. "She's worked wonders with Nicki, and I will always be grateful for that."

"Come on, Cord, who are you trying to kid? You're not asking about Becca because of Nicki. You're asking for yourself. You're interested in her."

Cord stood. "I am, but I'm too old for her."

"Stay away from her then, and let her go back to Houston."

"I wish it was that simple."

"It is. You're not over Anette's death, and you know it. Don't drag Becca into your misery. She doesn't deserve that, either."

Cord didn't say anything. Everything Colton had said was true. Anette's death still weighed heavily upon him. But he couldn't put Becca out of his mind.

Colton got up. "I have an early meeting in the morning. I'd better go."

They shook hands. "Cord?"

"Hmm?"

"Don't encourage Becca. She's an affectionate, outgoing, giving person and—"

Cord broke in. "You don't have to tell me a thing about Becca."

"Good, so I don't have to worry."

"No, you don't have to worry."

Cord went to bed with that thought on his mind. He wouldn't encourage Becca. He wouldn't do anything with Becca—except think about her every minute of every day. That would be his own personal hell. As if he needed another one.

THE MORNING BROUGHT a complete change of plans. Nicki woke him by jumping on his bed. That hadn't happened in so long that for a second he thought he was dreaming.

"Daddy, Daddy, wake up!" she called brightly. "We've got to go."

Cord opened one eye and glanced at the clock. It was four in the morning. He flicked on his bedside lamp and pushed himself into a sitting position. "What's wrong, baby?"

"We've got to go riding. I'm all ready."

Cord noticed that she was dressed, although her top was on backward and her boots were on the wrong feet. He gathered her in his arms. "It's too early, and Daddy has to work today."

"You promised, Daddy. You promised you'd teach Becca to ride."

God, he was hoping she'd forgotten about that. How should he handle this? "Not today, baby. Daddy has to work." It was a feeble excuse, but it was all he could think of at this hour.

Nicki stuck out her lip. "I wanna go riding."

"Nicki…"

She started to sob, hard and loud.

Cord caught her face in his hands. "Stop that this instant."

At the sternness in Cord's voice, her sobs immediately ceased.

"I'll get Smithy to saddle Half Pint so you can ride."

"But Becca," she whimpered.

Cord took a long breath. "I'll get Smithy to saddle a horse for her and teach her a few things."

Nicki smiled.

He pushed back her tangled hair. "I don't want you crying to get your way. I won't have that. When I won't let you do something, I have a very good reason for it."

"'Kay, Daddy."

BECCA SAT BOLT UPRIGHT when she heard the crying. She quickly got out of bed and ran to Nicki's room. Nicki wasn't there. Her heart jolted against her ribs. Where was she? She noticed Cord's door was open, so she walked in—and stopped abruptly. Nicki was sitting on the bed talking to Cord, who had nothing on from the waist up. Her breath lodged in her throat as she stared at the dark blond hair that curled down his chest.

"Hi, Becca," Nicki said cheerfully. "We're gonna go riding."

Becca blinked. "I thought I heard you crying."

"You did," Cord said, trying to tear his eyes away from Becca in the T-shirt. Her breasts were pressed against the material and her dark hair was mussed around her face as if she'd been making... He cleared his throat. "She was just having a tantrum, trying to get her way."

"What did she want to do? Oh, Nicki, you're all dressed. Sort of."

"She wanted to go riding at four a.m. That's what the crying was all about."

Nicki shook her head. "I not do that anymore."

"Oh," Becca murmured. "Good."

Nicki clapped her hands. "We gonna go riding, and Smithy's gonna teach you. Daddy's gotta work."

Who the hell was Smithy? Then everything became clear. Cord was opting out of teaching her; he'd given the job to someone else. She took large strides over to the bed and plucked Nicki out. "Let's get you back to your room."

"Don't want to," Nicki protested. "I'm not sleepy."

"Then, you can keep me company," Becca said as she bundled the child into her room.

She looked down at Nicki's booted feet. "For heaven's sake, you've got your boots on the wrong feet."

"No, I don't," Nicki answered, pointing at her feet. "That's *my* feet."

Becca smiled as she slipped the boots off and curled up in bed, with Nicki beside her. She started to change Nicki's clothes, but the little girl was already dozing off.

How dare he! How dare he think he could just get rid of her. Just hand her off to someone else because he didn't want to be with her. That made her angry. *Well, forget it, Cordell Prescott, you won't find it quite so easy.*

BY THE TIME SHE AND NICKI went down for breakfast, she had a plan. Cord had said he'd show her the ranch, and she would hold him to it.

Edie was at the breakfast table, to Becca's surprise. Maybe she was making an effort to be part of the family. Becca hoped so.

"Della, do you know where Cord is working today?" she asked as she poured syrup over Nicki's pancakes.

"In the north pasture, in the bottom."

"Can you tell me how to get there?"

Della turned from the sink. "Why?"

"Because Cord said I could use one of the Jeeps to bring Nicki to have lunch with him."

"I see. It's kinda hard to explain."

"I know where it is," Edie told her. "I'll go with you."

"That's great." Becca beamed. "We'll make it a family outing. Want to come, Della?"

"Lord, no. I got too much to do around here."

"Can't it wait? We could pack a big picnic lunch and take it to the guys. Gus would probably like a hot sandwich or something."

"He does like my steak sandwiches, and I could fix chicken salad for us." Della was getting interested.

"Hot dog for me," Nicki piped up with a mouth full of pancake.

"Okay," Della said. "Let's do it. It's been ages since I've watched the cowboys in action."

By ten o'clock, they were packed and ready to go, except for one little problem. Nicki wanted to ride Half Pint. In the end, Becca decided to let her, especially since Edie and Della were with them. Surely they could handle any problem that arose. Smithy, the man who cared for the horses, as Becca found out, wanted to go along, but Becca assured him everything was under control.

There were a few tense moments as Becca adjusted to driving a stick shift again. Della sat in the back, Edie in front. They just smiled tolerantly at the jerky ride. They were very good sports. Soon she got the hang of it and they were off, with Nicki racing ahead on Half Pint.

She followed Della's directions, and they drove through pasture after pasture of cattle. She'd never seen so many in her life. She had to stop repeatedly to let the animals cross the road. They took their time, unafraid of the Jeep. Each pasture was fenced off with a cattle guard so she didn't have to open gates. Becca had thought the trip would take maybe fifteen minutes, but thirty minutes later, they were still driving and there didn't seem any end in sight. Grassland gave way to bushy creeks, and then suddenly they drove into a clearing and Becca knew they'd arrived. Cowboys and cattle were everywhere. Several cattle were milling about in a pen. Cowboys were riding into the large herd in the pasture and separating cows with calves and guiding them toward the pen. A Jeep with a trailer behind it was parked to one side. The lowing of cattle filled the air, and excitement tingled along her nerves.

Nicki galloped to where Cord sat astride a big red-and-white paint horse. The tingling inside her became a jangling of sensations. God, he was so handsome—everything she'd ever dreamed about in a man.

She put the Jeep in gear and drove slowly forward. Cord had noticed Nicki and nudged his horse toward her. Then he saw the Jeep. It was all too obvious that Cord wasn't pleased. He removed his hat and wiped his hand across his forehead in a weary gesture, and in that instant Becca wished she'd gone back to Houston.

Cord didn't want her here.

CHAPTER NINE

BECCA PARKED THE JEEP near the other one, and they got out. She and Della removed the basket of food and the ice chest with the drinks and set it on the flatbed trailer. Gus rode over, followed by three dogs with mottled blue coats.

"What brings you ladies here?"

"We brought you lunch," Della answered, and Becca was glad. She felt so foolish; she'd come to get back at Cord and that was such a teenage thing. She could see that now. The man had made it plain how he felt, and she had to accept it. When she returned to the house she'd pack her things and leave. She hoped Nicki would understand.

Just then, Cord and Nicki galloped over.

"The ladies brought us lunch," Gus told Cord. "Ain't that nice?"

"Yes, very," Cord replied in a cool voice.

Nicki wriggled down from the saddle, and Becca caught her before she hit the ground.

"Nicki, you know better than to get off your horse without someone to help you," Cord reprimanded. "And never leave your horse untethered. You know better than that, too."

"Yes, Daddy," Nicki said in a pitiful voice.

Cord immediately swung from the saddle and helped her tie Half Pint to the trailer. Becca could see he didn't like snapping at his daughter. She knew it was a reaction to her unwanted presence.

"We got a few more calves to brand, vaccinate and tag, then we'll stop for lunch," Gus said. "You ladies can watch the fun." Gus clicked his tongue. "Let's go, boys," he said to the dogs.

"That's Gus's dogs—Bubba, Beau and Boo-Boo," Nicki said as she crawled up beside Becca on the trailer. "They're work dogs, so you can't play with them."

"Why is that?" Becca asked.

Nicki shrugged.

Della spoke up. "Gus is very particular about his dogs. They're Australian Blue Heelers and known for their expertise in handling cattle. Gus believes if you pamper them, they won't work, but he pampers them more than anyone."

Becca tried to listen, but her focus was on Cord as he remounted and followed Gus to the pen. A cowboy opened the gate and they rode in, the dogs waiting outside. Within minutes, Cord and Gus had separated the mother cows from their babies. Another cowboy opened the gate on the other side, and the cows were herded into a different pasture. The cows bellowed in an agitated manner and ran along the fence line trying to get to their babies.

Becca's attention was diverted back to the pen as the action started. She noticed a fire just outside the fence with a branding iron stuck in it. Gus and Cord dismounted, then Cord waded in among the calves and grabbed one around the back legs, jerking him to the ground. Things happened so fast that Becca had a hard time keeping up. A cowboy handed Gus the iron and he seared a Triple Creek brand on the calf's hind rump. At the same moment, another cowboy handed Cord a needle and something that looked like a gun. Cord injected the calf and snapped a tag in his ear.

"What's he doing?" she asked Della.

"Vaccinating against disease and putting a tag in his ear to show when he was injected. As soon as a calf's born, a tag with its mother's number is put in its ear. That way, the calves can be identified.''

Gus knelt down with his pocketknife. "Gus is castrating the calf to keep him from becoming a bull," Della told her. "When the calf is weaned from its mother, he goes into a feed lot for several months, then he's shipped to the slaughter and packing houses. It's how meat gets into the supermarket.''

In a matter of seconds, the whole thing was over. Cord let the calf up, and the cowboys quickly shooed the calf out the gate to his mother. Cord grabbed another and the process started again. It seemed a bit inhumane, but she knew it was necessary. The calves had to be castrated, and the vaccinating kept down disease. As a doctor she understood that. The tag and branding was for identification. Cattle rustling must be a constant danger with so many cattle. Joe Bates's appearance had underlined that particular reality.

It was all fascinating. Cord worked with a speed and expertise that probably took years to learn. Soon the calves were all vaccinated and branded, and Cord and Gus saddled up and rode back to the women, the other cowboys hard on their heels. Della opened the basket and spread out the food. The cowboys professed their thanks as they each took a steak sandwich and a drink. Several spared Becca a knowing glance, but she merely smiled back. They all wore shabby jeans, boots and tattered hats, their skin was leathery from the sun. They epitomized a dying saga—that of the Old West.

Nicki ate half her hot dog and fell asleep. Becca pulled the child against her, letting her nap. She'd had a busy morning.

As the cowboys sat in the grass eating, Della and Edie joined them. Edie seemed to know many of them, since she asked about their families. Cord sat with the group, while Becca sat on the trailer holding Nicki and feeling alone. She couldn't eat; she felt far too miserable.

Suddenly Cord got to his feet and walked toward her. "Let me take Nicki so you can eat," he said brusquely.

"No, she's fine and I'm not hungry."

He sat on the trailer. "Why not?" he asked, more kindly this time.

She couldn't hold everything in anymore. "I know you don't want me here, but I—I wanted to see something of ranching before I left."

Cord felt his throat close up. "You're leaving?"

She hadn't meant it to come out now, in front of everyone, but nothing was going as she'd planned. "Yes, Nicki will be fine and I need to get back to Houston."

He drew a deep breath. "Does this have something to do with Colton?"

Frowning, she tucked her hair behind her ear. "No, it has nothing to do with Colton."

"Then…"

She stared directly at him. "Then, what?"

Cord looked up at the blue sky, saw the bright sun and heard the cowboys talking, but all he felt was the pain in his chest. If she left, his world would come apart. He didn't know much, but he knew that. He was tired of all the confusion, all the aching inside him. Somehow, when he was with her, it wasn't so bad. So letting himself live again couldn't be bad, either.

His gaze swung back to her. "Then, don't go."

She swallowed at the suffering in his eyes, but she had to ask. "Why?"

"Nicki needs time to adjust," he lied with as much dignity as he could.

And so do I.

Becca realized he was lying—but she didn't mind. There was something happening between them, some emotional connection, and they both were aware of it. She could cope as long as he didn't push her away

"Will you teach me to ride and not pass me off to Smithy?"

A grin ruffled his mustache. "Sure, and I'm sorry about that. I—"

Before he could finish, a rider emerged from the woods and galloped toward Cord. Becca thought it was a man at first, but it turned out to be a woman. She was easily six foot, stoutly built and probably in her late forties. She drew up in front of Cord.

"Howdy, Mona," Cord said.

Mona tipped her hat and stared at Becca holding Nicki.

"Oh, this is Dr. Becca Talbert." He made the introduction. "She's spending some time with Nicki. And Becca, this is Mona Tibbetts. Her ranch adjoins ours."

"Nice to meet you, Mona," Becca said, smiling.

"Likewise," Mona answered. "You seem awful young for a doctor."

"I hear that a lot."

"Glad Cord found someone to help the kid. She's been having a rough time."

"Yeah," Becca said, gathering Nicki closer. "We're working on all that."

"Good," Mona murmured, her eyes moving back to Cord. "That black bull I bought from Hudson has broken the fence and gotten into your pasture."

"Dammit, Mona! I don't want him breeding my cows. He's got a wild streak and I don't want that in my cattle."

"I know, Cord, and I'm sorry. You warned me and I wouldn't listen." She shook her head. "He had such good markings, though."

Cord stood. "Do you know where he is?"

"No, but my cowhands are looking for him. I just wanted to let you know."

"Thanks, Mona. If we run across him, we'll pen him."

"Okay. Just call me." She turned the horse abruptly and rode off.

Nicki stirred and opened her eyes.

Cord poked her in the ribs. "Hey, sleepyhead. How am I gonna make a cowhand out of you if you sleep all the time?"

"Daddy," she said impatiently. "I'm hungry."

"Della brought some homemade cookies, and I believe she has some milk for you." He reached to take Nicki out of Becca's arms and as he did, their eyes locked and everything faded away except for the feeling that flowed between them.

"Daddy," Nicki said again. Cord quickly gathered her into his arms and they walked over to the group still sitting in the grass, listening to Gus tell his stories. Becca didn't hear much. Her heart was singing too loudly.

Soon after that, the guys went back to work, and she helped Della and Edie pack up the remains of the lunch, which consisted of wrappings and empty cans. The cowboys had a healthy appetite. Becca was secretly glad when Della and Edie decided to stay for a while. The cowboys herded more cows and calves into the pen. It was thrilling to watch Cord. He was so natural on the horse, so in control. She couldn't take her eyes off him. The process with the calves started again and time flew by. Soon the last calf in the pasture was taken care of and the portable pens were taken apart and put on the trailer.

"Oh my, look at the time," Della said. "I've got to get back and fix supper."

"Why don't you and Edie take the Jeep?" Cord said.

"Becca can ride with me. I want her to get the feel of a horse."

"Sure thing," Della answered. "See ya'll back at the house."

They clambered into the Jeep, which sputtered to life and roared off. Nicki was on Half Pint, ready to go. Becca glanced up at Cord on the big horse. "Is there a correct way to get on this thing?"

Cord's mustache twitched. "Yeah," he said, sliding his boot from the stirrup. "Put your foot in there and swing up behind me."

"Which foot?"

"The left one."

"Put my foot in there and swing up," she repeated. "Just like that?"

"Yeah."

"It's easy, Becca," Nicki said.

She looked up again and Cord seemed a hundred feet in the air. How could this be easy?

Sensing her nervousness, Cord held out his hand. "Come on, give me your hand and I'll pull you up."

That was all she needed. She placed her foot in the stirrup and gave Cord her hand, and with one smooth movement she was on the back of his horse. Her arms locked tight around Cord's waist. The ground had never seemed so far away.

"Becca, you have to loosen your arms. I can't breathe." Laughter edged every word.

She swallowed. "Do you have to?"

"Occasionally."

She slowly loosened her grip, then the horse moved and her arms tightened again.

"Relax," Cord coaxed. "Apache won't do anything I don't want him to do."

Apache! Oh God, she was on a horse named Apache.

Slowly they began to trot, and the movement of the horse reminded her of being in a boat—an easy flowing rhythm she could identify with. Her body relaxed as the creak of leather soothed her nerves and the musky scent of horse filled her nostrils. She reveled in the hard muscles of Cord's chest and back. Oh, she liked this.

The scenery was spectacular with green grasses, tall oaks, birds and cattle here and there. The landscape brought a sense of peace that was unequaled.

"You okay?" Cord asked.

"Yes," she answered. "It's so beautiful out here."

"Yep, there's nothing like it. I've always loved the outdoors. Clay and Colton were different. They preferred to stay in the house and read or play games. I hated school, but they loved it. I didn't like the confinement."

"So what did you do after high school?"

"Went into the army."

That was a surprise. She had assumed he'd never left the ranch.

"It was a learning experience, and what I learned was that I never wanted to be anywhere but on this ranch. It's in my blood, as Pa used to say."

"Why is the ranch called Triple Creek?"

"Three major creeks run through the property. My ancestors were looking for a good water supply and they found it here. There're also some ground-fed springs. Water's important to a rancher."

Becca heard the love and pride in his voice. It was clear that his heart was in this land.

Nicki raced ahead and shouted, "C'mon!"

"She's very good with a horse," Becca remarked. "She takes after you in that."

"Yeah," he replied somberly.

"Why didn't Anette like her to ride? Nicki obviously loves it."

"Because Anette didn't want her involved in anything she couldn't participate in, too, and she was deadly scared of horses. Anette was sacred of a lot of things. I guess Nicki was about two years old when I just took her and put her on a horse. Anette was furious. She said if anything happened to Nicki she'd never forgive me. She had this fear of Nicki getting hurt. She was so protective of her.... That's why it doesn't make sense that she'd kill herself. Nothing about her death makes sense."

"It does seem strange," Becca said.

They rode in silence for a while, and Becca wondered what had happened to Anette Prescott. What had made her do such a terrible thing? The truth would probably never be known.

"How you doing back there?" Cord asked.

"Great," she answered, and her arms tightened instinctively around him. Would he ever get over his wife's death? Would there ever be room for another woman in his life?

They rode up to the barns, where Mona and several cowhands were waiting for them.

Mona glanced at Becca on the back of the horse. "Something wrong?"

"No," Cord said. "Just giving Becca a tour of the ranch."

"Oh, well, we found the bull and we've got him in your pen. I'll pick him up in the morning, if that's okay."

"Sure, no problem."

"I'd do it this evening, but we have that cattlemen's meeting tonight."

"Damn, I'd forgotten about that."

"You are going, aren't you?"

Cord sighed. It was the last thing he felt like doing. He'd

rather be with Becca. Still… "I'm the president. I have to be there."

"I'll see you tonight, then." She tipped her hat to Becca and rode off, the cowhands behind her.

"Daddy, Daddy, watch," Nicki called.

Cord turned the horse toward Nicki. She threw her leg over the back of the saddle and slid quickly to the ground.

"See?" Nicki smiled. "I can get off all by myself. I'm not little anymore."

"I can see that."

Becca was wondering how *she* was going to get off. If a child could do it, she resolved, then so could she. She did as Nicki had done—swung her leg over the back of the horse and slid to the ground. But she moved too quickly and lost her balance, falling backward. She landed on her rear, feeling more than a little undignified.

Cord dismounted. "Are you all right?" he asked, but she could hear the laughter in his voice. Nicki laughed without restraint, and Becca sent her an exaggerated look of disapproval.

"Yes," she answered, as he helped her to her feet. She brushed off her backside. "I just bruised my pride."

They stood staring at each other. She finally cleared her throat. "Thanks for the ride. I enjoyed it."

"My pleasure, ma'am."

A warm fluttering started in her stomach, and she couldn't tear her eyes away. She wanted him to kiss her so badly….

Nicki leaned against Cord's leg. "I'm tired, Daddy."

Cord looked down at his daughter. "Who's gonna unsaddle your horse?"

"Gus will," she mumbled.

"No, Gus didn't ride your horse. You did. Now you have to take care of him. He has to be rubbed down and fed."

"'Kay, Daddy."

Becca thought that was a little unfeeling, but she knew Cord was trying to teach Nicki about responsibility. She also knew that he'd do most of the work.

Becca made her way to the house, as father and daughter led their horses to the barn. She wished Cord didn't have to go out tonight. She wanted to be with him.

But there was always tomorrow, she consoled herself.

THE NEXT MORNING Cord hung around the house waiting for Mona to pick up the bull. Becca and Nicki went out to look at the animal. He was massive with enormous horns and he pawed at the ground in anger. Evidently he didn't like being penned up.

Mona drove up soon afterward with a trailer. She immediately began talking to Cord, so Becca left them to their business. Nicki wanted to see Half Pint; hand in hand, she and Becca strolled into the pasture. Half Pint was grazing some distance away and wouldn't come when Nicki called. Nicki ran back to the barn to get a feed bucket.

As Becca turned to follow, she saw the black bull—and he was running directly toward her. Fear shot through her and she fell instinctively to the ground. The bull charged over her. She felt the heaviness and the sweaty heat of the animal, and her breath locked in her chest.

Stark terror rippled along Cord's spine as he saw the bull run over Becca. He dashed over to Apache and jumped into the saddle. "Gus!" he shouted, swiftly turning his horse toward the bull. Gus immediately joined him. The bull charged Apache, but Cord managed to move out of the way. He pulled out his rope and swung it at the bull, and between him and Gus, they drove the bull back into the pen.

Cord had one thought—to get to Becca. She *had* to be

okay. He was out of the saddle before Apache came to a stop, and threw himself down beside her. "Becca, Becca," he murmured, gently rolling her over.

"Oh," she moaned, and sat up.

Cord wrapped his arms around her. "Thank God you're okay." He drew back. "Did he step on you?" He glanced at her body.

Becca brushed grass from her blouse and jeans. "No, I don't think so." Her voice came out hoarse and unsteady.

Cord swept her into his arms and carried her to the barn. Mona hurried toward them.

"Cord, I'm sorry. I have no idea how this happened."

Cord set Becca on a bale of hay. "I want to know how that gate came open and I want that bull off this ranch."

Gus laid a hand on his shoulder. "She's fine, boy. Calm down."

Cord took a long breath. "Mona, I want that damn bull off this property—now. Gus will help you load him. I want him gone. Do you understand me?"

"Sure, Cord," Mona answered, and turned away.

Nicki came running over and crawled up beside Becca. "Oh, that mean bull! I don't like him."

Becca slipped her arms around Nicki, just needing to hold on to someone. Her body was quivering and she couldn't make it stop. Cord knelt down, gazing into her eyes.

"Are you all right?"

"Yeah." She tried to smile and failed.

"Let's get you to the house."

She staggered to her feet but her legs buckled, and Cord scooped her up and started toward the house. Nicki ran behind them.

"What happened?" Della asked as they came through the back door.

"That bull ran over Becca and Daddy's real mad." Nicki spoke up before Cord could.

"Oh my God."

"I'm taking her upstairs."

Once they reached her room, Cord carefully placed her on the bed. "Are you sure you're okay?" he asked in a worried voice.

"I'm just a little jittery, that's all," she assured him.

Della, Edie and Nicki entered a moment later. Della had a cup in her hand.

"We brought you a hot..." Nicki glanced up at Della. "What is it?"

Della gave Becca the cup. "A hot toddy. It'll calm you down."

"Thanks, Della." She took a sip. It was definitely brandy and something else—and it did calm her. Her body hadn't stopped trembling, but with Cord looking at her so tenderly, she didn't mind.

"I'll be back in a minute," Cord said suddenly, and left the room.

He met Gus at the back door. "Is that bull gone?"

"Yep, and Mona's pretty upset. You were kinda hard on her."

"One blow from that bull's hooves, and Becca could be dead. I don't take that lightly."

Gus removed his hat and scratched his head. "It was a bad thing, but the doc's okay."

"How did the gate get open?" Cord asked.

Gus shrugged. "It wasn't latched properly and that bull's good at finding holes."

"Still."

"It was an accident." Gus watched him for a second, then added, "You've been champin' at the bit lately, and it's time to let that horse run."

Cord scowled fiercely. "What the hell are you talking about?"

"You got some heart-bustin' feelin's for the doc."

Cord didn't say anything because he couldn't deny it.

"I'd better get back to work," Gus muttered. "I'll check on those calves we worked yesterday and see that Burt gets started cuttin' that hay, 'cause I know *you'll* be hanging around the house."

Cord walked around to the patio and sat down. He rubbed his face with a shaky hand. Gus was right. His heart was about to burst inside with the feelings he had for Becca. He'd never felt like this about any woman. He gazed off to the pool and watched as the sun glistened off the water. But all he could see was the bull charging straight for Becca. He would see that for a very long time.

He could ride and rope with the best of them, but he was powerless to stop a two-thousand-pound bull. That chilling thought had gripped him as he rode frantically for the animal. His only thought was to keep the beast away from Becca—to keep her safe. *Heart-busting'*. Oh God, he loved her. He'd known it in that instant as he felt his heart being ripped from his body. It didn't matter that she was too young. Nothing mattered but the way he felt.

He took a tortured breath. It was a relief to admit it, but beyond that he didn't know what to do. He knew she was attracted to him, but her life was in the city and his was here. He had brought one city girl to Triple Creek, and he'd sworn he would never do that again. Where did that leave them? Becca wasn't like Anette, though. She didn't seem to be afraid of anything.

Yet they were so different, and sexual chemistry couldn't change that. Could love?

CHAPTER TEN

BECCA SPENT THE REST of the day being pampered by everyone in the house, especially Cord and Nicki. She told them repeatedly that she was fine, but Cord insisted she take it easy. She spent the afternoon on the patio and found herself alone for a few minutes. Cord had gone to answer the phone, while Nicki was kicking a ball around.

Blanche came through the French doors with a glass in her hand. She wore tight stretch pants and a tank top. She sat in a chair opposite Becca, the ice in her glass tinkling, and crossed her legs. "Heard you had a little mishap, sugar."

"Yes," Becca said guardedly, wondering where Blanche had heard it because everyone seemed to avoid her.

"Did it scare the crap out of you?"

Becca's eyes narrowed. "What are you getting at?"

"Time for you to go back to the city, don't you think?"

"You've said that to me more than once. Why do you want to get rid of me?"

She met Becca's eyes boldly. "Because you're not the woman for Cord."

"Why, Blanche? Why am I not the woman for Cord?"

"You're not, so leave before anything else happens to you." Blanche stood to go back inside, but Becca stopped her.

"Why do you have to be so...so hard and cruel?"

"That's me, sugar, and you'd do well to remember it."

Becca shook her head. "I don't think that's you at all. It's just a front you put up so no one'll get near you, not even your sons." She paused, then added, "I've seen you looking out the window when we've been doing things."

"In your mind that means what?"

"That you care more than you want anyone to believe."

Blanche gave a fake-sounding laugh. "Oh, sugar, you haven't got a clue about me or Cord. This ranch is his life. Anette couldn't get him away from here and neither will you."

"Is that it? You're afraid I'll persuade Cord to leave?"

From the look on Blanche's face, she knew she was right. Blanche was afraid of losing Cord. Becca moved to the edge of her chair. "I would never ask Cord to leave Triple Creek. He loves this place, and love is about giving, not taking."

"Every love I've known was about taking and it's a lesson that's served me well over the years."

"Has it? Then, why aren't you happy?"

Blanche took a swallow of her drink. "Look around you, sugar. Everything you see belongs to me—and that makes me happy."

"I don't think so," Becca told her. "I think you'd love it if your sons called you Mom. I think you'd love to be part of their lives. That's why you're desperately trying to hold on to the last piece of family you have—Cord."

"Shut up," Blanche hissed, and stormed into the house.

Well, well, well, Becca thought. Blanche loved her sons, but she would never tell them. Why was that so difficult for her? Maybe it had something to do with her upbringing, or maybe she was just afraid. She was certainly afraid of losing Cord; that was obvious from her reaction. But Becca knew that Blanche would never admit it.

THE NEXT FEW DAYS passed quickly. Cord was very attentive and he no longer seemed angry at himself for being attracted to her. She and Cord had very little time alone, however. Edie was now eating every meal with them and even Blanche had made a couple of appearances at the dinner table. On the third evening, they sat in the den and listened to Nicki, who regaled them with stories about her day. Then she insisted on playing the animal game and chose animals that had to be acted out by each person. She said Edie was to be a mule and Blanche a goat. The ladies didn't demur. They played along, and by the time it was over they were all laughing, Blanche as much as anyone. Becca thought this was the way it should be—laughter should always fill this house. And she had to give both Edie and Blanche credit.

Cord kept his word and taught her to ride. The next morning he brought out a reddish mare. "This is Ginger," he told her, rubbing the horse's neck. "She's gentle and affable. You shouldn't have a problem with her."

Becca started to laugh.

"What's so funny?" Cord asked.

"My best friend's name is Ginger."

"I'm sorry, but that's her name."

"I can't call her Ginger. How about…Ginny?"

"Sure, whatever." There was laughter in his eyes. "Come on," he invited. "Rub her head and neck. Get acquainted with her."

Becca did just that. The animal was so gentle Becca couldn't help falling in love with her.

"Okay, time to ride," Cord said. "You sit in the saddle and I'll ride behind you. That way you can learn to control her." She climbed into the saddle without mishap, then Cord swung up effortlessly behind her and they were off at a slow canter.

"A cowboy uses the neck rein technique," Cord told her. "That way, he can hold the reins in one hand and use the other to rope or do whatever he has to." He held both reins in his left hand. "To turn the horse to the right, you merely lay the reins on the right side of her neck and Ginger—Ginny—will go in that direction. Likewise for the left. Pull the reins toward you to stop." He demonstrated, and Ginny reacted instantly to the touch and pull of the reins. She followed his instructions, and it was the most exhilarating experience of her life. With Cord's breath on her hair and his arms around her, she thought she could do this forever.

Each day she got better at controlling the horse. Riding was a matter of balance, which she was learning. She couldn't wait to get Nicki up in the mornings, dressed, fed and to the stables. One of the first things Cord taught her was that if you ride, you take care of your horse and equipment. Handling a saddle wasn't easy, but she was determined and soon she mastered the skill, although Cord or Smithy always ensured she had the belts girded tight. The saddles were kept in the barn on long wooden sawhorses. Each cowboy knew exactly where his spot was and everyone respected the property of others. As Gus put it, *A cowboy don't mess with another cowboy's stuff.*

Becca was beginning to know the cowboys by name: Shorty, Snuffy, Hank, Rocky, Billy Bob, Joe Bob, Clint, Dusty, Big Jim, Little Jim, Burt and Weazel. They were between the ages of twenty and sixty. None seemed to be married, though some were divorced, and they lived in the bunkhouse attached to the barn. Saturday was their night to dress up, go into Houston and hit the bars and dance halls looking for a woman. They talked quite openly about their escapades. Clint and Dusty were the Casanovas in the group, and it was a given that they wouldn't return to the bunkhouse on Saturday night. But the cowboys were always betting on who else would "get lucky."

Becca enjoyed their antics and camaraderie. She realized she should return to Houston, but she didn't do anything about it. She and Cord were becoming closer and closer, and she wanted to spend some time alone with him. With Edie and Nicki around, privacy was nil. Soon, she kept telling herself. It would happen soon. She'd waited a long time to experience these feelings and she didn't have to question her needs or desires.

She knew what she wanted. She wanted Cord.

CORD WENT THROUGH EACH DAY as if in a dream. Becca loved to ride and she seemed to love the ranch and the cowboys. For their part, the cowboys adored her. He had a hard time getting them away from the barn to actually go and do their work. They were all eager to help if she needed anything and they were gonna be some lovesick pups when she left. Not to mention him. Mrs. Witherspoon had called twice asking about her return date, but he'd told her to take a little more time with pay. He kept postponing it, but he knew Becca had to leave. Her life was in the city. He'd sworn he would never put himself in this position again, but Becca was different. She had a big heart and a loving spirit and everyone responded to that—even Blanche. Blanche was now playing with her granddaughter... something Cord had thought he'd never see. Edie was riding again, and they were having meals as a family. All because of Becca.

And his heart, which had been closed for so long, was slowly opening. He wasn't sure what to do about it. He decided to take it day by day, hoping when the time came, that he would have the strength to let her go.

BECCA PACKED A LUNCH prepared by Della and Edie for
the cowboys. Della helped her put the heavy ice chest and
basket in the Jeep. Nicki, of course, wanted to take Half
Pint, and Becca agreed when Edie decided to ride with
Nicki. The child was very comfortable on her horse, but
Becca worried about the risks she took.

She followed some distance behind Edie and Nicki. They
were going to a different part of the ranch today where the
cowboys were spraying the cattle with a medication against
flies, ticks and other pests. Hooping, hollering and distressed mooing could be heard before they reached the site.
The pens were set up in a clearing and cattle were herded
in, sprayed and released.

Several cowboys were milling about the campsite. Becca
parked the Jeep and joined them, surprised to see Mona
there. The older woman apologized for what had happened
with the bull.

"It was an accident," Becca told her.

"I know, but I'm just glad you're okay. I took that bull
to auction and sold him right away. I should've listened to
Cord."

Nicki rode up to Becca and jumped off her horse. "I'm
hungry."

"We have to get the food out of the Jeep first. Can you
wait?"

"'Kay," Nicki chirped, and ran to Gus to tell him something.

"Cord and I thought we'd never hear that again." Becca
laughed. "Now we can't seem to fill her up."

"You've worked wonders with her," Mona said.
"Cord's lucky to have a brother with such an understanding
girlfriend."

Becca didn't know quite how to answer that, so she
didn't. It wasn't any of Mona's business, anyway. Soon the

rest of the cowboys rode over with enthusiastic greetings and shy grins. Dusty and Clint hauled the food and drinks out of the Jeep before she had to ask. Cord dismounted and walked toward her. Just the sight of him sent a shock of excitement right down to her toes. She was amazed at how her body reacted to him and no one else.

"I see you don't need any help." Cord smiled as he watched the cowboys quickly spreading out the food.

"I think they're very hungry." She smiled back, lost for a moment in the light in his eyes.

"Hot damn," Gus interrupted. "Fried chicken and biscuits. That Della's a peach of a gal."

"You should be grateful," Becca told him as they sat on the grass. Gus's dogs lay beside him, waiting for scraps. "She and Edie fried chicken all morning."

"Edie, I'd give you a big kiss if I didn't have a wad of chewing tobacco in my mouth."

"No, thanks, Gus. I'll pass," Edie muttered, and everyone laughed.

"Do you know how bad that tobacco is for you?" Becca had to ask.

"C'mon, Doc, don't preach at me."

"I've seen men with half their faces removed because of cancer caused by chewing tobacco."

"Ain't nobody taking part of my face off. I'm dyin' with my boots on. Besides, at my age it's a roll of the dice, anyway."

"Just so you know the dangers."

Gus turned and spit the tobacco in the grass. The dogs sniffed it, then settled back down. "Satisfied, Doc?"

"Don't do it for me. Do it for yourself and Della."

"Right now I'm doing it 'cause I wanna eat fried chicken."

There was another burst of laughter, and then everyone

started to eat. Nicki sat in her lap with a chicken leg and a biscuit. Soon her head nodded against Becca's chest.

"My child always seems to fall sleep on you," Cord said.

"I don't mind," Becca said, licking her fingers. She was beginning to love Nicki so much, she wondered how she'd be able to leave her. She didn't want to think about leaving Cord. Tonight, she vowed, they would find time alone to talk and...the *and* part made her feel warm all over.

Mona asked Cord a question and that brief moment was gone. After lunch the cowboys headed back to finish spraying the cattle, but not before they'd helped clean everything up. Mona left, saying she had her own work to do. She apologized again for the incident with the bull. Nicki awoke and wanted her chicken leg, which Becca had ready for her.

Once the cowboys had finished spraying, they dismantled the portable pens and moved on to another pasture. Becca, Edie and Nicki followed the procession, reluctant to go back to the house. Becca enjoyed watching; the horses seemed to know exactly what to do and when, and the rider became part of his horse. One day she wanted to ride like that.

The dogs were also a pleasure to watch. They worked on commands from Gus, darting in and out of the herd, making sure that no cow or calf broke free.

The clouds grew dark, and Cord decided it was time to call it a day. Again Edie and Nicki rode ahead and Becca followed in the Jeep. The cowboys were still collecting the pens and storing them on the trailer. A few raindrops hit the windshield, and Becca hoped they could all make it back to the barn before the rain started in earnest.

The brakes seemed weak. She rounded a curve in the dirt road and applied the brake, but her foot went right to the floorboard. She pumped the brake several times, but it was useless. In her panic, she veered off the road and began to roll into a ravine. She tried to guide the Jeep back, but she was going downhill so fast that her efforts were jerky. She saw the huge oak a moment before the Jeep crashed into it.

Her head hit the steering wheel and sharp pain ripped through her. Everything floated around her in a fog. *God, please, don't let me lose consciousness.* But she couldn't focus, and try as she might, she couldn't stop the blackness that overtook her.

Cord.

CORD LEFT THE COWBOYS at the shed storing the pens, then rode toward the barn, eager to see Becca. He'd only been away from her for a little while, but even that was too long. Tonight he'd make time for the two of them. If he didn't kiss her and soon, he'd go crazy.

Before he could reach the barn, Nicki came charging toward him on Half Pint. "Daddy, Daddy," she shouted, and he immediately knew something was wrong.

"Whoa, slow down, baby," he said, stopping her. "What is it?"

"Becca, Becca…"

"What about Becca?" He had an uneasy feeling in his gut.

"She, she—we looked…and…"

Nicki wasn't making any sense; he was relieved when Edie rode up. "What's going on, Edie?"

"Becca didn't come back."

"What do you mean, she didn't come back?" That uneasiness turned into outright fear.

"We waited here for half an hour or so, then we rode back. We couldn't find her anywhere."

"She has to be *somewhere* between the site and the ranch!"

"I know, but she's not on the road."

"Daddy, where's Becca?" Nicki wailed.

He rode closer and put his hand over hers. "Go to the house with Edie and I'll head out to look for Becca."

"No, Daddy, no! I wanna look for Becca, too."

"Baby, listen to me. It's fixing to pour down rain, and I want you to go with Edie. I'll find Becca."

"You promise."

"I promise."

He nodded to Edie, then turned Apache and rode hell-bent for the shed. "Gus!" he shouted.

"Yeah?" Gus came out of the shed.

"Saddle up."

"What the hell for? It's startin' to rain."

"Becca didn't come back," Cord said urgently. "Something's happened and we have to go after her."

Gus whirled around. "Sure thing. I'll get the boys."

Within minutes they were saddled and ready to ride. Cord gave orders to check the road on both sides from the area where they'd been working to the barn. The rain began, a hard, driving rain, and darkness fell, hindering their efforts. An hour later they still hadn't found her. Cord thought he'd go out of his mind.

"Where the hell could she be?" he asked Gus.

"Don't know. The rain's washed away all the tracks. Ain't much we can do in the dark."

"Like hell." Cord exploded. "If anyone wants a job on this ranch, they'd better keep looking."

"Didn't say nobody's quittin'. We'd all ride through a blizzard for that gal. Just sayin' the weather and darkness ain't helping."

"She's just farther off the road than we think. Let's start

again, and remember to tell everyone to fire three shots if—
when—they find her.''

"They know the signal. Don't worry. We'll find her.''

Another two-hour search proved futile. The rain had
stopped, but it was difficult to move a horse through the
woods in pitch-black darkness. Cord was wearing a slicker
but his boots and hat were soaked. Apache was also wet
and tired, but Cord kept pushing him on. He *had* to find
Becca. He cursed himself for not having had someone drive
with her. After all, she didn't know this ranch. He
should've taken better— Suddenly a deer jumped in front
of them, and Apache reared onto his back legs.

"Down, boy, down.'' Cord talked to him in a soothing
voice, trying to calm him, but he felt just as nervous as the
horse. *Where was Becca?* Fear gripped him like a vise, a
fear he remembered well. He'd felt it the day Blanche had
said "Something's wrong with Anette.'' But this was different. This feeling encompassed his heart, his body, his
soul. And he knew what it was—love like he'd never
known before. He'd admitted it earlier, but now he knew
it beyond a shadow of a doubt. Becca was younger and a
city girl, but none of that seemed to matter anymore. He
just wanted to see her face again. *Oh God, please let her
be okay.*

BECCA AWOKE to a throbbing in her head. She raised her
hand to her forehead, and pain shot through her. Something
dripped onto her hand. Blood. Everything came back with
startling clarity. The brakes. The tree. As a doctor, she
thought of neck and back injury, but she felt she was safe
in that area. There wasn't much she could do. She had to
staunch the bleeding; that was her next concern. It was so
dark, though. She felt for the glove compartment and
opened it, then fished around until she found a rag and

something else—a flashlight. She held the rag to her head and wondered where she was and why no one had found her.

She winced as she tried to move, but managed to get out of the Jeep. She trained the light on the vehicle and saw that it was smashed against the tree and almost completely covered with bushes. She didn't even remember running through the bushes. The ground was wet, so that meant it had rained. God, where was she? Should she try to walk? Which way should she go? She saw no alternative and began to trudge up the ravine until she became so dizzy she had to stop. She took a couple of shaky breaths and sank to the ground as the darkness wrapped around her. She held the rag to her forehead and flicked the light on and off hoping someone would see it. The wind whistled through the trees with an eerie sound and lightning flickered across the sky. Another rainstorm wasn't far off.

She remembered another time she'd been in a rainstorm—the day she'd found out she was Emily's daughter. Filled with so many tumultuous emotions, she'd taken Owen's boat out in a storm, trying to run from the truth, but the truth was inescapable—like her love for Cord. She loved him and she had to tell him. Emily had told her she'd know when love was right. She finally understood what Emily meant. There was no indecision or doubt; she knew Cordell Prescott was her soul mate. Now she had to convince him of that...but first he had to find her.

She flashed the light several times, pointing it at the sky, then turned it off. She didn't want to run down the battery. She did that every ten minutes or so. She knew Cord was out there and he *would* find her. She just had to wait.

CORD GUIDED APACHE through the bushes, trying not to think the worst, but if she was hurt and needed medical help, time was running out. An armadillo appeared in front of them, and Cord pulled his horse to an abrupt halt.

He patted Apache. "Just an armadillo, boy." He looked down to see if there were more and noticed something in the bushes. He slid down from the saddle and began to drag the bushes aside. His breath caught in his throat when he saw the Jeep rammed against the tree. The passenger door was open and Becca wasn't inside. He looked in, resting his hand on the doorframe, and drew back as he felt something wet. It had to be blood. Oh God.

He glanced around. She couldn't be far. Then he saw it—a light flashing some distance away. He started to run, following the light. When he saw her, he sped up, then fell down beside her, his heart pounding so fast it was actually painful.

"Becca, Becca." He threw his arms around her. "Are you all right?"

"I bumped my head, but other than that I think I'm fine." Her voice quavered as she spoke. The rain was beginning again, mingling with the blood on her face.

"Are you sure?" He made a quick inspection of her arms and legs. "Nothing broken?"

"No," she breathed, dropping the bloody rag she'd pressed to her forehead. Cord quickly removed his slicker and draped it over them. She nestled in his arms, needing him more than she'd ever thought possible.

The rain beat down on them, but they were cocooned in their own private world. "What happened?" he whispered into her hair.

"I was making a turn and the brakes gave way. I pumped and pumped, but the Jeep wouldn't stop or slow down. Before I knew it, I was off the road careering down the ravine. I remember hitting the tree, then everything went black."

"Oh, Becca." His arms tightened around her. "I don't know what I would've done if anything happened to you."

That note in his voice made her feel suddenly weak. "I'm a little shaken, but I'm okay," she assured him again.

The rain continued to pelt down, but Becca hardly noticed. All she cared about was the man holding her so tenderly. Her hand slid up his chest to the warmth of his neck. Despite the stab of pain, she raised her head, and his lips covered hers urgently. She clung to him, eyes closed, and his mustache felt like velvet against her skin. She wanted him to touch every part of her. She gave herself up to pure sensation, and the world spun away.

Cord was melting into pure need—a need for Becca. Her hands, her softness, blocked out everything except the emotions inside him. His body hadn't been this alive in years.

He heard a sound and jerked his head up.

"What is it?" she asked.

"Someone's calling," he answered in a troubled voice. What was he doing? He'd been so glad to find her, he'd forgotten to alert the others. "It's probably Gus. I've got to let them know you're okay."

He began to get up, but she held on, kissing him passionately. His lips lingered on hers for a second longer. "Becca," he groaned. "You keep doing that and we'll stay lost forever."

"Sounds good to me," she whispered.

His hand touched her face and he drew it back when he felt the blood on his fingers. He scrambled to his feet. "I've got to get you to a doctor."

"Cord."

But he wasn't listening. He whistled and Apache came galloping up. He pulled a rifle from his saddle, then fired three times in the air. The sound ricocheted through Becca, returning her to the world of reality. As always, she and

Cord had had a moment—that was it. She'd wanted to spend the night with him, but things had turned out so differently.

Would there ever be time for the two of them?

CHAPTER ELEVEN

CORD SWEPT HER UP into his arms and mounted Apache. How he did that she didn't know, but one minute she was on the ground and the next she was in the saddle. They set off at a slow, careful pace, and within minutes, they were surrounded by cowboys.

"You found her," Gus said. "Thank God."

"Yeah, the brakes went out on the Jeep and she crashed into a tree. The Jeep's in the bushes. I've got to get her to a doctor." With that, he kneed Apache and they took off. She could tell they were going faster than before by the rhythm of her body, but as long as Cord held her, she wasn't afraid. Behind them she could hear the clap of hooves and she knew the cowboys were following them home.

When she saw the lights of the ranch in the distance, a peaceful feeling came over her. Cord didn't stop at the barn. He galloped straight to the house. As he began to lift her from the saddle, Nicki ran from the house, screaming, "Becca, Becca, Becca."

Della, Edie and Blanche were right behind her.

Becca slid to the ground, and Cord caught Nicki before she could crash into her. When he let the child go, Nicki wrapped her arms around Becca's legs. "Where *were* you? We looked and looked. Where *were* you?"

"Baby," Cord said. "Becca had a wreck in the Jeep and I've got to take her to the doctor."

"Oh, are you hurt?" Nicki glanced up at her, frowning.

"I bumped my head and your father thinks I should get it checked out."

"I wanna go, Daddy! I wanna go."

"Now, baby…"

"No, no, no. I wanna go," Nicki wailed.

Becca felt as though the top of her head was about to spin right off, but she had to deal with Nicki. She couldn't leave if the child was upset.

Before she could say anything, Blanche stepped up. "Come on, sugarplum, stay here with us. You'll just be sitting in a stuffy old room at the hospital. Stay here and we'll play that animal game again. Wanna bet I can be a better cow than you?"

"No, you can't. I'm the best cow. Daddy said so."

Cord knelt beside her. "Go with Blanche, baby," he said. "It's way past your bedtime."

"'Kay," she agreed, then flung her arms around Becca's legs again. "You coming back, Becca?"

Becca swallowed and bent down, trying not to wince at the pain in her head. "Yes, I'm coming back."

"You promise."

"I promise," Becca said with a catch in her voice, and kissed Nicki's cheek.

"I love you, Becca."

Becca had to swallow again. "I love you, too, sweetie. Now go with Blanche. I bet she'll make you some hot chocolate if you ask nicely."

Blanche took Nicki's hand, as the cowboys rode up. They were wet and tired and looked at her with woeful eyes.

"Thanks for searching for me," she said shyly. She was wet, muddy and tired, too—not to mention in pain—but she'd never felt so cherished.

Dusty tipped his hat. "Our pleasure, ma'am."

"Yep," Gus said. "You're a sight for sore eyes, Doc."

"Okay, everyone," Cord broke in, taking her by the arm. "I've got to get her to the hospital." He led her to his truck as Gus grabbed Apache by the reins and the cowboys rode to the barn.

Soon they were on the highway to Houston. Becca felt herself drifting off but knew she shouldn't fall asleep.

"Talk to me," she said. "I have to stay awake."

"I was just thinking about the changes you've made in the Prescott house. Blanche is taking care of my daughter." He shook his head. "Never thought I'd live to see that. And she and Edie haven't had a cross word in days. They can actually eat a meal in peace—or close enough. I'm not sure how that happened, but I know you've worked some sort of miracle. And Nicki. I'm so grateful for what you've done for her."

"I guess I'll have to put my magical skills on the market," she said lightly.

"I'd be the highest bidder."

"Why?"

He took a deep breath. "Because I don't want you to leave Triple Creek." Then he quickly added, "But I'd never ask that of you. I know you have a career and a life waiting for you."

"What if I stayed voluntarily?"

The truck swerved to the right; Cord straightened it immediately. "Don't say things like that while I'm driving!"

"It's true." She wasn't ashamed to admit it. "I'd give up everything to be with you."

His hands tightened on the wheel. "I don't want another woman giving up anything for me."

"I'm not Anette, Cord."

No, she wasn't. She was young, vibrant and captivating,

and he wanted to spend the rest of his life with her. He stopped at a red light and turned to her, but the words lodged in his throat. "Oh my God," he muttered.

"What?" she asked in a startled voice.

"Your face," he said. "The side of your face is blue and there's blood oozing from one spot. Are you in pain? Why didn't you tell me you were in pain?"

"Calm down. I'm sure it's just a bad bruise."

As soon as the light turned green, Cord made it to the hospital in record time. She directed him to The Methodist so she could at least see someone she knew.

A wheelchair was brought out when they arrived, and a nurse took Becca inside, where Cord filled out the necessary forms.

Before they'd even reached the waiting area someone called, "Becca Talbert, is that you?"

Becca turned to see an old friend. "Hi, Candace. Yes, it's me."

Candace eyed her wet and muddy appearance and studied the bruise on Becca's face. "What happened to you?"

"I had a car wreck. I'm waiting to be seen."

"We can't have that," Candace said. "Come on, I'll take you back and have a look."

"Candace, really it's..."

But Candace wasn't listening. She was already wheeling Becca down the hall into an exam room. Cord followed.

"Candace, this is Cordell Prescott and Cord, this is Dr. Candace Barker." Becca made the introductions.

"Nice to meet you," Cord replied.

"Same here, but I'm afraid I'll have to ask you to step outside while I exam her."

"Sure," he said, glancing at Becca. "Would you like me to call your parents?"

"No, please don't do that."

"Okay, I'll be right out there."

"Thanks, Cord."

After he left, Candace asked, "How did you manage to get rescued by a tall, handsome cowboy?"

"It's a long story."

Candace laughed and began to examine her. Becca felt there wasn't anything seriously wrong, but she had to be sure so she agreed to the tests Candace ordered. Her main concern was getting back to Cord. They'd started to talk in the truck and she wanted to finish their conversation. He'd said he didn't want another woman to change her life for him. But it wasn't about *changing,* in Becca's opinion. It was about accepting, about making compromises and being together. In a matter of three weeks, she'd fallen madly, wildly in love. She hoped Cord felt the same way. He hadn't *said* he loved her.

She had to talk to him.

CORD SAT IN THE WAITING AREA and noticed that people were staring at him. He must look a sight. He was wet and muddy from head to toe. He'd tried to wipe off his boots, but they were still caked with mud. He'd lost his hat somewhere and his hair was slicked back and dark with rain. None of that mattered.

There was a telephone in a corner of the room, and he wondered if he should call Emily and Jackson. No, Becca had said not to, so he had to respect her wishes. But he felt they needed to know she was hurt. God, would this terrible night ever end?

He didn't understand what had happened. They'd never had a problem with that Jeep before. If the brakes gave way, something had to have caused it. He strode over to the phone and called the ranch.

Edie answered. "Hi, Edie," he said. "How's Nicki?"

"She's fine. Blanche is upstairs reading her a story."

Cord was taken aback for a moment. Blanche was reading to Nicki? There was something wrong with *that* picture, but he wasn't going to question it. "Hard to believe, isn't it?"

"I know, and don't ask me what kind of story she's reading 'cause I'm not interfering."

"Thanks, Edie. I appreciate your restraint. Things are definitely changing in our house."

"Becca said it's time to let go of all the bitterness and hatred, and she's right. I'm too old to keep this up. Besides, Blanche is your mother and Clay's and Colton's."

"Yeah," he said, trying to digest this startling revelation of Edie's.

"How's Becca?"

"They're examining her. We'll be back as soon as we can. Is Gus around?"

"He's in the kitchen with Della. They were just fixing to leave. I'll see if he's still here."

Cord waited, and it wasn't long before Gus came on the line. "Hey, Cord. How's the doc?"

"Being examined," he answered, then added, "Gus, would you do something for me?"

"Sure, anything. You name it."

"At first light, get the boys to pull the Jeep to the barn and ask Smithy to go over it with a fine-tooth comb. I want to know why those brakes failed."

"You think it wasn't an accident?"

"I don't know, but there has to be a reason the brakes didn't work. Smithy keeps our vehicles in good running order, and he'll figure out what went wrong."

"Sure enough. We'll get to the bottom of this. You just take care of the doc."

"I will. See you in the morning."

He hung up with a somber expression. He had to have some answers—for himself and for Becca. He ran both hands over his face in a weary gesture, trying not to think about their conversation in the truck. But he couldn't block out her words. *What if I stayed voluntarily? I'd do anything to be with you.* He wanted to grab at everything she was offering, but he had to do what was best for her. He still felt so confused, so bitter, over Anette's death. Colton was right; he couldn't drag Becca into his misery. But how did he let go of something he wanted with all his heart?

WHEN CORD WAS ALLOWED to see Becca, she was sitting on the side of an exam bed, wearing a bandage on her forehead. Her skin was so pale, it terrified him. His heart jackknifed into his throat, and he knew in that instant that he'd never be able to walk away from Becca. He could remind himself of all the reasons he should, but when he looked into her dark eyes all those reasons disappeared.

"Ah, Mr. Prescott," Dr. Barker said when she noticed him. "Becca has a bad bruise and a slight concussion. She'll be fine in a few days. She just has—"

"I know the drill, Candace," Becca broke in.

Candace winked at Cord. "She's on the stubborn side, so make sure she takes it easy."

"Don't worry. I will."

"I'll sign these release forms and you can be on your way." Candace rolled the wheelchair over.

"I can walk. I don't need that thing."

"Hospital procedure," Candace said calmly. "You know that."

Cord practically lifted her off the bed into the chair.

"Thanks," she said to Candace.

"No problem." Candace smiled. "Working with Dr. Arnold doesn't mean you can't visit us poor souls still here in the hospital.''

"I'll remember that." Becca returned her smile.

As they left the emergency room parking lot, Cord asked, "Would you like to go by your parents' place?"

"It's the middle of the night, Cord. I'm not waking them up."

"I'm sure they wouldn't mind."

She turned to look at him. "I'm not ten years old."

"I didn't—"

"Are you trying to get rid of me?"

"No, of course not. I just want you to feel better."

"What'll make me feel better is to go home to Triple Creek." The word *home* had slipped out, but she wouldn't take it back. Even without her realizing it, that was what Triple Creek and the people there had become to her.

When they stopped at a red light, she caught his gaze and could almost feel the wall he was trying to erect between them. "Don't do that."

"What?"

"You're trying to think of everything you can to keep us apart—Anette, Colton, my career, my age—and they're simply excuses to mask what you're really feeling."

"I want what's best for you."

Her eyes didn't waver from his. "You're what's best for me."

"Becca." He reached out his hand to touch her face. She linked her fingers with his.

"When my head stops throbbing, we'll talk about this again. But right now, I just want to go home and go to bed."

Cord didn't say another word. He couldn't. Happiness

was unfurling inside him with such speed that it made nonsense of everything he was thinking.

WHEN THEY ENTERED through the back door, the lights were on and Blanche was sitting at the kitchen table in a black negligée drinking coffee. She rose.

"How you doing, sugar?"

"A bit of a headache, but I'm fine."

"Well, I'm off to bed." Blanche yawned. "Didn't want to go to sleep in case Nicki woke up."

"Thanks, Blanche," Cord said. "That means a lot to me."

Mother and son stared at each other for a moment, then Blanche walked out of the room.

Cord picked up her cup and sniffed it.

"What are you doing?" Becca asked.

"Seeing what she drinking 'cause she's sure not acting like herself."

"What's that saying? Don't look a gift horse in the mouth."

His mustache twitched. "Yeah, I should leave well enough alone. Now, it's time to get you to bed."

Becca slowly made her way up the stairs with Cord supporting her. When they reached her room, he said, "Just undress and get in bed."

"I can't."

"What?"

"I can't go to bed without a bath."

"Surely that can wait. You're dead on your feet."

"I can't rest or sleep without a bath. I'm filthy."

"All right." He sighed. "But I'm not leaving."

"Fine." She moved into the bathroom and closed the door. Turning on the taps full blast, she stripped out of the dirty clothes. Then she eased into the water. Her body was aching and the hot water felt heavenly.

"You okay?" Cord called through the door.

"Yes. Stop worrying."

"I'm gonna take a shower. Be right back."

"Okay."

Cord rushed to his room, removing his clothes as he went. The wet boots were difficult to pull off, but he managed. He stepped into the shower, shampooed his hair and washed, doing everything as fast as he could because he didn't want to leave Becca for too long. He quickly dried off, slipped into a pair of clean jeans and a T-shirt, then darted back to her room.

He tapped on the door. "Becca, you okay?"

"Yes, but could you hand me my T-shirt? It's in the top dresser drawer."

"Sure." He found it without a problem, opened the door a crack and handed it to her.

"Thanks." As she slipped it over her head, the room spun crazily. She gripped the vanity to keep from falling. "Cord!" came out as a desperate cry.

He pushed open the door and took in the situation at a glance. She was trembling and her skin had gone a pasty white. He gathered her into his arms and carried her to the bed.

Pulling the sheet over her, he said, "Get some rest. Reaction is setting in."

"Please don't leave," she begged.

He nodded and sat down on the bed. "I'll stay until you fall asleep."

"I'd like that." She sighed, then added, "But I don't like that you're so far away."

He didn't, either, but he was trying very hard to keep his head clear, which was a wasted effort where she was concerned. He stretched out on his side and draped one arm over her wasit.

With her head beneath his chin, she placed her hand on his chest. Her fingers felt his taut muscles and she drew strength from his closeness. "Oh, yes." She sighed heavily. "I like this much better."

He kissed her forehead. "Go to sleep."

"Cord."

"Hmm."

I love you echoed through her head as she drifted into sleep.

Cord knew she was asleep but he continued to hold her. Whatever she'd been about to say had curved her lips into an enchanting smile. Unable to resist, he gently touched her mouth with his own. She moved against him and every nerve in him came alive. He hadn't thought it was possible to have this overpowering need and love for anyone. With Anette it hadn't been this strong. Or if it had, he'd forgotten, with all the other problems in their marriage. Problems they couldn't work out. Problems that had ultimately led to her death. He never forgot that fact. He didn't want Becca to feel that kind of unhappiness. He knew they were two very different women, yet he couldn't rid himself of those doubts.

At the hospital, when he'd looked into Becca's eyes, he had known he couldn't walk away from her. His feelings for her went too deep for that. But one fear tortured him day and night. Could he make her happy?

Oh, Becca, where do we go from here?

CHAPTER TWELVE

THE NEXT MORNING Becca woke up to a slightly disoriented feeling, which surprisingly was not unpleasant. She reached out her hand, somehow thinking Cord was there, but he wasn't. It was cool where he'd lain, and she yearned for his presence. She pushed herself to a sitting position, brushing hair away from her face. Her body was achy and sore but otherwise she felt fine. Her head wasn't even throbbing anymore.

"Becca, Becca." She heard Nicki shouting a moment before the child burst into the room. Cord followed close behind.

Nicki ran to her side. "Daddy said I can't jump on the bed. Oh…" Her eyes grew big when she saw Becca's face. "Oh, you got an ouchie. Does it hurt?"

Becca leaned over and kissed her. "No, I feel okay this morning." Her voice slowed as she noticed what Nicki was wearing. She had on a red silk gown, and the thin straps had been tied into a knot to fit Nicki's small size. "Where'd you get that outfit?"

"It's Blanche's," Nicki said excitedly. "She let me sleep in it." She ran her hands down the red silk. "Isn't it pretty?"

"Yes, very," Becca said enthusiastically. She glanced at Cord, who was frowning. Their eyes met and she smiled, wanting him to know it was all right for little girls to play dress-up.

He smiled back, and her heart raced.

"Baby." He addressed Nicki. "Becca has to rest today. She can't play or go riding."

"That's okay, Daddy," Nicki informed him. "Blanche is gonna show me how to put makeup on."

"What!"

Nicki's face crumpled at the note in Cord's voice. "She said it was okay."

Cord took a calming breath. "Nicki, you're too young to wear makeup."

Nicki shook her head in agitation. "I'm just gonna *play* with it."

"I'm sure Daddy understands that," Becca said, her eyes catching Cord's and sending a message.

"Yeah," he said slowly, receiving the message and shifting his eyes back to Nicki. "Now it's time for you to get dressed."

"'Kay, Daddy. I can dress myself, then I'm gonna wake Blanche." Nicki ran from the room.

Cord opened his mouth to stop her, then closed it.

"Aren't you going to tell her that Blanche doesn't get up until noon?" Becca asked when she saw the glint in his eyes.

"No." He walked over to sit on the bed. "I think I'll let her surprise Blanche." He dropped a quick kiss on her lips. "How are you?"

She looped her arms around his neck and kissed him deeply in response. He groaned, gathered her close and took the kiss a step further. Delicious warm feelings swirled around them, and Becca didn't want the kiss to end, but Cord began to draw back.

"Much better, I'd say." He grinned.

"Yes, now that you're here." She stroked his shaven cheek and one finger traced his mustache. He caught the finger in his mouth, then kissed her palm and trailed kisses up her arm to her shoulder. Her body quivered from the sensation.

"I could stay here all day," he whispered into her neck.

"There's a thought," she said breathlessly.

"Hmm." He gave her a final quick kiss and got to his feet. "I've got a child to take care of, so stop tempting me."

"Cord, it's all right for Nicki to play with makeup and to wear fancy clothes. That's normal for a girl her age."

"I just don't want her to grow up too fast."

"I know, but Blanche's taking an interest in her is good."

"Yeah, I have to be careful what I wish for." A grin split his face and he added, "Take it easy today. Nothing strenuous. And maybe you should call your parents."

She frowned. "Cord."

"Think about it," he said as he left the room.

Becca stared at the phone, then picked it up with a sigh. She knew her parents would be up and it was probably a good time.

Her father answered the phone; she could tell he was startled by her voice.

"Is something wrong?" was the first thing he asked.

She told him about the accident, and her mother immediately came on the line.

"Becca, are you okay?" Her voice was full of anxiety.

"Yes, Mom, I'm fine."

"Why don't I come out to the ranch and check you over?"

"I'm fine. I just have a bruise on my head."

"Your father and I can be there in no time."

"You're not listening to me," Becca said impatiently.

"I'm sorry. I get a little nervous when one of my children's been injured."

"But I'm fine," she repeated again. "So you've got nothing to be nervous about."

"When are you coming home?" Emily asked, suddenly changing the subject.

"I'm not sure."

"You've been there three weeks and you said Nicki's doing better. Isn't it time to come back to Houston?"

Becca took a long breath. "No, the time's not right. When I decide to leave, I'll let you know."

"You sound annoyed."

"I am." Becca didn't lie or disguise her feelings, as she had so many times in the past. "I wish you'd let me make my own decisions and trust my judgment."

There was a long pause.

Finally Emily said, "I always trust your judgment."

"No, you don't," Becca said. "You're questioning my decision to stay here."

"Only because I want you home where I can take care of you."

"I'm not Scotty's age and I can take care of myself. If I couldn't, you'd be the first person I'd call."

Another long pause.

"I love you, Becca."

Becca blinked back a tear. "I love you, too, but I'm not a little girl anymore."

"You will always be my little girl."

"But now, please, let me be an adult."

"That's so hard, angel."

"I know, but it's what I need."

"Okay, then, I'll try, but you'll have to bear with me if I falter at times."

"I will, Mom. Always."

"Call me when you get back to Houston."

"I will. Bye."

Emily hung up the phone, turned in to Jackson's arms and promptly burst into tears.

"Emily, what's wrong?"

"Our little girl is all grown-up," she sniffed. "She doesn't need us anymore."

His arms tightened around her. "She will always need us, but we have to release our hold—let her live her own life."

"I don't like this part of being a parent."

"Ah, but this is where it gets good. Grandchildren will be next, and I can't wait."

"Grandchildren!" Emily drew back in shock, and Jackson laughed at her. It wasn't long before she was laughing with him.

CORD HELPED NICKI finish dressing, persuading her to wear a T-shirt and shorts rather than the frilly pink sundress she'd originally chosen. They were halfway through breakfast when the phone rang. It was Gus.

"Can you come to the vehicle shed as soon as possible?" he asked.

"What's up?"

"You need to see this for yourself."

"I'll be right there."

Cord left Nicki with Edie and Della, and hurried to the shed. He was sure it had to do with the Jeep, which made him anxious. Gus met him in the yard.

"How's the doc?"

"She has a bad bruise on her head and a slight concussion, but she's going to be fine. Just has to take it easy."

"That's great."

"Did you get the Jeep pulled in?"

"Yep, that's what I want to talk to you about. It didn't take Smithy long to find the problem."

"What was it?"

"The nut on the brake line tubing has been loosened. The brake fluid drained out."

Cord stopped in his tracks and stared at Gus. "What!"

"The nut was loosened," Gus repeated. "There're fresh marks on it. Smithy says it was done recently."

"You mean it was loosened intentionally."

"Looks that way."

"My God, who would do that?"

"I'd say we got a snake in the chicken house."

"But who?" Cord said under his breath as he walked into the building. Smithy showed him the line, and it was plain as day that it had been loosened. Smithy assured him it couldn't have been jarred loose. He'd checked the line last week and the nut was tight with not a mark on it. For a moment Cord was completely staggered. This was *intentional.* But he couldn't let his thoughts run away with him; he had to have more facts.

He walked some distance away, and Gus came with him. "What do you think's going on?"

Gus removed his hat and scratched his head. "Got me. Ain't nothing like this happened around here before."

Cord glanced off to the horses frolicking in the pasture. "Doesn't make sense. Who'd want to hurt Becca? Everyone likes her." He said the words he'd been trying to avoid, to deny. *Someone was trying to hurt Becca.*

"Yeah, maybe that's the problem."

Cord's narrowed his eyes at Gus. "What do you mean?"

"All the cowboys are smitten with her. Maybe one of 'em thought he'd come to her rescue. Be the big hero and all."

Cord shook his head. "That's hard to believe. I trust every cowpoke on this property."

"Me, too, but we have to face facts. We were the only ones around that Jeep yesterday."

"It must've been loosened sometime after it left Smithy's shop," Cord said almost to himself.

"That's what I'm saying. Becca drove straight to the bottom where we were working. No one else came near the Jeep except us, the cowboys and Edie. Mona was there for a little while, but she left when we went to the last pasture."

Cord dismissed them immediately. "Mona doesn't even know Becca, and I doubt if Edie has any idea how to loosen a brake line."

Gus thought for a minute. "Maybe someone wasn't trying to hurt the doc. Maybe they were trying to hurt you."

"What do you mean?"

"Joe Bates." Gus said the name that tied Cord's stomach into a hard knot of anger. "He said he'd get even, and he knows you drive that Jeep occasionally. He's a shifty character, and he could've slipped in and out of here easily. He knows the ranch."

"I suppose," he muttered, trying not to let his anger get the best of him. He had to think this through with a clear head. Still, none of it was logical. Joe Bates was all talk and basically a coward. He knew that if he pulled anything, Cord would come looking for him. But what if he was drunk? He'd been bold enough to show up at the ranch the other day. Surely the man wasn't so stupid as to try something like this. Nevertheless, Cord decided he'd let the sheriff know. But he'd start by questioning his cowhands.

"Get all the boys into the bunkhouse. I want to talk to them."

"Now, why don't you let me do that? I probably can get more out of 'em."

"I'll talk to them personally," he responded in a stubborn voice.

"Don't lose your temper. These are good boys," Gus reminded him.

"Maybe one of them isn't," he said in that same stubborn tone. When Gus began to speak, he held up his hand. "Whatever. Just get them in the bunkhouse—now."

Gus ambled away without another word.

Cord went into his office, which was attached to the tack room, and called the sheriff. Then he walked over to the bunkhouse with a hollow feeling in his gut. He had to get to the bottom of what was happening here. Now that he knew the Jeep's crash couldn't be dismissed as an accident, he had to acknowledge that Becca's life could be in danger. He had to keep her safe and he would do everything in his power to achieve that—even if it meant her leaving the ranch.

CORD ENTERED THE BUNKHOUSE with a dark expression on his face. The house consisted of a kitchen, large living area, two bathrooms and two big bedrooms with four bunk beds in each. The cowboys were gathered in the living area.

Cord didn't sit, nor did he say a word. He'd known each of these men a very long time and for a moment he just stared at them.

Dusty was the first to speak. "What's up, boss?"

Cord took a step closer. "It's about yesterday."

"The doc's all right, ain't she?" Clint asked anxiously.

"She has a slight concussion and a bad bruise on her face, but she's going to be fine."

"Great," Joe Bob put in.

"I want to thank all of you for your efforts in finding her last night." Cord thought he should mention that first.

"Ah, shucks, boss, it weren't no problem," Rocky said.

"What happened? Did she lose control of the Jeep?" Big Jim asked.

"No, she didn't lose control," Cord replied, letting his gaze sweep over them. "The nut on the brake line was loosened."

Cord watched their faces in the shocked silence that followed his words. A minute later, Dusty jumped to his feet.

"What the hell? Somebody did that on purpose?"

"Yeah," Cord replied.

"Well, I'll be a son of a bitch," Hank said. "Tell us who it is and we'll string 'em up."

"I don't know who it is. That's why I'm talking to you."

The silence became suffocating. Then Clint got to his feet. "Are you saying you suspect one of us?"

Gus intervened. "Now, don't go getting' a burr in your jeans. But we were the only ones around that Jeep yesterday, and it's not exactly a secret that you all are smitten with the doc. If one of you did something a little crazy, just tell us. That's all Cord's asking."

"I'll handle this," Cord said to Gus, a little offended that he'd interfered. He turned back to the men. "I'm just asking for the truth."

"Hell, boss," Clint said. "We may be cowboys, but we're not stupid. We can all see the doc only has eyes for you, just like the song says. She's a nice lady and we all like her. Not one of us here would harm her in any way."

"I believe you," Cord said without having to think about it. These men *wouldn't* hurt Becca. "Did any of you notice anything suspicious—anything out of the ordinary?"

"No, we were working," Rocky said, and each man in turn shook his head.

"Any of you noticed Joe Bates around lately?"

"He was at the feed store the other day when I picked up that load of feed," Little Jim muttered. "He said some snide things about you, and I told him if he didn't shut up, I'd smash his face in. He said you'd get what was coming to you."

Cord frowned. "This was on Tuesday?"

"Yeah. Want me to find him and rough him up a little?"

"No, the sheriff will talk to him. And he'll probably talk to each of you. Just be honest."

"Sure," Dusty said, then asked, "You do believe us, don't you?"

Cord nodded. "Yeah," he said, and walked out, Gus on his heels.

Outside, he turned to face Gus. "Next time I'm talking to the boys, please don't interfere."

"I'm sorry. I was only trying to help."

"Gus..." He took a deep breath, not sure why he was so upset. "I'm just—never mind. I have to talk to Becca."

He strolled toward the house, stopping as the sheriff drove up. Cord explained what had happened in more detail and showed him the Jeep. They talked a bit about Joe Bates, then Gus took the sheriff over to talk to the cowboys and Cord headed back to the house. He wanted to tell Becca personally; she deserved to hear it from him.

Before he could make it to the house, Mona drove up, pulling a cattle trailer. Cord could see a bull inside. He didn't have time for this. But he and Mona had been friends since they were kids. Mona and his brother Clay were the same age and she was more Clay's friend than his, but Cord occasionally helped her with ranching problems. He'd tell her what was going on, and she'd understand that he didn't have time to look at a bull today.

"Howdy," he said, as she got out of the truck. Mona

was a strong, independent woman, and Cord had always admired that about her. Even after her father died, she'd continued to run the ranch with as much expertise as a man.

Mona glanced toward the sheriff's car. "Something wrong?"

"Yeah, there's been an accident." He told her about the night's events.

"Oh, no. Is Dr. Talbert all right?"

"She's fine."

"I'm so sorry, Cord. I know how appreciative you've been of the doctor's help."

"Not a very good way to show my thanks."

"No, but I'm sure the sheriff will find the culprit."

"Mona, did you notice anything yesterday?"

"I was only there for a little while."

"Did you notice anyone around the Jeep?"

She shook her head. "No, can't—wait a minute. Gus was putting an ice chest in the back as I rode away. But I'm sure that means nothing."

Cord thought about that for a second, but dismissed the possibility. Gus wasn't like that. He only wanted to help Becca. Didn't he? Cord shook his head to clear it of such traitorous ideas.

He glanced at Mona. "You seen Joe Bates lately?"

"Yeah, he was over at my place yesterday asking for work."

"He was?" That might be the answer to all his questions—Joe Bates.

"Yes, but don't worry. I didn't hire him."

"Damn, this is all so confusing."

"I guess I'll leave you to sort it out. I only stopped by to show you this new bull."

"Put him in your pen and I'll try to look at him tomorrow."

"Thanks, Cord, and try not to worry too much."
"Bye, Mona."

BECCA SPENT MOST OF THE MORNING on the phone. Not
long after she'd talked to her parents, Grandpa George
called, and she knew her father had told him what had
happened. He insisted that he didn't want to bother her but
just had to hear her voice. She assured him she was fine,
and Grandpa George believed her. That was what she loved
most about him—his trust in her judgment, his faith in her
good sense. She suddenly realized that was the major problem with her parents; they'd never fully believed that she'd
adjusted to the revelations that had changed her life. They
wanted to be there for her, to comfort her, to help her. But
with two such wonderful people, she had adjusted a long
time ago. Now they had to trust her to live her own life.
Becca felt good about this morning's conversation, in
which she'd taken a stand on this very issue. The past,
present and future seemed clearer in her head, and Cord
had a lot to do with that. He eased her restlessness. And
she needed that. She needed Cord.

Later, Rose and Owen called to see when she was coming to Rockport, but she knew they were really asking about
the accident. She told them she was okay and that she
wasn't sure when she'd make it to Rockport. Not before
her birthday, which was in August. They didn't try to dissuade her, and she was grateful for that. She understood
that everyone genuinely cared about her well-being, that
her family wanted her to be happy. And she finally was.
She couldn't wait to see Cord again.

After talking to Ginger, she curled up on the sofa in the
den, leafing through a medical journal. Nicki crawled up
beside her.

"You don't feel good, Becca?" There was a note of

anxiety in her voice, and Becca knew she was remembering her own mother and all the times Anette didn't "feel good."

She kissed her cheek. "I feel great—and you know what?"

"What?"

"I think we need some chocolate. What do you think?"

"Yeah. We need chocolate."

There was a bowl of candy kisses on the coffee table. Becca was sure they hadn't been there yesterday. She reached over and grabbed a handful. She unwrapped one and handed it to Nicki, then popped one in her own mouth.

"Mmm, mmm, that's good." She sighed.

Nicki nodded. "Real good." She stretched out her arms. "It's gonna make your butt *this* big."

Becca made a face. "I sincerely hope not."

Nicki burst into giggles and Becca joined in. She loved this child so much. How was she ever going to leave? She gathered Nicki close and held her tight. A lot had happened in a short period of time, but she knew with overwhelming certainty that her heart would always be here with Cord and his little girl.

CORD CAME THROUGH the kitchen door and stopped short. Blanche and Edie were sitting at the table drinking coffee. It was a sight that took a moment to get used to. There were no hurtful words flying around—just an amicable silence.

Blanche glanced at him. "Cord, you should tell that kid of yours that some people don't get up at the crack of dawn."

Cord suppressed a grin. Blanche wore a lavender negligée, her hair was mussed and her face devoid of makeup. In all his forty-two years, he'd rarely seen that. Blanche never left her room unless she was perfectly dressed, coiffed and made up.

"And maybe you should be careful what you say to her. She was just excited about the makeup you mentioned." He glanced around the room. "Where is Nicki?"

"She's in there bothering Becca, thank God," Blanche groaned. "I don't think my eyes are fully open yet."

"They're not," Edie remarked. "You look like you've been rode hard and put up wet, as Gus would say."

"You're not exactly fresh as a daisy," Blanche shot back.

"It's almost noon and this is as good as I get," Edie added with a touch of humor.

"Okay, ladies." Cord held up both hands. "I need your help."

Blanche eyed him strangely. "Something's wrong, isn't it."

He told them about the Jeep.

"Oh my God," Blanche and Edie said in unison.

"Are you sure?" Della asked.

"Yeah, there's not much doubt about it."

"I tried to warn her but she wouldn't listen to me," Blanche mumbled.

Cord frowned. "What are you talking about?"

"This ranch is not a place for a city girl like Becca."

Cord decided to let it pass. He didn't have time for that conversation and preferred not to hear Blanche's opinions on the matter, anyway. He had to talk to Becca.

"Could you occupy Nicki while I speak with Becca?"

"Okay," Edie said. "I'll take her riding."

"That's not a good idea. The sheriff's still here and I don't want to upset Nicki. It might remind her of Anette's death."

"Oh my." Edie put a hand to her mouth. "This is awful."

Blanche got to her feet. "Go get the kid, Edie, and bring her to my room. I'll find some old makeup and paint her up like a clown."

Edie's eyes narrowed. "I will not take orders from you."

"Don't start," Blanche warned.

Cord intervened. "I'll bring Nicki. And for God's sake, get a grip. I don't need this right now."

"I'm sorry, Cord," Edie said immediately.

"Yeah, whatever," Blanche added disagreeably. "I'll be in my room, and believe me, the kid knows where it is."

"I'll send her along," Cord said a moment before he headed for the den.

Becca and Nicki were sitting on the sofa with their heads together. One blond, one dark. His heart melted as he watched them. Becca had brought so much into this house. She had reached Nicki when no one else could and she had touched him in a way that even now was hard to understand. He knew he'd never be the same. Whatever had happened in Becca's past, she had a great capacity to love, to laugh and to share. Now he had to tell her that someone had sabotaged the Jeep—and possibly tried to kill her. How would he do this?

With the truth. Becca would expect no less.

CHAPTER THIRTEEN

"DADDY," NICKI SHOUTED, and scrambled off the sofa when she saw him. She ran into his waiting arms.

"How's my baby?"

"Fine. Becca and me are eating chocolate. Want one?" She held a candy kiss in her hand.

"No, thanks, but Blanche might. She's looking for you."

Nicki frowned. "She was grouchy when I waked her."

"Well, she's in a better mood now and she's getting out some makeup."

"Oh boy." Nicki wriggled from his arms. "I'm gonna get pretty." She glanced back at Becca. "Wanna come?"

"No, sweetie, but you have a good time."

"'Kay." She charged out the door to Blanche's room.

Cord sat beside Becca. He removed his hat and laid it on the sofa, then turned to look at her. His heart constricted at the sight of her bruised face. He gently touched it with the back of his hand. Who had done this to her? Through him swirled anger, which he had to control.

She caught his hand and kissed each finger with slow thoroughness, and for a moment he forgot everything but her. "Becca," he said huskily. "We have to talk."

Something in his voice alerted her. "What is it?"

He linked his fingers with hers. "I had the Jeep pulled to the shed, and Smithy took a look at it."

"Did he find out what was wrong with the brakes?"

Cord nodded but he didn't say anything else.

"Well?" she prompted.

"Did you notice when the brakes got weak?" he asked.

"They worked fine going down there, but when I started back they weren't holding too well, and finally they didn't hold at all."

"I see."

She watched him for a few seconds. "Cord, what are you trying not to tell me?"

He looked directly into her eyes. "The nut holding the brake line was loosened and the brake fluid leaked out."

She blinked. "Loosened? What do you mean?"

"Smithy checked the vehicle last week and everything was fine. Someone loosened the nut."

"On purpose?"

"That's what it looks like."

She took a moment to digest what he was saying, but it was all so unreal. "Who would do that?"

"I don't know. The sheriff's talking to all the cowboys."

Her eyes widened. "The sheriff is here?"

"Yes, I want to get to the bottom of this, but I don't want you to worry. It wasn't necessarily intended for you. Anyone could've been driving the Jeep—including me."

"That doesn't make me feel any better," she said shortly. "Oh, no! Could it have been that Joe Bates?"

"Becca—"

"It could have, couldn't it?" she interrupted. "That's why the sheriff's here."

"Maybe," he admitted. "We're not sure. I…"

She could see he was having difficulty with the words, so she slid her arms around him. "What is it?"

"I just have this bad feeling," he whispered into her hair, not even realizing he was pouring out his heart. "It's the same feeling I had when I found Anette. I couldn't find any answers then, but I knew something wasn't right. Just like I know something's not right now.''

''You said anyone could've been driving the Jeep.''

''I think it's best if you go back to Houston.'' The words slipped out before he could stop them. Becca's safety mattered more than his need for her.

She drew back. ''You want me to leave?''

He kissed her cold lips. ''That's the last thing I want, but we have to do whaterever will keep you safe.''

''I feel safe with you.''

''Becca, please—''

''I'm not leaving,'' she said in that stubborn voice he'd heard before.

''Becca…''

''No, I mean it. I'm not running away like a frightened animal. If someone doesn't want me here, then they'll have to tell me to my face.''

''Why do you have to be so stubborn?''

''That's just me.''

''I know,'' he replied, shaking his head.

''Besides, I'm not abandoning Nicki. She's so much better, but I have to prepare her before I go.''

Who's going to prepare me?

Nothing was said for a moment as Cord wrestled with his conscience. He wanted her out of harm's way, but he didn't have the strength to force her to go.

''Cord, I'm not Anette,'' she said calmly. ''It takes a lot to scare me. I'll admit I'm a little afraid, but not enough to run away and hide.''

He didn't say anything—just held her hand so tightly that it went numb.

''I know you have a lot of unresolved issues and feelings about Anette.''

''Yeah,'' he admitted in a tortured voice.

This was the right moment to mention something that was bothering her. "Why haven't you done anything about Anette's things? Nothing's been touched since her death."

"I couldn't stand to go in there," he said brokenly.

"It's time," she whispered. "Go through her things. Put her to rest for good. You said you didn't have any answers about her death. Sorting through her belongings might give you the peace you need."

"This isn't about Anette. This is about your safety," he said in a frustrated voice.

"You said you had the same bad feeling about both."

He took a long breath. "Yeah, and I wish I could make it go away."

"You have to start somewhere."

"I can't go into that room." His voice was so low that she barely heard him.

"Yes, you can," she insisted. "You want answers about Anette and I think that's where you'll find them."

He frowned.

"Her whole life on this ranch is probably in that room. I'm sure you'll discover that she loved you and Nicki. It's time to recognize those feelings and put them behind you. It's time to live again." She kissed the corner of his mustache. "I want you to live again—with me."

"Becca." He covered her mouth with his own. She opened hers and gave him everything he wanted and more—

Della cleared her throat from the doorway, and they immediately drew apart. "The sheriff is in the kitchen."

"Be right there," Cord said in a hoarse voice. He gazed into Becca's darkened eyes. "You have a knack for getting me completely sidetracked."

"Nice, isn't it?" She smiled provocatively.

"I'm sure the sheriff wants to discuss the accident. Are you up to it?"

"Yes." She smoothed his mustache with her finger. "And I'm serious about Anette's room. It has to be done."

"I'll think about it," he conceded as he got to his feet and helped her up.

Becca knew they had no future without resolving the past. And she desperately wanted a future with Cord. The intentional tampering with the brake line was something she had to face, too. She had an eerie feeling that this incident and Anette's death were connected. How, she had no idea; it wasn't a rational conclusion. But she sensed that the place to start was Anette's room.

THE DAY PASSED IN A BLUR. The sheriff questioned them all, but there wasn't much anyone could tell him. Becca had seen no one suspicious around the Jeep and neither had Edie. The sheriff believed Joe Bates was probably the perpetrator. He didn't feel any of the cowboys had reason to do such a thing. He intended to find Joe Bates and see what he was up to.

Becca felt better, but she could see Cord was still suspicious. She knew his emotions were tied to Anette and she had to get him past that. She *had* to talk him into entering Anette's room.

Soon after the sheriff left, Nicki walked into the kitchen, and all Cord and Becca could do was stare. She had on a red dress of Blanche's that came down to the floor and she tottered on high heels. Beads adorned her neck and arms, and long silver earrings dangled from her ears. Her face was heavily made up and a purple streak had been sprayed in her blond curls.

She held out her arms. "Aren't I pretty?"

Cord couldn't speak.

"Yes, sweetie, very pretty," Becca said in a whisper.

Cord found his voice. "What's that in your hair?"

"Color. Ain't it neat?"

"No, I don't like it," Cord said before he could stop himself.

Nicki's bottom lip began to tremble.

"What Daddy means is that it's different," Becca said. "Once he takes another look, I'm sure he'll like it." She gazed pointedly at Cord.

"Yeah...yeah..." He spoke slowly, knowing what Becca wanted him to say, but the words were like sawdust in his mouth. He couldn't see his little girl behind the glitz and glitter.

Edie entered the kitchen and stopped dead in her tracks, her eyes on Nicki. "Oh my Lord."

"Look at me, Edie," Nicki called.

"Is it Halloween?" Edie whispered in Becca's ear.

"Nicki's been playing dress-up with Blanche," Becca explained.

"Oh my Lord," Edie said again.

"My sentiments exactly," Cord murmured.

Blanche breezed in at that moment. "Well, sugarplum, did you dazzle everyone?"

"I don't think *dazzle* is the correct word," Cord told her.

"Daddy doesn't like my hair," Nicki informed Blanche.

"Ah, your daddy's a cowboy and they like simple things. But you and me, we're movers and shakers."

"Yeah." Nicki beamed, obviously glowing in her grandmother's attention. "We move and shake. I'm gonna show Della." Nicki stumbled for the den.

"Have you no sense?" Edie hissed when Nicki left.

Blanche stepped close to her. "You know, Edie, I could spruce you up, too, but it's kinda hard making a silk purse out of a sow's ear."

"And it's hard to make a lady out of a harlot," Edie shot back.

"Time out," Cord said loudly. "The main thing is that Nicki's happy." He paused, then added, "In the future, Blanche, try not to get so...overenthusiastic. I'd better find her before she breaks her neck in those heels." Cord hurried out with Edie behind him.

"How you feeling, sugar?" Blanche asked when they were alone.

"Much better."

Blanche pulled out a chair and sat down. "I guess it helps that Cord's so attentive."

Becca shook her head. "I'm not letting you goad me. But I'm proud of the interest you've taken in Nicki."

"Don't read too much into it, sugar."

"Oh, but I do."

"Then, that's your problem," Blanche said. "If I were you, I'd get the hell outta here before anything else happens."

"Is that another warning?"

Blanche's eyes met hers. "Take it any way you want, but that brake line was tampered with for a reason. It was intended for you or Cord. Either way, it's not good. You'd be better off in Houston."

There was a tone in Blanche's voice she hadn't heard before. "Are you worried about me?"

Blanche stood. "Sugar, I don't worry about anyone except myself. You're the worrying type, though, but you won't have to worry about the kid. I'll look out for her. Just go where it's safe." She disappeared out the door.

Well, well, Becca thought. Did wonders never cease? Blanche was afraid of showing emotion. That was why she'd left so quickly, but she couldn't hide her fear from

Becca. Did Blanche know more than she was saying? Becca had a feeling she did. But what?

CORD AND BECCA HAD TO WASH and rewash Nicki's hair to get the purple out. After the second scrubbing, Nicki insisted she didn't want "no more of that stuff." Cord tiptoed out of the room a little later as Becca was reading Nicki a story. Nicki drifted off to sleep, but he still wasn't back. Becca put the book away, glancing at the inscription. Again she felt that a woman who loved a child this much would not intentionally kill herself. It had to have been an accident. But tampering with the brake line wasn't. God, why did she keep putting the two together? They'd happened so far apart and they weren't related in any logical way. Then, why couldn't she shake the ominous feeling?

Becca had a quick bath and put on a big T-shirt. She studied her face in the mirror and saw that it was much improved. The bruise was fading and the swelling had gone down. She'd always been a fast healer.

She went into the bedroom, wondering where Cord was. They hadn't said good-night and she was hoping that just maybe they'd spend this night together. She hadn't expected him to leave so suddenly. Where was he?

CORD STOOD AT HIS BEDROOM window, staring out into the darkness. His mind seemed numb, overwhelmed by the confusion of his thoughts. Was someone out there trying to hurt Becca? Or were they trying to hurt him? He didn't have any answers—just like before. *Everything* was just like before. The not knowing was the intolerable part. What was out there that he couldn't see? And *why* couldn't he? If there was a traitor on his property, he had to know. Around and around his thoughts went, until he threw back his head and clenched his fists. He had to know.

The place to start is Anette's room.

But that had nothing to do with Becca, he told himself. Then realization dawned. In a way, it did. Until he resolved his feelings about the past, he had no future. And all he could see in his future was Becca. All he *wanted* was Becca. Cord knew what had to be done—and he was finally ready to do it.

He opened a drawer and took out a key. A key from the past. The key to the room he'd shared with Anette.

BECCA SAT CROSS-LEGGED on her bed, trying to read an article she'd been working on all day. But her eyes kept straying to the door. Was Cord not going to say good-night? She couldn't believe how much that hurt her.

Just as she became absorbed in the article, there was a tap at the door. Her head jerked up, and she smiled as Cord stepped into the room.

"Hi," he said, walking over to the bed and taking in her smooth legs. A warmth settled in his loins, but he forced himself to ignore it. First things first. "I've been thinking," he said as he sat down.

"Have you?" She ran her hand across his broad shoulders, loving the way his muscles tensed.

He caught her hand. "Yes, and you're right."

"About what?"

"Anette's room."

She hadn't expected this. "You mean…"

"Yes. It's time for me to get rid of her things and close that door of my life forever."

"Oh, Cord."

"I've been so angry with her that I couldn't go in there. Now I feel I can, and I want to do it while Nicki's asleep, but I need your support."

"Of course." She squeezed his hand.

He raised an eyebrow. "Ready?"

"Now?"

"Yes. I've got two big boxes in the hall."

"Okay," she said, getting off the bed. When he decided to do something, he meant business. But she was so glad. Cord needed to be free, and this was the beginning of that freedom.

She followed him down the hall to the locked door, where two boxes waited to be filled with the remnants of Anette's life. When he removed a key from his jeans and opened the door, a smell of dust and something Becca couldn't define greeted them. Cord flipped on the light, and for a moment they both stood and stared. The room was decorated in pink and deep blue, and the floral bedspread on the king-size bed was tumbled as if someone had recently been sleeping on it. Pictures of Nicki covered one wall, but Becca's eyes were drawn to the dresser. Three bottles of whiskey were still there—two were empty, but the third had about a fourth of the liquor still left. Becca realized that was the source of the foul smell. The room had a sense of doom about it.

Cord felt a suffocating sensation and he wanted to run, to forget he'd ever shared this room with Anette. He remembered the many arguments, the temper tantrums and the tears. Bad feelings about his marriage threatened to overtake him. Then he noticed the pictures of Nicki and the panic eased. Anette had given him Nicki, and he could never regret that. There *had* been good times, but they were so hard to remember, because the pain had darkened even those.

Aware of his turmoil, Becca slipped an arm around his waist and went into his arms. Without her shoes, she barely came below his chin. "Are you sure you want to do this?"

she said into his chest. His heart was beating so fast that she couldn't even count the rate.

"Yes," he muttered, and knew that he did. It was time. Gently releasing her, he pulled the boxes into the room. Without any real organization, he started opening drawers and throwing clothes into the boxes. Becca joined in until they'd emptied the dresser and armoire. Cord scowled at the whiskey bottles, then slammed them to the floor.

"Damn her, damn her," he cried in a strangled voice. "How could she do this to Nicki?" All the emotion he'd been trying to hold back suddenly burst forth.

Becca immediately hurried over to him and held him tight. "I don't think she knew what she was doing," she told him.

He clasped her just as tightly for a second, then let her go. "Sorry. I just lost it when I saw the bottles." His hand trembled as it touched the dresser. "I don't know where they came from. We didn't keep liquor in our room, and the whiskey's not a brand Blanche stocks downstairs, so Anette must have bought them herself."

Becca knelt and picked up the bottles, which hadn't broken. As she did, she noticed something against the dresser. Several pills were lying on the carpet, almost hidden in the deep pile. "Look," she said, picking one up. "There're pills on the floor and they're an antidepressant. I recognize the tablet."

Cord glanced at the pill and drew a deep breath. "She must've been taking as many pills as she could and following them with liquor. All this time, I was hoping it was an accident, but it must have been intentional."

"I suppose," Becca murmured in a weak voice.

"What? You don't think so?"

"I just keep remembering the books she bought for Nicki and the inscriptions. It's hard for me to imagine a woman with that much love abandoning her child, but depression alters personality.''

Cord sucked air into his lungs and released it. ''I'm glad I did this. I know she committed suicide for some reason of her own. A reason I wouldn't understand. But now I have to accept it, even though I'll always wonder if I could have changed things.''

''Probably not,'' she said. ''So you have to stop blaming yourself.''

''Yeah, I've carried that burden around for too long.''

''I agree,'' she said. She lifted the jewelry box on the dresser. ''I'm sure you want to save this for Nicki.''

''Yes, I put Anette's wedding and engagement rings in there after the funeral. I definitely want Nicki to have those.''

Their wedding picture stood on a corner of the dresser. Cord picked it up and placed it in a box.

''Cord,'' she admonished. ''I'm sure Nicki will want that, too.'' She knelt by the box and retrieved it, then studied the two people in the photo—a much younger Cord in a suit and tie, but still just as handsome and stirring to her senses. Anette was blond and very pretty. Nicki looked a lot like her.

Becca touched the photo. ''So you like blondes?''

There was a note of uncertainty in her voice, and Cord wanted to reassure her. He knelt behind her, pulled her hair away from her face and gently kissed her neck. ''Not anymore,'' he whispered.

She leaned back against him, and he slipped his arms around her. ''Oh, that was the right thing to say,'' she teased.

''It's the truth.'' He kissed the side of her face as she rested her head against him.

''Still, I think you need to keep the photo for Nicki.''

"Okay," he said. "But I believe her memories of her mother are fading. These days all she thinks about is Becca, Becca, Becca. You've overshadowed all the pain in her life." His arms tightened around her. "Just like you've overshadowed all the pain in mine."

"Oh, Cord." She turned in the circle of his arms and met his lips with a need that was unequaled by anything she'd ever felt. When that need was about to consume them, Cord drew away and scooped her into his arms. "Let's continue this somewhere more comfortable."

"But we haven't finished the room."

"We'll finish it in the morning," he told her. "Right now, all I want to do is love you."

CHAPTER FOURTEEN

HE CARRIED HER TO HER ROOM and placed her on the bed. His lips found hers while his hand slid beneath the T-shirt to her breasts. Pinpoints of pleasure shot through her as his thumb gently massaged, then his lips followed. The featherlight stroking of his mustache against her skin sent her senses spiraling out of control. She never dreamed it could be like this—she couldn't think, she could only feel.

"Oh, Becca," he whispered. His lips trailed down her abdomen. "I want to take it slow and make this perfect for you, but it's been so long for me, I don't know if I can. I've never wanted anyone the way I want you."

She had to tell him the truth. She forced herself back to reality, which wasn't easy with her body pulsing at a new rhythm.

She swallowed. "I want you just as much. But..."

His tongue stopped its exploration of her navel and he raised his head. His hair was disheveled from her hands and his eyes were glazed with passion. "But?"

"This will be my first..." She couldn't finish. Admitting such a thing at her age was embarrassing, somehow.

"Are you saying..."

She nodded.

He immediately tried to pull away, but she held on to him. "Oh, no, Cordell Prescott. You're not doing that to me. This is *my* choice, my decision. My mother always told me I'd know when the time was right. The time is now and the man is you. Do you know why?''

He shook his head, mesmerized by the fire in her eyes.

''Because I love you.''

He closed his eyes and sagged against her. ''Oh, Becca.''

''It's true,'' she told him. ''My heart flutters when you walk into a room. My knees get weak when you smile at me. I hurt when you hurt, and I can't stand the thought of being apart from you. There's a special connection between us. I don't know how it happened, it just did. Yes, you're older than me and more experienced, but you are my soul mate.''

Cord felt his heart beating in unison with hers. They *were* one. He'd felt it for a very long time. But could he take from her what she was so willing to give?

He drew back and stared into her darkened eyes. ''I've made so many promises about you. I promised myself I wouldn't get involved with Colton's girlfriend or someone so young, and most definitely I wouldn't fall for another city woman. But I broke all those promises.''

She kissed the corner of his mustache, his cheek, and then her tongue tantalized his ear with gentle strokes.

''Becca.'' His head tilted toward her as the emotions she engendered in him overshadowed his doubts. He took a deep breath. ''I have a feeling I'm going to break another one.''

She smiled and rained kisses along his neck to his jaw. Her lips met his in a long, heated kiss and her hands quickly unbuttoned his shirt, her fingers reveling in the taut muscles before she unfastened his belt.

''Wait.'' He breathed raggedly. ''I have to take off my boots.''

''No problem.'' She laughed as she slid to the floor, grabbed a boot and began to pull.

"A cowboy's dream," he remarked. "A woman to remove his boots."

"I thought a cowboy's dream was to have a woman warm his bed."

"Ah, they're one and the same thing." Cord grinned. "First she removes his boots, then she warms his bed...among other things."

The task completed, Becca stood and removed her T-shirt. "I can do *other things*." She met his grin, which slowly turned to an expression of awe.

"My God, you're beautiful," he whispered. He reached for her, pulling her between his legs. His lips found her sensitive breasts and then he quickly removed her panties, and his lips and hands tantalized her body until her knees buckled and they fell back onto the bed.

She helped him out of his jeans, and his body was hard, firm and aroused. Her hands touched and explored and excited feelings she'd never experienced before. "Becca, are you sure? I don't think I can—"

Her finger covered his lips. "I don't want you to stop. I want you to love me."

He cradled her face in his hands and gazed into her eyes. "Do you know how much I love you?"

She smiled the most beautiful smile he'd ever seen. "No, but you can show me."

"Becca, Becca." His tone was ragged as he rolled her onto her back.

He was gentle and tender, just as she'd known he would be. The first thrust of pressure tightened her muscles, then Cord kissed her deeply and her body melted into a shimmering receptacle. The next thrusts she accepted with unbound pleasure that echoed through every nerve ending and intensified until she cried his name with an urgency that carried her to a realm she'd only dreamed about. Cord moaned his release a moment later, but they held on to each other, still needing that closeness.

"Are you all right?" he said, his breath warm against her neck.

"Oh-h, yes. Cowboys definitely do it better."

He grinned at her. "How do you know? You have nothing to compare it with."

"Oh, I just know." She smoothed his hair back. "That's why I waited so long. I've been waiting for you."

"Becca…"

"Don't ruin this moment with regrets," she warned.

He kissed her softly. "I won't. I've just never met anyone like you before."

"Good." She sighed. "Now I just want to go to sleep in your arms and feel your breath on my skin."

He moved to the left side of the bed and pulled her in to him. "That can be arranged."

She snuggled against him. "Thank you," she whispered.

"I'm the one who should be saying that." He kissed her neck. "Go to sleep, my Becca. I'll be here when you wake up."

She fell asleep with that thought in her head. *He will be here.*

Cord got up and turned off the lights. When she murmured softly, he gathered her back in his arms. Tomorrow he'd probably have those regrets and curse himself for taking something so precious from her, but tonight he would cherish this moment and this woman.

BECCA WOKE UP to a lethargic achy feeling and it was a wonderful sensation. She stretched languorously and reached for Cord. He wasn't there. *Oh, no.* He'd said he'd be here. He couldn't have—then she spotted him in the bathroom shaving, and her heart rebounded.

For a few minutes she just watched him. Shaving cream was slathered across his chin and he was methodically shaving away a night's growth. All he had on was his underwear. Light brown hair covered his lean body in all the masculine places—places she'd explored last night. A warm ache dissolved in her lower abdomen as she remembered his gentleness. Their lovemaking was everything she'd ever thought it would be, and she was so glad she'd waited for Cord. Sex with love was exactly as Emily had told her—more than a physical act, it was a coming together of two hearts, bodies and souls.

Her hands ached to touch him. She slipped out of bed and walked naked into the bathroom. She curled her arms around his waist from behind, drew in his tangy masculine scent and kissed his back. "Good morning."

Cord's whole body jerked alive at her soft touch. He wiped shaving cream from his face with a towel and turned to her. His breath caught in his throat at her sheer loveliness. Her hair was mussed, her eyes bright, and she was beautiful to her soul. He didn't know how he'd got so lucky, but he wasn't going to question his feelings anymore. They were too damn good.

"Good morning," he murmured as he kissed the fading bruise on her face. Then his hands caressed her smooth shoulders and worked their way down her arms to her waist and pulled her nude body against him. He leaned against the cabinet, holding her close, marveling at all the emotions that tripped through his body—emotions that had been dormant for too long.

His eyes slid to her breasts. "When I saw you in tight jeans, I thought that was as good as it got. Then I saw you in that big T-shirt with those gorgeous legs and I knew it couldn't get any better than that. But this—" he kissed each breast lingeringly "—is my favorite. You without a stitch on is pure heaven."

Her body shivered with delight as she stood on tiptoes and linked her hands behind his head. "I kind of like you that way, too."

"Do you?" He grinned mischievously.

"Mmm." His lips smothered the sound against her mouth in an open, revealing kiss that she welcomed. "I like that, too." She giggled as she felt his hardness against her.

He groaned and the kiss deepened. Her fingers tangled in his hair and his hands were equally at work on her body. Slowly he turned, and they moved toward the bed, still in each other's arms. They tripped over his boots and fell backward onto the bed laughing. But the laughter died as more urgent demands took over. Cord kissed, touched and caressed until everything spun away but the love that bound them together.

Later—how much later she wasn't sure—she lay in the crook of his arm, savoring this special time with the man she adored. Nothing would ever equal the experience of finding love and having it returned. She suddenly knew what her restlessness was all about—Becca the woman had been struggling to emerge…and now she had.

"I don't want to, but I've got to go," he said with a tremor in his voice. "I'd have a hard time explaining to Nicki what I'm doing in your bed."

She turned her head and kissed him. They hadn't talked about the future, but they would. In the meantime, their love would grow until it encompassed everyone around them. Last night had been a big step, and each step now would guide them toward the future.

Cord hurriedly slipped into his jeans and grabbed his boots and shirt from the floor. "I'll get Nicki up and fed

so you can take it easy," he said. "Then I'll ask Edie and
Smithy to take her riding, 'cause I want to finish cleaning
out Anette's room." He reached down and softly kissed
her warm lips. "Oh," he muttered. "If I don't go now, I'll
never get out of here. See you later." Another quick kiss
and he was gone.

She pushed up against the headboard and sat for a long
time with her arms around her waist, just enjoying these
wonderful new feelings. Cord loved her and she loved him.
But she felt an uneasiness, a vaguely unsettled sensation,
which she knew must be related to Anette's death. She had
to put that out of her mind. Cord had finally accepted it;
that was the main thing. Today they'd clear out the rest of
Anette's things and, as Cord had said, close that door forever. After that, they'd talk about the future. Instinctively,
she realized that Cord would not want her to give up her
job—just as she'd never ask him to leave this ranch. She
could easily commute. It would take her thirty to forty-five
minutes to get to work each day, depending on traffic, but
she wouldn't mind. She'd do a lot more to be with Cord.

A smile spread across her face, and she knew she had to
talk to someone. She picked up the phone and punched in
Gin's number. It was early, but she knew Gin would be
getting ready for work. Not that she planned to tell her
every little thing. She just wanted to tell her best friend that
she'd finally fallen in love. Madly, deeply, forever in love.

The phone rang several times, then a sleepy voice came
on the line. "Hello."

Becca was startled. That wasn't Gin's voice—but she
knew it well. "Colton, is that you?"

"Becca?" He sounded just as startled.

"Yes."

"Oh—you're...probably wondering what I'm doing
here."

"No, I—"

He broke in. "I...uh, Ginger's having a problem with her car and I stopped by to help her."

Becca frowned. Colton was lying. He didn't know a thing about cars and he'd be the last person Gin would call. Wouldn't he?

"I'm glad you could help her," she said for lack of anything else to say. "Is Gin there?"

"Yeah, yeah, she's right here."

There was a moment of strained silence. "Hi, Bec," Ginger said, her voice tentative.

"Has the world stopped turning and no one told me?" she asked in a teasing manner.

"What do you mean?"

"You asked Stuffed Shirt for help. That has to mean something drastic."

"Well, stuffed shirts are good for something." Becca heard a muffled laugh. "I've got to go," Gin added quickly. "I'm running late. I'll talk to you when you get back to Houston."

Becca hung up the phone with a smile. Something was definitely going on between Colton and Ginger. And they didn't want her to know about it. Why? She was happy for them; she had to make that clear as soon as possible.

SHE AND CORD DIDN'T GET TO Anette's room until later in the day. Nicki clung to Becca, not wanting to do anything without her. Becca figured this had to do with her injury, and she spent the morning reassuring Nicki. They played games, read stories and laughed. She didn't want Nicki to lose any ground. Becca knew it was time for Nicki to be in a play group, which would help prepare her for school in August.

After lunch, she and Cord walked to the stables with

Nicki and Edie. They watched her ride for a little while, then headed back to the house. Smithy promised to keep an eye on Edie and Nicki.

They held hands and couldn't seem to stop smiling. Blanche gave them a knowing look, as did Edie and Della—but that was fine. Everyone could see they were in love.

In the hall Cord pulled her into his arms and kissed her deeply. "I've been wanting to do that all day."

"Me, too," she whispered against his lips.

"We could go to your room," he muttered hoarsely.

"We could," she agreed, "but let's finish Anette's room first...."

"Good idea," he said, moving down the hall. "I don't want to think about this anymore after today."

As Becca followed, she remembered the pictures of the Prescott men. She'd never asked Colton, but she wanted to know. "Cord, why are there no portraits of Prescott women?"

He shrugged. "I'm not sure. It just seems to be a tradition to hang portraits of the men."

"That needs to be changed," she said in a tight voice.

He raised an eyebrow. "Does it?"

She poked him in the ribs. "Yes, and I'm sure Blanche and Edie would agree."

"Oh God, I can feel a family uprising about to start."

"It doesn't seem fair to me," she went on, ignoring him. "Prescott women have produced Prescott men, so..."

He gave her a quick kiss. "It isn't, but nothing in this family is done the way it should be."

"That needs to be changed, too."

He shook his head. "You've already changed a lot of that, and if anyone can change the portrait situation, you can, but for now, let's concentrate on Anette's room."

They worked until they had everything in boxes. Becca noticed that all of Cord's things had already been removed from the room. Cord taped up the boxes of clothing and accessories and carried them to the garage to be taken to a charity. Anette's purse and several small photo albums were still in a drawer, and Becca couldn't help flipping through the albums. There were pictures of Cord, Anette and Nicki and their life together. Anette's expression was often tense, and she was smiling in only a couple of the photos. She seemed to be constantly unhappy. Becca assumed that was a result of her depression—Anette's obvious anxiety and inability to feel happiness.

Cord said he didn't want the albums, so Becca added them to the things they were saving for Nicki. She didn't know what to do about the purse so she handed it to Cord. Dumping its contents on the bed, he pulled out the credit cards and license to destroy. The makeup and miscellaneous items he threw in the trash. Photos, he put in with the albums. He picked up an envelope and tore it open. Inside was a letter.

Becca leaned over his arm to read.

Stop bothering me and making those vile insinuations and remarks. I can't take any more. If you don't stop, I'll tell Cord. I'm serious. You don't frighten me. A

"What does that mean?" she asked.

Cord shook his head. "I have no idea and there's no address on the envelope." He took a long breath. "Someone was bothering her. Who? And why? God, this is so bizarre."

She rubbed his arm. "I know, and I guess there's no way we'll ever find out."

He tossed the letter onto the bed. "That's what makes me so damn angry. I just want to know."

Becca wrapped her arms around him, wishing she could give him some answers. All she could offer was comfort. "Let's finish up and get out of here," she suggested.

"Sounds good to me," he murmured in a distant voice, staring at the letter.

She left him with his thoughts and stepped inside the walk-in closet. At the bottom she found two handmade quilts.

"These are so lovely," she said, picking up one of the quilts. "Who made them?"

"Anette," he answered solemnly. "The doctor thought it would be good for her to have a hobby. She really enjoyed it for a while, then she just lost interest."

"We definitely have to keep these for Nicki," she said, gathering up the quilts. As she stood, she noticed something that had been concealed beneath them. "What's that?"

It was a small metal box. Frowning, Cord took it into the bedroom. "I'm not sure. I've never seen it before." He laid it gingerly on the bed.

Still holding the quilts, Becca stood beside him and they both stared at it. "Is it locked?" she finally asked.

Cord sat down and tried the lock, and the lid popped open. There were papers inside. He took a deep breath for strength. He didn't know what these papers were, but somehow he felt they were going to change his life. He wanted to slam the lid and throw the box away, but he couldn't. He had to face what was in the box—for himself, his child…and Becca.

He withdrew the first paper and unfolded it. Setting down the quilts, Becca sat next to him and read the document. "It's your marriage license," she said.

"Yeah," he murmured with relief. Maybe this wouldn't

be as bad as his gut was telling him. The next paper was
Nicki's birth certificate. At the bottom was a large document. Cord slowly unfolded it and as he began to read, his
body started to tremble and he couldn't stop the anger that
coursed through him.

"What is it?" Becca asked worriedly.

"It's Pa's will." The words were low and bitter.

Becca's first thought was to wonder what Anette was
doing with Claybourne Prescott's will; her second was to
ask why Cord was so angry. His hand clenched the paper
and a look she'd never seen before came over his face.

"Cord." She placed her hand on his arm. "Tell me
what's wrong."

"This says…" He had to swallow before he could continue. "This says the ranch was left to me and Edie. Clay
and Colton were given trust funds, and Blanche a monthly
allowance."

"Oh." Becca suddenly understood what was wrong.
"Did you never see your father's will?"

"Yes, but it wasn't anything like this. Everything was
left to Blanche, and his children received trust funds." He
paused, staring down at the will. "You see, Blanche Duffy
and Claybourne Prescott made a deal. He would leave everything to her if she married him and gave him a son. The
will was drawn up when Clay was born—and that was the
will I saw. This one throws me."

"Oh," she said again.

"This is dated twenty years ago."

"Then it was made later than the original will," she said.
When she noticed the shock on his face, she wished she
hadn't spoken.

He stood and started to pace. "Looks that way, but what
the hell was Anette doing with it? She never mentioned a
thing about Pa's will. What does this *mean?*"

She got up, too, and flung her arms around his waist, stopping him in midstride.

"I don't understand any of this," he mumbled into her hair.

"I don't, either, but there *has* to be a reasonable explanation," she told him.

"Yeah," he muttered, his eyes dark. "And I know exactly where to get it." Still clutching the will, he grabbed the letter from the bed and stormed out of the room.

"Cord," she called, but he was gone. Becca could guess where he was going—to find Blanche.

CHAPTER FIFTEEN

CORD CHARGED INTO THE KITCHEN, where Della was dicing onions. "Where's Blanche?" he asked abruptly.

"In her room, I think." She eyed him strangely.

"Go outside and find Edie and tell her to come to the house. And please stay at the stables with Nicki."

Della put down the knife. "What's wrong?"

"Just do as I ask. I'm not in the mood for a lot of questions." Cord knew his voice was hard but he couldn't help it. Inside he was a cauldron of emotions.

"Sure, sure," Della said as she headed out the door.

Cord turned and saw Becca standing in the doorway with a worried frown. His stomach churned with the love he felt for her, but it didn't diminish the other emotions. "I have to handle this in my own way," he told her.

"I know," she said. "Just try not to lose your temper."

He went down the hall and banged on Blanche's door. "I want to talk to you now." When there was no response, he banged again. "*Now,* Blanche."

He joined Becca in the den and paced as he waited for his mother. She finally arrived, dressed in a tight black dress and heels. She was obviously getting ready to go out.

"What the hell's the rush?" she complained, staring at her red nails.

"You want to explain this to me?" He shoved the will in her face.

"What is that?"

"Pa's will. His last will and testament," Cord burst out. "It reads a little differently from the one we saw after his death. So I think you'd better explain—and fast."

Blanche's skin took on a grayish hue. "Where did you get that?" she asked, sinking onto the sofa.

"I found it in Anette's room."

"That bitch. She said she was gonna destroy it."

Cord took a jerky breath and tried to maintain some control. "What was Anette doing with it in the first place?"

"She was looking for Nicki's birth certificate for school and came across it in my safe. I'd left the damn thing open."

"Why didn't she tell me?" He couldn't understand that. Why would Anette keep this a secret from him?

"You're the last person she wanted to know."

"What!"

"Think, Cord," Blanche said. "If you found out you owned half this ranch, she knew you'd never leave. Her main goal was to get you away from here. My secret was safe with the snotty little—"

"Shut up!" Cord shouted. "So this is Pa's last will?"

"That's it," Blanche said in an impertinent tone.

"And the will you showed us?"

Blanche remained quiet.

"Tell me!" he shouted again.

"That was the will Claybourne drew up when Clay was born," Blanche said.

"And? Dammit, Blanche, you'd better tell me what happened because I'm losing my patience."

"After…after you boys were grown, Claybourne changed his mind. He went to the lawyer one day and changed everything, then told me what he had done. He said Clay and Colton weren't interested in the ranch, and you and Edie were. He said I would always be taken care of and I didn't have to worry. But I did. I wanted to leave him because he'd broken our deal, but I had nowhere to go and I'd never see my boys again. I..." Blanche turned away, her shoulders heaving.

Cord gave her a minute to recover; he needed one, too.

"I didn't know what to do." Blanche continued. "I knew Edie wouldn't let me stay here. So I did the only thing I could. I used the first will."

Cord sucked air into his tight lungs and realized he was still holding the letter from Anette's purse. "Explain this."

Blanche frowned. "I don't know what that is."

"You were bothering Anette—threatening her—and she couldn't take anymore. You pushed her over the edge."

"Now, wait a minute," Blanche said indignantly. "I didn't threaten her. She's the one who threatened me. I don't know what that letter means, but it has nothing to do with me."

Edie came in, and Becca caught her and held a finger to her lips.

Cord glanced at his older sister and decided he could only deal with one thing at a time. "So let me get this straight. Pa left me and Edie the ranch, and you took it upon yourself to lie, to deceive us."

Blanche clasped her hands, twisting them nervously. "I didn't have any choice," she mumbled.

"What are you talking about?"

"I gave up my life for Claybourne and all he left me was a pitiful allowance. I couldn't live on that. I had to do something and—"

"A pitiful allowance?" Cord interrupted harshly. "A whole family could live on what he left you. You have free room and board and the ranch pays for your Cadillac and credit cards. What else do you need money for?"

Blanche stared at the big diamond on her hand. "It was more than that."

"How?"

She looked directly into his eyes. "I haven't been a good mother. Hell, I haven't been a mother at all, and Edie hates me. You two would've kicked me out before Claybourne was ever buried. This ranch has been my home since I was a girl." Her voice quavered on the last word.

Cord ran both hands through his hair. "You believed I would kick out my own mother?"

"Yes," she said without hesitation.

Cord swallowed hard. "I lost track of the number of times Pa said to me, 'When I'm gone, son, look out for your mother. Take care of your mother, son.' Do you think I would go against anything he ever asked of me?"

"I didn't know," she said weakly.

"He cared about you, and if you'd given any of us a chance, we would have, too."

Blanche trembled and she seemed to have difficulty breathing. "When Claybourne and I talked about getting married, he said he'd leave everything to me if I gave him a son. Over the years, Edie has made that look as if I was a greedy bitch out to get everything Claybourne had. It was Claybourne's idea, but in truth it was the only reason I agreed to marry him. I wanted freedom from the men and the bar, and I wanted a better way of life. Claybourne said he'd treat me like a queen. He said I wouldn't have to lift a finger. And he kept his word. He treated me better than I'd ever been treated in my whole life and I began to care for him. It wasn't just a bargain anymore, it was real, but I didn't know how to tell him that.

"When I got pregnant with Clay, I was nervous. I was still just a kid and I didn't want to be a mother. I didn't know anything about it. All I knew was how to tend bar.

Claybourne said not to worry, he'd take care of everything. After Clay was born, he whisked me off to a spa for a month to recover and hired a nanny for the baby. He was just so grateful to have a son. He did the same thing with each child. I never had a chance to bond with my babies. I never…I never got to hold my babies.''

Silence stretched for endless seconds and Cord had difficulty absorbing the heartfelt words. ''Did you really want to?'' he finally had to ask.

Blanche met his gaze. ''Yes.''

''Then, how could you do this to me—and Edie?''

''I was fighting to stay here,'' she said quietly. ''That was my only reason.''

''Why hold it over our heads for years?''

Blanche twisted her hands again. ''Because…that's the only way anyone noticed I was here.''

The emotion in Blanche's voice startled Cord, and he was at a loss for words.

''You horrible, horrible woman.'' Edie broke in, unable to stay quiet any longer. She glanced at Cord. ''Is it true? There's another will? Pa left me half the ranch?''

Cord handed her the will.

''Oh God. Oh God,'' she said, and started to cry. ''I thought he'd forgotten about me. But he didn't. He knew how much this ranch meant to me. Oh God, I can't believe it.'' She sank unsteadily into a chair and stared at Blanche. A sly smile tugged at her lips. ''Well, the tables have turned. And you're right, Blanche. I want you out of here as soon as possible.''

Blanche got to her feet. ''Gloat all you want, Edie,'' she said. ''I could've kicked your ass out of here when Claybourne died, but I respected his wishes. I gave you just as much money as my boys, and I put up with your holier than thou attitude not out of the kindness of my heart, but because I knew Claybourne wanted it that way. All these years you've alluded to the men in my life. Well, after I married Claybourne, I was faithful to him, and there hasn't been anyone since his death. Hell, I not only gave him a son, I gave him three. So believe all the bad things you want. You've always looked at me as the enemy, as someone who took your place with your father. You never looked at anything from my point of view. I was young and a stranger in your house. I knew I had to be strong to survive. I did a terrible thing with the will, and I'm not apologizing for it.'' She took a breath and continued. ''You've taken far more from me than I've ever taken from you. So gloat if it makes you feel better.''

''What do you mean, I took from you? I never took a thing!''

''You took my babies,'' Blanche said quietly.

''Because you didn't want them.''

''I wanted my babies, but I just never knew how...'' Blanche blinked back a tear and Becca could see she was fighting not to cry, still struggling not to show any emotion. ''Christmases were the worst. Claybourne just assumed I didn't want to be part of the festivities. I always watched you boys open your gifts from the hallway.'' She looked at Cord. ''I gave you your first saddle—the one with the silver on it. I had a hell of a time dragging it into the house. Claybourne thought Edie bought it, and Edie thought Claybourne bought it. One never questioned the other. I also bought Clay and Colton their first computers. There were always presents from me under the tree, but no one ever knew and I—'' Her voice cracked and she shook her head.

She'd bought him the saddle; that was all Cord could think. He remembered how excited he'd been when he saw it. He'd loved that saddle. He'd used it until he got too big for it, and Nicki used it now. *Blanche bought the saddle for him.* He'd never even dreamed his mother thought about him. His emotions were overwhelmed by so many new feelings.

"I'll pack my things and get out of here," Blanche added in a rush.

"No one's going anywhere," Cord said, and Becca couldn't have loved him more than at that moment.

"Sit down, Blanche," he added. "We have to sort this out." He looked at Edie. "I know how you feel and I also know you're not hard-hearted. Blanche has a lot of explaining to do and we're both going to listen." He turned back to Blanche. "How did you get Pa's lawyer to keep the second will a secret?"

Blanche moved uncomfortably. "After Floyd Dawson drew up the will, his job was done. Claybourne didn't ask him to keep it or to see that his wishes were carried out. Then Claybourne put the original in the safe, but he didn't destroy the old one. I didn't know what I was going to do when your father passed away—and then I saw both wills. Claybourne and I had made a deal, and I decided to stick to our agreement. It wasn't something I consciously planned. I was desperate and I did it before I could really think about it. I was home free until that stupid Anette started snooping around."

Cord closed his eyes briefly. "At this point, Blanche, it would be in your best interests to make an effort to stay on my good side. Snide remarks about Anette aren't accomplishing that."

"I want her out of here, Cord," Edie said, her voice hard.

"Let me handle this, please," he said to Edie. Then he addressed Blanche. "So Dawson knew about the second will and said nothing."

"It's not his job to enforce it."

"Morally, ethically, it's his job! Hell." He shoved a hand through his hair.

"She needs to be in jail," Edie said. "She's committed a crime. I know she has."

"Edie," Cord said sharply, his eyes never leaving Blanche. "We made this easy for you, didn't we, Blanche?"

"Yes. After the funeral, Clay and Colton were eager to get back to their jobs. They looked at the will and said to let them know when I'd taken care of everything." Blanche let out a long breath. "And you were so broken up over Claybourne's death, you didn't want to talk about wills or anything else. You let me handle all the details."

"Do you know why that was?"

Blanche shook her head.

"Because we trusted you," Cord said. "I trusted you not to do something like this to me."

Blanche bit her lip, and Cord could see she was wrestling with her conscience. He was glad to learn she had one.

"We all knew about the first will," he went on. "We'd heard the story all our lives. And we also knew how much Pa loved you. It never crossed our minds that he'd change his will."

Blanche pushed back her hair nervously. "He never believed I loved him. He thought someone so young couldn't love a man his age. I didn't love him at first, but I grew to love him more than I'd ever thought I could. I wouldn't have stayed here, otherwise."

"Ha," Edie interjected.

Cord ignored Edie, trying to take in everything he was hearing. This Blanche was throwing him. This Blanche had feelings. He was angry with her, yet he found he couldn't maintain that anger. Still, through all the tumultuous emotion, he had to be clear on one thing.

"I'm not sure what to believe right now, but I want you to tell me the truth about Anette."

Blanche gave him a puzzled frown. "What about her?"

"The letter. Did you have anything to do with it?"

"No! I wouldn't lie to you now. Whoever Anette wrote that letter to, it wasn't me."

Cord was unsure and needed more detail, more corroboration. "You're the one who found her. What made you go to her room?"

"When I got in that day, Della and Edie had Nicki in the kitchen and Nicki was crying, wanting her mother. I asked where Anette was, and Edie said she'd been in her room most of the day. I decided the lazy bi—" She paused and changed her tone. "I decided she wasn't getting away with that. She was gonna take care of her kid. I found her on the floor with the whiskey bottles and the pills. I immediately called you, and you rushed her to the hospital. That's all I know. I never realized she drank so much."

"Maybe because you made her life a living hell," Cord snapped.

"She wasn't the saint you thought she was," Blanche shot back. "What do you think she did when she found the will? Did she tell you? No. She held it over my head, threatening to tell you, and she enjoyed every minute of it. Finally I told her to go ahead—that would put an end to her dream of leaving. She knew I was right and she didn't have to write me a letter to tell me that. Whatever we had to say to each other, we said face-to-face."

Cord sighed tiredly. "Where did the liquor come from?"

Blanche blinked. "What?"

"The liquor that was in our room is not the kind that's kept in this house. Where did it come from?"

"How would I know? She did have the ability to buy

things. Wait a minute—'' Blanche's eyes narrowed. ''Are you saying *I* bought her the liquor?''

''I'm not saying anything. I just want answers.''

''Well, I don't have them.''

Silence. Cord stared at his mother and tried to piece everything together, but nothing was fitting, nothing made sense. He sighed again. Before he did anything else, he had to sort out the will.

''Edie and I have to talk,'' he finally said. ''And I have to call Clay and Colton. Everyone has to know the truth, and we have to deal with it.''

''Fine,'' Blanche said. She turned and left the room. Becca followed her.

BECCA FOUND HER SITTING on her bed, twisting the rings on her fingers, a broken expression on her face.

Blanche glanced up as Becca stepped into the room. ''If you've come to add your opinion, sugar, you'd better hurry because I'm not gonna be around much longer.''

''You don't know Cord very well if you think he'd make you leave,'' Becca said. Blanche had done a terrible thing, but Becca understood her motive and she knew Cord did, too. Her whole life, Blanche had been fighting to survive, and keeping the will a secret was just another instance of that.

''Yeah, well, what I know about my sons could be stored in a thimble.''

''Then stop trying to alienate yourself from them.''

Blanche gave her a puzzled look. ''What are you doing here, sugar?''

''I'm not really sure. I'm so angry at what you've done to Cord. He's suffered so much over Anette's death and he doesn't need this. But somehow…'' Becca paused, unsure of her next words. "Somehow I understand why you did it."

"Oh, please." Blanche laughed scornfully.

Becca let that pass. "Just tell me one thing."

"What?"

"Do you know anything about Anette's death?"

"I told Cord I don't, and I'm not lying about that."

For some reason Becca believed her. She'd had a lot of doubts about Blanche and she wanted to resolve them. "Ever since I've been here you've been trying to get me to leave. You've even made insinuations about something happening to me. Why?"

Blanche stared at her rings, then raised her head, her eyes holding Becca's. "Cord and I have had our disagreements, but he's the only son I have who even knows I'm alive. As long as I had control, I could keep him here. But the moment I saw you together, I knew you had a different kind of power over him. A kind Anette never had. You could take him away from here—away from me. He didn't deserve another city woman screwing up his life. I wanted to protect my son from any more pain."

Becca had already guessed most of this, but she was relieved to hear Blanche admit it.

"Yet you've hurt him." Becca couldn't help saying it.

"Yeah." Blanche flipped back her hair. "That proves what a good mother I am, doesn't it?" She spoke in a careless tone, but her attempt at indifference didn't fool Becca.

"Three little words could solve all your problems."

"And what would those be?"

"I love you."

Becca expected a comeback, but none came. The broken look returned to Blanche's face, and she seemed to be struggling for composure.

"Let your sons know you love them," Becca urged. "Love can work miracles."

When Blanche didn't respond, Becca walked out. She was sympathetic—surprisingly so—to the older woman, but her main concern was Cord and what he was going through. How would he handle this? Whatever he decided, she knew she'd be there for him—no matter what.

CORD SAT FACING HIS SISTER, searching for the right words. Before he could find them, Edie spoke.

"I want her gone."

"I know you do, but please understand that she's my mother." Cord didn't know why he was pleading Blanche's case, but that biological bond was there and he couldn't ignore it.

"She was never a mother."

"Maybe because she was never given the chance or maybe because she didn't know how." He rubbed his hands together. "Did she really give me the saddle?"

Edie shrugged. "I didn't buy it. Like she said, I assumed Pa did. I suppose she could have."

He gripped his hands tightly together. "I think we need some time to cope with all of this."

The phone rang, and Cord knew Della was outside with Nicki.

"Excuse me," he said. "I'd better get that." Edie seemed lost in her own thoughts, so he stood up and went to the kitchen to answer it.

"Triple Creek Ranch."

"Cord, this is Sheriff Reyes."

Cord quickly collected his thoughts. "Hi, Sheriff. Found out anything yet?"

"Yeah, we located where Bates is living. His girlfriend said he was out taking care of business, although she couldn't give us any details. We're still watching the place, but I wanted you to be aware of what's happening and to be on the lookout for him. He might show up again, because I have a feeling the business he's talking about is you. All my sources say he really has a grudge against you."

"Thanks, Sheriff. Don't worry, he's not getting near me or my family."

"Give me a call if you even spot him."

"I will."

Cord hung up and walked out onto the patio. He sat down, burying his face in his hands. The world seemed to be crashing in on him. Last night his life had seemed full of potential; his future had promised happiness. He had found something so precious in Becca. But now he'd discovered that his mother had betrayed him and Bates was out to get him. He didn't know how much more he could take, especially if Becca was hurt in the process. He'd do anything to keep her safe, and he wasn't letting her out of his sight until Bates was caught.

He surveyed the landscape, the ranch. He had put his heart and soul into this place and now it was his—and Edie's, too. In the end, that was what Pa had wanted. Somehow, that didn't make him feel better. How could his mother do this to him? And Anette? He didn't understand her part in this. She knew how much he loved the ranch. Why wouldn't she tell him what she'd learned? Was Blanche's accusation true—that Anette was trying to manipulate him into leaving Triple Creek?

The unanswered questions were tearing him apart.

BECCA HURRIED INTO THE DEN looking for Cord, and found Edie silently crying. Becca's heart went out to her. Two stubborn women and both wanting the same thing—to be loved. She knelt by Edie's chair and hugged her.

"He really loved me." Edie choked out the words. "I thought he'd forgotten about me, but he loved me." Edie clutched the will in her hand, so Becca knew what she was talking about.

"Of course he loved you. You were his daughter," Becca told her softly.

"After he brought *her* here, things changed. I became invisible to Pa and I hated her."

"*Hate* is a very destructive word."

"It's how I feel, especially after what she's done to Cord."

"But Cord will forgive her," Becca said confidently.

Edie wiped her eyes. "You seem sure of that."

"I am." She placed her hand over her heart. "Because I know him in here. He'll never be able to turn his back on his mother."

"She's an awful person," Edie muttered.

"Have you ever given yourself a chance to get to know her?"

"No, and I don't want to."

"Let go of the bitterness, Edie. Don't be the one to tear this family apart."

Edie stared ahead with a defiant expression, and Becca got up and left her with her memories. The Prescott family was hurting, and try as she might, she couldn't bring them together. Maybe she was trying too hard. She had to let it happen naturally; she couldn't force them to love one another.

She finally found Cord on the patio. He was staring off into space with a shattered look on his face. His sorrow and confusion wrenched her heart, and she opened the door and went outside to him. When she slid into his lap, his arms gripped her tightly.

"How could she do this?" he whispered.

"For love," she murmured, tangling her fingers in the hair that curled into his collar.

"What?"

"Power and control is love to Blanche. Somehow, by having control, she thought she could keep her boys coming back here and she'd be able to keep you under her thumb. Blanche hasn't had much love in her life, and she did everything she could to hang on to the little she had. She used devious methods, but she was desperate."

"Don't ask me to forgive and forget," he said stubbornly.

"That's exactly what I'm asking you to do."

"Becca…"

"When I found out that Emily was really my mother, I was so angry and hurt. I lashed out at everything and everyone around me. I wanted to hurt Emily and Rose like they'd hurt me, but when I saw the pain in Emily's eyes and saw what my behavior was doing to her, I realized that bitterness was an emotion that could destroy us all—if I let it. I didn't want that. I loved Emily and Rose and knew they were fighting just as fierce a battle as I was. Once we forgave each other, everything else fell into place."

He stroked her hair. "I'm so sorry you had to go through that, but this is different."

"No, it isn't," she insisted. "Blanche is your mother, and no matter how angry you are, you can't change that."

"No, no, I can't," he muttered. "I still can't believe she bought me that saddle. I was with Pa when I saw it in the store. I said I wanted it, and he said I was too young for a saddle like that. I'd have to wait until I got older. Then, there it was on Christmas morning. A gift from Santa."

"So he must've told Blanche about the saddle," she mused. "And he had to have known she bought it."

"I suppose."

"He probably knew her better than anyone—knew how afraid she was to show her feelings."

"She wasn't afraid of Pa. I've seen her get in his face when she was displeased with something."

"Like what?" she asked. She could imagine Blanche standing up to almost everyone, but she couldn't see her standing up to Claybourne Prescott.

Cord didn't answer, and she glanced at his face, which had gone a grayish white. "Cord," she said in an urgent voice. "What is it?"

"The arguments," he whispered. "The arguments were about us. I remember one time—Clay must've been about sixteen, and Pa wanted him to work on the ranch but instead he was building computers in his room. When Pa found out, he was furious. He said he was going to throw the computers in the creek and take a rope to Clay to beat some sense into him. Blanche got between them, and I can still hear her words. She said, 'Don't you dare. If you touch one hair on his head, I'll leave you.' Pa stormed out of the room, but afterward he was more open-minded about Clay's computer skills. I'd forgotten about that. And there was the time Colton tried his hand at smoking. He set his bed on fire, and Pa was livid at his stupidity. Pa took his belt off and said he was gonna teach him a lesson. Blanche took the belt away from him and said he wasn't hitting Colton and that Colton would be grounded for a month and wouldn't get an allowance until the damages were paid for. Pa never liked his decisions questioned, but he gave in to Blanche."

"Did you father ever hit you?"

"No, he had a bad temper and always did a lot of threatening, but he never hit any of us."

"Maybe because he knew Blanche wouldn't stand for it," she remarked. "In her own way, Blanche was there for each of you when you needed her."

"I never saw it that way back then, and neither did Clay or Colton."

"Maybe it's time you did."

He cupped her face and kissed her gently. "I wish I had your loving spirit."

She kissed him back, and for a minute they were lost in each other. He rested his forehead against hers. "Oh, I needed that."

"Me, too."

"Cord."

"Hmm?"

"Blanche didn't destroy the second will."

He pulled back to look at her. "What do you mean?"

"It was the original. So why didn't she destroy it? No one ever would have known, but something in Blanche wouldn't let her do that. It's called character. Granted, Blanche had to dig deep to find it, but she did. I wonder if your father left both wills in the safe as a test for her."

"Maybe," he murmured. "But I can't think about it anymore."

Blanche was a contradiction that tied him in knots. Who was the real Blanche? He didn't know, and maybe he'd never understand what motivated his mother. But he was very clear on one thing: Becca was the stabilizing force in his life. She brought him joy, and she gave him perspective on the whole family mess. For now, he would just concentrate on her.

He held her tighter. "The sheriff called a little while ago. They located Bates's address, but he wasn't there. Sheriff

Reyes wants us to be on the lookout for him. Evidently Bates has been spouting off to everyone that's he's gonna get even with me.''

"Then, he was the one who tampered with the brake line?"

"That's the way it's looking, and I don't want you going anywhere without me or someone else." He kissed the side of her bruised face. "I could kill him for what he's done to you."

"We'll just let the sheriff handle it, and I'll stick to you like glue." She pressed herself against him. "Oh, yeah, I like that idea."

He growled deep in his throat as his lips found hers, but the sound of someone coughing discreetly drew them apart. Mona was standing some distance away, watching them.

"I'm sorry," she said. "I don't mean to interrupt, but no one answered the door."

"That's all right," Cord said as he straightened.

He made no move to get up and Becca saw no need to get off his lap. Their relationship was intimate, and she certainly didn't want to keep that a secret.

"Blanche and Edie are dealing with a lot right now and I guess they didn't feel like answering the door," he explained.

"Is something wrong?"

Cord told her about the will.

"Cord, I'm so sorry," Mona said. "How could Blanche do that?"

"I'm still trying to figure it out."

"But I am happy for you. I know how you feel about this ranch."

"Thanks, Mona."

"When you didn't come by today, I knew there had to be some kind of problem."

"Damn, Mona, it completely slipped my mind. I'll try to get over there in the next couple of days."

"No hurry. Just take care of your family first."

"I will."

"Goodbye." Mona tipped her hat. "Dr. Talbert."

"You've known Mona for a long time?" Becca asked, as Mona walked away.

"Since we were kids. She and Clay are the same age. She had a crush on him when they were younger and she still asks about him."

"But Clay didn't feel the same way?"

"No, he preferred feminine blondes."

"Really? Must be something in the Prescott genes."

He grinned. "Not entirely. These days, this Prescott prefers dark hair and dark eyes and…" The rest of his words were drowned as she kissed him.

"And a lot of that," he added in a whisper.

Becca settled against him, feeling content. "Mona seems so stern and…sad."

"She's had a very difficult life," Cord said. "She was the only child of a man who wanted a son, which he never bothered to hide."

"I thought she *was* a man the first time I saw her."

"Sometimes she thinks she is. She runs her ranch better than almost any man I know. A few years back, she fell in love with a guy at the feed store. I told her what the hell, go for it, but then she found out he was married and she was devastated for weeks. Since then, I think she's given up on any chance of love or marriage."

"That's such a pity."

"Becca, Becca, Becca!" They could hear Nicki shouting as she came through the gate, her ponytail bouncing. Becca got up and met her halfway, and Nicki ran into her arms.

"You should've seen me," Nicki gushed. "I roped. Gus is teaching me. Gus said I was fast as greased lightning."

Becca kissed her cheek. "I'll bet you are." Her nose twitched as a pungent smell reached her nostrils and she noticed the dirt—or something else—on Nicki's jeans.

"What's that smell?"

Nicki brushed at her jeans. "I fell in the dirt when I jumped off Half Pint."

"I think it was more than dirt, little bit," Gus said from behind.

"It don't matter," Nicki said, then spotted Cord. "Daddy, wait till you hear!" She immediately ran to Cord.

Cord held her close. "I heard, baby."

"I can rope real good," Nicki mumbled into his shoulder.

Cord just continued to hold her. He loved his child with all his heart, just as he loved the woman staring at him with those sparkling, gorgeous eyes. He was truly blessed. The anger inside slowly eased as he realized that. It was hard to stay angry when he had so much. Somehow, he had to find a way to keep this family together. He knew that was what Becca wanted and now he wanted it, too. Truly wanted it, in a way he never had before.

"Let's get you cleaned up," Becca said, and took Nicki's hand.

"Gus said he ain't seen nothin' like it. He said…" Nicki was chattering away as they went into the house.

Gus removed his hat. "What's goin' on, Cord?"

Cord told him about the will.

"Good God Almighty, what's wrong with that woman?"

"It's a big mess" was all Cord said.

Gus shook his head. "By golly. Ain't this somethin'?"

Cord didn't want to tell him Blanche might have been harassing Anette. He still wasn't clear on that.

"Yeah, but there's someone else I want to talk about," he muttered.

"Who?"

"Joe Bates."

"Have they found the bastard?"

"No, but they found where he lives. His girlfriend said he was out taking care of business and the sheriff feels that business might be me. So I want everyone to be on the alert."

Gus stood. "Don't worry. He won't get past us again."

"Thanks, Gus, and I'd like to apologize for snapping at you the other day."

"No problem. We were all wound tight about the doc."

"I just can't stand the thought of someone hurting her."

Gus patted him on the shoulder. "Yeah. Well, ain't nothin' gonna happen to the doc as long as we're around. You can take that to the bank."

As Gus walked off, Cord hoped he was right. He'd feel a whole lot better when Joe Bates was caught.

CHAPTER SIXTEEN

THAT NIGHT, after they'd put Nicki to bed, Cord and Becca sat in the den curled up on the sofa. Blanche and Edie were in their rooms. They hadn't even come to supper. Nicki kept asking questions about it; she'd gotten used to Edie and Blanche eating with her. Cord just told her they had other plans for the evening. Nicki was disappointed because she'd wanted to tell them how well she could rope. That was the only thing on her mind, and she didn't notice any tension in the house, which was a relief to Cord.

Becca ran her fingers through Cord's hair. "What are you thinking about?"

He kissed the palm of her hand. "I called Colton and Clay while you were reading to Nicki."

"How did they react?"

"They were shocked, but both said basically the same thing. Pa left them a trust fund, which they got, and they're satisfied with that. They said that whatever Edie and I decide to do about the ranch is up to us and they'll support us. But we plan to meet and discuss it. Colton asked about you. Evidently your father mentioned the accident."

"What did he say?"

"His usual warning. Also that it's time for you to return to Houston, but he didn't seem as adamant as before."

She told him about the phone call to Ginger and that she thought Colton and Ginger were sleeping together.

"That's your best friend?"

"Yes, and Gin and Colton are always at each other's throat. I guess they finally found something not to argue about."

He looked into her eyes. "Are you happy about that?"

She smiled. "What do you think?"

He kissed her deeply, then asked in an aching voice, "What am I going to do about Blanche?"

She stood and took his hand. "Let's go upstairs and forget about Blanche and everything that's happened today. Let's just think about us. Tomorrow things might look different."

Arm in arm they went up the stairs. Inside her room, he took her into his embrace. "I love you," he said. "I can't get through this without you."

That was all she needed to hear. Somehow they'd survive this—as long as they had each other. They still hadn't talked about the future; that was for later. There were too many other things that took precedence. At the moment, Houston seemed a lifetime away.

THE NEXT MORNING Cord was up and dressed before she even woke. She stirred, and he kissed her lips.

"I'll get Nicki up for breakfast, then I'm going into town to talk to Pa's lawyer. He's got a lot of explaining to do."

She sat up. "Okay, but I'll miss you."

His eyes strayed to her breasts and he kissed each one slowly, his mustache a brush of delight. "If you don't stop, you'll never leave," she teased.

"I know." One last kiss, and he was strolling toward the door. At the door he added, "Don't stray too far from the house. Gus and the boys are on the lookout, but Bates could be anywhere."

"I won't," she promised as she headed for the bathroom. After getting dressed, she went down to the kitchen, looking forward to a cup of strong coffee. Nicki was there munching on cereal and telling Della about her roping at the same time.

"Morning, sweetie." She kissed the top of Nicki's head, then filled the largest mug she could find with fresh coffee.

"I'm gonna rope again today, Becca. Gus said I could, and you can watch me 'cause I'm real good. Gus said so."

Gus entered the kitchen. "How you doing, Doc?"

"Fine, thanks, Gus."

He glanced at Nicki. "Ready to go, little bit?"

"Yep." Nicki slipped out of her chair and looked at Becca. "C'mon."

"I'll finish my coffee and be right behind you."

"'Kay." She ran out the back door and Gus followed.

Becca watched as Della nervously wiped the table. "Della, are you all right?"

She faced Becca. "What's gonna happen to this family? Everything was going so well, but now—how could she do that to Cord?"

"I can't condone what Blanche did, but I don't think she meant to hurt anyone. She wanted to remain part of the family and she was afraid there wasn't much chance of that if the will surfaced. She should have trusted Cord, though. I thinks she knows that now."

"It's just awful, and so is the stuff with Joe Bates. What else is going to happen?"

Becca put an arm around her shoulder. "Nothing. The Prescotts are due for some good luck. Now I'd better check on Nicki. She might have Gus all tied up."

She got a partial smile out of Della. As she walked to the stables she wondered if Cord was at the lawyer's yet. She hoped he could find some answers to help him sort through this.

Several of the cowboys waved and she waved back. Dusty rode up. "You feeling better, ma'am?"

"Much better, and tell all the boys thanks for searching for me."

"No problem, ma'am. Have a good day."

He rode off, and Becca climbed onto the fence. Gus and Nicki were some distance away on horses. Gus twirled a rope over his head and swung it at a post. It circled the post swiftly and accurately.

Nicki had a much smaller rope, but she guided Half Pint toward the same post and swung the rope like Gus. Wobbly it landed on the post. "Did you see, Becca?" she called excitedly. "Did you see?"

"Yes, sweetie, I saw."

"I'm like greased lightning Gus says."

"Gus should know." Becca stayed for a while longer. Sometimes Nicki hit the post, sometimes she didn't. The misses didn't count, but the hits drew lots of shouting. Becca suspected she'd learned that from Gus.

Watching Nicki, she suddenly had the urge to call her own mother. She hadn't talked to her since the accident and needed to hear her voice. She felt deeply grateful for the love they shared; being around so much bitterness had made her realize what their lives could've been like if they hadn't had the strength to forgive. Cord, too, would forgive his mother, she thought. When he was ready, when he'd worked through his anger and his sense of betrayal.

"Sweetie," she called, "I'm going to the house to make a phone call. I'll be right back."

"'Kay," Nicki yelled, not taking her eyes off Gus.

Becca made her way to the house, where she met Della at the back door, clutching a large purse. "Today's my grocery day," Della explained. "See you later."

The house seemed eerily quiet as she walked upstairs.

Edie and Blanche were still in their rooms. She started for the phone, then saw Anette's albums lying on her dresser. She'd been planning to store them for Nicki, but with everything that had happened she hadn't had the chance. On impulse, she picked them up and sat on the bed. The first two were typical photos of a family. The third one wasn't an album at all. It was some sort of journal. There were notations in what she recognized as Anette's handwriting. Becca settled back and began to read.

I hate this place. Why can't Cord see that? Why doesn't he take me away from here? If he loved me, he would.

She scares me. Every time I see her, my skin crawls. She says nasty things and I don't know how to respond. Why can't she just leave me alone?

I want to tell Cord, but I can't. She said she'd get even if I did—that she'd hurt my baby. I have to keep Nicki away from her.

Little by little she's driving me crazy. The pills don't help anymore. I have to tell Cord. He's the only one who can stop her.

I love Cord and I love Nicki. Why can't I fight back? Why am I so weak? She's evil. I know she's evil.

There were more entries, all of them much the same. Becca slowly closed the album. "Oh, Blanche, what have you done?" she said under her breath. She had championed Blanche, thinking there was some good in her, but the woman had obviously driven Anette to her death by her abrasive behavior. How could Becca have been so wrong about her? Maybe she *was* evil. But Becca rejected that idea. She'd seen a side of Blanche no one else had—her vulnerability. Something wasn't fitting here.

The troublesome thoughts went around and around in her head. She placed the albums on the dresser again and wondered what to do about them. Cord had to see these, but she didn't want to cause him any more pain.

As she struggled with what to do, she remembered the quilts Anette had made and went along to Anette's room to retrieve them. She put the quilts and everything they'd saved for Nicki in a box and stored it in her closet. She left the journal on her dresser; Cord had to see it, she decided.

She called her mother and talked for half an hour or so. As she hung up, she heard a sound—a loud *thump*. She thought Nicki might have followed her into the house, and quickly opened her door to check. She was startled to see Mona in the hallway.

"I knocked, but there doesn't seem to be anyone around," Mona said.

Becca wondered why she hadn't just left instead of coming into the house uninvited. "I'm sorry, but this isn't a good time," she said in a cool voice.

Wordlessly, Mona pushed her way into the room and locked the door.

"Wait a minute! I—"

"Shut up," Mona screeched in barely controlled rage.

Becca took a couple of steps away from her.

"You couldn't leave him alone, could you?"

Becca shook her head. "What are you talking about?"

"Cord. You just had to have him."

"My relationship with Cord is none of your business."

"That's where you're wrong, *Doctor*." she said the last word with disdain. "I've waited all my life for Cord and I'm not waiting any longer. I took care of that mousy thing he brought home from Dallas and now I'm gonna take care of you."

One thing registered on Becca's mind. "What did you do to Anette?"

"I warned her that if she didn't leave, I'd hurt her."

"And you did, didn't you?"

A sinister smile tugged at her thin lips. "Yeah, it took me years, but I got rid of her."

Anette had been writing about Mona, not Blanche. It had been Mona all along driving Anette to the edge—but did Anette take that final step herself?

Becca moved back still farther. "How did you manage that?"

"It was easy. I made her swallow as many pills as I could, then I forced liquor down her throat until she passed out. I should've done it years ago."

She said the words with such joy that Becca began to tremble. The woman was insane. Insanely in love with Cord. And Becca was locked in this room with her.

Mona saw the fear in her eyes. "You've got a right to be afraid. You should've left when I let that bull out of the pen."

"You did that?" She gasped.

"Yeah, Cord was so busy staring at you, he didn't see me undo the latch."

"And the Jeep?" she asked shakily.

She nodded. "I rode off, but I walked back. Everyone was at the pens. The cowboys were so eager to show off for you that no one noticed when I slipped under the Jeep. All it took was a couple of twists with a wrench."

Becca was speechless. It wasn't Joe Bates—it was Mona. She knew words were futile because the woman had completely lost touch with reality. But Becca had to talk. That was what she did best. She had to talk until someone came to help her. *Cord, please hurry home.*

"But it didn't work." She found her voice. "It only drew Cord and me closer."

"Shut up!" Mona yelled.

"Cord hasn't fallen in love with you in all these years and it's not going to happen, even if you kill me."

"He will. You're young and pretty and you've turned his head. When you're gone, he'll come to me."

"He didn't when Anette died."

"Shut up," Mona yelled again. "I'm tired of listening to you."

Becca swallowed, desperately searching for a way to keep Mona talking. "You said you've been waiting for Cord all your life, but wasn't it Clay you loved first?"

"Yeah, I had a thing for Clay, but he wasn't a rancher and I knew he wasn't the man for me. Cord was different. We have the same interests, and he cares for me. Clay never did."

"Are you sure Cord cares for you?"

"Yes," she replied smugly. "I made up this story about a guy at the feed store I was seeing. I told Cord the guy was married, and Cord got very upset."

"He was upset that you might get hurt," Becca said, remembering the story Cord had told her. "Cord has a very soft heart, but he doesn't have those feelings for you, and you know it. That's why you made up that story."

"Stop talking," Mona shouted, pulling a large syringe from her pocket.

Fear became something real and vivid, and if someone didn't come soon Becca didn't have many choices. Mona was so much bigger, and the hope of holding her off was a pitiful dream.

"One injection and you'll die a peaceful death."

"What's in the syringe?"

"Just can't stop with the questions, can you?" Mona sneered sarcastically. "But since you're so curious, I'll tell you. It's sodium pentobarbital—a euthanasia solution."

"Where did you get something like that?"

"I had a problem a couple of months ago with a few cows having deformed calves. The vet left the drug with me in case it happened again. That way I could put the calf down myself. You see, the vet trusts me. Everyone does."

"There'll be an autopsy. Cord will find out what you did."

"It can't be traced to me," Mona retorted. "I told the vet I used it. It's all on paper. Besides, Joe Bates worked for a vet once. He knows how to get the drug. Everyone'll think he did it."

"You won't—"

The words were cut off as Mona grabbed her by the hair and threw her onto the bed. In an instant, Mona had straddled her, clamping both of Becca's hands in one of hers. Mona was strong, and Becca's attempts to break free were futile.

Mona laughed, a cruel sound. "Go ahead, Doctor, fight until you don't have any breath left. In a minute it won't matter, anyway."

"You can't do this," Becca said in a shaky voice. "Think about Nicki. She can't take losing someone else. She's just a little girl."

Mona removed the plastic cap on the needle with her teeth and spit it on the floor. "She's a nuisance and I'll have to find a way to get rid of her, too. Ship her off to school or something 'cause I'm not having her whining around me."

"You bitch!" Becca shouted. "You conniving, evil bitch." She bucked and twisted and turned, determined to get away, but then she saw the needle coming toward her and she screamed with every ounce of strength she had.

BLANCHE STROLLED INTO the kitchen and poured a cup of coffee, then started for the den, coffee in hand, to add a spot of brandy. She stopped abruptly and stared. Edie was lying on the floor, blood oozing from her head.

"Oh my God," Blanche cried, dropping the coffee. It splattered all over her slacks and feet, but she didn't notice. She threw herself down and raised Edie's head. "Edie, what happened?"

Blood soaked through Blanche's clothes as she cradled Edie in her arms. She jumped up and ran into the kitchen for towels and wrapped them tightly around Edie's head. "Edie, can you hear me?"

Edie moaned.

"What happened?"

"I…came down…and someone hit me. A big person."

"Oh God, you're bleeding so bad. I've got to get you to a hospital."

At that moment, Cord walked through the back door, feeling a lot better. Dawson had confirmed everything Blanche had said—even her fear of being kicked out of the house. Cord had had a few choice words to say to him, but the lawyer had said he'd merely made out the will. Claynourne hadn't asked for him to enforce it. He'd said Blanche had shared a few confidences with him; that was all. He wasn't privy to what she'd decided to do. He'd figured it was a family situation. And Cord realized it was. The thing, though, was that Blanche hadn't lied to him about any of this. It meant a lot, but right now, he just had to see Becca.

He stopped short as he entered the den, then dropped down beside Blanche and Edie. "What the hell happened?"

Blanche wrapped another towel around Edie's head. "I'm trying to stop the bleeding," Blanche cried. "Call 911!"

Cord grabbed the phone from the table and dialed. "They're on the way." He saw that Blanche was soaked with blood and that her hands shook as she held the towels tight. He put his hands over hers.

"What happened?" he asked again.

"I don't know." Blanche choked out the words. "When I came in, I found her like this. She said someone hit her— a big person."

A big person. Joe Bates.

Fear shot through Cord. "Where are Becca and Nicki?"

"I don't know. I don't know," Blanche sobbed. "Cord, I think she's lost consciousness."

Cord felt Edie's pulse. "She's still breathing. Stay with her until the ambulance gets here. I've got to find Becca."

As Cord stood there, a scream echoed through the house. "Oh my God, what's that?" Blanche asked.

But Cord had already left, taking the stairs three at a time. He tried Becca's door; it was locked. Stepping back, he swung at the door with his booted foot. It splintered away from the frame and he shoved it aside and stepped in. For a second he stood motionless, unable to believe what he was seeing. Mona was holding Becca down and trying to inject something in her arm. Becca was fighting like a hellcat.

Cord grabbed Mona by the shoulders and jerked her away from Becca.

"Don't come near me. Don't come near me," Mona screeched in a voice Cord had never heard. She held the needle in front of her like a weapon.

Cord didn't know what was going on, but his main concern was Becca. He reached out an arm and gathered her close, keeping an eye on Mona. "Are you all right?" She was trembling severely, so he tightened his hold.

"Yes, yes, now I am," Becca said in a hoarse voice.

"What's this about?"

"She killed Anette and she was trying to kill me," Becca managed to say.

"What!"

"It's true," Becca whispered. "She made Anette swallow pills, then she poured liquor down her throat until—"

"Why? Why would you do that?" Horrified, Cord stared at Mona. Her eyes were glazed and she had a feverish look.

Mona didn't answer. She took the needle and drove it into her own arm.

"Mona!" Cord shouted but it was too late. The medicine in the syringe was gone. Her eyes rolled back as she crumpled to the floor. Cord released Becca and knelt beside the woman.

"Why, Mona? *Why?*"

"I've waited and waited…all my life. I'm the only… woman for you. I love…you." Her head fell sideways.

Cord knelt there in shock. He and Mona were friends; they'd always been friends. He'd never led her to believe anything else. They had never even kissed, so he didn't understand how she could have these feelings for him. Yet she'd killed Anette and almost killed Becca. How could he have been so blind? Pain ripped up from his abdomen and gripped him—so tightly that his breath locked in his chest.

Two arms slipped around him, and he clasped Becca's hands, taking the strength and comfort she offered. After a moment, he got slowly to his feet and they moved away from Mona. "Are you sure you're all right?" he asked.

"Yes, a little shaken, but I'm fine."

"It's been Mona all along," Cord said quietly. "Joe Bates had nothing to do with any of this.

"No," Becca responded. "She let the bull out and loosened the brake line hoping to scare me away. And it seems she'd been harassing Anette for years, trying to get rid of her. The letter in Anette's purse was to Mona." Becca picked up the journal from the dresser and showed it to Cord.

Cord read for a minute then slammed it shut. "God, why didn't Anette tell me? Why did she let this go on? I don't understand."

"I think she wanted to be strong enough to handle it on her own. Also, Mona threatened to hurt Nicki if she said a word to you."

"Oh, no…"

Cord's words were cut short by the sound of sirens. "God, Mona must have hit Edie before she came up here. She's bleeding heavily. Blanche is with her. We'd better see how she's doing."

They ran down the stairs, where they found Blanche still holding Edie's head in her lap. Blood was everywhere. Becca immediately sank down beside Edie and took her pulse. "Was she talking to you?" she asked Blanche.

"Yes."

"Did she make sense? Did she knew where she was?"

"Yes."

"Her pulse is weak. Edie, can you hear me?" Becca asked loudly.

"Yes." Edie opened her eyes and then slowly closed them.

"The ambulance is here," Cord told her, running to open the front door.

The paramedics hurried through with a stretcher. Becca introduced herself and explained the situation. "She's received a sharp blow to the head. She's floating in and out of consciousness, but she's coherent. She'll need a c-collar and a back board to guard against trauma to the neck and spine. And I need a 4X4 to bandage her head."

"Yes, ma'am," the paramedic responded, and within minutes they had Edie in the ambulance.

"I'm going with you to apply direct pressure to stop any bleeding."

"We're trained to do that."

Becca sent him a glance that brooked no argument. "All right, let's just go," the paramedic said with a sigh.

Blanche sat there trembling, and Cord helped her to her feet. "Is she gonna be all right?" Blanche asked in a trembling voice.

Becca glanced back and made an instant decision. "Come with me, and we'll make sure she's okay." Blanche went with her meekly, not speaking.

"I'll call the sheriff about Mona and take care that Nicki doesn't see any of this," Cord told Becca as she stepped into the ambulance beside Edie and Blanche. "I'll see you at the hospital."

The ride in the ambulance was a silent one. The paramedics gave Edie oxygen and started an IV. Becca checked her vital signs and found they were stronger.

"Becca, are you sure she's alive?" Blanche asked. "She's so still."

"Yes, she's just very weak, but Edie's tough."

"Tough as an old boot," Blanche remarked, but Becca noticed that the resentment usually in her voice wasn't there anymore. Could something good come out of this tragedy?

As soon as he'd called the sheriff, Cord dashed out the back door, needing to find Nicki. He had to know she was okay. He met her running to the house and his first thought was relief that she hadn't come sooner. Breathing hard, he scooped her into his arms. *His little girl was safe.*

"Daddy, you're squeezing me too tight," Nicki complained.

"Sorry, baby." He loosened his hold immediately. "I'm just so glad to see you."

"I've been roping." She held out both hands. "My hands are getting red, and Gus said we had to stop."

"That's a good idea. You don't want blisters on your hands."

"'Kay, Daddy. Where's Becca? I want to show her my hands."

His heart felt heavy. He had to tell her something. "Edie had an accident and Becca went to the hospital with her."

"What happened?" Gus asked. He'd been standing there watching.

Cord took a breath and lied. "She fell and hit her head."

"Oh, she got an ouchie?" Nicki asked.

"Yes, she's got an ouchie, and Daddy has to drive to the hospital to check on her. So I want you to go with Gus and—"

"No, I want to go, too," Nicki said in a sullen voice.

"You can't, baby. The hospital isn't a place for children. I'm sure Gus will take you riding until Daddy gets back."

Nicki frowned and played with a button on his shirt.

"C'mon, little bit," Gus said in a cajoling voice. "Let's ride to the bottom and visit the boys. Why don't you show me how fast you can ride?"

That did the trick. Her eyes grew bright and she slipped from Cord's arms. "I can ride real, real fast. You'll see!" With that, she was racing to the stables.

Cord started to call her back, but Gus said, "Don't worry. Smithy's at the barn. He'll watch her. What's going on?"

Cord told him about Mona.

"God Almighty! Mona? I can't believe it."

"Yeah, it takes some getting used to."

The sheriff drove up with a second ambulance behind him. As Cord had directed, they parked at the front of the house. "I've got to go. Just take care of my child and get her away from this. I don't want her to see a thing."

"I will, and phone when you have news about Edie."

Cord hurried back to the house and opened the front door for the sheriff and the coroner. Within minutes they had Mona's body bagged and out of the house.

"There'll be an inquest into Mona's death," the sheriff said. "It's routine, but it has to be investigated."

"I understand."

"I'll call off my boys on Joe Bates."

"Yeah," Cord said in a distant voice.

"Mona Tibbetts." The sheriff shook his head. "I never would've thought it. She seemed like such a nice lady."

"She had us all fooled."

"You just never know," the sheriff said as he walked out the door.

Cord rushed upstairs to straighten Becca's room. The sheriff's men had removed the syringe, but he wanted to ensure that there were absolutely no signs of what had happened.

He picked up the journal. Why hadn't he known what Mona was doing? Was he so insensitive to Anette's needs that he'd dismissed everything as her paranoia? He sank onto the bed. He had, in effect, helped Mona kill his wife. The truth of that hit like lightning, searing everything inside him. He couldn't give in to those feelings now. Later, they'd tear him apart. But now he had to get to Edie—and Becca.

CHAPTER SEVENTEEN

CORD MET BECCA AND BLANCHE as Edie was being taken up to her room. They'd had to give her blood, and the doctor said it was a good idea if she spent the night. Edie was groggy, but awake. Her head had been stitched; she was going to be fine.

Becca slid one arm around Cord's waist. "You okay?" He didn't answer, and she knew he wasn't. She could feel him distancing himself from her. He had so much to deal with, so much to assimilate, and she hoped he wouldn't push her away.

She didn't have time to think about it as they got Edie settled into a room.

Blanche tucked in the blanket on Edie's bed.

"Why are you being so nice, Blanche?" Edie said crossly. "You're not staying at Triple Creek."

Blanche paled and took a step back from the bed. Becca inhaled a deep breath. It was like dealing with two children, which was something she was good at.

"That's not nice, Edie," Becca told her. "If Blanche hadn't applied those towels to your head, you would've lost a lot more blood and you might not have made it."

"Why didn't you just let me die, Blanche?" Edie asked. "It would've been to your advantage."

"Honestly, Edie, it never crossed my mind. It should have. I'm surprised it didn't."

"Me, too," Edie murmured. "You're still leaving Triple Creek," she added as an afterthought.

"I know, Edie."

"As soon as possible."

"I know."

There was a pause, then Edie asked, "Where will you go?"

"I'll probably get an apartment in Houston. I've never been on my own before. It'll be a new experience."

"An apartment?" Edie thought about that for a minute. "I don't think Pa would want you living in an apartment."

"Well, Pa's not here, now is he?" Blanche said cheekily.

"Enough!" Cord said angrily. "I've had it. I'm tired of all the fighting and bickering. It stops *now*. I can't deal with any more. Blanche isn't going anywhere. She's staying at Triple Creek. Pa would want it that way and frankly so do I. Blanche is my mother. Even though I have a hard time with what she did, she is still my mother. Do you have a problem with that, Edie?"

"No. No, I guess not," Edie answered quietly.

"I've got to get some air," Cord said, and strode out of the room.

"What's wrong with him?" Edie asked.

Blanche started to tell her about Mona, and Becca quickly followed Cord. She found him in a waiting area, pacing.

"Cord," she said softly. She moved to put her arms around him, but he backed away. A tiny fear took root inside her.

"Is Blanche ready to go?" he asked in a cool tone. "I've got to get back to Nicki."

She tried again. "Cord."

He held up a hand. "No, Becca, I don't want to talk. I just want to go home."

Becca watched him for a second and knew he was fighting a battle within himself. She would give him time. But she wanted to hold him, to comfort him, and it was so hard not to.

"I'll get Blanche," she said, and walked away.

LIKE THE JOURNEY in the ambulance several hours before, the ride to Triple Creek was silent. No one spoke a word and the silence was getting to Becca. Cord was shutting her out. She could feel it as strongly as the heart beating inside her. He was in pain and he needed to share that pain in order to assuage it. How did she make him see that?

Nicki was excited at their return and had a million questions. She couldn't understand why Blanche and Becca were so dirty. The blood had dried to a dark stain, and fortunately Nicki thought it was dirt. Blanche and Becca went to get cleaned up and left Cord with all the questions.

Supper was another silent event, except for Nicki's chattering. Afterward, Becca took her upstairs to put her to bed. Cord didn't follow. The broken door to Becca's room had been removed and Nicki didn't notice that it was missing. As Becca was reading Nicki a story, Cord came in to kiss his daughter good-night.

Cord looked at Becca, "Can I see you downstairs?"

"Sure," she said. When she'd finished the story, she joined him in the den. She sat on the sofa and Cord paced in front of her.

She held her breath waiting for his words because she sensed she wasn't going to like them.

Cord knew what he had to do, but the words wouldn't come. In his head he had it all worked out; his heart was another matter. When he closed his eyes, he could see Mona about to inject Becca with the needle. If he'd been a few seconds later, Becca would be dead—like Anette. Because of him.

Suddenly, he turned and said, "I want you to go back to Houston."

Becca bit her lip, trying to maintain control of her emotions. "Why?" she asked simply.

"Because it's what I want."

"Why?"

"Dammit, Becca, you don't belong here!"

Her eyes met his. "Then, why do I feel as if I do?"

They stared at each other for endless seconds, then he dredged up every ounce of courage he possessed and said, "You don't. You belong in Houston with an elite circle of friends. You're not cut out to be a cowboy's wife."

Her eyes didn't waver from his. "Then, why am I in love with a cowboy?"

"I want you away from this place," he shouted. "There's nothing but pain and suffering here. Can't you see that? I couldn't for so long, but I can now. I killed Anette. I couldn't see what Mona was doing to her. I should have. I should've been there for her. I won't hurt you like that. I'd die before I let that happen."

Becca stood. "Then, why are you hurting me now?"

He drew a ragged breath. "I'm not, and you'll see that in time."

"I won't," she said. She tried to touch him, but he backed away.

"No, don't touch me" came out as a strangled plea, and she knew nothing was going to change his mind. She tried desperately to restrain the tears that were threatening to overtake her. But she wasn't leaving without a fight.

"So Mona wins."

"What?" He seemed disconcerted.

"She wanted to break us up and she's doing exactly that."

He blinked. "That kind of logic might work on Nicki, but not on me. I can't handle you being here. I just can't take any more. Go, please."

She wanted to argue with him or throw a temper tantrum like Nicki, but she could see how badly he was hurting. He needed time to adjust to the turbulent events that had happened. And she told herself again that she would give it to him. Even though she didn't want to. Walking away from the man she loved would truly be the hardest thing she'd ever have to do.

He turned to leave the room.

"Cord," she called.

He stopped.

Please, he prayed. *Just go.*

"I'm not leaving without saying goodbye to Nicki. She's been through too much—I can't desert her. She has to understand and accept why I'm leaving."

"I know that, and I wouldn't expect any less of you." With that, he left the room, and Becca's heart broke into so many pieces that the pain became unbearable. She sank onto the sofa and began to cry.

CORD WALKED QUICKLY to the barn and flipped on the light. He grabbed a bridle off the rack, then moved to the gate. He whistled and Apache came trotting up. Slipping the bridle over his head, he guided him into the barn. As he slung a saddle onto Apache's back, Gus strolled in.

"What're you doing?" Gus asked.

"Nothing," Cord muttered.

"Shouldn't you be at the house with Becca and Nicki?"

"There is no Becca anymore," Cord said as he swung into the saddle.

Gus frowned. "What're you talking about? Cord, what's wrong with you?"

Cord didn't answer. He pulled his hat low and kneed Apache. As the horse cantered out, Cord embraced the evening's warmth. He gave Apache his head and they headed toward open range at a full gallop. Faster and faster Apache ran, and his hooves hitting the ground were the only sound in the darkness. They cut through the air like an arrow—sharp and steady. On and on Cord rode, driving the horse as well as himself. He had to keep going. He had to keep the memories at bay.

Apache was panting and sweaty when Cord finally pulled up. He sat for a moment rubbing Apache's neck. "Sorry, boy. I'll let you rest."

He slid from the saddle to the grass, walked a few yards away and sank to the ground. He buried his face in his hands, unable to ignore the truth any longer. He had almost gotten Becca killed. He couldn't get that thought out of his head. He loved her and wanted to make her happy, but he had endangered her life. Just like he'd endangered Anette's.

He couldn't drag Becca into his misery. She deserved better than that. Colton had warned him; he should have listened and not gotten involved with her. Now he was hurting her, but she'd get over it. She had a brilliant career waiting for her and she'd find the right man in Houston. *He wasn't the man for Becca.* He lay back on the cool grass and watched the dazzling display of stars. A coyote howled mournfully in the distance, echoing the pain in his heart. He wasn't the man for Becca, he told himself again and again. Even if she was the woman for him.

BECCA HURRIEDLY TRIED to wipe away the tears as Blanche walked in, but she didn't succeed.

"What's the matter, sugar?"

Becca didn't see any reason to lie. "Cord asked me to leave."

Blanche's eyes grew big. "You're joking."

"No, he's all torn up about Mona and Anette. He's blaming himself, and I can't reach him."

"Hell's bells, you're not leaving, are you?"

"Yes. I can't stay here if he doesn't want me to. And if I can't reach him, our love means nothing."

"Sugar, give it some time and it'll work itself out."

She wiped away another tear. "I'm not sure. I have to be back in Houston in a few days, anyway. I was just hoping not to leave under these circumstances."

"Cord loves you. I know he does."

"Yeah." She blinked back more tears. "But I don't think he'll let himself remember that." She took a breath. "Would you do me a favor?"

"Sure, sugar, anything."

"I have to tell Nicki in the morning and I'd appreciate it if you were there for moral support. I'm not sure how she's going to take it."

"I'll set my alarm. I'll be there."

Becca swallowed. "Also, would you be there for her when I'm gone? She'll need someone besides Mrs. Witherspoon."

"Sure, sugar. I'm getting into this grandmother thing."

"Thanks, Blanche." She stood. "Now I'd better go pack."

"Becca," Blanche said, and Becca turned.

Suddenly Blanche hugged her. "You know something? You're the only woman I've ever really liked."

Becca was thrown for a second, but she returned the hug and hurried away. She had to or she'd cry her eyes out.

BECCA DIDN'T SLEEP MUCH. She'd packed all her things; everything was in her car. The only thing left was to talk to Nicki, and she wasn't looking forward to that. But it had to be done.

She was hoping she'd have a chance to talk to Cord one more time, but he was nowhere in sight. He didn't show up for breakfast, and she wondered where he was. It wasn't like him to miss getting Nicki ready in the morning, but then, Cord wasn't acting like himself. She'd thought they were soul mates and could reach each other on any level, but pain had obliterated the bond they shared. There had to be a way to get it back. The love she had for Cord wasn't going to disappear.

Becca took Nicki into the den and pulled the child onto her lap. Blanche stood in the doorway.

"What're we gonna do today?" Nicki asked, and Becca's throat closed up.

Becca rubbed her little arm. "Remember when I first came here and I told you I was a doctor and I took care of girls and boys like you?"

"Uh-huh."

"Well, it's time for me to go back to my job."

"Why?"

"Because those girls and boys are waiting for me to take care of them."

"But you take care of *me*." Nicki's bottom lip began to tremble.

Becca kissed her cheek. "You will always be my favorite patient, and Blanche will bring you to see me and you can call me anytime you want."

"You bet, sugarplum," Blanche said heartily as she came in and sat down. "I'll load you up in the Caddy and we'll head to town. You can see Becca's office and you might even meet some of those kids Becca treats."

"That's a marvelous idea," Becca said, remembering the

play group she'd been thinking about for Nicki. "There's a play group in my building, and you can come and play every day or whenever you like."

Nicki twisted her hands. "There's kids there? Kids I can play with?"

"Yes."

"But..."

Becca could see Nicki wasn't quite sure; her eyes were already bright with tears. *Don't cry, Nicki,* Becca was praying. If she cried, Becca knew she wouldn't be able to leave. Tough love really was tough when the heart was involved.

"You know what, sugarplum?" Blanche said. "I've got this red feather boa that would look super on you, and I bet I could find some red high heels, too."

"Oh boy!" Nicki's eyes lit up and she slid from Becca's lap. "I can wear your heels?"

"You betcha, but you'd better give Becca a hug before she leaves."

Her little arms encircled Becca's neck. "I love you, Becca."

Becca fought back tears. "I love you, too, sweetie."

Blanche led Nicki away. At the door Nicki waved at her and Becca waved back, her heart in her throat. Nicki wasn't going to cry, but *she* would if she didn't get out of here soon.

She ran into the kitchen and hugged Della.

"I'm so sorry," Della said. Becca had told her the whole story.

"Sometimes things don't work out the way we plan."

"We'll miss you."

"Bye!" Becca ran out the door to her car.

She backed out and headed for Houston and her life. But she couldn't help thinking that the scene in her rearview mirror *was* her life—the only life she wanted.

CORD WATCHED HER LEAVE from an upstairs window. She was gone. She was safe. His heart wobbled inside him, but he was doing the right thing. They'd had a moment out of time and he would never forget it. But his loss would torture him for the rest of his life. That was exactly what he deserved.

BECCA WENT DIRECTLY to her apartment and unpacked, but she was restless. She suddenly had to see her mother. She drove to the clinic, but Emily was with a patient so she waited in her office. There was a family photo of the four of them on Emily's desk. Becca picked it up, staring at the smiling faces. They were happy, and she needed that happiness right now.

Emily entered the office and stopped, her surprise almost comical. "Becca! What are you doing here?" she asked in a startled voice. "Oh, it's so good to see you," she said as they embraced.

Emily drew back. "Your hair's longer and you look... different."

"How?" Becca asked.

"I don't know, but..." Emily gazed into her eyes. "You're all grown-up."

"Yeah, Mom. I don't even say *jeez* anymore," Becca said with a touch of mirth. "I'm all grown-up."

"I guess I've never really accepted that before."

"No, I don't think you have."

"Oh my, I have a grown-up daughter." Emily pushed dark hair away from Becca's shoulder. "And she looks so sad."

Unable to stop herself, Becca burst into tears, and Emily held her tight.

"What is it, angel?"

"I'm in love and...and it hurts."

Emily seemed to need a moment to absorb this, then she led Becca to a chair and got her a glass of water. "Tell me all about it."

Becca didn't leave anything out. She told her mother every detail except the intimate part, which belonged to her and Cord alone.

"Oh my." Emily brought a hand to her chest. "I'm so thankful you're okay, and your face has healed nicely, too."

Becca took a sip of water. "I know you and Dad will be upset that Cord's older, has a marriage behind him and a five-year-old daughter—but I love him and I love Nicki."

"Your father and I want you to be happy. That's all we've ever wanted for you."

Becca frowned in puzzlement.

"What is it?" Emily asked.

"All these years I've been trying to be the daughter you wanted. I didn't want to disappoint you again."

Emily pulled up a chair and faced her. "Angel, you have *never* disappointed us."

"Yes, I did," Becca refuted. "When I found out you were my mother, I did all those crazy things to hurt you."

Emily gently removed the glass from Becca's grasp and set it on a table, then she took her daughter's hands in hers. "That was a traumatic time for all of us. You wouldn't have been human if you hadn't responded in some way. You had so many emotions to get out of your system." She squeezed her hands. "You have never disappointed Jackson and me," she said again. "Our love is unconditional." She eyed Becca for a moment. "Did you choose medicine because you thought I wanted you to?"

Becca considered that and she had to be honest. "In part, I guess I did. I always wanted to be like you, but I enjoy being a doctor and I don't regret that decision."

"I'm glad, because you're very good with kids."

"For a while now, I've felt this restlessness and I couldn't figure out what it was."

"Have you figured it out now?"

"Yes." She looked at her mother. "I'd fit myself into the mold of being Emily's daughter. Your little girl. But the woman in me was clamoring to be released. I kept pushing her back, because deep inside I believed that once the *woman* surfaced, I'd lose something precious."

"And did you?"

"No." Becca smiled. "I gained so much more. And I know that no matter what happens, you and Daddy will always be there for me, whether I'm a little girl or your grown-up daughter."

Emily patted her hands. "Yes, we will."

"Oh, Mom, love is hard."

"Yes, but it also brings great rewards."

"I'll try to remember that."

"You're coming to dinner and I don't want to hear any excuses. Scotty hasn't seen you in ages and Grandpa George is in town."

"Yes, I've missed everyone, and I can't wait to hold Scotty." She needed to hold Nicki, too—and most of all, Nicki's father.

Cord, how can you do this to us?

THE NEXT FEW DAYS weren't easy. Becca had trouble sleeping and she didn't feel like eating. She talked to Nicki and to Blanche every day; the child was doing fine. Becca was grateful for that. Blanche said Mrs. Witherspoon hadn't come back and that Cord kept Nicki with him most of the day. When Nicki wasn't with him, she stayed with Blanche. Becca didn't know why he'd chosen to do this, rather than rehire the nanny or send Nicki to a play group, but she was sure he had a reason—one that made sense to him, anyway. Blanche also said that Edie was home and recovering well. The Prescotts had gone on without Becca, and she'd never felt so alone in her life. She had her family, but Becca— the woman Becca—needed a whole lot more.

She called Gin several times but was unable to reach her. The Fourth of July arrived, and Becca planned to stay home in her apartment, but the family was having a barbecue at her parents' so she went. She enjoyed seeing everyone. When she got there, Emily, Rose and Aunt Maude were in the kitchen preparing lunch. Jackson was at the grill keeping an eye on the meat. Grandpa George and Owen were playing ball with Scotty. So Becca sat on the patio swing by herself, staring off into space and wondering what Cord and Nicki were doing. Did they miss her?

Jackson sat down beside her. "When I see that look on your face, I really want to hurt Cord Prescott," he said.

She glanced at her father. "But you won't," she said with certainty.

"No, because I love you too much."

"Thanks, Daddy," she murmured.

There was silence for a while. Then she asked in a low voice, "How do you feel about Cord and me?"

"When your mother first told me, I wasn't too happy," he confessed. "It was the age issue, but after I thought about it I changed my mind. I know Cord, and he's a good man. I guess what I'm saying is that the only thing I want is your happiness and if Cord makes you happy, then I'm all for it."

"I love him, Daddy," she said softly.

"I know."

"I never thought love would be like this—with such incredible highs and devastating lows."

"Angel, we all go through it. Just give Cord some time

to get over this. And remember, once you find true love, never let it go.''

She managed a smile. "This is from personal experience?''

"You're damn right it is,'' he replied strongly. "I thought I'd die when your mom pushed me away after we found out you were our daughter.''

"But you got through it?''

"Yeah,'' he said. "It took time, but now we have you and Scotty...and so much more.''

Her parents had endured much, but now they were happy. Would things work out as well for her and Cord? She honestly didn't know.

She turned to face her father, knowing she could talk about anything with him. "You've known the Prescotts a long time.''

"I met Clay in college. He was younger than me, but we became good friends.''

"Did you ever meet the older Mr. Prescott?''

"Yes, lots of times. He gave Clay his share of the money to start our computer company. He'd come every couple of months to see how we were doing.''

"Did Blanche come with him?''

"Sure. I don't think he went anywhere without her.''

"What was she like then?''

"Same as she is now,'' he told her. "Rough around the edges. She said what was on her mind and couldn't care less if it offended anyone, but Mr. Prescott adored her. She was so much younger than him, but they got along really well.''

"What was Mr. Prescott like?''

"Well...'' Jackson thought for a minute. "He was his own man—did things his way. Didn't care what people thought. At times he was hard and overbearing, but he loved his sons. Whenever he came to San Antonio, he'd throw Clay into a panic with all his instructions on how we should run the business. But when he left there'd be tears in his eyes as he shook Clay's hand and asked if he had enough money to pay the bills and eat. He didn't want Clay doing without.''

Becca ran her hand along her bare leg. This was what she needed—to talk about Cord and his family. "Mr. Prescott didn't ever hug him?"

"No, he wasn't a very demonstrative person."

She remembered Colton saying the same thing about himself, so it must be a Prescott trait. But Cord was very loving, and so gentle with Nicki. That was probably what had first attracted her.

"Tell me what Cord was like when you met him."

"Young, handsome and hardworking, and the ladies always gravitated to him. Clay and I decided it was the cowboy thing."

"Oh, I don't think I want to hear that."

Jackson lifted her chin with his fingers. "Cord was so unassuming, he never suspected all the ladies were interested in him."

"Yes, he's like that," she said quietly. "He never knew Mona cared for him in a romantic way."

"That's not his fault," Jackson was quick to point out.

"I know that, but how do I make *him* see it?"

Jackson took her in his arms. "Just let the wounds heal, angel."

"But, Daddy, this is so hard."

"It'll get better," he promised. "Now, why don't you go relieve Dad and Owen? Scotty's making them run far too fast."

"Okay." She brushed away a tear. "Thanks for talking to me. I needed that."

"I know," he replied with a father's wisdom.

BECCA WENT TO WORK in Dr. Arnold's office and settled into a routine. Dr. Arnold was a well-known pediatrician and several doctors worked under her. Becca was honored to be one of those doctors. As the newest member of the team, she took patients who couldn't get in to see the other doctors. Slowly she was meeting the little patients and getting to know them. The days were busy, but nights were agonizing. She kept waiting to feel the feathery touch of Cord's mustache or to wake up and see him in the bathroom shaving, but each morning she felt a little more alone and a little more empty.

Early one morning, Ginger breezed into her apartment and slammed her purse on the bar. "Well, so you're back in town and I'm the last one to know."

"I called several times," Becca told her.

"Oh." Gin looked surprised. "I went out of town for the Fourth. So…how are you?"

"Things have been rough lately."

"Colton told me what's been happening. Are you okay?"

Becca sat on the sofa and curled her feet beneath her. "I'll never be the same again."

Ginger eyed her strangely as she sat down, too. "You seem different."

"Pain does that to a person."

"You're in pain?"

"Yes, right about here." She placed her hand over her heart.

That strange look turned to guilt, and Becca knew what was on Gin's mind—her affair with Colton.

"This isn't about Colton, Gin. It's about Cord."

Ginger crossed her legs nervously. "I don't know what you're talking about."

"Colton and I are friends like I've always told you," she said tolerantly. "We've never shared a passionate kiss and we've certainly never slept together."

"That has nothing to do with me!"

"Really? Then, why is your face almost as red as your hair?"

Ginger glanced up; their eyes met and they burst into laughter.

"I'm sorry," Gin murmured. "It just happened."

"What are you apologizing for? I'm happy for both of you."

"It's your fault, anyway."

"My fault?"

"Yeah. Colton called to see if I'd been watering your plants and that made me mad as hell, so I gave him a piece of my mind. Then he stopped by your place while I was here and we got to talking and he offered to take me out to dinner. I surprised myself when I accepted. After that, one thing led to another. Colton's very nice once you get to know him." Her eyes grew dreamy. "I make him laugh and he makes me take life more seriously."

"I assume going away for the Fourth was with Colton."

"Yeah," Gin said in a hesitant voice. "Are you *sure* you're okay with this?"

"Yes, I'm fine," Becca assured her. "Colton isn't the Prescott who's broken my heart."

"Cordell Prescott is a fool."

Becca's face darkened, and Gin immediately backpedaled. "I know he's gone through a lot, but can't he see how much you love him?"

"Right now, he's suffering so much I don't think he can see much of anything."

There was a long silence, then Becca suggested, "Why don't we go out for dinner tonight?"

"I'm sorry." Gin's face fell. "I have plans to meet Colton at his place, but you can come with me. I'm sure he'd be glad to see you."

"No, thanks, I'm not in the mood to be a fifth wheel. Besides, I have some medical reading to catch up on."

After Gin left, Becca quickly got dressed for work, but her mind was filled with thoughts of Cord. How long would the pain last? How long before the ache inside her disappeared? How long was a lifetime? Forever. She would feel this way forever, or until Cord was back in her life.

CHAPTER EIGHTEEN

CORD STOOD WATCHING Nicki play from the den. The sheriff had called and said that Mona's death was ruled a suicide. Apparently they were trying to locate a distant cousin who would inherit the Tibbets ranch. Also, Bates and his girlfriend had moved to Montana. It was over, the sheriff had said, but Cord knew it would never be over for him.

His gaze shifted to Blanche, who was sitting in a lounge chair also watching Nicki. That was the only good thing that had come out of this mess. He and Blanche had gotten closer, and Blanche now helped him with Nicki. They were still waiting for Clay to fly home so they could have a meeting about the will. But in the meantime, Edie and Blanche were getting along. He hadn't heard one argument lately. They were pulling together as a family—just like Becca had wanted them to. God, why couldn't he stop thinking about her?

He hardly noticed when Blanche came in. All he could see was Becca's face, her eyes, her smile. He was walking a tightrope of emotion and didn't know how long he could stay balanced. But he was afraid he was going down and could do nothing to stop himself. He focused on Nicki. His daughter was all that kept him sane.

"Cord, where are you?" Colton yelled from the kitchen.

Cord turned as his brother came into the den. Colton walked straight up to him, his right fist connecting with Cord's jaw. Cord wheeled from the blow.

"How could you?" Colton said through clenched teeth. "I told you to leave her alone. Becca doesn't deserve this."

Cord's eyes darkened. "The first punch is free, but if you try it again, I'll knock you on your ass."

The two brothers faced each other. Cord was the taller, bigger one, but Colton had blood in his eye.

Blanche immediately got between them. "Stop this right now! Nicki could come in any minute."

Cord swung away and went through the French doors to the patio.

Blanche placed her hands on her hips. "Your brother's in pain. Can't you see that?"

"I'm not really worried about his pain," Colton said angrily.

"Yes, you are. That's why you're here. You know Cord and Becca are right for each other. I understand that's hard for you to accept but—"

"If he loves her, how can he do this to her?" Colton broke in.

"Think about everything Cord's been through. In time, he'll realize he can't live without her."

"I don't know. He's stubborn as a mule."

"Maybe, but I hope you got all the anger out of your system."

Colton rubbed his knuckles. "No, and I think I broke my hand."

"Come to the kitchen," she said. "I'll make you some coffee and put ice on it."

Blanche walked away, but Colton just stared after her with a perplexed expression.

Blanche glanced back at him. "What's wrong?"

"I don't think I've talked this much to you in all my life. Who are you? I don't know this person."

"I'm your mother and you're my son, and that's how we're gonna act from now on."

"Oh," Colton said, and followed her into the kitchen.

CORD PUT NICKI TO BED, and luckily she didn't mention Becca. Every time she did, he shriveled up inside. And tonight he'd almost reached the end of what he could tolerate. Colton had a right to be angry, and the bruise on Cord's jaw was a small price to pay for what he'd done to Becca.

He went down to the kitchen and discovered Blanche there.

"Sit down," she said.

"Blanche, I'm not—"

"Sit," she ordered. "I have a few things to say and you're gonna listen."

He took a seat.

"How long are you gonna blame yourself for Anette's death?"

"Leave it alone."

"No, I won't," Blanche told him. "I don't think you even realize how disturbed Anette was."

"What are you talking about?"

"Did you finish reading this?" She set the journal in front of him.

He pushed it away. "I don't want to see that again."

"That's too bad, because you're listening to what it has to say."

"Blanche…"

But Blanche was reading from the book. "'I should tell Cord, but I won't. He says he loves me, but he might take Mona's side. If he does, then I'd have to kill them both because I'll never let her have him. I need more pills. Maybe then these thoughts will go away.'" Blanche laid the book down. "Does that sound like a person you could help? She was on medication when you met her. You knew that. Her condition only got worse. Her pregnancy might have been a factor, but she wanted the baby. And Mona didn't help matters. But you certainly had nothing to do with that."

Cord didn't say a word.

Blanche went on. "You've always been a very kind person. When you met Anette, she had practically no one and she wanted a family. You gave her that, but Anette needed a lot more. You got her psychiatric help, but it wasn't enough." Blanche was silent for a moment, then added, "You can't stop living because of what happened. Let it go. Put it in the past where it belongs."

Cord got up and left the kitchen without a backward glance. He walked to his room and fell fully clothed onto the bed. Memories of Anette consumed him. Blanche was right; he'd been kind to Anette. She'd seemed so lost and alone, and he'd wanted to help her, but she had other problems he hadn't really considered. After they were married, her depression and paranoia grew worse. How much Mona had to do with that, he wasn't sure. Obviously Anette and Mona were engaged in some private battle he wasn't even aware of. Why couldn't he see what was happening right under his own nose? Because they'd made a point of keeping it from him. And there was nothing he could have done to change that.

The truth of that jolted him and he sat up. *He couldn't have changed a thing.* But if he'd known how Mona felt— that thought wouldn't let him go. He'd known Mona all his life. The kids at school had teased her and he'd told her she was pretty. He'd done it out of kindness. Just to make her feel better. Could that have been the start of her infatuation with him? Had she read more into it than he'd actually intended? He didn't see how, since there was no romantic involvement between them and Mona was some years older. She'd even been smitten with Clay. He'd dated other women and the only interest he and Mona had in common was ranching. They'd never touched or kissed. How could she have deluded herself that their friendship was something more? He'd never encouraged her in that way.

Still, for whatever reasons, she'd developed an obsession with him. Why hadn't he seen the signs? Mona had spent too much time at Triple Creek. She'd relied on him to help her make decisions—or pretended to. And he'd fallen for it. But anything he'd done, he'd done out of kindness. Around and around went the thoughts until he felt as though his head would burst.

His emotions were wavering dangerously, taking him places he didn't want to go.

Just when his capacity for strength had reached its limit, he glanced down and saw his boots, and suddenly Becca's face swam before him.

A cowboy's dream. A woman to remove his boots.

The memory of her smile eased the turbulence inside him, but he couldn't complete the circle by accepting her in his life. He wouldn't hurt another woman—especially Becca.

He got up and ran down the stairs to the stables. He was saddling Apache when Gus walked in wearing his boxer shorts and boots. He held a shotgun in his hand.

"God Almighty, boy! I thought we had a prowler."

"Go back to bed, Gus. It's just me."

"Where you going?"

Cord swung into the saddle. "Go back to bed."

Gus rubbed his bald head. "You gonna ride that horse to death."

Cord signaled Apache and they shot out of the barn.

"Or yourself," Gus muttered. "When's all this gonna end?"

BECCA LOVED HER JOB and all the kids she saw. They were so innocent and trusting, and depended on her to make their aches and pains go away. She'd hoped that once she threw herself into her work and submerged herself in other people's problems, the pain inside her would ease, but it didn't. Each day that passed without a message from Cord made her heartache worse.

The bright spot in her life was Nicki. Blanche brought her to the play group three days a week, and Becca made sure she had time to spend with her. Nicki was always so thrilled about visiting her, and she chatted on and on about everything. When she mentioned Cord, Becca's heart fluttered with something that wasn't going to disappear—love. Almost a month had gone by, and if it hadn't been for her work, Becca would have been overwhelmed by grief and disappointment.

On Monday morning of the Fourth week, she stopped by the hospital to check over a newborn, a healthy little boy. No problems and all his vitals were strong. She told the mother to call the office and they'd set up scheduled appointments for the baby. When she reached the clinic, the nurse informed her they had a full morning. It started with three-year-old Casey, who had a cold; the mother was worried because it wasn't clearing up. The child was in day care and exposed to all sorts of things. Becca couldn't do anything about that, but she assured the mother her little girl was fine and that she would get better. Next was two-year-old Eric, whose ear was red and swollen. The boy was constantly pulling on it. Becca quickly saw the problem— a dried black-eyed pea was stuck in his ear. Becca was able to extract it without admitting him to the hospital. And another two-year-old, Noah, had a rash all over his body. His hands, feet and face were not affected. It took a while for Becca to figure it out. Finally she asked if he had any new pajamas. The mother said yes, he'd gotten some for his birthday. She prescribed an ointment for the rash and told the mother to get rid of the pajamas. The boy was allergic to the fabric.

Her days were mostly the same, caring for babies and children. Occasionally she dealt with teenagers. Today she saw a fifteen-year-old girl who'd been sick with vomiting for a week. The mother insisted she had the flu and needed something for it because the girl couldn't miss any more school. Becca gave the girl, Katie Adams, a thorough exam and ran some tests. She suspected Katie was pregnant. The mother was very domineering, and Becca could see her daughter was afraid of telling her. While Mrs. Adams went to get coffee, she talked with Katie, who admitted she was pregnant. Becca told her she had to tell her parents. What followed was a big scene. The mother screamed and yelled, but it didn't change the fact that the girl was pregnant. Becca set up counseling for them, hoping they could work things out.

It was one of those days she was glad to go home.

JULY HAD TURNED into August, and she'd still heard nothing from Cord. Her family went to Rockport, but she stayed in Houston. She had to be here if Cord called, but she finally realized that wasn't likely to happen. She had a decision to make. She could go on waiting or—or what?

Then she discovered a certain fact that changed her whole perspective. Her body had begun to tell her something and she knew what it was. She and Cord hadn't used any protection when they'd been together. Doctor or not, she hadn't even thought about it. Love had blinded her to that need. She took a pregnancy test and confirmed it: she was having a baby. That knowledge sent her into orbit with delight, then just as quickly brought her down to earth. How did she tell Cord? He was dealing with so much already, and she had no idea how he'd take the news. She definitely would not tell him with the intent of getting him back. Cord had to decide that on his own.

She sat on the sofa with her hand on her flat stomach and knew she wanted Cord's child with all her heart. "We'll be fine," she whispered. "I love you already and your father will, too, but I'm not sure there's time for him to realize that before you're born."

She thought of the fifteen-year-old and so many girls like her. Sex came with a price—responsibility. Emily had told her that once. Maybe that was why she'd waited so long. At her age, sex was a choice she'd made consciously and with full awareness. She could handle the consequences.

She considered Emily and what it must've been like to be pregnant at seventeen. Becca was older, self-supporting, mature, but what if she'd been seventeen and unmarried— and had to face Rose? Becca trembled. For the first time, she could really imagine the fear and turmoil Emily must have experienced. It was a revelation.

"Don't worry." She patted her stomach. "You and I will never be parted." But, oh, she didn't think she could wait eighteen years, as her mother had, for Cord to rejoin their lives.

She curled up and wondered how her parents were going to react. A smile spread across her face. There would be no harsh words or judgments, because she was their daughter and they loved her. She'd tried so hard to be perfect for them, but she didn't have to be. They loved her just the way she was—faults and all. And they'd love her baby.

HER BIRTHDAY came and she spent it with her family. She wasn't very good company, but no one seemed to notice. She just kept thinking she was twenty-nine, pregnant and alone. The thought didn't depress her; it gave her something to look forward to—the birth of their child.

Nicki started classes in Houston at the private school Anette had wanted her to attend. Nicki was eager to have Becca meet her teacher. So far, Becca had managed to put her off.

Blanche had also enrolled Nicki in ballet classes. The school was having a party to allow students, teachers and parents to meet each other, and families were welcome. Nicki had begged her to come, and Becca couldn't tell her she wasn't part of the family. It didn't help that Blanche kept insisting. Becca said she'd have to check her schedule, but she'd already decided she couldn't go. Cord would be there, and if she saw him she'd fall to pieces. Her emotions were very precarious these days.

The night of the party, Colton and Ginger stopped by. Colton frowned at her. "What? You're not dressed." She had on jeans and a knit top.

She knew exactly what he was talking about. "I'm not going."

"You have to. Nicki's expecting you."

"Colton…"

"So what if Cord's there?" Gin said. "Thumb your nose at him. Come on, I'll pick out something sexy for you to wear." Gin disappeared into her bedroom.

Becca turned to Colton. "I can't do this."

"Sure you can, gorgeous. Just smile and everything'll be fine."

Still she hesitated.

"I'm mad as hell at Cord," Colton told her, "but I can't even imagine what he's going through. I know one thing, though—you're the only person who can reach him. He has to see that life goes on. One look at you is all he needs."

She smiled. "I never knew you were a matchmaker."

"I'm not. I'm just trying to help two people I care about."

"Bec, are you coming?" Gin called from the bedroom.

Colton raised an eyebrow. "You'd better go. You know how she is when she gets going on something."

She hugged him. "I'm so happy for you and Gin."

"You were right. I needed someone to make me laugh. Ginger makes me feel like the kid I never was, and it's a wonderful feeling." He paused, then looked into her eyes. "For so many years I thought my future was with you but…"

"We'd have been miserable together," she finished for him.

He grinned. "That about sums it up. Now, what's it gonna be? Are you planning to let Nicki down?"

"I would never let Nicki down," she said, and it was true. As Gin had said, so what if Cord was there? She had to see him eventually, and tonight was a good time to start. She couldn't keep the excitement from rushing through her at the prospect.

SHE DECIDED—or rather, Ginger decided for her—to wear a maroon slim-fitting dress with a short-sleeved jacket. Ginger said she didn't need the jacket, but she wore it, anyway. The dress was low-cut and she didn't want to appear—well, she wasn't sure so she wore the jacket.

When they arrived, the party was in full swing. Little girls in tutus were running everywhere. A teacher introduced herself, and Colton told her they were the Prescott family. Before the teacher could say anything, a screech was heard.

"Becca, Becca, Becca."

Becca bent and caught Nicki as the child hurled herself into her arms. "Look at me." Nicki ran her hands down the pink tutu. "We got them today and the teacher said we could wear them. Don't I look pretty?"

"Beautiful." Becca kissed her cheek.

"Watch, I can do this already."

She stood on tiptoe and raised her hands above her head. She tried to turn and toppled backward, but Colton caught her.

"You need more practice, munchkin," Colton teased her.

"Yeah," Nicki said, not deterred for a moment. "Come on. Daddy, Blanche and Edie are over here." She caught Becca's hand and pulled her forward.

CORD SAW HER COMING—saw everything about her with painful clarity. She looked as beautiful as she did in his dreams, and he wanted to run, to put as much distance between them as he could. But his feet stayed rooted to the spot and his eyes followed her across the room. There was something different about her, but he couldn't determine exactly what it was. Her dark hair was longer and hung enchantingly around her face; however, that wasn't it. Her body seemed fuller—or did it? He wasn't sure. God, he remembered what it was like to touch those breasts, those hips. He had to get out of here. He couldn't do this. But his feet wouldn't move.

BECCA SAW HIM and her insides melted with a need that only he could create. He wore dark slacks and a white shirt with his Sunday boots and hat. He held a glass of punch in one hand and there was a distant, brooding look in his eyes. He was so handsome.

What do I say to him? She had to say something.

She hugged Blanche and Edie, then turned to face him. They stared at each other for several seconds. Without realizing it, she placed her hand protectively on her stomach. Her tongue was thick and the words wouldn't come.

What do I say to him?

"How are you?" he finally asked.

Awful. Without you, I'm awful.

Before she could answer, Nicki broke in. "Becca, look." Becca tore her eyes away and glanced at Nicki, who was holding a pair of tap shoes. "I'm gonna take tap dance, too. These make lots of noise."

"I bet they do."

After that, the liveliness of the party took over. She shook hands with teachers and parents and met some of the little girls. Two of them were her patients, and she visited briefly with their parents. All the while, she avoided looking at Cord. She'd thought they would be able to talk but that barrier was still there. He wasn't letting her near him, and she didn't know how to break through. She didn't understand how she could love him so much, yet still be unable to reach him.

CORD SIPPED HIS PUNCH and watched her. He wanted to look away but he couldn't. Becca was talking to several little girls, Nicki in the center; he noticed that Nicki wasn't letting anyone get too close to Becca. They were all drawn to her like a magnet, just as he had been.

Ginger walked up to him. "I don't think we've been properly introduced, but I'm Ginger Daley, Becca's friend."

He spared her a quick glance. "Yes, I know who you are."

Ginger followed his gaze to Becca. "She's always been

like that. Just about every time we went to the mall, there'd be some kid who'd gotten separated from his mother and we'd spend our afternoon searching for her and making sure the kid was okay. And the baby-sitting jobs. I think our teenage years were spent with Becca taking care of every kid in Rockport. I can't tell you the number of Saturday nights that ticked me off. But that's Becca.'' She took a sip of her punch. ''I could probably stand here all night listing Becca's good qualities, but I believe you already know them.''

''Yeah,'' he murmured. He knew all about Becca, and he didn't need another person telling him anything. He glowered at her. ''Is there a point to this, Ginger?''

''There sure is,'' she replied without hesitation. ''You're an idiot, Cordell Prescott.''

His eyes narrowed. ''Excuse me?''

''You've been through hell. So what? A lot of people have. Get over it. Can't you see you have heaven waiting for you?'' Without another word, she walked away.

If one more person tried to interfere in his life, he was going to snap. He didn't need... Becca raised her head and their eyes met across the room. All he could see was pain. Deep, inner pain.

Pain he'd caused.

All the emotions he kept locked up came pouring into his heart. He couldn't breathe for a moment and he had to force himself to inhale deeply. He was at the crossroads of his life and he knew it. The past still had a strong hold on him, but there was nothing he could do about it. He finally saw that. The present, though, the pain he saw in Becca's eyes and the pain he felt in his heart—that was something he could change. *You have heaven waiting for you.* Suddenly the mist around him cleared. The past would not keep him a prisoner.

His heart leapt with this awakening. Circumstances had clouded his judgment and blinded him to what was important in his life. He'd no control over Anette or Mona. He had done everything he could to help his wife, but she'd chosen to keep secrets from him. He had no power over that. And he certainly had nothing to do with Mona's insane behavior. It was all so clear now, and he knew what he had to do. And he had to do it immediately.

He walked over to Colton. "Could you take Blanche, Edie and Nicki home? I have somewhere to go."

"Sure, but what the—"

Cord didn't wait to hear the rest. He strolled quickly to the door.

Becca saw him leave and her heart sank. He couldn't even stay in the same room with her. All her hopes died. He wasn't going to give them a chance. She had to get away before the tears took over. She kissed Nicki goodbye and used her cell phone to call a cab. Colton wasn't too pleased, but she had to be alone to deal with the fact that the life she wanted with Cord was only a fairy tale—as Blanche had once warned her.

CORD DROVE TO THE CEMETERY and walked to Anette's grave. He stood for a long time breathing in the warm August air. The wind picked up and blew stray leaves around his feet. He was no longer overwhelmed, but he had to confront his emotions concerning Anette. That was the only way to put all this behind him. He remembered when he and Becca had brought Nicki here. Talking had helped his child; maybe it would help him, too.

He remembered the words Nicki had said and they echoed his own feelings. "I'm not mad at you anymore," he whispered from his soul. For so long he'd been angry at Anette for what she'd done. But now he understood that she hadn't killed herself. Mona had murdered her. He sucked air into his lungs. He couldn't let that destroy him because there was nothing he could have done to change it. Nothing. He couldn't go on blaming himself, punishing himself.

"I'm not mad at you," he repeated, and the rest of the hurt began to leave him. He put his hat on his head and walked back to his truck.

BECCA UNDRESSED and slipped on a T-shirt, then curled up on the sofa. The tears she'd been holding back suddenly burst forth, and she cried for herself, for Cord and for everything that was lost. She knew Cord was softhearted and felt things deeply, but she'd believed he would find his way back to her. Tonight that hope had dwindled to nothing. He was going to continue blaming himself for everything. He refused to let himself live again.

She sat straighter and dried her tears. She wanted to call her mother and tell her about the baby. She had to tell *someone*. But she wanted to tell Cord first. A baby was probably the last thing he wanted to hear about, though.

She curled up again. She couldn't help thinking that unhappy pregnancies ran in the family. Rose and Emily had both gotten pregnant out of wedlock. Why was it that history had a way of repeating itself? But this baby was very much wanted....

THE RINGING OF THE DOORBELL woke her. Groggily she sat up and pushed hair away from her face. It was after twelve. Probably Colton and Ginger making sure she was okay.

She got up and looked through the peephole, and her whole body froze. Cord was standing outside. Was something wrong with Nicki? That was the only reason he'd be here, the only reason she could think of. She quickly opened the door.

For a moment they just stared at each other. He wore the same clothes he had at the party and clutched his hat in one hand. "Can I talk to you, please?" he finally asked.

"Sure," she answered, moving aside to let him in. "Is it Nicki?" She could hear the anxiety in her voice.

"No, she's fine."

He was so much taller, and without her shoes she was reminded of that. His mere presence in her apartment took her breath away.

He noticed her red and puffy eyes. "Have you been crying?"

She tucked hair behind her ear and didn't know quite how to answer that—so she didn't. "Cord, why are you here?"

He twisted his hat. "I'm not sure where to start," he said. "But this thing with Anette and Mona hit me pretty hard."

"I know that."

"When I thought Mona could have killed you, too— well, I just couldn't handle it. I hurt every woman who's ever loved me and I couldn't handle that, either. I felt so much guilt and blame that it overshadowed everything."

Becca's heart started to beat with alarming speed.

He raised his head and she saw his eyes. The pain was gone. Thank God, the pain was gone.

"Tonight when I saw you, I realized I'm still hurting you. I can't do that anymore, either."

"You can't?"

His eyes held hers. "No, I love you and—"

"Don't say that." She broke in fiercely, surprising herself. "How can you love me and still hurt me? Anette didn't hurt me. Mona didn't hurt me. *You* did. You hurt me and…'' Emotions overwhelmed her and she couldn't go on.

"Please, forgive me,'' he said in a tortured voice. "I do love you. You may not understand why I had to send you away, but at the time it was the only thing that made sense to me." He paused, then added, "I love you, Becca. Nothing will ever change that."

At the look in his eyes and the passion in his voice, everything in her crumbled away, the anger and the grief and the hurt. All that remained was the love. She threw herself into his arms and words were stilled as their lips met in hungry, aching need. Cord lifted her off the floor as the kiss went on and on. She wrapped her arms around his neck, her fingers tangling in his hair, giving herself up to this moment, his kiss.

Somehow they were on the sofa and she wasn't sure how they'd got there. All she wanted to do was hold him, touch him…and love him.

"Oh, Becca." He groaned as his hands slipped beneath her shirt to her breast. "I'm been starving for this, dying for you."

"Then, why did you push me away? That hurt so much."

He rested his forehead against hers. "It's hard to explain, but when I found out about Mona and Anette, I felt a terrible guilt. It was eating me alive and I didn't want to drag you into my agony. I wanted you to have a normal life, away from the insanity that plagued me."

She kissed the corner of his mustache. "I have no life without you."

"I finally realized that, too. About myself, I mean. After everything that happened, I didn't think I deserved one, but now I do—a life with you."

That was exactly what she needed to hear. Her world suddenly righted itself. Except for one thing...

"Say you love me and forgive me," he whispered.

"I love you and I forgive you," she answered, and for the next few seconds there was only blissful silence as their lips met. She didn't want this to end, but she had to tell him. "We have to talk," she said in a hoarse voice.

He shook his head. "No talking or thinking. I just want to love you."

She wanted that, too, and it was tempting to wait and tell him later. But they couldn't start their life that way. She had to be honest.

"We have to talk," she repeated in a stronger voice.

Her voice got his attention, and he drew his lips away. "What is it? What's wrong?"

She didn't know how to tell him, so she said the first thing that came into her mind. "You haven't mentioned marriage."

He seemed to relax. "I assumed we would. Isn't that what you want?"

"Yes, but it would be nice to be asked."

"Oh, I'm sorry," he said and stood up. "I'll be right back."

Startled, she asked, "Where are you going?" But he was already out the door. She didn't know what to think, but he'd said he'd be back. So she waited.

In a minute, he *was* back. He laid a box of chocolates and a dozen long-stemmed white roses in her lap. Then he got down on one knee and took her hand. "Rebecca Talbert, will you marry me?"

She pushed the candy and roses aside and made a dive for him. "Yes, yes, yes," she said as they kissed long and deep, then she asked, "Where did you get the candy and roses?"

"I brought them as a peace offering."

"Very wise."

They kissed again and Cord settled back on the floor, against the sofa, with her on his lap.

"You sure you don't want to rethink that decision? I come as a package deal—Nicki and the rest of my crazy family."

"And one more," she said softly, leading up to what she had to tell him.

"One more what?" His tongue found the sensitive area behind her ear.

"One more child." She tried to keep her senses clear, but that was hard to do with Cord's breath on her skin.

"Child? What child?" he asked in a hazy voice.

She swallowed. "Our child."

"We don't have a child."

"In about seven months we will."

The room suddenly became very quiet, and she rushed on. "Now, Cord, don't freak out on me and please don't go all silent. Let me reach you."

"You're pregnant?" His voice came out low and shaky. "How did this happen?"

She lifted an eyebrow. "Want me to give you a biology lesson?"

"No, I mean…are you okay?"

"I'm fine."

"But this is too soon for you."

"I'm ready for a baby—your baby."

"Oh, Becca." He cradled her head in both hands. "I love you so much."

"Then, you're okay with this."

"I'm so happy I could walk on water. A new life. A new beginning. That's what I need—with you and our family."

They kissed slowly, then held each other close. "I love

you, Cordell Prescott,'' she said, and for several heavenly moments not another word was spoken.

Slowly she reached for the chocolates. ''Do we eat these chocolates and make love, or make love and then eat the chocolates?''

He took the box out of her hands and smiled. Soon the whole world faded, leaving just the two of them in a private universe of their own making. Shadows of the past might appear from time to time, but their love, strong and lasting, would now have the power to chase them away.

EPILOGUE

Two years later

BECCA PUT THE FINISHING touches to the table. The flowers, candelabra, china and linen were perfect—just the way she wanted it. It was Thanksgiving and both families, Cord's and hers, were coming. It was the beginning of a new Prescott tradition, and she enjoyed preparing the house and getting a meal ready. She paused for a moment, thinking back, and gave thanks for everything in her life.

She had married Cord a month after that August night, in a small chapel with family and friends. She'd worn her mother's wedding dress, even though it was tight around the waist. Her parents reacted exactly the way she'd known they would to the pregnancy—lovingly and supportively. Rose was another matter. Even though she'd tried to hide it, she wasn't pleased, but she adored her great-grandson. The day she had Cordell Jackson Prescott was one of the happiest of Becca's life. Nicki was infatuated with her little brother; Becca and Cord wanted Nicki to be comfortable with him, and she was. It helped, too, that she was the big sister.

Becca had a hard time adjusting her work schedule. She'd spent so many years becoming a doctor and she loved it, but she loved her family more. So she compromised. She worked full-time until C.J., as they called their son, was born. Now she worked four half days, and was on call one weekend a month, to assist Dr. Arnold. Sometimes it turned out to be more than that, and Cord was understanding. He didn't want her to give up her work. And it helped that he was always close to home.

They had renovated the second floor. They'd ripped out walls and made a new master suite and nursery. Becca now felt as if she was a part of this history in the house. She, Blanche and Edie had hung portraits of all the Prescott women in the upstairs hall. Cord smilingly approved of their efforts.

Colton and Ginger had eloped a year ago and spent a lengthy honeymoon in Europe. She and Ginger were now sisters-in-law. That seemed so natural, given how long they'd been friends.

Della came in wearing a flowered dress and white apron. "What do you think?" Becca asked, surveying her handiwork.

"Just beautiful." Della sighed. "Everything's so different around here. It's a pleasure to come to work these days."

Becca put an arm around her waist. "And it's a pleasure to have your help. Maybe one of these days I'll learn to be as good a cook as you."

"Mommy, Mommy," Nicki called.

On their wedding day Nicki had asked, "Are you my mommy now?" Becca had replied, "Yes." From then on, Nicki had called her Mommy. Anette had receded in her memory. Anette's portrait—painted from a photograph— hung upstairs, and they put flowers on her grave during holidays, but she knew Nicki had very little recollection of her. In a way that was good, but Becca didn't want her to completely forget her real mother. The things she'd saved from Anette's room were in a sealed box in her closet. At the appropriate time, she and Cord would give them to Nicki.

Nicki burst into the room, her blond curls everywhere. "Daddy can't do my hair right, Mommy. I want you to fix it. I want to wear these, and Daddy doesn't know how they work." She held out the hair clips Blanche had sent her from Paris.

Blanche and Edie were now traveling together. Two women who had spent years hating each other had become traveling companions. They still argued from time to time, but their arguments were trivial, almost as though the habit was too deeply ingrained to stop. Forgiveness had come slowly to the Prescott family, but in the end it had arrived.

Clay had finally flown home and he, Cord, Colton and Edie had sat down with Blanche to work out the details of the will. There were no recriminations against Blanche. Her sons did their best to understand her motives. Then Edie shocked everyone by saying she was satisfied with a trust fund. She was too old to run a ranch and it really belonged to Cord. It was enough that Pa had remembered her. So Cord gave up his trust fund, which was divided among Edie, Colton and Clay, and he took full possession of the ranch. Everyone seemed happy with that arrangement, and all the boys were finally getting to know their mother. Blanche had changed so completely that the hard, crude person Becca had first met was nonexistent. Once Blanche had learned that she didn't have to own everything for the family to care about her, she realized what a fool she'd been and what a treasure she had in her sons. Edie was just tired of the long battle and gave in gracefully. After spending two weeks in Europe, the two women had traveled to Alaska to see Clay, Nina and the girls. They were all flying home for Thanksgiving.

Becca combed Nicki's hair and secured the clips. "How's that?"

Nicki looked in the mirror over the buffet. "Just like I wanted," she said, studying herself.

Nicki was starting to take an interest in her appearance. Poor Cord. He wasn't ready for this—and neither was she.

Apparently satisfied with her hair, Nicki turned to Becca. "When are Blanche and Edie coming home?"

"Colton and Ginger are picking everyone up at the airport, so they should be here in about an hour."

"I'm glad 'cause I miss them."

"Me, too, sweetie."

Secretly she knew that Blanche and Edie traveled—at least in part—to give them time as a family. She'd told them they didn't have to do that, but they didn't listen to her, and Becca loved them all the more. She'd been raised as an only child and she wanted to belong to a big family. Now she did, and she couldn't be happier.

"Scotty and me can go riding after dinner, can't we, Mommy?"

"Yes, but remember your cousins from Alaska will be here, too, so you have to include them." Nicki and Scotty were "buddies," as Nicki put it. Becca had worried about the two being jealous of each other. At first they were, but that soon ended. Nicki was taken with Scotty's computer skills, and Scotty was amazed at Nicki's riding and roping ability. They were always eager to show the other new things.

"Okay," Nicki agreed.

Childish screeches could be heard a moment before C.J. flew into the room without a stitch of clothing except for his cowboy boots. He threw himself at Becca's legs and peeked around her to his father standing in the doorway.

At the sight of Cord, Becca's heart fluttered with excitement. It was the same every time she saw her handsome cowboy. He hadn't changed a bit in two years, except that the sadness in his brown eyes had been replaced by a joy that was echoed in hers.

With a smile, Becca ruffled the blond curls on her son's head. "Cord, our son doesn't have any clothes on."

He walked farther into the room, laughter filling his eyes. "While I was working on Nicki's hair, he took his pajamas off and put on his boots. Before I could think of a way to get his pants over his boots, he darted out the door. I'm gonna have to bring my rope to the house so I can lasso him. Might be the only way I can keep up with the boy."

As Cord drew closer, C.J. screeched again and ran into the den.

"God Almighty, boy, you're naked as a jaybird." They could hear Gus, and Becca groaned.

"I'll get him," Nicki said.

Cord kissed the top of Nicki's head. "Thanks, baby."

Cord stared after her as she chased C.J. "She's only seven and I'm afraid to blink. If I do, she'll be all grown-up."

Becca wrapped her arms around his waist from behind. "Oh, I think we have a while yet."

"Yeah," he murmured. "When I remember what it was like a couple of years ago, I get cold chills."

"That's all behind us."

He turned in the circle of her arms. "Your parents call you *angel* and you really are." He bent his head and softly kissed her as she leaned in to him.

"You're gonna get so lucky tonight," she murmured wickedly.

"I get lucky every night," he teased. "I have to be the luckiest guy on the planet." And he was. The situation with Anette and Mona had almost destroyed him, but Becca's love had saved him. Every day when he woke up with Becca in his arms, he knew he was truly blessed.

She watched his face. "You're in a good mood."

"I guess I am," he admitted. "I never thought we'd have family occasions in this house. Now the whole Prescott family and yours will be here. I'm very grateful for that. And Clay's thinking about moving back to Texas. It would be wonderful if we were all together again."

"Yes, it would," she said. "It would give our kids a chance to grow up with their cousins."

"I think Blanche has a lot to do with their decision."

"Probably, and since Nina's parents have passed away, they want their girls to be around family. Clay's girls think Blanche is cool."

He caressed her face. "I think *you're* cool. And beautiful, brilliant, loving and…"

She kissed the vee in his shirt and traveled upward.

"Oh," he moaned. "When you do that I get completely sidetracked and—" Just as his head dipped toward her, they heard more screeching and laughter from the den. Nicki was still chasing C.J. trying to catch him.

Cord gave her a quick kiss. "I'd better corral our children."

"Cord, why can't we make C.J. understand that he has to wear clothes?" she asked woefully. C.J. didn't like clothes. He preferred to run around in nothing but his boots.

"Beats me. I never had this problem with Nicki."

"I don't know where he gets it from," she said. "I was always very discreet as a child." She poked him in his ribs. "He probably gets it from you."

"Uh, I don't think so. I don't remember preferring the buff."

She looked into his eyes. "Why is it I can handle other children, but not my own?"

He stroked her cheek with the back of his hand. "He's not even two years old. Give it time. He won't be doing this in a few years. Isn't that what you'd tell a worried parent?"

"Yes." She sighed, knowing he was right. It wasn't anything to worry about. "One of us had better get him dressed before company arrives." As the words left her mouth, the doorbell rang.

They could hear C.J. running in his boots to the door.

"Oh, no," Becca muttered.

"Relax," Cord said. "Everyone's seen him without his clothes on." Then he took her into his arms and kissed her deeply. Her arms crept around his neck as she returned the kiss. As always, they were in their own world.

"I love you," he whispered against her lips. "Just wanted you to know that before the craziness of this day starts."

"I love you, too," she whispered back. "You've made me so happy. I'm glad I waited for you."

"Me, too. I never thought it was possible to be this happy," he replied. "You've changed my whole life—not to mention my whole family."

She smiled into his eyes. "I never dreamed I'd fall in love with a cowboy."

He settled his hands around her waist. "How's the experience so far?"

"Exciting, stimulating, fulfilling, passionate—and you'd better keep it that way."

"I promise, for the rest of our lives." He sealed that vow with a searing kiss. "Now we'd better go rescue whoever's at the door from our naked son."

Arm in arm, they strolled to the front door. Becca had finally found the passionate love she'd been looking for. Like Emily, she would love one man—forever.

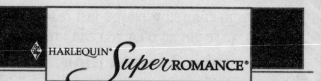

COOPER'S ❧ CORNER

The newest continuity from Harlequin Books continues in September 2002 with

AFTER DARKE
by *USA Today* bestselling author
Heather MacAllister

Check-in: A blind date goes from bad to worse for small-town plumber Bonnie Cooper and city-bred columnist Jaron Darke. When they witness a mob hit outside a restaurant, they are forced to hide out at Twin Oaks. Their cover: they're engaged!

Checkout: While forced to live together in close quarters, these two opposites soon find one thing in common: *passion!*

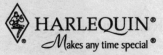

HARLEQUIN®

Makes any time special ®

Visit us at www.cooperscorner.com

CC-CNM2R

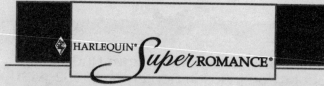

HARLEQUIN *Super*ROMANCE®

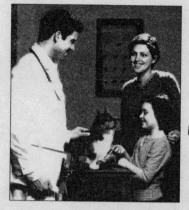

CREATURE COMFORT

Creature Comfort, the largest veterinary clinic in Tennessee, treats animals of all sizes— horses and cattle as well as family pets. Meet the patients— and their owners. And share the laughter and the tears with the men and women who love and care for all creatures great and small.

Listen to the Child
by Carolyn McSparren

Dr. Mac Thorn—renowned for his devotion to his four-legged patients and his quick temper—is used to having people listen to *him*. But ex-cop Kit Lockhart can't hear him—she was injured on the job. Now Mac is learning to listen, and Kit and her young daughter have a lot to teach him.

Coming in September to your favorite retail outlet.

Previous titles in the Creature Comfort series

#996 THE MONEY MAN (July 2001)

#1011 THE PAYBACK MAN (September 2001)

HARLEQUIN®

Makes any time special ®

Visit us at www.eHarlequin.com

HSRCREAT